TRUTH ABOUT
MEN & DOGS

ANDREA SIMONNE

Liebe
Publishing

Truth About Men & Dogs

By Andrea Simonne

ONE

~ Philip ~

D og piss.
   I took another swig from the bottle.
Definitely dog piss. With a hint of something else.
Cherries?

There was a case of this stuff in the kitchen. When Gavin and I met with Drink Virtue, a small beverage company, they'd served us a drink that tasted like apple cider. Not this swill. *Who the hell makes a wine spritzer that tastes like dog piss?*

It was bad enough I was drinking a wine spritzer at all.

Still, their numbers were excellent, and my gut told me they were on to something. They'd found an untapped market—not an easy thing to do.

I leaned back on the deck chair. The view of the water was picturesque. The wind rustled through the trees like a lullaby, but I grunted with annoyance.

I needed to get off this godforsaken rock.

My back pocket buzzed, and I reached around for my phone, except it wasn't there.

Just me grabbing my own ass.

This phantom buzzing had been going on all morning. My mom and sister stole my phone right after we arrived in Truth Harbor yesterday. Right before they announced there was no party for Gavin, my business partner and best friend, that it was only a ruse to get me here. One he was in on apparently—and yes, I'd be dealing with him later.

I took another swig from the bottle of cherry-flavored piss, trying to decide what my options were.

I felt like the benevolent ship captain whose crew had turned mutinous.

Vacations weren't my thing. I didn't want to hurt anyone's feelings, but it'd been less than a day, and I was already bored out of my mind. There was no way I'd last a whole week. It turned out my cousin Doug lived here—as if that didn't tell me everything I needed to know about this small town. Doug was the biggest sad-sack loser I'd ever met. Don't get me wrong, I loved my cousin, but I'd never known anyone so consistently miserable.

There was only one ferry a day out of here, and I'd like to be on the next one tomorrow morning. If I could get my hands on a car, I could leave tonight. There was another escape route, though it involved back roads and hours of driving. Chartering a plane was a possibility. Even a helicopter. It sounded excessive, and admittedly, I'd only used them in an emergency. Last-minute deals or contract signings that couldn't happen if I were stuck in Seattle traffic.

I took in the water view and imagined myself trapped here for the next week with nothing to do but stare at the clouds as they drifted by.

Hell, this *was* an emergency.

No doubt my mom and the pest would be furious at me for escaping their good intentions. That gave me pause. My mom had just retired from her job as a schoolteacher, and I knew it was an emotional time for her.

My eyes went down to the bottle in my hand. "Fizzy Lizzy," I read aloud. "To your health and celebration." It was a health tonic, a vitamin wine spritzer of sorts. When Drink Virtue pitched the idea to us a few weeks ago, Gavin and I liked it enough to offer it to our investors, but we agreed something needed to be done about the name.

"What are you doing, silly?"

I glanced around the deck to see who was talking to me. Except there wasn't anyone. I was alone.

Huh?

I heard feminine laughter, and then she spoke again. "That's not a good idea."

I realized the sound was coming from below the second-floor deck where I was sitting. She was on the sand talking to someone.

Her voice drifted up to me with a sultry tone. "You bad boy. You have to stop that and mind your manners."

My ears perked up. Whoever these two were, they had no idea they weren't alone.

There was more feminine laughter and then some scuffling noises. Something that sounded almost like a growl.

The house we were staying in was a vacation rental, so maybe the couple below didn't know it had been rented out. They thought they had the place to themselves for their afternoon tryst.

I remained quiet, enjoying myself. She had a pretty laugh. Girl next door, with a hint of something naughty. I tried to imagine what she looked like—hopefully blonde with a voluptuous body, and a tiny white string bikini.

"Come on, silly," she said in a teasing voice. "That's enough."

I smirked. I should go inside and give them their privacy, but screw that. If they wanted privacy, they shouldn't be out here playing grab ass.

There was some heavy breathing coming from below, and I tried to picture the scene. The blonde's face was flushed. The ties on that string bikini were pulled apart by a masculine hand that looked an awful lot like mine.

"Stop that now," she said, her voice firmer than before.

Her lips were pink, I decided. And she had pale tan lines around her breasts, which were full and heavy as they fell into my eager hands.

"I mean it. That's *enough*."

I paused my imagination and frowned. Blondie didn't sound happy anymore.

"Get your nose away from there."

Your nose?

"Aaaah!" she shrieked.

I jumped up and ran over to the side of the deck. I was ready to help, but nothing could have prepared me for the sight below.

It wasn't a lust-filled couple at all but a woman lying on the ground. She was tangled up in some kind of rope as she twisted in the sand like a giant snake. Instead of a lover beside her, there were three small, puffy black dogs that yipped maniacally as soon as they saw me.

What the fuck?

I rushed down the back stairs and ran toward her. "Are you all right?" As I got closer, I realized it wasn't rope but the dogs' leashes she was tangled up in.

She squealed, pulling on them, still trying to free herself. One dog had its paws on her chest, licking her face.

The other two yipped excitedly again.

"*Sit!*" I commanded in a deep voice, pointing at the ground.

Like a light switch, the two dogs fell silent. The third stopped its licking and looked at me with surprise. I glared down at it. Finally, it sat too. All three of them stared up at me with their mouths hanging open.

"Wow," the woman breathed. She was staring at me just like the dogs. "That was amazing."

I bent down in front of her and took the leash from her hand. "Are you okay?" I unclipped each end so I could get her untangled.

"How did you do that?" she asked.

I didn't answer, still trying to deal with the leashes. Her sweatshirt had ridden up over her hip, revealing an expanse of creamy white skin.

"I can never get them to listen to me." Her voice was clear and pretty. "They're like cute little demons."

"You have to let them know who's boss," I said, still working to untangle her. My knuckles brushed against the smooth skin on her hip though I tried to ignore it. Despite any voyeuristic tendencies, I wasn't an actual lech. "They need to respect you."

"They're my stepsister's dogs, and they definitely don't respect me." She sighed. "In fact, I'm sure they hate me."

After freeing her, I clipped each dog's leash back to the handle before returning it to her. "It doesn't matter if they hate you. They'll still respect you if they know you're in charge."

"You think?"

I stood up and offered her my hand. She took it, and soon we were standing beside each other, though I saw her wince.

"Are you okay?"

"Oh, I'm fine."

Neither of us said anything more, and I sensed her embarrassment. She wasn't looking at me but down at her feet.

I took the opportunity to check her out. She was on the short side, a little younger than me, with an air of someone who was having a bad day. To be honest, she wasn't exactly the hot blonde in my fantasy.

First of all, there was no string bikini. In fact, she was wearing baggy gray sweats that reminded me of a lesbian gym teacher I had in high school, and not in a good way. Her hair might have been blonde, though I couldn't tell because it was pulled back into some kind of severe librarian bun, and that wasn't in a good way either.

The truth was she was plain, possibly homely, and not my type at all.

"Thanks for your help," she said, brushing the sand off her body. I was rewarded with a glimpse of plump cleavage when she bent over.

As we continued to stand there, it occurred to me that I might have found the solution to my problem. "Do you have a phone I could borrow?"

She looked up at me with large eyes. They were light brown with flecks of gold. "You want to borrow my phone?"

"I just need to make a quick call."

The dogs were already getting antsy beside her. One of them had wandered over to sniff something on the ground, pulling on the leash. Another yipped but quieted as soon as I gave it a stern look.

"Sure, I guess so." She stared at me in a lost way.

"It'll only take a quick moment," I assured her.

She continued to stare. Finally, she blinked a few times and came to her senses, pulling a girly turquoise phone from her pocket.

I smiled. *Hallelujah.* Soon I'd be free. Free from this hillbilly town. Free from this absurd vacation I'd been tricked into. I could go back to my normal life.

But then there was yelling behind us. Another female voice, and unfortunately, this time I recognized it immediately.

"Stop! Don't give him that phone!"

Dammit. I put my hand out. "I just need it for a second," I said urgently. "That's all."

But the librarian gym teacher didn't hand it over. Instead, she gripped it tighter, watching as the pest ran up to us wearing a T-shirt, shorts, and big flowered rain boots though it was sunny and warm outside.

"Please do *not* give him that phone. I'm begging you!"

I rolled my eyes at her theatrics. "Don't listen to this crazy girl." I still had my hand out. "I've never seen her before in my life."

"Philip!" She turned to me in outrage.

Librarian gym teacher's brows knit together as her eyes flashed to mine. "Do you two know each other?"

"Of course not," I said.

"This is my brother!"

"Your brother?" She seemed conflicted.

I softened my voice. "I helped you a moment ago, remember? The least you could do is lend me your phone." I was tempted to snatch it from her hand, but I wasn't that much of a dick.

"Please don't give him that phone," the pest pleaded. "It's a matter of life and death!"

TWO

~ Claire ~

"I'm sorry," I said, ignoring my rescuer's outstretched hand. "I'd better not."

Storm clouds brewed as he followed the movement of my phone back into my hoodie pocket. Clearly he wasn't happy. His eyes met mine. They were striking—light blue surrounded by thick dark lashes.

I tried not to gawk at him again. It was embarrassing enough the way he'd found me writhing on the ground.

The young woman beside him had to be his sister, because she had the same dark hair, same blue eyes, and the same pink flush high on her cheeks.

The only difference was the expression on their faces. While she was grinning and gushing thanks to me, he wasn't. In fact, the storm clouds hadn't left.

I forced myself to turn away, though I could still feel his eyes on me.

I wished I'd made some effort to put myself together before I left the house. My stepmother, Violet, had asked me to take the dogs for a walk, and I didn't expect anyone to be here. The Talbots, the owners, rented it during the summer, but I hadn't seen anyone around until now.

How was I to know there'd be some cute guy? Not that I was interested. But at least he was nice enough to help me with the demon dogs.

"Philip, you promised you'd give it a *chance!*" The sister's hair was pulled into a messy topknot that shook when she spoke, emphasizing her words like the dot on an exclamation point.

"I did no such thing."

"It's for your own good!"

I didn't want to get involved in some kind of family quarrel, but I had to admit I was curious. "Why is it a matter of life and death if I loan him my phone?"

My rescuer shook his head. "It's not."

"It is too!" The sister turned to me. "He almost died!"

Apparently this was amusing, because he laughed. "You'll have to forgive the pest. She's a *drama* major."

"The doctor at the ER said you needed to rest, that you should take it easy."

Philip rolled his eyes, glancing up at the sky in amazement.

I wondered what was wrong with him. He certainly didn't look unhealthy. In fact, he looked *very* healthy. Fit and muscular. Not super pumped up like some guys you see—which, to be honest, I didn't care for. Guys who were too overdeveloped looked kind of weird to me.

My rescuer didn't look weird. He was perfect, with just the right amount of solid muscle. Plus he was handsome, and I mean crazy handsome.

I wished I'd put on eyeliner. Not to mention the way I was dressed all in gray like a mental patient.

"Do you know how long it's been since he took a vacation?" the sister asked. "Never! That's how long. What kind of lunatic workaholic *never* takes a vacation?"

"I don't need a vacation," he said. "My life is a vacation."

"You're hearing this, right?" She looked at me as if I were her accomplice, so I nodded. "He's going to work himself into an early grave!"

I studied Philip some more, trying to figure out what the problem could be. High blood pressure? Heart problems? A life-threatening case of hemorrhoids? Admittedly, none of those things seemed likely, but if an ER doctor was involved, it must have been something.

"I'm sorry you're not feeling well," I said to him. "I hope your health improves."

Philip opened his mouth, but his sister spoke first. "Thank you. My mom and I are doing our best to take care of him, but he's fighting us every step of the *way!*"

One of the demon dogs barked at her tone, and the other two began to pull on their leashes again. I glanced down. "I should probably get going. I was just walking the dogs. My name's Claire." I switched the leash over and held my hand out. "It's nice to meet you both. I live a few houses up the road."

"Oh, really? I'm Eliza," the sister said with a smile. Unsurprisingly, her grip was light and mercurial. "It's nice to meet you."

"Philip," he murmured as he shook my hand. His grip was firm and concise.

My dad used to tell me a lot could be said about a person by their handshake, so I took note of theirs. A firm grip was good, as long as it wasn't too firm like a hand strangler. Although a strangler was better than a dead fish or, even worse, a bear trapper—someone who imprisoned your hand with both of theirs. Worst of all though was the elbow groper, a person who shook your hand and then groped your elbow too, like a politician.

After a moment's deliberation, I decided their handshakes were acceptable.

"It's nice to meet you both." I gave Philip a quick smile, trying to hide my embarrassment. "Thank you for your help with the dogs."

"No problem."

"Oh, don't go yet!" Eliza's topknot wobbled. "You're the first person we've met since we arrived."

The dogs were getting restless, each of them yanking in a separate direction. Soon it would be anarchy again.

"We're renting the house for the month," she continued. "You should join us for dinner sometime."

"That sounds nice," I said, still struggling with the leashes. "But I really ought to get going."

Philip gave a short whistle from the side of his mouth. Three little demon heads turned in his direction. He didn't say a word, just pointed at the ground. To my amazement, they each trotted back over.

"Wow," I breathed. "That's a trick you'll have to teach me. Maybe next time."

I started to move away. Unfortunately, there was a sharp pain in my left ankle as soon as I put my full weight on it.

"Hey, wait," Philip asked with concern, stepping toward me. "Are you hurt?"

I waved my hand. "I'm fine. I twisted my ankle a little when I fell, but I'm okay." I continued to hobble toward the beach with the dogs leading the way. I was desperate to leave. They seemed like nice people, but I wanted to get out of here. Besides needing a shower, mascara, and a change of clothes, Ivy would be by soon to pick up her dogs.

"Maybe I should drive you," he offered, following me.

"Oh, I couldn't put you out like that." The dogs, happy to be leaving, had begun to drag me along the beach while I limped behind them like some kind of freak.

"We'll both drive you!" Eliza clomped up beside me. I noticed for the first time how she wore floral rain boots.

Philip was still following me and reached down for the dog leash handle. "My sister and I would be happy to take you home."

"Um, that's okay. Really." I resisted his attempts to take the leash.

"I think she's in pain," Eliza said, turning toward her brother. "You should carry her to the car."

"*What?*" I squeaked. "That's not necessary. I'm totally fine!"

His eyes roamed my length as we continued the tug-of-war for the dog leash. He appeared to be assessing me, probably wondering whether I'd break his back. I was a curvy girl, and let's just say I hadn't seen single-digit jean sizes since sixth grade.

To my amazement, he moved in closer. "Maybe I *should* carry you." His eyes were still focused on my body, and it looked like he was studying the front of my hoodie.

"No!" I gulped. "That's okay. I wouldn't want you to have a heart attack or aggravate your hemorrhoids."

"My what?"

"We can't let her walk off with an injured foot!" Eliza's topknot bounced frantically. "She needs our help. We have to *do* something!"

I continued to stagger down the beach, trying to get away from them as fast as possible. Before I knew it, the dog leash was snatched from my hand, and to my utter astonishment, Philip had swooped in and plucked me right off the ground.

"Aaaah!" I shrieked, my arms flailing out. "What are you doing? Put me down!"

"You're hurt," Eliza lamented. "Please let us take you home."

My God, are these people crazy?

THREE

~ Claire ~

"I can walk," I insisted. "Seriously!"

"It's no trouble," Philip said as he moved us both toward the front of the house.

I could barely believe this was happening.

Despite my stream of complaints, I had to admit the whole thing was pleasurable. He didn't seem to have any difficulty carrying me at all, and he smelled really good. A clean, crisp guy smell that was doing something funny to my insides.

It had been a long time since a man carried me. Not since my wedding day nine years ago when Ethan brought me over the threshold for our honeymoon.

"Don't strain yourself," I said, wrapping my arms tighter around his neck, trying not to enjoy the ride so much or the feel of his strong body. "I wouldn't want to aggravate your high blood pressure."

He didn't say anything, and I wondered if that was it. High blood pressure. It made sense, and it explained why his mom and sister were trying to force him to take a vacation—especially if he was a workaholic.

We arrived at a silver SUV parked in front of the house, and he gently put me down on my feet. My breath caught.

"I'm sorry I'm so heavy," I said, flustered.

He gave me a strange look. "You're not heavy." Then he opened the passenger door for me.

I gawked at him again, though luckily he didn't see me this time.

As he held the door, I climbed inside. Eliza had the dogs behind the SUV and was telling them to hop in, which they did enthusiastically. The demon dogs loved car rides.

Philip went to the driver side, but apparently neither of them had the keys.

"I should tell mom we're leaving," Eliza said, clomping away toward the front door. "I'll be right back."

I was sitting in the passenger seat now with Philip in the driver side. There was an awkward silence between us. I shifted in my seat. My left foot ached, and I thought about work, hoping this wouldn't be a problem. Even the dogs were silent waiting for the car to start moving.

Philip's arm rested on the steering wheel as he gazed out the front windshield.

"So what do you do?" I asked to be polite.

"I'm in finance."

"Doing what?" I was no expert, but I knew that covered a big area. My best friend Leah used to work in finance.

He shrugged. "You could say I find opportunities."

Eliza came out from the house, but she wasn't alone. A middle-aged woman with shoulder-length salt and pepper hair followed behind her.

"What kind of opportunities?"

He smirked as his eyes met mine. "All kinds."

Eliza swung open the passenger door. "My mom wants to meet you."

I smiled at their mom and introduced myself again. They sure were a friendly bunch, if not a little eccentric.

"I'm Sylvia," she said, taking my hand in a firm and steady grip. "It's nice to meet a neighbor. Truth Harbor is a lovely town."

There was a snort from Philip's direction.

I glanced at him with surprise. Granted, my hometown was small, but everybody thought it was charming with its beautiful harbor along the waters of Puget Sound. Over the years it had turned into something of a tourist destination during the summer months. Unfortunately, there were rumors that a real estate group was trying to buy up half the town. They wanted to build a shopping mall. They also wanted to build condos and hotels along the waterfront. It would change our town's entire character. It had become a controversial issue among locals.

"Thank you," I said. "I grew up here, and I've always loved it."

"My nephew moved here a few years ago," Sylvia told me. She had the same light blue eyes as her children. "It was on his recommendation that we decided to come here for vacation."

"That's right!" Eliza exclaimed. "I forgot to mention our cousin lives here. Maybe you know him?"

I smiled politely. Truth Harbor had grown, and there were enough new people that I very much doubted I knew their cousin.

"His name's Doug Bradley. He owns a small contracting business."

I opened my mouth in surprise. "Doug, the owner of Bradley Wood & Paint?"

"Yes, that's him!" Eliza jumped up and down. "You do know him!"

"Doug is your cousin?" I met him a few months ago when my stepmother, Violet, hired him to build some bookcases for her. She kept inviting him around, and I finally realized she was trying to fix us up. I liked him, but not in a romantic way. I'd hired him recently though. "He's doing some work for me. I'm finishing a second room so I can use it as an office for my business."

"You have a business?" Philip shifted toward me with interest.

"Yes, it's a maid service. Mostly private homes." I nodded toward the house they were renting. "I call it Your House Sparkles."

"Those can be profitable." His gaze was penetrating. The blue in his eyes was the exact color of the sky above us. "Though the competition is fierce, and job turnover is high. It's often difficult to maintain quality employees, and you need good insurance, which can bleed into your bottom line. How long have you been doing it? What's your valuation?"

"My what?" I stared at him.

"Philip, leave the poor girl alone," Sylvia interjected. "She doesn't want to discuss her business with you. And you're supposed to be on vacation, so try and act like it."

"How many employees do you have? What does your SWOT look like?"

"Um...." I glanced toward his mom and sister, who both had pained expressions on their faces.

"Maybe you should show me your financials." He lowered his voice. "I'll bet I could help your bottom line."

My financials? And why did it sound like he was asking to take a peek under my skirt?

Sylvia smiled helplessly. "I apologize for my son. He seems to think we all exist on the same data-driven plane as he does."

"It's okay. I guess I should know all that stuff. My company is new and pretty small. I only have three employees, including myself."

Although I wondered if I even counted as an employee. I wasn't sure. I'd have to ask the accountant I'd spoken with about how to save on taxes.

"It was very nice to meet you," Sylvia said, still smiling at me.

"Same here," I replied. "I hope you guys enjoy your stay."

On the car ride home, Eliza chattered exuberantly from the back seat. She told me how she'd just started her summer break from college and how she'd been switching majors for a few years but had finally settled on drama.

"I even got a television commercial recently. My first acting job that's paid!"

"Congratulations." I turned to look at her. "What's the commercial for?"

"A lighting company. I play a young mom who's putting her baby down for the night. Do you want to see it?" Eliza pretended to hold a sleeping infant in her arms. She gazed at it lovingly, then gave me a fierce look. "Night light for a *good* night."

I took in her performance, trying not to smile.

She grinned. "That was my line. What do you think?"

"I like it."

"They told me I won the part over three hundred actors. Can you believe it?"

"I can see why. You're very talented."

"Oh." She shrugged and seemed embarrassed, glancing toward the window. "I'm okay. It was nice to earn some money. I'm putting it toward tuition."

"I told you that's not necessary," Philip's deep voice growled beside me.

"It *is* necessary. I want to start paying my own way."

He was silent, and I suspected it was a discussion they'd had before. "Turn here." I pointed at the driveway that led to the main house. Luckily the black wrought-iron gate was open.

"Wow, this is where you live?" Eliza's voice was breathless behind me as we approached Sullivan House. "It's amazing."

"Thank you."

"Your maid service must be doing very well," Philip commented as he pulled into the circular driveway near the front entrance.

"Oh, it's not like that. I grew up here. My father bought the house before I was born. It's over a hundred years old."

"What does your father do?"

"He is... or was an attorney. He passed away three years ago."

I glanced toward the house. It was definitely impressive. Two stories with a sweeping colonial facade. Six bedrooms situated so they all looked out onto the harbor. People always commented on its beauty.

"I'm sorry to hear that," Eliza said, and I could tell she meant it. "That must have been hard for you."

"It was." I didn't say anything more. My father's death wasn't something I liked to discuss. "You can pull off onto that side lane there. I don't live in the main house."

Philip followed my instructions and turned onto the small dirt road that led to the carriage house tucked out back in the woods. At one point it had been an artist studio, but now I lived there.

There were already two cars parked in the dirt driveway that led up to my tiny house. My own turquoise Kia, which had the Your House Sparkles logo on it, and a red BMW parked right beside it that belonged to Ivy. I wasn't sure why she'd parked down here.

We pulled up behind my Kia, and Philip turned to me with a grin. "Would you like me to carry you to the front door?"

My eyes drifted down to his neck and shoulders, the strong feel of them still fresh in my memory. I was tempted to say yes but knew that would be weird. "No, I can manage. Thank you for driving me."

He nodded.

Eliza and I both got out of the car, and I waited as she opened the back to let the dogs out.

"Wow, this is really where you live?" She took in the cottage and the surrounding woods.

"It is," I said, taking the leash handle from her. Obviously it wasn't as impressive as the main house, but I loved my little home and was grateful for it.

"It's amazing. It looks just like a gingerbread house from a fairy tale."

"Thank you. It used to be an artist studio."

Eliza swooped in and gave me a hug. "I'm so glad we met today."

"Me too," I murmured, surrounded by her youthful fragrance.

She pulled back and grinned. "I hope we'll be friends."

"That would be nice."

The dogs pulled on their leashes as I watched Eliza climb into the passenger side of the car. Glancing around, I didn't see Ivy and figured she must be up at the main house visiting with her mom.

I waved goodbye to them as they backed out of the driveway, then limped behind the dogs up the cobblestone path to my door. The cottage did look like a gingerbread house. It was brown with white trim and had a pointy roof and curling eaves. I'd planted flowers and climbing vines out front, which only added to the effect.

I went to unlock the front door when, to my surprise, it opened on its own.

"There you are!" Ivy was standing on the other side. Her long shiny blonde hair fell around her shoulders like a splash of light. "I was wondering where you were."

"How did you get inside?" I asked, angry to discover she'd let herself into my home without permission. "You can't just enter my house whenever you feel like it."

"The spare key is in the same place it's always been. I didn't think you'd mind." She bent down on one knee and began speaking baby talk to her dogs, who gathered excitedly around her.

"Yes, I do mind. Don't do it again."

She glanced up at me as if I were being unreasonable. "I don't see the problem. You have a key to *my* house, after all."

I clenched my jaw. The only reason I had a key to her house was because she'd hired my maid service to clean it for her twice a month. Not that I went there myself or anything. I accepted the job because work was work, but there was no way I was going to clean her house personally.

She stood up and wiped her hands on her designer jeans. "Whose car was that? I didn't recognize it."

"It's the people who are staying at the Talbots' rental up the street."

"What?" Her slender nose wrinkled with distaste. "You let *strangers* bring my dogs home?"

"They brought me home too."

She sniffed but didn't comment.

Apparently it was okay if strangers brought me home, but the dogs were another matter.

Typical Ivy.

I pushed past her and limped into the kitchen, which was only a few feet away. My home was a small studio and nearly claustrophobic, but I preferred to think of it as cozy.

Ivy glanced down at the way I was limping but didn't comment on that either. "Thank you for taking the dogs for a walk. My mom told me you've been helping her with them. Ethan and I appreciate it."

I tried to say "you're welcome," but the only thing that came out was an irritated grumble. I walked those dogs to help Violet, not Ivy. The fact was I didn't want her here. Not in my house, or my hometown, or sleeping next to the man who was once mine. Ethan and I had been high school sweethearts since our senior year. We married during college, where I helped support him while he got his accounting degree. I thought we'd be together forever, but forever turned out to be only seven years.

I was over it, I reminded myself. And I was definitely over *him*. I wouldn't take Ethan back if someone offered me a billion dollars.

Why did they have to move back though?

Things were finally looking up. People in town had stopped giving me pitying looks, had stopped referring to me as "poor Claire" under their breath. It felt like I was starting to find myself again.

And then Ivy and Ethan returned. After living in Bellingham, they decided to move back to Truth Harbor three months ago. They bought a house. Ethan set up shop as an accountant in town, and it was clear they intended to stay.

Violet and my younger stepsister, Daphne, were thrilled to have Ivy back. They tried to convince me it was for the best, that we needed to put what happened behind us, that we needed to move forward as a family. Forgive and forget.

We, I scoffed to myself. What they really meant was *me. I* needed to forgive and forget. Except I could never forgive them for what they did to me. For Violet's and Daphne's sakes though, I tried to get along with Ivy.

At least she'd been saddled with Ethan's last name. It was the only silver lining I could find in this ugly mess. Her last name used to be Sullivan, but not anymore.

Ivy Spivy.

I wanted to giggle every time I heard it.

"Oh, and when your maid comes by my house tomorrow, will you please tell her to clean each of the bathroom sinks?" Ivy was admiring herself in the small mirror by my front door, smoothing down imaginary frizz in her silky straight hair. "I think she forgets every time."

I took a deep breath. "Of course."

"You really should train your employees better."

I gripped the kitchen counter.

Ivy reached out and yanked one of the many sticky notes I had stuck all over my house off the wall. "What are these ridiculous things?" She read it aloud. "'The future belongs to those who believe in the beauty of their dreams.' Eleanor Roosevelt." She looked up at me. "What is this?"

"It's a motivational quote. They inspire me."

Ivy made a face. "Seems pathetic."

It figured she wouldn't understand. Starting a new business was a lot of work, and it helped to remind myself that I was working toward something.

"And I'd appreciate it if in the future, you didn't let strangers drive my dogs around," she said. "You don't even know those people."

"In the future, you should find somebody else to watch your dogs when you go on vacation. I don't want to have to be the one who walks them every time." Violet barely tolerated those dogs, and Daphne was even worse at managing them than I was.

"Why are you acting like this?"

"Because I did you a favor, and you're complaining."

Ivy sighed. Her expression changed to one of pity, the one she wore when she thought I was hanging on to the past.

"Come on, Claire." Her voice softened into that sugary tone I disliked. She only used it when she wanted something. "We're sisters, remember? *Family.*"

I went quiet.

She sure knew my weakness. My soft underbelly. I was an orphan, and Violet, Ivy, and Daphne were all I had. So I listened to them when they told me that all families had their problems. "Let's put it in the past," Violet had said to me. "It's what your dad would have wanted. He always wanted you girls to be like real sisters."

Ivy was still standing there giving me her pity look.

My breath shuddered. I *don't* want him! I felt like screaming at her. Ethan was a cheater and not worth my time, but she didn't believe me. She always acted like I hadn't been enough woman to keep him, like I was harboring some deep jealousy of her for stealing him—which couldn't be further from the truth.

I limped over to get a glass down from the cabinet. "Those people aren't strangers anymore. They were being kind." I turned on the tap. "It's not like I was out there hitchhiking."

The dogs started to yip and scratch at the door, trying to get outside.

"Whatever," she said. "I'm going up to the house to see my mom."

And with that she left. *Thank goodness.*

I drank some water, then opened the fridge and took out a container of fruit. After covering the mirror by the front door again so my birds wouldn't fly into it, I went over to my own little babies—my parakeets, Quicksilver and Calico Jack.

"Hi, sweeties," I said, opening their cage.

Calico Jack immediately hopped onto my hand. "Kiss, kiss," he squawked at me.

Quicksilver came out next but flew to my bookcase. He wasn't as affectionate and tended to be a troublemaker.

"Look what I have for you two." I opened the container of fruit. Quicksilver immediately came down to me.

I fed them by hand for a bit, gently petting and cooing to them. Both birds were rescue animals I'd adopted from the shelter in town.

When they were done snacking, they flew up to the rope I'd strung across the room. I put the fruit away, figuring I'd take a shower next. My keys were still in my pocket, so I pulled them out along with my phone, except there was a problem.

My keys were there, but no phone.

"What the heck?"

I frantically searched my hoodie pockets, then my sweatpants. *Did it fall out? How could that have happened?* I began to panic. That phone was my life. Losing it would be a nightmare.

I retraced my steps and thought back to the car ride and then to the way Philip had carried me up the beach with such gallantry.

And that was when I knew the truth.

He wasn't being gallant at all.

"That asshole stole my phone!"

FOUR

~ Philip ~

U*nbelievable.*
   A full hour and it wasn't happening. I tried every key
combination possible.

The simplest way in should have been to bypass the voice assist, a
security loophole most people didn't know they should close, but
apparently the maid wasn't most people. There used to be a way to
bypass the emergency dialer using a set of keystrokes and the home
button. It was tricky. The timing had to be just right, and it only gave
you access to the phone's regular dialer, but that was all I needed.

Except that didn't work either.

I stared at the phone in frustration.

Dammit.

The metal backing grew warm in my hand as I pondered my next
move. I was sitting in my bedroom. I'd told my mom and the pest I
was taking a nap. The girly rhinestone-studded case sat beside me on

the pillow. The maid's favorite color must have been turquoise, as I'd noticed her car was the same vibrant shade.

Picking up the case, I slipped the phone back inside. My original plan was to hack the dialer and then call for transportation out of here. Afterward, I'd drive over to the maid's house and return her phone, making up a story about how it had fallen between the seats of the car.

Okay, I admit it. Not my finest hour.

Unfortunately, now I'd have to return it with nothing to show for my efforts.

I got up from the bed and slipped the phone into my front pocket, using my T-shirt to hide the bulge before leaving the room. Once out in the hall, I heard a male voice coming from downstairs.

"How was your nap?" my mom asked when I entered the house's comfortably decorated living room. The furnishings were mostly blue and white with a coffee table made from a large chunk of driftwood. "Look who dropped by for a visit."

It was my cousin Doug, which explained the male voice I'd heard. I walked over. "Hey, Dougster, how you doing?"

He stood up, and we gave each other a quick hug.

Doug was a year older than me and had a skinny doe-eyed look about him that reminded me of a young Jackson Browne. He looked the same as he did when I saw him last year in Seattle. We lived near each other as kids and basically grew up together.

He sat back down again. "Oh, I'm okay, I guess."

Taking the chair next to him, I noticed he was drinking one of the dog-piss wine coolers. I wanted to ask what he thought of it but didn't get a chance because he started telling me about his pollen allergies. A subject he'd apparently been talking about for some time.

I smiled politely, glancing around. My mom and Eliza were also smiling politely. Doug wasn't smiling because he was too busy boring everyone to death.

"And the allergy medication makes me sleepy," Doug went on in his sad-sack voice. "I'll start sneezing and my eyes will water. Sometimes my nose gets clogged. A clogged nose is no picnic, I can tell you that." He gave a dry huffing laugh.

He seemed pitiful. So pitiful none of us had the heart to shut him up. Not even me.

My sister, whose intolerance for boredom was legendary, shifted position. She had something hidden low next to the couch. She kept glancing down, and I realized she was texting on her phone. Sneaky brat.

Not that I could blame her.

My mom nodded with sympathy at my cousin's continuing nasal saga. She turned to me. "Would you like a muffin? Doug made them."

I glanced at the basket on the table. "No thanks. I'm good."

My mom's eyes widened, and I could sense the instant hurt emanating from Doug.

"I mean sure." I leaned forward to grab a muffin. "I'll have one. Definitely."

"They're oatmeal flax," he said. "I call them my kick-starter muffins since they keep you regular—if you know what I mean." He gave a brief chuckle.

I took a large bite of muffin and forced myself to chew. It was bland and tasteless with a texture not unlike wet cat litter.

"What do you think?" he asked.

"Great." I choked down the first mushy bite. "Delicious."

From the corner of my eye, I could see the pest trying not to laugh.

"Baking is something that helps take my mind off my troubles." He stared at me with his usual hangdog expression. "Hey!" He brightened. "Maybe I should sell my muffins. What do you think, Philip? You're the business expert."

I didn't reply. I got this a lot. People trying to pitch me their lame ideas. I usually shut them down quickly—brutally when necessary. In Doug's case, however, I only gave a noncommittal grunt, not wanting to be unkind.

"I haven't been getting much work lately," he lamented. "I guess people just don't want to hire me anymore."

He seemed about to continue with his new subject, and I leaned forward, eager to take part and offer suggestions, but then Doug sighed wearily and shifted back to his allergies. I tried to ask him more about why business was slow, but he couldn't be deterred.

As I tuned him out, I wondered what had brought him to this sorry state. He was my blood relative, after all. My dad's sister's son. Shouldn't he have some of our drive? Some of the famous North ambition? I hated my father, but I couldn't deny the sonofabitch was a go-getter.

Part of the problem was his mom—my aunt Linda. She definitely had the North ambition, except her main ambition seemed to be manipulating and controlling her only child. At least he had the sense to move away from her, even if it was to this small town.

My cousin began to drone on about the sinus spray he used every morning.

I was on the verge of asking my mom to kill me with the fireplace poker, but then the front doorbell rang. *Anything*, I thought. Anything had to be better than listening to my cousin monologue about the snot in his nose all evening. I tried to get up and answer it, but the pest was faster.

"I'll get it!" She leaped off the couch like the winning contestant from a game show. "Nobody move!"

"I wonder who that could be." My mom leaned back, trying to see the front door.

A moment later, my sister came into the living room escorting an attractive young woman.

Doug obviously knew who she was, because he jerked up from the couch, banging his knee against the driftwood table. "Claire! What are you doing here?"

Claire? Why did I know that name? I studied the young woman who, for some reason, was staring at me with a pissed-off expression.

My mom and Eliza also seemed to know her and were talking

animatedly as I continued to try and place her. Was she a friend of my sister's?

"Did you change your mind about dinner?" Eliza asked eagerly. "I hope so."

"No, I seem to have lost my *phone*." Despite being angry, the woman's voice was clear and pretty.

It was the maid. The one who I'd thought was plain. The one whose stolen phone was currently in my front pocket.

Shit.

"Nice to see you again, Claire." I nodded smoothly, trying to decide how to handle this.

She didn't reply, just continued with her murderous gaze, which I was starting to enjoy. Outside of family, most people were too intimidated by me to glare at me like this.

She opened her mouth like she wanted to say something.

"How's your ankle?" I inquired. "I hope it's better."

Her mouth closed abruptly. She glanced around at the others, obviously frustrated. "It's fine," she muttered.

"Have a seat." My mom got up and encouraged her to come over to the couch. "You should stay off that foot."

Claire limped over and sat down next to Doug, who had transformed into a nervous twitching rabbit.

"Are you... did you..." He swallowed. "Did you hurt yourself?"

She turned to him and explained about twisting her ankle earlier today.

"Gosh. I'm really sorry to hear that." He gulped, wringing his hands and nodding vigorously.

I'd never seen my cousin so animated. He seemed at war with himself about how to behave and kept sneaking furtive glances at her.

As a result, I decided to look at her myself.

Long curly blonde hair. Short curvy body. She was wearing fitted jeans with a peach T-shirt. It was no surprise I hadn't recognized her, because she looked completely different.

Claire smiled at something my mom said, and I shook my head in amazement. Damn, she wasn't plain at all. I couldn't believe I'd gotten it so wrong.

Not that she was my type. Despite all her glaring, I could tell she was too sweet for me. A few too many hearts and rainbows with a unicorn thrown in for good measure.

Not my thing.

I turned my attention back to Doug, because it clearly *was* his thing. He was still twitching all over.

"Would you like a... uh... muffin?" he asked Claire, his face red. "I made them myself." He fumbled for the basket, nearly dropping it in her lap.

"I didn't know you baked." She took one out along with a napkin.

Doug nodded enthusiastically. "Oh, I do. In fact, Philip told me he thought they were delicious."

At the mention of my name, her eyes narrowed, and she shot me another skewering look.

I wanted to grin with delight, but instead I kept my expression neutral. She may have her suspicions, but she had no proof I had anything to do with her missing phone.

"He thinks I should start selling them to people," Doug continued with enthusiasm. "That we should go into business together, that my muffins would be a sure thing!"

I raised an eyebrow. He got all that from my indifferent grunt? I didn't contradict him though. I could tell he was only trying to impress her, and I suspected when it came to women, Doug needed all the help he could get.

Claire took her first bite of muffin, and her eyes widened as she slowly chewed.

The pest jumped up. "Let me get you something to help wash that down. Is a wine cooler okay?"

Claire, who was still chewing, nodded eagerly.

Meanwhile, Doug watched her like a puppy awaiting its master's approval.

The maid wore an uncomfortable smile, still trying to choke

down the first bite. When Eliza appeared with the dog-piss wine cooler, Claire grabbed it from her. I watched the way her mouth pressed against the rounded edge. The way her hand gripped the long bottleneck.

My mind went straight into the gutter.

I couldn't help it.

My gaze slid down her body. As always, my imagination didn't fail me, and I easily pictured her without that peach T-shirt, then without any clothes at all.

Wait, let's go back to that white string bikini from earlier.

She put the bottle down and licked her lips. They were pink and pretty, and I enjoyed the sight of them. I glanced over at Doug, who obviously enjoyed the sight as well.

"What do you think?" he asked, staring at her with eager adoration. "Is that the best muffin you've ever eaten?"

"It's...." She seemed to be searching for the right word.

"Delicious?" he offered.

"Yes." She smiled. "Delicious."

Doug beamed at her.

"What do you think of the beverage?" I asked, curious. Maybe I was the only one who thought they tasted like dog piss.

She looked down at the bottle in her hand and licked her lips some more. "It tastes like a pencil eraser."

I chuckled.

"I thought they were strange too," my mom said in agreement. "Where did these come from?"

I explained how Gavin sent them over, that the manufacturer was looking for investors. "They're supposed to be somewhat healthy. A healthy alcoholic beverage."

"I certainly wouldn't give them any money," my mom said. "Not unless they fix the taste."

"Me either," Claire agreed.

"Is everything okay?" Doug asked, turning to her. "You said your phone was missing."

She nodded. "I was hoping I could look around outside. I must have lost it when I was here earlier checking on things." Her eyes narrowed on mine.

"Sure," I said. "Maybe it fell out of your pocket when I carried you."

"It might be on the beach," the pest offered. "Or maybe in the car. We'll help you look."

"We'll find it," Doug said quickly. "Don't you worry, Claire!"

Everybody got up and headed to the front door to go search outside for the missing phone that was now burning a hole in my front pocket. I was still trying to decide how to handle this.

"I know, let's call your number," my sister said, snapping her fingers. "That way we can hear it ringing."

I froze midstep.

"Great idea." Doug's head bobbed with enthusiasm.

My sister had her phone out in a flash and was asking Claire for her telephone number.

My pulse ratcheted up. "I'll join you guys in a minute," I said, trying to sound casual as I pointed over my shoulder at the bathroom.

Once inside, I yanked the door shut and pulled the phone out of my pocket just as it started buzzing like a motherfucker.

This was unbelievable.

There was a knock, and I turned on the sink full blast. "What is it?" I yelled through the door.

"What are you doing in there?" It was the pest.

"Taking a whiz." I spoke loudly over the running water.

"Where are the car keys?"

I'd kept them earlier, not that I was planning to leave with my mom's car, though it was tempting. "On the dresser in my room."

After a few minutes, when it was clear the house was empty, I left the bathroom and headed down the back stairs behind the house. Thankfully everything was quiet. It was dark outside, and the air smelled like the beach. I placed the maid's phone artfully on the ground near where we'd been standing together earlier.

That task completed, I headed back upstairs and grabbed a flashlight before going out through the front door.

"Any luck?" I asked as I walked over to the car. All four doors on my mom's SUV were open, and the women were looking under the seats.

"It doesn't appear to be here." My mom stood up and shook her head. "I'm so sorry, but I don't see it."

Claire bit her lip. "That phone is my entire life. What am I going to do?"

"Have you guys checked behind the house?" I asked.

"Not yet." My sister closed the doors and started shining her phone's flashlight on the ground near the car. My mom and Claire joined her in the search.

"I'll do it." I glanced around for my cousin, who for some reason was down near the end of the driveway by some bushes. "Doug and I will search out back." I headed over and told him to help me check behind the house.

"But I haven't finished looking around these bushes yet," he said, studying the edge of some thick foliage.

"Forget that. She was never over here."

Doug was crouched and pushing some leaves aside. As I watched his determined expression, the perfect plan hatched in my mind. A plan that would set this whole thing right.

"Come on." I grabbed his arm, yanking him to his feet. He resisted, but as with most things in life, I was stronger and more determined.

"Hey, where are you taking me?" he complained. "Let go! Claire's phone might be back there!"

"Dial her number again," I called over to my sister as I headed out back, dragging Doug alongside me like a skinny broomstick. He was a few inches taller than me.

As we approached the back of the house, I ignored his complaints as he continued going on about searching those damn bushes.

"I know what you're doing," he spat out. "You don't want *me* to find the phone."

I glanced over at him.

"You're going to find it yourself tomorrow when no one else is around. Then you can be the big hero!"

He wore an angry expression, and I was surprised he had the balls to speak to me in that tone. "What the hell are you talking about?" I gave him my full attention now.

"I saw the way you were looking at her." He swallowed hard. "At Claire. You want her. Don't deny it."

My brows went up, because obviously I did find her attractive.

"But she's not one of your women," he went on. "Claire isn't like that. She's sweet and kind, and I won't let you treat her that way. She's been through enough."

I slowed my pace. "You've got it all wrong."

"No, I don't. I know you, Philip, and I know you've been with a lot of women. But Claire deserves someone who wants her as more than just a distraction until the next ferry arrives."

I stopped walking completely.

"Just leave her alone." His voice quivered. "That's all I ask."

He was breathing heavily, and I studied his unhappy expression. "You really like this woman, don't you?"

"She's special. I'm smitten with her."

I lowered my voice and leaned toward him. "Don't worry, I'm not making a play for Claire." My eyes flashed down the beach, to the spot where her phone sat waiting to be found. It was time to put my plan into action. "Why don't you go check over by the deck post?" I nodded. "I'll stay here and look by the house."

"Fine." My cousin sighed, then trudged off. I turned my flashlight on and moved it along the walking path as I waited for Doug to find the phone. It shouldn't take long.

As I pretended to search, I thought about what he'd just said to me. About my using the maid as a distraction until the next ferry arrived. To be honest, the thought had occurred to me.

I wouldn't even consider going after her now. Not when I knew Doug wanted her.

I glanced down to where he was still bumbling around, searching for the phone. Why hadn't he found it yet? From where I stood, it looked like he was standing right on top of the damn thing.

It was no secret I dated a lot. I liked women, and they liked me. I didn't hear any complaints—well, I did occasionally, but most of them knew I wasn't the marrying kind, and that wasn't going to change.

"I found it!" Doug suddenly shouted. "Hey, everyone, I found it!"

Finally. For Christ's sake.

"Great!" I called down to him.

Doug came running up from the beach. "I found it!" he yelled, holding it up high. "I found Claire's phone!"

"Dude, that's great."

He galloped past me like an Irish setter and was still yelling as he rounded the corner to the front of the house.

I grinned. Stealing that phone was a dick move, but this whole thing was turning out perfect. I had a solid gold feeling in my gut, the kind I always got right before a deal was coming together, one I knew would be a winner.

The women were all gathered around Doug as I walked over to join them.

"He didn't want to check behind the house, but I insisted," he was telling everyone. "Philip thought we should check by those bushes down there, can you believe that? But I said, 'Let's look out back,' and I was right!"

It sounded like he was recounting a war story, and a false version at that, but I didn't stop him. It was good to see my cousin pleased with himself for a change.

"Thank you, Doug," Claire said. "I can't tell you how relieved I am."

"I'm just happy I was here to help." He gave her a satisfied grin.

"I appreciate it." She stepped close to him and wrapped her arms around his neck to give him a hug. I saw his eyes widen, and then they widened even more when she planted a quick kiss on his cheek.

I'd never seen my cousin so happy.

I glanced at my mom and sister, the three of us exchanging a look of understanding. Doug may have been a tiresome bore, but he was also one of us. He was family. And more than anything, I wanted him to get the girl of his dreams.

FIVE

~ Claire ~

My ankle still bothered me. The pain wasn't anybody's fault, but in my mind, I couldn't stop blaming that rotten phone thief, Philip. Even though Doug found it, I knew Philip was guilty. I wanted to accuse him, but how could I? As soon as I arrived at the house, I realized I had no evidence at all that he took it.

"You're limping, Claire," Mrs. Lamb said as she watched me wipe down her kitchen counters. "Are you all right? You don't need to go to the store today if you aren't up to it."

Mrs. Lamb was one of my many elderly clients. Normally, I preferred to clean alone and disliked having any client follow me around, but she was a favorite and enjoyed making friendly chitchat.

"It's no trouble at all," I said, loading her dishwasher. I already knew she was running low on milk and eggs. Her son, Elliot, wouldn't be by until sometime next week.

"Well, only if you're sure. I left a list there for you. Did you see it?"

"No worries. I've got it right here." I patted my front pocket.

Mrs. Lamb was a retired history teacher, and as I cleaned her house, she often told me interesting historical facts. She knew a lot about Truth Harbor and the people who settled here. It was fun learning who they named the streets after or about the ships that came into our harbor, which had something of an infamous past.

I took my apron off, folding it before adding it to my cart of cleaning supplies.

I wasn't always a maid. I used to help manage a small insurance office. During the last year of our marriage, Ethan and I were trying to have a baby, and he convinced me to quit my job. It might not sound very modern, but I couldn't wait to have children. I had been eager to be a mom and begin a new phase of my life.

All that changed when he left me for Ivy.

Suddenly I was divorced, broke, and unemployed.

My former boss wasn't hiring, and I didn't know what to do. But then I saw an ad to be a maid. I'd enjoyed housekeeping since I was a kid. It might sound like a strange hobby, but I had a shelf full of books on how to keep house and knew how to clean anything.

The job was hard work, but it suited me. My life had spun out of control, but as I scrubbed and polished, at least I could turn one small corner of the universe into something that made sense.

Mrs. Lamb started to rise from the dining room chair, and I went over to help. Her favorite soap opera was starting in a few minutes, and I set her up in the living room.

"I'm headed out now," I told her. "But I'll be back soon with your groceries."

I pushed the wire cart of cleaning supplies out to my car so I could load everything in the back.

Doug had called earlier and left a message about coming over to look at the room I'd hired him to work on. It was a mistake to kiss him on the cheek last night. I meant it in friendship, but I probably shouldn't have done it. I suspected he might have a crush on me, and I didn't want to lead him on.

Since my divorce, I hadn't dated—though I'd forced myself to sleep with someone last year. A photographer acquaintance of Leah's. She set up the blind date, convincing me I'd like him since he was from Scotland and had a sexy accent. I purposefully drank too much, and it became my first one-night stand ever. Except I felt nothing. Not during the sex or afterward. I told myself it didn't matter. All that mattered was Ethan was no longer the last man I'd been intimate with.

I headed over to the grocery store. After parking, I checked my schedule. I had a meeting with a new client that afternoon.

After I finished shopping and was pushing the groceries out to my car, who should I see but the phone thief himself—Philip.

He wore black jeans and a dark gray T-shirt, casually leaning against that silver SUV. He was staring at a phone, of all things. Apparently he'd gotten his hands on one after all.

I tried to detour around him, hoping he wouldn't see me.

"Claire," he called out.

I gave a curt nod, hurrying past, but to my annoyance, he didn't take the hint.

"Your ankle's still bothering you," he said, coming up alongside me. "I can help with those bags."

"No, thank you. I've got it."

Except he didn't go away, reaching out to try and take the cart from me instead. Talk about pushy.

I sped up even more, limping along as fast as I could.

By the time I got to the car, my ankle was killing me, and I was out of breath. I opened the rear to unload the bags. Philip took the first one, but I grabbed it from him.

He picked up a different bag, and I grabbed that one too, wrestling it from his hands. My behavior was bizarre, but I didn't care.

He stopped moving and stared at me. "I'm only trying to help."

"You've done enough," I said, shoving the bag inside my car.

He went silent. I glared at him only to discover he was smiling at me. It looked like he was enjoying himself.

There was a flash of white from his teeth, and his cheeks had that natural flush some guys get which I'd always found appealing.

I regretted my attraction to him, because in the light of day, with my normal wits about me, I could see what a gigantic pain in the ass he was. The kind of man who steamrolled over anyone who got in his way.

"Is there something you'd like to say to me?" he asked, smirking now.

I loaded the last bag in the car and slammed the rear closed. I turned and met his eyes. They were ridiculous. Sky blue fringed by those sooty lashes. Intelligence shone out from them.

We considered each other. He was taller than me, but then every-body was taller than me.

"You're a thief!" The words spewed out before I could stop them. "A *rotten* thief."

His brows went up, but he didn't seem surprised by the accusation.

"You stole my phone."

"My cousin found your phone on the beach."

"You set that up. I don't know how, but you must have."

He didn't reply, his gaze wandering down to the turquoise polo shirt I was wearing.

"What kind of person are you?" I ranted. "Pretending to help someone but then actually stealing from them. You should be ashamed of yourself."

"Don't you think you're overreacting? It's not like you didn't get your phone back."

"So you admit you stole it."

He shrugged. "I'm not admitting anything."

What he did upset me, but it was like he wasn't even paying

attention. He was studying the logo on my shirt. "Your House Sparkles," he read aloud.

Taking a page from some of the larger maid franchises, I'd had these turquoise polo shirts created for the employees of my small company to wear. I figured when people saw them, it was free advertising.

"But that doesn't really work, does it?" he murmured, tilting his head slightly.

"What do you mean?"

"As a name, it's lacking."

I couldn't believe this jerk. What an asshat. "I don't know what you're talking about. It's a perfectly good name."

"No." He appeared to be thinking it over. "It's terrible."

Who did this guy think he was? "Who do you think you are? I don't need to stand here and be insulted."

"You need something stronger. Something that announces what your business is right away."

I rolled my eyes. *Whatever.*

"Your House Sparkles could be anything," he continued. "It's a lousy name for a maid service."

"No, it's not. And I don't care what you think." I grabbed the grocery cart to push it back up to the store. He didn't follow, and I had the distinct impression he was staying back to watch my ass, though I hoped not. My ass was ample—quite ample. Let's just leave it at that.

When I walked back to my car, he was still standing there. He was holding his phone again, but there was a sly grin on his face.

"I'll be going now," I informed him in a frosty tone as I moved past him to get to the driver side.

Philip nodded. His eyes lingered on me before abruptly turning away. "Another time" was all he said before heading back to his SUV.

I stood for a moment and watched his ass, though I shouldn't have. His ass was perfect. It was a pleasure watching it encased in those black jeans.

"I'm sure the devil has a perfect ass too," I muttered as I got inside my car and slammed the door shut.

UNFORTUNATELY, I kept thinking about Philip's comment that my business name sucked. Was it true? When I took over the maid service from Jane a few months ago, I'd changed the name from Jane's Maid Service to Your House Sparkles. I had decided to make a real go of it.

The other two maids who'd worked for Jane—Laurie and Kyle—couldn't care less about running the business. They worked part-time since both of them had families and wanted a job with flexible hours and little responsibility. So after Jane called it quits, they were more than happy to let me take over. I didn't have any family to distract me. No children or husband. Let's face it—I had no life at all. I was grateful too, because right after I took ownership of the maid service, Ivy and Ethan moved back to Truth Harbor.

It might have sounded pitiful, but running my own business—no matter how small—made me feel like less of a loser.

Not that I knew what I was doing. I'd been learning how to track expenses, and I always made sure everyone got paid on time, but I was barely scraping by. I'd taken out some ads to try to bring in new business. Then I had the great idea to paint my car turquoise and have the Your House Sparkles logo added to it. I figured it was an advertisement everywhere I went. But all that cost money.

As a result, things were tight. Even with me living in the carriage house, it was a stretch to get by every month. When my father passed away, he left me half of Sullivan House, but he left the other half to Violet with instructions that she be allowed to live there as long as she wanted. I'd inherited some money in a trust, but I needed all of it to cover my yearly portion of the taxes and insurance. I'd also taken out a small loan for the room addition on the carriage house.

I was determined to grow my maid service, determined to never rely on a man financially again.

The new client I was meeting lived on the edge of town in a housing development not far from Ivy and Ethan. The houses were all minimansions. Nice, but a little soulless for my taste.

"Hello," I said aloud to myself, practicing my greeting as I pulled into the driveway. "I'm from Your House Sparkles. My name's Claire, and I'm the owner."

I got out of the car and glanced around. Each house was large with a similar architectural style. All the lawns were green with immaculate landscaping.

After I rang the bell, a well-groomed woman about my age opened the door. I gave her my rehearsed greeting and then put my hand out. "Are you Mona?"

She nodded. Mona was a tall, slender brunette with a limp-fish handshake so lifeless, I worried whether someone should check her pulse.

"You're the maid?" She lifted her nose slightly and took in my appearance in a way that suggested I was emitting an odor.

"Yes. It's nice to meet you."

She opened the door wider, and I stepped inside the entryway. It had a parquet floor with a large crystal chandelier overhead.

"Let me show you the house."

"That sounds great." I had my clipboard with me, ready to check off the number of rooms she wanted cleaned and what she wanted done in each one. "How did you hear about our service?" I asked, following her up a staircase with thick beige carpeting. I always tried to find out how people heard of us so I could tell which one of my ads was working.

She glanced over her shoulder at me. "My friend Ivy recommended you."

I hid my irritation. After all, I should have been glad Ivy was sending business my way. In fact, this was the third new customer in a month that came from Ivy selling me to the women she socialized with.

After following Mona down a long hallway, I noticed double doors ahead of us. She swung them open and led me into an elaborate master bedroom. To be honest, it was a mess. Not that I was judging, since I was here to fix the mess. She then led me into the large attached bathroom, which was equally messy.

"Here is where I'd like you to start."

I balanced the clipboard on my arm and made note of the type of tub she had so I could bring the right cleaning materials next time. There was marble and porcelain, plus the floors were ceramic tile, which I'd found was best to vacuum first and then clean with a microfiber mop. I made a note of that too.

She stood there with her arms crossed, staring at me as I wrote.

"My understanding is that you'd bring your own cleaning supplies," she said, still staring.

"That's right." I finished writing and looked up at her from the clipboard.

"Well, where are they?"

"Excuse me?"

"Where are your cleaning supplies?" She spoke slowly like I was an idiot. Her round blue eyes were spaced far apart and bulged out. They reminded me of a fish—just like her handshake.

"Oh, I'm not here to clean right now. I'm here to find out what your needs are so we can do the best job for you when we do come back and clean."

She gaped at me with those bulging eyes. Her lips were puffed up and probably fake. I watched the way her mouth opened and closed. Weird. She really looked like a fish.

"How often do you think you'd like us to come in and clean?" I lifted my pen, ready to write down her response. "We can do weekly, biweekly, or monthly." I explained how our prices were prorated by how often she needed us. "Most people do bi—"

"You're not cleaning today?" she asked, clearly agitated. "I thought you were here to clean."

"No, as I just explained, and as I also explained in the email we sent you, this is only a preliminary meeting to determine your needs. Afterward, we'll schedule your cleanings."

"My *needs*?" she hissed. "My *needs* are that I want my house cleaned right fucking now!" Her blowfish lips rapidly opened and closed.

I took a deep breath and studied my clipboard. I had two choices. I could thank her politely for her time and walk out of here, or I could smile and figure out a way to make her happy and keep this job. I didn't enjoy having these kinds of clients, but unfortunately, they were a reality.

My ever-dwindling bank account was also a reality.

I ran through the day's schedule in my mind to see if there was some way I could accommodate her. Laurie and Kyle were already booked, and neither of them worked after their kids got out of school. I had two more jobs today, and then I was meeting Leah and Theo for dinner tonight.

I sighed to myself. They wouldn't like it, but I would have to cancel.

"I have a couple more jobs today," I told Mona, "but I could come back and clean your house this evening. Would that be acceptable?"

She glanced down at her well-manicured hands, fingering the big rock on her finger. "I suppose I'll give you another chance, but *only* because Ivy recommended you."

We set up a time for later that evening. Afterward, she showed me the rest of the house and what she wanted done, complaining the entire time about how she wasn't happy with this miscommunication, how she expected more professionalism next time. "I'll be inspecting your work," she said, swinging her dark hair over her shoulder, "so don't think you can get away with laziness. I have *very* high standards."

Part of me felt like sticking my pen right into one of her big fish eyes, but I continued to smile politely. I'd learned after working with the public that you had to kill them with kindness.

I CALLED Leah on the way to my next job, telling her the bad news that I'd have to cancel dinner. We usually met at the town's main diner, a place called Bijou's Cafe that had outstanding desserts.

"Seriously? This is the third time in a row."

"I know. I'm sorry."

"Is it because of work?"

"A new client I met today." I briefly explained the situation and the misunderstanding between Mona and me.

"Damn, she sounds like a real witch. Maybe you should fire her and move on. You don't need people like that in your life."

"Maybe." I did occasionally "fire" clients, though I tried to avoid it. "I'm not going to build a business turning customers away."

"I just hate you slaving away for someone so awful. I guess it's no surprise that Ivy sent her."

I didn't reply. Leah hated Ivy, and the feeling was mutual. I'd known Leah since grade school, so the two of them were well acquainted.

"Have you noticed how all these new customers Ivy sends you are complete bitches?" Leah pointed out. "Every last one of them."

"At least she's trying to be supportive."

"I think she's doing it on purpose. She wants to torture you."

"I doubt that." Ivy always hung out with the mean girls at school. In fact, she was the head mean girl, so I shouldn't be surprised that all her friends were awful. "That last one she sent to me wasn't so bad."

"The one who wanted you to scrub her shower tiles with a toothbrush and baking soda?"

"At least she tipped well." In truth, she was horrible—so horrible that Laurie and Kyle both refused to go back after the first time they cleaned for her.

"Ivy has it in for you. She's always been jealous."

It wasn't the first time Leah had tried to convince me of this. I couldn't understand why Ivy would have any reason to be jealous. When we were younger, it seemed like she had everything—looks, brains, the whole package. She was the most popular girl in school, though, admittedly, a lot of people were afraid of her.

"I seriously doubt it. Why would she be jealous? Especially now."

"Because deep down in her black heart, she knows you're a better person than she'll ever be."

"I don't think she believes that or even cares."

"Trust me. That's why she's only happy if you're miserable."

It did seem that way, but our history wasn't all bad. I remembered camping with Ivy in the backyard during middle school after her mom married my dad, giggling all night as we talked about boys. Everything changed during high school though. I caught her in bed with some guy during the summer between junior and senior year, and after that she acted different toward me. They were inside the carriage house having sex, and I got the impression it wasn't the first time. I didn't see who it was, but I figured it was her boyfriend, Derek—the captain of the football team. Predictably, Ivy only dated star athletes. She was upset when I caught them, but I told her I'd keep her secret. And I did. I never said a word to anyone.

After high school, she left for college in California and stayed there. When my father died three years ago, she showed up out of the blue and announced she was moving back home. At first I didn't know what to make of it. At my dad's funeral, she wept as deeply as I did. It surprised me. He may have been her stepdad, but Ivy obviously loved him.

The memory of those tears was what pushed me to try and get along with her, despite what happened with Ethan afterward. Not that I'd ever forgive them for betraying me. There were days after my dad died, and after their affair came out, when I wanted to scream. But I was doing my best to move on.

"I couldn't get a hold of Theo," I said, figuring I'd change the subject. "I texted her but haven't heard back. Have you talked to her today?"

"She probably has her phone off or is busy with her bees."

"Probably," I said. "I'll try calling her later."

Theo, short for Theodora, was an entomologist specializing in honey bees. She worked for the university, which had a small research facility outside of town. The mention of Theo's phone made me think of that thief Philip again. "Listen, do you think I should change the name of Your House Sparkles to something else?"

"No, of course not."

"Someone told me they thought it wasn't a good name. That it wasn't strong enough."

"I think it's charming. Who the heck told you that?"

"No one. Just some guy."

"A guy?" Her tone perked up. Despite my insistence on not dating, she was always on the hunt for me. "Do tell. Is he cute?"

"No, he's an asshat," I said, pulling into the driveway for my next cleaning job.

"A hot asshat, I hope."

Philip obviously was hot, but I wasn't going to admit that.

"Hmm, your silence is loud," she said, and I could hear the grin in her voice. "Deafening."

"He's Doug's cousin."

Now it was Leah's turn for silence. She'd met Doug recently when she hired him to build some extra storage space for her yarn. "Well, don't worry. Neil has a cute single friend, and I want you to meet him."

"Absolutely not." I turned the car engine off. "And I have to go to work now."

"It's not a date or anything. Just a couple of beers."

"Forget it."

"Come on. He's got nice shoulders and a Spiderman tattoo."

"I don't care."

Leah lowered her voice. "I'll bet I could convince him to wear an eye patch and a fake peg leg."

I smiled. I kind of had a thing for pirates.

"And not that I was *looking* or anything." She coughed lightly. "But I'm pretty sure his package is hefty size."

"Sorry." I chuckled. "I'm not interested. Hefty size or otherwise."

I WAS STILL CHUCKLING when I cleaned the next house. Leah could always make me laugh. Neil, the guy she was currently dating, was a vet who took care of all the animals on the small farm she bought a few months ago. Alpacas and llamas for spinning wool. She'd also acquired seven cats. To be honest, I sometimes wondered if she was only dating him to get a break on her vet bills.

Leah had left Truth Harbor for college and then lived in Seattle, working for an investment company, but she gave it all up to come home recently and live her dream. Her twin brother was the deputy sheriff in town. She was divorced like me—though her marriage had been a short one.

As I sprayed the bathroom mirror and wiped it down, I thought about the guy she wanted me to meet. I liked nice shoulders. An image flashed in my mind of Philip's shoulders when he carried me. The way they felt beneath my hands, muscular and sturdy.

I pushed the thought away. He was a thief. And an asshat.

Overall, I didn't have much experience with men. Ethan was my high school sweetheart and the only man, besides that one-night stand, I'd ever slept with. I sometimes wondered if that was why he cheated on me. I knew it was the cheater's fault, but sometimes lying alone in bed at night, a part of me wondered what I'd done wrong. I thought I'd been a decent wife, and hoped I'd be a good mother someday too.

I'd never admitted it to anyone, but my biggest regret from the marriage was that we never had kids. During the divorce, people kept telling me how lucky I was there were no children involved, how it made things so much easier, but privately I couldn't help feeling like Ethan had doubly cheated me.

After finishing the next two houses, I wasn't looking forward to cleaning Mona's gigantic McMansion. It had been a long day, and I was tired.

I gave myself a pep talk as I sat in my car by the harbor, eating a peanut butter sandwich and drinking coffee. It was nearly dusk, and the sky was pink and blue. I came to this spot a lot, gazing out at the sailboats and wishing I was on one of them. I grew up sailing and missed it.

I took a sip of coffee and reminded myself how hard work led to success. How this wasn't just a job for me, that I was trying to build something.

Sometimes when I couldn't sleep at night, I went on motivational websites and read other people's success stories. I'd learned how it was common for small business owners to work extra hard in the beginning so they could reap the rewards later.

After finishing my sandwich and shoving the wrapper back into my pirate lunch box, I double-checked to make sure I had all the cleaning supplies I needed. Everything in order, I started up my car, still sipping coffee as I drove.

Lost in thought, it wasn't until I pulled into the driveway of Mona's house that I noticed another car already parked there. I turned my engine off, then paused. It looked exactly like Ivy's red BMW.

No, it couldn't be.

My eyes flashed over to the front porch, and my stomach dropped.

Sure enough, Ivy was standing there.

Worse, she wasn't alone.

My cheater ex-husband was standing right next to her.

SIX

~ Claire ~

Ethan.
Despite the two of them moving back to town three months ago, I haven't seen or spoken to him even once. I knew I'd have to see him eventually, but I was hoping to put it off as long as possible.

Ivy's head turned my way from where they were standing on the porch. She definitely saw me.

Ugh. What am I supposed to do now?

More than ever, I wished I hadn't agreed to clean Mona's house tonight.

I took a deep breath. There wasn't anything I could do. It was unprofessional to show up late.

Gripping the handle, I opened my car door. My legs felt strange, and I tried to let the solid feel of the pavement calm me as I walked around to the back. I took my time getting out my cleaning supplies, setting up my wheeled cart.

My stomach clenched, but I forced myself to stand up straight and put a confident smile on my face. I'd read that faking a positive emotion could make you feel the real thing.

The two of them were standing together, and as I approached the house, it was obvious they were dressed for a night on the town. Ivy's pale hair shimmered. She wore a tight black dress with high-heeled sandals and was dazzling as always. Meanwhile, my turquoise shirt was stained with sweat. There were smudges on my pants from the last job, where I'd cleaned the bathroom floor on my hands and knees. I wished I'd at least freshened up. The eyeliner I put on this morning had worn off hours ago.

"Claire!" Ivy called out to me. Her shrewd gaze took in my work clothes and the cart I was pulling behind me. "What a coincidence meeting you here. Are you working for Mona?"

"Yes, that's right." I kept my tone even. I glanced at Ethan, but he faced the other way, talking to a man beside Mona who must have been her husband. Despite how exhausted I felt, I smiled brightly. "One last job tonight. I really enjoy running my own business."

"Ethan, it's Claire." She tugged on his arm. "Isn't this a coincidence?"

"Who?" I heard him say.

Finally, he turned around.

My smile faltered. He looked exactly the same. His wavy brown hair was a little shorter, but his hazel eyes, his tortoiseshell glasses, and his overall good-guy face were the same I'd once fallen in love with. His sweet, nerdy smile was the only thing missing.

"Claire?" He stared at me with a stunned expression.

"Hello, Ethan." *You cheating bastard.* "How are you?" I smiled brightly again and held on to my fake confidence with a death grip, like I was dangling from a skyscraper.

Ethan grinned. "Wow, it's great to see you, Claire."

I nodded, not quite willing to go that far in my niceties of politeness.

"What are you doing here?"

I didn't have a chance to answer, because fish-face Mona noticed me from the doorway. "There you are, *finally*." Her round eyes bulged while her puffy lips opened and closed. "I've left instructions for you with our nanny. You'll also need to take care of the diaper area."

Ivy turned to Mona and spoke in a teasing voice. "Now don't be too hard on Claire. She's a good worker and always does an excellent job cleaning."

"Cleaning?" Ethan's eyes widened, roaming over my dirty clothes, then to my cart of supplies. "You're here to *clean?*"

"Yes," Ivy explained to him. "That's what she does now."

I was about to tell him how I owned my own company, how I had two employees, but the words stuck in my throat.

"Claire is a maid," Ivy said with triumph. "She owns her own business. Isn't that great?"

Those familiar hazel eyes were still on me, and I hated what I saw in them. The way his whole face changed as the truth sank in. "You're really a maid?"

"Yes, I am." I still tried to keep my facade. My fake confidence had slipped away though, and I was falling fast, plummeting from that skyscraper. Of all the times I'd imagined seeing Ethan again, it was never like this. There was never pity in his gaze or in his voice.

"And you own your own business," Ethan said softly. "Good for you, Claire."

I wanted to punch him in the nose. Punch him in that good-guy face, because he wasn't a good guy, and I had to learn it the hard way.

I straightened my spine, even though my cheeks burned with humiliation at his pity.

"Well, come on, then," fish-face Mona said, waving me over impatiently. "Bring your supplies into the house. We haven't got all night."

Everyone stepped aside to make room so I could move clumsily past them, dragging my wheeled cart behind me like some kind of beggar girl. To top it off, I was still limping.

There's no shame in honest hard work, I told myself as I entered the house. *None whatsoever.*

IT TURNED out Mona had a three-year-old daughter named Champagne. Seriously. Who named their kid that? She was a holy terror too, with an endless stream of demands from which she was never satisfied. No toy or book was good enough. All food and drink landed on the floor. She threw a tantrum over the slightest thing, and I felt sorry for the nanny, who seemed at her wit's end.

I tried to help her where I could, but mostly I worked on the house. It took me forever to clean that huge McMansion. Mona may claim to have high standards, but from what I could tell, she was a complete slob. I scrubbed and mopped with ruthless intensity as I relived my humiliation on the front porch.

I have nothing to be ashamed of, I reminded myself. *They should be ashamed for what they did to me, not the other way around.*

When I was done cleaning, it was almost nine, and Mona and her husband still weren't back from dinner. I put my invoice on her kitchen counter and let the nanny, Taylor, know I was leaving.

"Here." I dug out a business card and handed it to her. She was only in her early twenties, but I couldn't help noticing how responsible she was. "I run a maid service. It's not a bad way to earn some extra money."

She took my card with raised brows. "A maid service? I'm not sure if I'm interested."

"No pressure," I said with a shrug, wrapping the cord for the vacuum cleaner. "Just think about it. You can set your own hours, and there's a lot of flexibility."

I didn't actually need to hire anyone, but hopefully I would soon, and good people were hard to find. I figured if she wanted work, I could give her a few hours, and we'd go from there. I'd read online that successful business owners were always thinking two steps ahead.

"Okay." Taylor nodded, still studying the card. Her eyes flashed up to mine. "I'll think about it."

By the time I finally made it home, I was half dead with exhaustion. My arms ached, and my fingers were so stiff I had trouble unlocking the front door to the carriage house. Occasionally after work, I stopped at the main house to see Violet and Daphne, who had moved back home recently, but it was too late tonight.

"Hey, babies. Mama's here," I said, coming inside and turning the lights on.

"Kiss, kiss!" Calico Jack squawked. "Kiss, kiss!"

I closed the curtains and made sure the mirror was covered before I went over to the cage to let my parakeets out. I felt guilty when I was gone all day, and I tried to let them out whenever I was around.

I put my hand in the cage, each bird stepping up on it one at a time. So far I hadn't had to do much training, as both birds were already trained when I got them.

"Kiss, kiss," I cooed, encouraging the words I'd taught Calico. I stroked his bright green feathers. Quicksilver had already flown over to one of his favorite perches in the room. I glanced up at him. "No chewing, please." Unfortunately, he liked to chew and had already gone through one perch.

The bad thing about having a small studio home was I couldn't close off any separate areas for the birds. At least I'd have another room once the interior was finished. My dad had started building the second room onto the carriage house years ago but never completed the project. Despite the cost, I decided to go ahead with it since it would be a perfect office space.

After Calico flew over to see what Quicksilver was up to, I went into the kitchen and grabbed a Kit Kat bar from my chocolate drawer. I usually waited until my birds were asleep before sitting outside to eat my bar, enjoying the night's quiet, but today had been too stressful.

As I took the first bite, debating whether I should pour myself a glass of wine, there were car tire sounds on the gravel road in front of my house.

I went still. It was kind of late for visitors. An engine turned off, and then a car door closed. Footsteps on the path.

Who could it be?

Glancing at the birds, I moved nervously toward the window and slid the curtain back slightly.

I nearly choked on my Kit Kat.

My ex-husband was standing on my front step.

He knocked.

What on earth? I took another bite of chocolate, chewing rapidly. I usually liked to break my Kit Kat bar into pieces, but I was too distracted by this strange development.

"Claire, I know you're in there. I can see your car in the driveway, and the lights on in the house."

I remained quiet, hoping he'd go away.

He knocked again. "Come on, I'm not leaving until you talk to me."

I swallowed and spoke through the closed door. "What are you doing here?" Pushing the curtain back a millimeter, I took another peek outside and saw he drove the red BMW. "Is Ivy with you?"

"I came alone."

"What do you want?"

"Look, can you open this door so we can talk face-to-face?"

"We have nothing to talk about. Go home."

"I want to see how you're doing." He paused. "It's been a while."

"I'm doing fine. Now leave."

"Could you please just open the door?"

I opened it a half inch, not wanting my birds to escape. Their wings had been clipped, but I was still careful. "Go away! I have nothing to say to you."

His face was right there. "I just wanted to make sure you're okay. It was a surprise to see you tonight."

I didn't reply.

"Look, can we talk for real? This is ridiculous. Let me come inside."

Through the trees, I saw a light come on at the back of the main house. It was probably Violet spying on me. Great.

"I wanted to talk to you about something," he said. "It will only take a minute. It's important."

"Fine," I grumbled. "Give me a second." I'd hung up a thin curtain to block the front door from my birds and yanked it shut behind me. There was no way I was letting Ethan inside my house.

His eyes stayed on me as I stepped outside. His face was mostly in the shadows cast by the porch light. "Claire," he said softly.

I was still holding the Kit Kat bar in my hand. "Look, I have no idea why you're here, and I really don't care. I want you to leave."

"I didn't know you were working as a maid."

"That's why you came here?"

He lowered his voice. "How long have you been cleaning people's homes?"

"There's nothing wrong with it. And for your information, I'm also a business owner with three employees." I decided to include myself as an employee, wishing I'd padded the number even more. I should have added Leah and Theo, since neither of them would care.

"I always thought you went back to your old job." He shook his head. "What happened? I can't believe you're really a cleaning lady." He licked his bottom lip. "Look, do you need money?"

"*What?*" I went completely still. "What do you mean?"

"Do you need money? I could help."

I gasped as rage flooded through me. The kind of rage I hadn't felt since I found out he was cheating with Ivy. My pulse pounded. "Are you kidding me?"

He seemed surprised by my anger. "No, I'm not kidding. I want to help."

"You're offering me money? *Now?*"

He nodded. "Yes, of course. I didn't know your situation was so desperate."

It was a good thing I didn't keep a weapon in the house. "You rotten bastard. After everything you've put me through, now you show up here and act like you want to help? Like you give a damn? I don't want your money!"

"Be sensible, Claire." He ran a hand through his hair, with agitation. And what sucked was I recognized the gesture. He was so familiar to me, everything about him. Even his smell was familiar. "My practice is doing great. I can easily help if you need it."

"And what would Ivy say?"

"It's none of her business." His eyes went to mine earnestly. "Let me help. I want to."

And there it was. That nerdy grin. Ethan's good-guy face in full bloom. I trusted that face, loved it with all my heart, and in the end, it had betrayed me.

My teeth clenched. "Fuck. Off."

"What?"

"I said fuck off!"

Ethan blinked and seemed taken aback. "You never used to talk like that or have a temper. What's gotten into you?"

"Yes, I've changed. I'm not the stupid idiot I was when I married you!"

He seemed frustrated. "How did we get here? You used to be my best friend."

"You know very well how we got here."

He sighed. "Let me know if you change your mind. Like I said, I'm more than happy to help."

"Go fuck yourself."

He laughed a little, then turned and walked back to that shiny red car.

THE NEXT MORNING, I went up to the main house to join Violet and Daphne for breakfast. They usually ate around seven thirty, which was a bit early for me, but I didn't sleep well last night after Ethan's visit and was up earlier than normal.

The two of them were already sitting at the dining room table, Violet reading the newspaper while Daphne studied her phone.

"Claire," Violet said, eyeing me over her paper. "How nice to see you this morning. It's been a while since you've joined us for breakfast."

I pulled up a chair and grumbled my reply. I wasn't exactly a morning person.

"Hi, Claire." Daphne smiled. She was a year younger than Ivy and me and was the exact opposite of her sister personality-wise. I always thought she was prettier than Ivy, but for some reason, Daphne was shy. I figured it was from standing in her older sister's shadow so long.

"I noticed you had a visitor last night," Violet said, lifting her mug of coffee. "Anyone we know?"

Of course she'd noticed I had a visitor. Violet was smart, nosy, and rarely missed a thing.

"It was nobody." I yawned. I knew she couldn't see anything back there when the trees were thick with summer foliage.

"Hmm." She sipped her coffee.

I got up and went over to the dining room's sideboard, where all the breakfast food was laid out buffet style like a country inn. It was served this way every morning. Violet employed both a part-time cook and a full-time housekeeper.

When I first met her all those years ago, I worried she was marrying my dad for his money. I'd only been in middle school, but I knew what a gold digger was. It turned out I was wrong, and Violet had money of her own. She married my dad for love, and to be honest, they were happy.

I sat back down with coffee and a plate of food.

"Try the marmalade," Violet said, adding some to her English muffin. "Daphne made it. It's quite delicious."

I took the container from Violet and spread some golden marmalade over my toast, glancing at Daphne. "I didn't know you made jam."

"It's just a hobby I started recently."

I took a bite. It was the perfect mixture of tart and lemony sweet with a hint of something floral. It was unusual but tasty. "This is amazing. What flavor is it?"

"Lemon and rosewater."

I took another bite. "I can't believe you made this. Do you think I could get a jar?"

"Of course." She gave a shy smile. "I plan to make more soon, and I'll give you some."

"How's your maid service coming along?" Violet asked me. "Ivy mentioned the other day that she's been sending new business your way."

"Yes she has." I reached for the creamer, noticing how my arms still ached from last night.

"I'm glad to hear things are settling down between you two."

After peppering my eggs, I ate with purpose, trying not to think about Ivy or my ex-husband.

"I hear she and Ethan are thinking of trying for a baby," she said casually.

My hand tightened around my fork as I continued to shovel eggs in my mouth.

Violet sighed. She was originally from the south, and her voice still had a slight drawl to it. "Ivy's not getting any younger, after all. Now is the time to start if she's ever going to."

Ivy and I were the same age. Thirty-two.

"Are you still planning to finish that extra room, Claire?" Daphne asked. "My mom said you were thinking about it."

I nodded, grateful for the change of subject. "Yes, I am." I swallowed a bite of food. "In fact, I have a meeting with Doug today. He's coming by to look at the space and tell me when he can start work."

"Doug's coming by?" Daphne's eyes stayed on me. "What time?"

I shrugged. "Around noon, I think. Why?"

"Oh, I just wanted to ask him something." She quickly reached for her teacup. "About a house I listed."

Daphne was a real estate agent of all things. I couldn't think of a more bizarre job for her. In my mind, real estate agents needed to be aggressive and outgoing, neither of which described Daphne. Still, she seemed to make a living, so she must have been okay at it.

"Doug is such a nice boy," Violet said, holding her coffee. She smiled at me in a confiding way. "And I think he has a crush on you."

Doug was a thirty-six-year-old man, not a boy, but Violet referred to everyone younger than her like that.

"Oh, I don't know." I didn't want to admit to Doug's crush, since I wasn't exactly interested in him, and I didn't need Violet trying to push us together. She knew I didn't date, but I imagined they'd all feel less guilty if I had a man.

I noticed Daphne stiffening at her words.

"And what about you, Daphne? Have you heard back from Logan?" Violet asked.

"Not yet." She put her cup down. For some reason Daphne didn't date either. Something her mother was continuously displeased about.

Violet turned to me. "Logan's father is the head football coach for the Seattle team. He bought some property out here, and from what I've heard, he's building a beautiful home on it."

"Is that right," I murmured. I never kept track of rich people who moved to Truth Harbor, but it occurred to me I should probably start. There might be future business there.

"A realtor in Daphne's office sold him the property recently." Violet eyed her daughter with pride. "Logan came in with his father, and when he saw Daphne, he immediately asked for her number."

"That's great." I smiled at Daphne. "Say, do you think I could drop off some flyers for Your House Sparkles at your office?"

Her reddish blonde brows came together. "Gosh, I don't know. You'd have to ask my manager, Dave."

I nodded, adding it to my mental to-do list.

"You know, the chamber of commerce gives out a welcome packet to everyone who buys property here," Daphne offered. "You could contact them too."

"That's a great idea. I'll head by there today."

I ran through my daily list in my head. I had two houses to clean this morning, and last night's laundry needed to be dropped off. I'd recently started a barter deal with the local drycleaner's, where she washed all our dirty clothes for us, and we cleaned her elderly mom's home.

Violet gave me a pointed look before picking up her newspaper again. "Don't forget taxes and insurance on the house are due by the end of the month."

I sighed, not wanting to think about the large check I'd have to write.

Every year I owed money for my share of Sullivan House. When my father left it to both Violet and me, I doubt he knew it would turn out this way.

"Is everything all right?" Violet asked. "I'm happy to buy you out, Claire. You know that."

She'd recently offered to buy out my half of the house, and I had to admit, I was tempted. It would certainly clear up my money problems. I couldn't do it though. This was my family home. I loved Sullivan House. Where would I live? An apartment in town? Even the cozy carriage house wouldn't be mine anymore.

When I was younger, I always imagined raising my own family here. After Ethan finished college and we moved back to town, my dad had encouraged us to move in as a way to save money. There was more than enough space for everyone, but Ethan said no, that it was too old-fashioned.

"I'll send you the bill for the maintenance as well," Violet told me, flexing the newspaper in her hands as her eyes scanned the page. "We may need to install a new water heater soon."

"Sure." I stared at my empty plate, wondering how much that would cost.

The bills were stacking up. I had no choice. My business *had* to succeed.

SEVEN

~ Philip ~

"Chill out, dude, seriously."

Doug didn't seem to hear me though, as he continued pacing in front of the maid's gingerbread cottage. He had a meeting with her about some work she'd hired him to do. The ferry didn't leave until tomorrow morning, so when he invited me along, saying he wanted my advice about improving his business, I agreed.

"Do you really think I should ask Claire out?" he asked for the tenth time. It turned out this was the real reason he'd invited me today—I was to be Doug's wingman. "What if she says no?"

"What if she says yes?" I countered. "When it comes to women, you have to be optimistic. Think positive."

"I don't know." His face went into its usual hangdog expression. "I'm not like you. I'm not smart and successful. Women usually turn me down."

"That's not thinking positive."

"You're right." His head bobbed, and he punched his fist for emphasis. "I've just got to stay positive!" He continued to pace. An innocent man awaiting a jury verdict or more like the hangman's noose, if you asked me.

I leaned against Doug's truck and sighed with frustration. I wished I could get some work done. I promised I wouldn't, but it was a promise that was getting difficult to keep. Gavin and I were in the middle of a deal with a real estate group that was looking seriously profitable. I talked to him earlier, and even though I wasn't there in person, it sounded like things were on target.

It was a relief to get my phone back.

I had to threaten to go into town and buy a car before my mom and the pest finally agreed to discuss terms.

You'd think handling million-dollar deals for breakfast would make negotiating the release of a cell phone from a retired school-teacher and a flighty girl who endlessly changed college majors a cakewalk.

Think again.

I could be a dictator at times, but I liked to think of myself as benevolent. I'd met narcissistic CEOs who were less bloodthirsty and demanding than those two.

First I had to promise I wouldn't use my phone for work while I was on this "vacation." I had to agree I'd take off at least one day a week, plus one full weekend every month.

I was also told that I needed to start thinking about my future. Apparently I was a thirty-five-year-old man who lived like a little kid —my own mother's flattering words.

"It's time for you to settle down, Philip. Don't you want to find the right woman and get married?"

"Sure." I shrugged. "Someday."

"Because you're getting *old*," the pest added with relish. "Seri-ously frigging old."

My mom frowned at my sister. "Now stop that, Eliza. We'll be discussing ways to improve your life soon enough."

Her brows shot up. "Why? What's wrong with me?"

"Everything." I grinned. "In fact, let's pick on you for a change."

"Please. I'm the perfect one. We all know *you're* the one who's screwed up."

"No, I'm not. *You* are."

She stuck her tongue out, and like the immature kid I apparently was, I stuck mine out right back.

My mother sighed.

In the end, I agreed to all their demands. Not much of a negotiation.

The pest retrieved a plastic bag covered in sand with my phone inside. She'd buried it out on the beach. I wasn't thrilled about all this, but damn if I didn't grin with pride at my sister's hiding skills.

"I've taught you well," I said, holding the bag up for inspection. It explained why I couldn't find it anywhere inside the house. And believe me, I'd searched.

She fluttered her lashes. "You have."

So I was stuck in this backwater town one more day, listening to Doug freak out about a woman he was obsessively in love with—or at the very least had a painful hard-on for.

I glanced around outside of the maid's cottage. It was straight out of a fairy tale with a happily ever after and all that jazz. I could see why this appealed so much to my cousin.

Definitely not my taste. It would be like living inside a lollypop.

Though admittedly, when I ran into her in the parking lot yesterday, she wasn't exactly spewing rainbows and unicorns. More like fire and brimstone. It turned out she had quite a temper, not that I could blame her for being pissed at me.

"How should I phrase it again?" Doug asked, wringing his hands. "What should I say to her?"

I calmly explained how important it was to keep it casual with women. "Just ask her if she'd like to get coffee or maybe a drink. No big deal."

"What if she says no?"

"If she shoots you down, then act likes it's nothing. Don't let her know how much it matters to you."

He got a panicked expression on his face. "Do you think she'll shoot me down?" He gulped, staring at me like the oracle of all things female. Which, let's face it, I was. I'd spent many years studying the fairer sex, and knew what I was talking about.

"I think you've got a shot with her," I said, trying to be encouraging. In truth, I had no idea if he had a chance. If you'd asked me a few days ago, I would have said yes, but after seeing her temper in that parking lot, I'd say it was fifty-fifty whether she'd go for a guy like Doug.

"At least I brought her some of my kick-starter muffins. Maybe those will convince her."

I cringed. Those muffins weren't going to convince any woman of anything. "Just play it cool. Trust me."

Doug, being who he was, continued to work himself into a lather. Finally, I gave up and listened to my voice mail. Besides work, there were messages from a few women. A model I'd met at an art opening recently and another one who'd given me her number at some charity event. Two messages were from Madison, an attractive blonde I'd met at a dinner party last month. We'd been out a few times, but I didn't feel like talking to her right now. Instead I read the news and checked social media.

Eventually Claire's turquoise Kia pulled up in front of the house. "Sorry I'm late," she said, hurrying toward us with an armful of papers. "I got held up by one of my clients."

Doug's eyes bugged out in terror at the sight of her.

She still hadn't noticed me yet, and I let my gaze drift down to her voluptuous ass. I couldn't fault my cousin's taste in women. She was attractive. Short and curvy, and oddly, seeing her temper the other day made her more appealing to me, not less.

"Philip and I didn't mind waiting... not for you, Claire!"

"Philip?" She turned and finally saw me leaning against the side of Doug's truck. She scowled. "What are *you* doing here?"

"My cousin invited me." I shoved my phone into my front pocket and gave her a little smirk.

She was still scowling but then seemed to catch herself and turned back to Doug. "Come inside the house and you can see the room again."

"Buh... before we go inside, I'd like to ask...." He gulped. "I'd like to ask you a question."

"Sure, what is it?" She shifted the stack of papers to one arm.

"Do... do you think... do you...?" Doug's face went bright pink. He stopped talking and went back to his expression of terror.

She tilted her head. "Are you okay?"

His mouth opened, but no sound came out.

"Would you like a glass of water?" She went to unlock her front door.

I walked over to follow them inside, but Doug grabbed my arm. "I can't do it!" he hissed in my ear as Claire disappeared into the house.

"Of course you can."

"I tried, but I'm too nervous. I feel sick!"

"Ask her out later, then. Once you've calmed down."

"I think I'm going to throw up. I'll *never* calm down!" He stared at me with wild eyes. A crazed ascetic who seemed to live on nothing but those tasteless muffins. "*You* have to do it for me."

"What? No fucking way." I tried to pull my arm back, but his grip was surprisingly strong.

"Please, Philip. You saw what happened. She's going to shoot me down." He made this strange moaning sound like a dying moose.

Claire appeared in the doorway. "Is everything okay out here?"

"We're fine," I said, keeping my voice steady while Doug's fingers cut off the circulation in my arm. "My cousin just needs to tell me something."

Her eyes flickered over to Doug, whose moans had turned into gasps for air. "Is he really okay? He doesn't look so good."

"I think he took too much allergy medication." I gritted my teeth. "Just give us a second."

"Sure." She nodded with concern. "Let me get him that water and maybe a cookie."

"That would be great."

As soon as she disappeared from the door, I yanked my arm away from his barnacle-like grip. "Seriously, dude, pull it together."

"I can't," he moaned. "I just can't. You have to ask her."

"Claire detests me, so I'm the last person you want asking her out for you."

"Say you'll do it," he begged. "There's no one else."

This was unbelievable. I should have predicted something like this would happen.

"Please." Doug's bottom lip shook, and it looked like he was going to cry.

I let my breath out and gazed up at the sky. Blue and cloudless. I wondered whether I should tough love it here or not. How was Doug going to grow a spine if I did all the heavy lifting?

"Please, Philip," he continued to beg. "I swear, I'll never ask you for anything again."

I looked over at him. He was a pitiful sight.

"All right, fine," I said. "I'll do it."

DOUG WAS SITTING at Claire's kitchen table, slurping down a glass of water and eating a muffin. He'd gone back out to his truck for them and offered her one.

"I'll just save it for later," she said, wrapping it in a paper towel. I imagined it was going straight into the trash as soon as we left.

"Good idea," Doug grinned at her. He was still twitchy but seemed to have calmed down now that he knew I would take care of this.

It wasn't that I didn't want to help my cousin, but I'd always felt there were certain things in life you needed to handle yourself.

Women were definitely one of them.

As Claire stood in the kitchen, looking over some paperwork, I took in her small house. It was a tiny studio, and I could see why she wanted the extra space.

There was a galley-style kitchen with a dining area near the front door. The living room, which was also her bedroom, housed a large birdcage on one side. On the opposite wall were boxes filled with what appeared to be cleaning supplies. A giant brass bed dominated the center of the room. While the overall feel was sweet and cozy, it was different than I expected.

To be honest, there was something about that damn bed. My eyes kept going back to it. The frame was ornate with decorative vine work that trailed along the front and back. It was piled high with satin pillows and silky blankets in shades of red and purple. The effect was one of complete sensual abandon. It looked straight out of a Turkish harem or some kind of high-priced bordello.

My eyes cut over to Claire with her turquoise polo shirt and her hair pulled back into that spinster librarian bun. She was talking to Doug about how she'd like to get work started on the new room as soon as possible.

What in the hell was she doing with a sexy bed like that? There wasn't even a naked woman lying in it, yet I was practically getting a hard-on.

I imagined her lying in it. Naked with her arms over her head, gripping that brass frame so her lush body was on full display. A hot expression on her face.

We'd sink into the bed together while I sank into her.

I swallowed, feeling guilty for thinking about some woman my cousin was into. Maybe I needed to return that voice message from Madison. Clearly I'd gone too long without sex.

"Let's see this spare room of yours," I growled. "I don't have all day to stand around."

The two of them looked at me.

"Is this it?" I motioned to a door off to the side of the kitchen.

Judging by what I'd seen from the outside of the house, it had to be the new addition.

"Yes, that's it." She nodded.

Doug put his glass down and got up from his chair.

The unfinished room was a few degrees cooler than the rest of the house and smelled like pine. Gavin and I both worked for his dad's home construction company during high school, so I was familiar with this type of project. It was framed but still needed a lot of work. The insulation and drywall weren't completed, and the flooring hadn't been laid yet, though at least the wiring was in.

Doug came in and walked around, made a show of touching and inspecting the wood framing. "I spoke to my drywall guy this morning, and we should be able to get things started tomorrow." His voice squeaked. He turned and gave me a nervous look.

"Really?" She brightened and brought her hands together. "That's great. Sooner than I was expecting."

"Uh, yeah... tomorrow." He blinked and eye twitched in my direction, trying to relay a message.

"Say, listen, Claire." I stepped forward and rubbed my jaw. "I just had a thought. Would you consider meeting for a—"

"Will you go on a *date with me!*" Doug shouted at her.

She startled, her eyes widening. "What?"

"Would you have dinner with me... or... m-maybe a movie?"

She opened her mouth.

"Please," he begged, his voice trembling as he rocked back and forth on his heels. "We can do *anything* you want. Anything!"

"I don't really—"

"*Coffee!*" he yelled, remembering my advice. "We can have coffee!" He began to moan like a dying moose again.

She appeared stunned.

"Please, don't shoot me down," he begged, still moaning.

I was stunned as well. I'd never seen such a pathetic display from a grown man in my entire life. I couldn't believe the two of us were even related. I honestly wondered if Aunt Linda had gotten the wrong baby from the hospital years ago.

"I guess a movie would be... okay," Claire said, shifting uncomfortably.

"It would?" Doug gaped at her. "You'd go to a movie with me?"

"All right."

"Saturday night at six?"

She nodded.

"We're going to have a really great time. I promise! Don't you worry!"

Doug may have been sick with nerves, but I was sick after watching this. "So you guys are going on a date. That's nice," I managed to say.

"Yes, we are." He wore a big grin. "A movie. Claire wants to go to a movie with me. You heard her say it."

AFTER GOING over a few more details about the room, Doug and I headed back outside. Claire seemed subdued when we left. I didn't blame her.

Just as we reached the truck, a young woman was hurrying down the dirt driveway toward us. She was tall and slender with long reddish hair. Very attractive. She wore a tan business suit, and her gaze was focused on my cousin.

"Doug, I'm so glad I caught you before you left!"

He turned. "Oh, hey, Daphne. How's it going?"

"Just fine." She smiled, still catching her breath from running.

"Is there something I can help you with?"

She seemed nervous as she began to describe some house that needed a closet added to help increase its value. Her voice was quiet, but from what I could gather, she was a real estate agent.

"Oh, I'm so sorry," she said, turning to me. "I didn't mean to be rude. I'm Claire's sister, Daphne." She put her hand out, and I took it with surprise. The two of them didn't look alike, and I would never have pegged them as sisters.

Daphne turned back to Doug. "Do you think you could look at the house sometime soon? It wouldn't take long."

He scratched the back of his neck and appeared skeptical. "Gosh, I don't know. I'm starting work here tomorrow, and that's going to keep me real busy."

"They wouldn't need you to start on the closet for another couple of weeks." Daphne was smiling at him. "Maybe we could meet this weekend? I'll buy you a coffee, and we can discuss the job."

My cousin seemed to mull it over. Was he seriously turning down the opportunity for more work?

He shook his head. "Well, I can't this weekend. Claire and I are going to the movies on Saturday."

Daphne's face fell. "Oh, I see." She nodded. "I totally understand."

"Sorry, it looks like you'll have to find someone else to work on that closet." Doug pulled the keys for his truck out of his pocket, ready to leave.

I stared at him with disbelief. There was no way I was letting him turn down a job. "He'll be there Monday morning to give you an estimate," I informed Daphne.

They both looked at me with surprise.

Doug stood up straighter. "Now listen here, Philip, you can't just—"

"Text him the address," I told her. "He'd be *happy*"—I shot him a weighted look—"to build a new closet for your client. How many bids are they considering?"

Daphne's eyes widened. "I don't know. I've only recommended Doug so far."

"Great. Tell them he does excellent work and that he'll give them a fair price." Which was true as far as I could tell. Doug gawked at me, but I ignored him. "Be sure to keep him in mind for other work you hear about in the future."

"I will." Her gaze went back to Doug.

My cousin seemed upset, but I really didn't give a shit. Enough was enough. He wasn't going to get away with whining about his lack of work and then turn down a job right in front of me.

Predictably, he complained the whole way back to the house. He was still complaining when we went out to where my mom and sister were sitting on the back deck. My mom had her computer open in front of her while the pest was reading some kind of manuscript.

"You can't just take over and tell me how to run my business!" he whined. "You crossed the line, Philip."

"What happened?" my sister asked, looking up from her reading material.

I turned to Doug, exasperated. "I just did you a favor. If you put as much effort into your business as you do into complaining, you'd be successful."

He opened his mouth, then closed it.

"Philip," my mom reprimanded me from where she was sitting. "Please don't talk to him like that."

Doug smirked, bolstered by my mom. "Yeah, you shouldn't talk to me like that. Who do you think you are?"

My eyes settled on him, and I gave him my coldest glare, the one I used during contract negotiations when I suspected somebody was trying to fuck me.

He squirmed, turning away.

"This woman is my mother," I informed him. "That's the reason she gets to speak to me that way. It's time for you to stop whining and act like a man. Take some responsibility for yourself, for Christ's sake."

Doug blinked at me. His bottom lip quivered, and then his whole face crumbled. "You're right!" he wailed, collapsing onto one of the deck chairs. "Everything you said about me is true. I'm a complete failure!"

Shit. "Look, I didn't mean to be so harsh. But you were just telling us how you're not getting enough work."

"I'm my own worst enemy!"

"Why would you turn down a job?" I sat across from him, genuinely curious. I could feel my mom and the pest watching our conversation.

"I don't know. I just get nervous." He stared at me with those large brown eyes. "I'm worried I'll get my hopes up and then be disappointed when they hire someone else."

"But that's part of doing business. Competition is healthy. You just move on to the next opportunity."

My sister put down her manuscript and smiled at my cousin. "I don't think you're a failure. Not at all."

"None of us think that, Douglas," my mom said. "You have your own business, and you live in this lovely town."

"I suppose," he mumbled.

"Hey, and you just got Claire to go out to the movies with you," I added, trying to cheer him up.

He brightened. "I did, didn't I?"

I flashed back to the scene earlier and wondered how often he used that begging technique to get women to go out with him. It was horrifying to watch, but obviously it worked.

His expression turned smug. "It's a good thing I didn't listen to *you.*"

"What do you mean?"

"You told me I should wait and ask her later."

I leaned back in my chair. "That's only because you were freaking out."

"You told me I should play it cool. That women don't like guys who show emotion or get attached."

My mom and sister both made scoffing noises.

I shrugged. "That's not exactly what I said. Though it's basically true."

A phone rang somewhere in the house, and my mom got up. "Please don't listen to my son when it comes to women," she told Doug before going inside. "He doesn't know what he's talking about."

"Definitely don't listen to him." The pest leaned forward. "Everything my brother says about women is dead *wrong*."

"Excuse me." I turned to her. "And how would you know?"

"Hello? I *am* a woman."

I rolled my eyes. "Give me a break. You're a kid."

"I'm twenty-four!"

I grumbled a little. I knew my sister was in her twenties and even dated, but I didn't like to think of her as a grown woman with a bunch of loser guys chasing after her.

"The only reason my brother thinks women like commitment-phobic alpha assholes is because he happens to be one," she told Doug.

"Hey, I do all right. I'm not exactly hurting for female attention." The truth was I was seldom turned down when I asked a woman out.

"That's because the women you date are all just as screwed up as you are."

"No they aren't. What are you talking about?"

"All those shallow relationships? Most of them only want you for your money or what you can do for them."

"That's ridiculous."

"You know it's true." She reached for her glass of ice water. "Why do you think Mom and I want you to find a wife? It's obvious none of those vapid women are going to stick."

"Who says I want them to stick?"

"Going from one woman to the next without developing any real emotional ties." She took a sip and put her glass down. "Let's face it, you're no better than a dog."

"Jesus, could you be more flattering?"

"Why? It's true. You *are* a dog."

Doug was grinning ear to ear as my little sister raked me over the coals.

A moment later my mom came in, holding the phone to her ear with a worried expression. "It's for you," she told Doug. "It's your mother."

Doug's grin vanished, and he took the phone. "Mom?"

The three of us watched with concern. From what it sounded like, she was in the hospital and needed him to come to Seattle. "I'll leave right away," he said. "Let me go home and pack a bag." He continued to listen for another minute before he hung up.

"What's happening?" I asked.

He sighed. "She was feeling a little dizzy, so she called an ambulance, and they took her to the ER. They're running some tests to make sure she's okay."

Not to be unkind, but this wasn't the first time my aunt Linda had called an ambulance for herself. If ambulances gave out frequent-flier miles, she'd have a first-class ticket around the world. Nothing was ever wrong with her either. She was as healthy as an ox.

"Is there anything we can do?" my mom asked. "Do you need us to help you pack?"

"No, I can do it myself."

Doug's hangdog looked sadder than usual, and I felt like an asshole for giving him such a hard time earlier. "It's a long drive to Seattle. I could probably charter a small plane for you," I offered. "I assume there's an airfield nearby."

"Thanks, but you don't have to do that. I drive to Seattle a lot. My mom doesn't like me living out here, says it's too far away and that I should move back home—but I don't want to."

I nodded with understanding. If Aunt Linda were my mother, I doubt I'd want to live anywhere near her either.

Doug wore a gloomy expression. "This means I won't be able to start work on Claire's room tomorrow."

"I'm sure she'll understand," I said.

"She'll probably hire someone else now."

"I doubt it."

He shook his head. "You heard her. She's anxious to get started on that room. Why would she wait for me?"

"She'll wait."

He hung his head. "Not after I tell her I have to leave town for the next couple days."

I didn't reply. I thought about how relieved I was to be leaving myself. There were a million things I needed to do when I got back to the city.

Doug shifted in his seat, staring at me. "Listen." He swallowed and leaned forward. "I just had an idea. Do you think... maybe you could fill in for me?"

"What do you mean?"

"Fill in for me with the job at Claire's."

"I can't. I'm leaving tomorrow."

He licked his lips. "I know, but it would only be for a couple of days, and then you could leave. I'll be back on Saturday."

"Now that's a fine idea, Douglas," my mom said. She turned to me. "Why don't you do that and help your cousin?"

"But the ferry only runs on weekdays," I said with annoyance. "I'll be stuck here until Monday."

"You just said you could charter a small plane anytime," the pest pointed out.

My mom nodded. "And didn't you and Gavin do a similar type of construction work for his father years ago?"

I didn't bother responding because she already knew the answer.

"It's the perfect solution," she said.

"I swear I'll be back by Saturday," Doug told me. "You can use my truck too, since I'll take my car to Seattle. You'll mostly be managing the drywall guy until I get back."

All three of them were staring at me with a hopeful expression.

I sat up straight. It was time to lay down the law. "Look, I have a company to run. I need to get back to work. Forget it."

"Work from here," my mom said. "It's only a little longer, and I doubt Gavin would mind."

I doubted Gavin would mind either, but that wasn't the point. I didn't want to be stuck in Truth Harbor one more night, much less two.

"Please, Philip," Doug begged. "I promise I'll never ask you for anything again."

"You already told me that earlier."

"This time I mean it. I swear!"

My mom and the pest were looking at me like I was a monster for not wanting to stay and help Doug. I knew I'd never hear the end of it.

I blew my breath out in frustration. This was unbelievable. "Two days," I growled. "And not a minute more."

EIGHT

~ Claire ~

"I can't believe you're finally going on a date, and it's with Doug." Leah picked up her beer. "Especially after you turned down meeting Neil's friend with the shoulders and Spiderman tat."

It was a lively Tuesday night at Bijou's Cafe, and Leah, Theo, and I were finally having dinner together. I glanced around at the crowd. There was a line out the door, since Tuesday was free dessert night and the desserts were amazing.

"It's not really a date," I said, shifting on the red vinyl seat. "He just asked me to go to the movies."

"I think Doug is handsome," Theo offered. She dipped a french fry into her usual ketchup, mustard, and mayonnaise mixture. "Exceedingly dull, but still handsome. And it's good you're going on a date."

"It's not a date," I insisted.

"It sure sounds like one." Leah eyed me. "I thought you were done with men."

"I am done with men." I described what happened earlier that afternoon with Doug groveling and begging me to go to the movies, and how his cousin was there to witness the whole thing. "I was basically ambushed."

Theo's green eyes flashed at me through her glasses. Bits of copper hair escaped her messy bun, springing out like corkscrews. "Wow. He must really like you."

"Yeah, I guess." I let my breath out. "I felt sorry for him. What was I supposed to do?"

She shrugged and popped a fry in her mouth. "Say no?"

"A pity date," Leah mused. "Just don't get drunk and sleep with him like you did that photographer."

"Very funny."

"At least Ethan's not the last guy you slept with," Theo said, nodding and chewing. "In my opinion, that photographer was a necessity."

"Yeah," I sighed, not exactly proud of my one-night stand.

"What happened when you had to cancel the other night?" Theo asked me, picking up her burger. "Leah said you had a horrible client."

"Ugh." I told them all about fish-face Mona and how rude she was. "I wish I'd turned down that job, because now she's refusing to pay me for all the work I did. She claims she's not satisfied and wants me to go back and clean her house all over again for free."

"Hmm." Theo chewed her burger. "It sounds like Mona might need a mysterious *Periplaneta americana* infestation."

"I'm afraid to even ask what that is."

"American cockroach." She gave me a sly grin. "They fly in warm weather, and it's been rather warm lately, wouldn't you say?"

"Gross." As much as I disliked Mona, I wouldn't wish that on anyone. "That's sweet of you to offer, but please don't tempt me."

She shrugged. "Just say the word and I'll have a friend cook one up for you."

"Wow, you're like a Mafia hit man," Leah said with admiration. "How much do you charge for your infestation services?"

"A couple grand, but this one's on the house." She winked at me.

I knew she was joking. Or at least I was pretty sure. Theo had a dry sense of humor, and I couldn't always tell when she was serious or kidding. "What sucks is Mona's rudeness wasn't even the worst part of that evening." I told them about running into Ivy and Ethan there and how they were all dressed up for a night on the town.

Leah rolled her eyes. "I wish they'd never moved back here."

"Me too."

"How was it seeing Ethan?" Theo asked.

"It was weird. He looked the same. I expected him to have grown horns and a forked tongue by now."

Theo smirked. "He's probably hiding them. Was he wearing a hat?"

"No, but his hair was suspiciously fluffy." I didn't mention him coming to see me later that night and offering me money. I was too embarrassed.

My phone buzzed beside me, and I checked the display. It was Doug. This was the second time he'd called since the afternoon. I knew I should answer it, but I felt too guilty. I'd already decided to cancel our date. I didn't want to hurt his feelings though.

"By the way, what's the formula for that soap scum remover you told me about months ago?" Leah asked, getting her phone out. "That stuff was amazing. I need to make another bottle."

"Just mix equal parts white vinegar and blue liquid dish soap," I said. "You can microwave the vinegar until it's hot if you want it stronger."

"That's right." She nodded and began typing my instructions into her phone. "I forgot that part last time."

By the time we finished dinner, the line for Bijou's was still out the door. I had their famous strawberry shortcake for my free dessert, and it was sublime. Worth every calorie and gram of fat. When I saw Bijou's daughter, Isabel, I waved at her. We went to high school together. She used to bring her mother's shortcake to school events.

As we headed out past all the people still waiting, I heard someone call my name. I turned and saw it was Eliza.

The three of us walked over. Philip was there, along with their mom, Sylvia. I said hello and introduced everyone.

"I can't believe how busy it is out here on a Tuesday night," Eliza said. Her eyes were striking, though not quite as intense as her brother's. "This place is like a party town!"

"It's a little quieter in the off-season," I explained, "but we get a lot of tourists during the summer months." I could feel Philip watching me, though I ignored him.

"Well, it looks like I might be staying for a while longer," Eliza continued with excitement. "I'm trying out for a part in a play at the local theater."

"Really? That's great."

We chatted some more, and then, just as we were leaving, Philip nodded toward me. "See you tomorrow."

I nodded back. It was a curious thing to say, but all I could think was he must be coming by with Doug again. Luckily I'd be gone most of the day.

"Wow, he's cute," Theo said as we were walking back to our cars. "How long is he staying in town?"

"I don't know, and I don't care. Trust me, he's an asshat."

Leah turned to me. "Wait a minute, *that's* the asshat who told you to change your business name?"

"Yes." I was grumpy even being reminded of it. "He also stole my phone."

"What do you mean?" Theo asked.

I told them what happened after Philip carried me up the beach. "He won't admit to taking it, but I know he did it."

"Wow." Theo shook her head. "You're right. Total asshat."

Leah seemed to be deep in thought. "He looked familiar. What did you say his name was again?"

"Philip. He's here with his mom and sister. Apparently he was forced into a vacation because of some kind of health problem."

Theo pulled out her car keys from her front pocket, since she seldom used a purse. "Really? He doesn't look unhealthy. What's wrong with him?"

"I don't know. High blood pressure, I think. He's a workaholic."

"What's his last name?" Leah wanted to know.

"North."

Her eyes widened. "Wait a minute, *Philip North?*"

Theo and I stopped walking because Leah had stopped.

"Holy shit." Her tone grew excited. "Do you guys know who that is?"

"No." Theo and I glanced at each other. I had a feeling I wasn't going to like what I was about to hear.

"He runs NorthStone Capital—the company in Seattle I used to work for as an analyst."

I blinked with surprise. "Really?"

"I can't believe I didn't recognize him. I've never actually met him though." Leah grinned. "I always thought he and his partner, Gavin, were so cool. They're eccentric but crazy successful."

I tried to adjust my picture of Philip to accommodate this new information. No wonder he seemed so full of himself. "Eccentric how?"

"They're like outlaws in the financial world. They never wear business suits. They refuse to play by the rules—no secret handshakes or cigar smoking behind closed doors. *Finance Today* had them on the cover, and they wore torn jeans and leather jackets. Back then everyone was calling them Butch and Sundance and referring to NorthStone as the Wild Bunch."

"And that's Doug's cousin?" Theo seemed to find this amusing. "Who knew?"

"I know." Leah laughed. "I can't believe he never mentioned it."

I rolled my eyes. "No wonder he had the audacity to steal my phone. Not to mention the way he criticized my business name."

"Uh-oh." Leah went still and looked at me with concern. "Maybe you should change the name of your maid service. I mean, if Philip North thinks it's a dud, it probably is."

"What?" I couldn't believe what I was hearing. I shook my head. "Forget it. I don't even know him."

"Trust me, most people would pay a lot of money to hear his opinion about something like that."

"So what?" I thought about the way he stood inside my house looking bored and irritated. The way he'd insulted both me and my hometown. I couldn't care less about his opinion.

I WAS JUST out of the shower the next morning, combing my wet hair back into a bun, when my front doorbell rang. Figuring it was probably Violet or Daphne, I threw on my white silk robe.

When I opened the door, my pulse shot up. It wasn't Violet or Daphne but Philip. The financial outlaw himself.

"Can I help you?" I asked gingerly, hiding behind the door. My hand went to my chest area, making sure I was sufficiently covered.

"Good morning. I'm here to get started."

"Get started on what?"

"Your room."

My brows came together with surprise. "My room?"

"Yes. Didn't Doug call yesterday?"

"He did." I nodded. My eyes went behind him to Doug's truck sitting in my driveway.

"Okay, good."

I was confused. "Where's Doug? Why are *you* here?"

Irritation rippled across his handsome features. He wore jeans and a navy T-shirt that made his irises seem darker and bluer. There was a day's worth of black stubble on his face, and he did sort of look like an outlaw. What he didn't look like was a man who had any kind of health affliction, unless being an asshat counted.

"What did Doug tell you when you spoke yesterday?"

I got a prickle of unease, like maybe I was missing something in this conversation. "I didn't actually speak to him," I admitted.

"He didn't leave a message?"

I licked my lips. "I haven't had a chance to listen to his messages." I knew I should have, but I didn't feel like it last night, and then I forgot this morning.

Philip sighed. "Doug had to leave. His mother was in the ER."

"Oh? I hope she's okay."

"She's fine. But I'm here to take over for the next two days."

Now I wished I'd listened to those messages. I assumed it was Doug gushing about the date I was going to have to cancel. "Excuse me, but did you say *you're* going to take over the work on my room?"

"Yes, that's correct. For two days."

"But do you even work in construction?"

"No."

"Are you licensed and bonded for this?"

"No."

"Then why on earth would you take over for him? I didn't hire you. I hired Doug!"

"You're right." He nodded. "You did hire Doug, and I'm happy to leave if that's what you prefer."

I pulled my robe tighter around myself, feeling justifiably indignant. "Yes, I believe that *is* what I prefer. That's what I'm paying for, after all."

He stared down at the ground before hitting me with that electric gaze. "I know it's irregular, but Doug asked me to fill in since I have some experience with this kind of project. He figured you didn't want to wait until next week."

I considered his words but didn't say anything.

He looked through the paperwork he was holding. A clipboard and an iPad. Doug had used one when he was here yesterday to take photos and notes. "Look, I'm mostly here to make sure the drywall guy gets started on the insulation." He paused and pulled out a piece of paper, holding it up for me. "And I can assure you he is licensed and bonded because I checked it myself. So what's it going to be?"

I sniffed, eyeing the paper. "Well, I just don't know."

"All right, suit yourself." He turned around and began to walk away.

I thought of all the boxes of cleaning supplies stacked in my small living area, the bags of cleaning cloths, the extra polo shirts I'd ordered because they gave me a discount if I bought them in bulk. My laptop was crammed into the corner. I'd been forced to use one of the boxes as a desk.

He was halfway down the path before I spoke up. "Wait! Do you really have experience with this kind of project?"

He stopped and looked at me over his shoulder, then sighed. "Unfortunately, yes."

"Okay. I've changed my mind. It's only for two days, right?"

He appeared to be thinking it over. Finally, he shook his head. "Forget it."

I opened my mouth. "*What?*"

"You should just wait for Doug to get back. Although the drywall guy might not be available again for a while, but maybe you'll get lucky." He continued to walk toward the truck, and, to my annoyance, I had to chase after him in my bathrobe and bare feet.

"I want you to get started right away," I said, panicked at the thought of this going on for weeks.

He was near the front bumper with me right behind him when he abruptly turned. His brows rose as he seemed to take in what I was wearing. My robe wasn't a mini, but it was short and above the knee.

"I've reconsidered," I said quickly. "I'm okay with you filling in."

A smile played around the edges of his mouth as he stared at my bare legs. "All right, I suppose I could do it."

"Great." I hugged myself against the early morning chill and could feel his eyes on me. I wasn't exactly a leggy supermodel—

which, if everything Leah said was true, was probably what he was used to. But then something else occurred to me. "I don't want a repeat of the other day when you stole my phone." I gave him a pointed look. "That better not happen again."

His smile grew wider. His gaze went back to my legs, then trailed up until they met my eyes. "I guess that all depends."

My body tingled from the way he was looking at me, and I found it difficult to breathe. "On what?" I managed to say.

He leaned in closer, lowering his voice. "On whether you have anything else worth stealing."

His expression was sly and playful. He was close enough that I could smell him—soap and the scent of a clean male.

I had this crazy desire to touch him.

My mind flashed back to when he'd carried me on the beach the other day. The feel of those strong shoulders beneath my hands. I wondered what he'd say if I asked him to do it again.

"Maybe you should carry me back to my front door," I said, trying to sound saucy.

Philip's expression changed to confusion. "What do you mean?"

I sucked in my breath, mortified. "Nothing," I blurted, covering up my dumb attempt at flirtation. "I was just kidding."

His eyes went to my foot. "You want me to carry you? Is your ankle still bothering you?"

"No, it's fine. It was only a joke." I laughed, though it sounded more like I was coughing up a hairball.

He glanced back at the house. "Okay, then. I'll get started on that room."

"Yes," I said, my face burning. "That would be great."

"I need to make a phone call first and grab a few things."

"All right."

I went back inside and got dressed, chastising myself the whole time. It had been ages since I'd flirted with a guy. I sounded like a nitwit.

By the time I was dressed, Philip was at the door again. I decided the best way to handle this situation was to remain cordial and nothing more. I'd treat him like any other contractor.

"There's a fresh pot of coffee," I said politely, letting him in. He followed me to the kitchen. "Would you like a cup before you start?"

"No thanks, I don't drink coffee."

I nodded. "It's not good for your blood pressure anyway."

He was looking through the paperwork in his hand but stopped to glance at me. "My what?"

"Your high blood pressure. At least you're managing it. My father had it too and could be stubborn about it. In fact, he was also a workaholic. Just make sure you take your medication. That's very important."

He seemed mystified. "I don't have high blood pressure. Where did you get that idea?"

"From your sister. When she said they forced you into a vacation because of your health."

Philip chuckled and shook his head. "Food poisoning, not high blood pressure."

"What do you mean?"

"I mean I ate food from a couple of street vendors when I was in Mexico City recently and got mild food poisoning."

"Oh." I took that in, feeling slightly silly for my assumptions. "Well, eating from a street vendor in Mexico doesn't sound smart either."

He shrugged. "I normally have a cast iron stomach."

"Obviously it didn't protect you."

"Yes." His voice was dry. "That's been pointed out to me." His gaze shifted behind me, fixating on something in the other room.

I turned to see what it was, but the only things there were my bed and the large cage with my parakeets inside. "Those are my birds."

His gaze moved back to me.

"My parakeets. Is that what you're looking at?"

He nodded, but seemed to be studying me like he was trying to figure something out.

"They're shy around strangers."

He went back to his paperwork, and I began to wonder if Leah was confusing him with someone else. While he had a commanding presence, he didn't seem like some big-time finance guy. His dark hair was shaggy and in need of a haircut, and he wore a pair of beat-up Adidas sneakers.

Surely he'd at least have new shoes if he were that successful. And why would he be filling in for Doug?

As Philip talked about the construction project, I couldn't resist admiring his body. His T-shirt was fitted enough that I could see how solid he was beneath it. I'd bet he looked amazing. It wouldn't surprise me if he even had a six-pack. I almost wished I could ask him to strip down and show me.

"So I'll grab those for you today," he said. "Unless you want to get them yourself."

My eyes flashed to his face. I'd been so busy imagining him without a shirt that I hadn't heard a word he'd said. "Um... get what exactly?"

"The samples."

"Samples?"

"Yes, for the *flooring*." He seemed impatient. "What else would I be talking about?"

"There's no need to get snippy. And yes, I would prefer it if you got the samples."

His mouth twitched. "Did you just call me snippy?"

"You are being snippy."

As he chuckled, his phone began to play spaghetti western music. He answered it with a quick "What's up?"

I took that as my cue to leave.

On the drive over to my first cleaning job, I called Laurie and Kyle to remind them about some schedule changes this week. I also called a couple of my elderly clients to see if they needed me to make a grocery store run, which two of them did. It was a busy morning, and by the time lunch rolled around, I was glad for the break.

I parked my car in its usual spot along the water facing the harbor. My coffee from this morning was cold, but I sipped it anyway as I admired all the sailboats.

I thought some more about Philip, feeling mortified. I reminded myself he was still the asshat who took my phone. Then I remembered the situation with Doug and realized I was stuck. There was no way I could call and cancel our date while his mother was having health problems.

As I started the second half of my tuna sandwich, the passenger door of my car opened and some guy jumped inside.

"Hey!" I yelped in alarm. It took me a second to realize it was Ethan.

He grinned at me, closing the door. "I thought I'd say hello."

"Are you crazy? You nearly gave me a heart attack. You can't just jump into a person's car like that."

His expression turned sheepish. "Sorry, I didn't mean to scare you. I saw you parked here and figured we could talk."

"We have nothing to talk about. Get out."

Ethan's hazel eyes were imploring behind his glasses. "I know I handled things badly the other night. I didn't mean to insult you. Honestly, I just wanted to make sure you're okay."

I put my sandwich down, trying to control my temper. "I'm fine. Now please leave."

Instead of leaving, he slid his gaze over the interior of my car. "It's funny, I've seen this car around town before, but I never knew it belonged to you."

I picked up my sandwich and took another bite, determined not to let him ruin my short lunch break.

He grinned. "It's obviously hard to miss."

I chewed with determination.

He shifted in the passenger seat, smoothing down his gray suit and dark green tie. An expensive gold watch on his wrist. Shiny loafers on his feet. He looked more like a successful financier than that scruffy outlaw back at my house. He didn't have that sense of command though. Philip struck me as formidable. Ethan still came across as the charming good guy, always ready to please. Ironically, I used to love that about him. I loved how he was always ready to help a friend or family member in need. That was why I believed him when he told me he was helping Ivy move her stuff into her new place. I was proud to have a husband like that. Little did I know he was helping her in other ways too.

"So how is business going?" He leaned back, getting more comfortable. "You know, I'd be glad to do your taxes for you or offer advice. There's no need to pay someone. That's just throwing money away."

I didn't say anything and continued to eat my sandwich.

"It's no trouble at all. You don't even need to make an appointment."

It would be a frigid day in hell before I let him touch my taxes. I picked up my cold coffee. "No thank you. I've already found someone."

"Are you sure? Because I want to help, Claire. Any way I can."

"I'm *very* sure."

He nodded, his eyes on my face.

Neither of us spoke, and there was a weird intimacy sitting in my car with him like this. I didn't want it, but I couldn't deny it either. It came from years of being together, years where I'd believed this was the man I'd be spending the rest of my life with.

"I don't know why you're here," I said, "but you need to get out of my car."

His eyes were still on me. "You've changed. You're harder than you used to be."

"And whose fault is that?"

He leaned closer. "I'll bet you're still soft on the inside."

I was tempted to pull out my pepper spray and blast him in the face. Let's see if he still called me soft.

I shoved the plastic wrap from my sandwich back in with the rest of my lunch. "What do you want?"

"And you're still into pirates, I see." He nodded toward my lunch box.

"Look, we're not friends, okay? I'm not going to sit here and make nice with you. I'm sure Ivy wouldn't appreciate you being here either."

"It doesn't have to be so awful between us. I've been thinking about all the good times we used to have. Do you ever think about us?"

"No." I mostly tried to forget he existed.

He looked out at the ships in the harbor. "Remember the first time you took me sailing on your dad's boat back in high school? The way you saved me from being decapitated by the sail?"

"The boom," I corrected him.

"And then I almost fell overboard." He chuckled. "Thank God, you knew what you were doing, or we'd have been lost at sea."

It was true. He'd been a terrible sailor right from the start.

He lowered his voice. "And then that night on the water together. Just you and me, talking and gazing at the stars and... doing other things." He smiled. "That was amazing."

It was the first time we were intimate together. The first time I'd been intimate with anyone.

"We have so many great memories. How did this happen?" Ethan seemed frustrated. "I never meant for things to be so wretched between us."

I sighed. This had always been one of his biggest flaws. Instead of taking responsibility for his own life, he shifted the blame. "None of this happened to you like you're some kind of innocent bystander."

"Being back here and seeing you again... it's like I've woken up to discover everything has spun out of control. This was never how I imagined my future."

"You made a choice, remember? You chose Ivy." Or she chose him, which was also accurate. Probably more accurate. Though it didn't really matter.

He shook his head, still gazing out at the water. "It's like I've been in a dream state or something, and now I'm finally awake."

I rolled my eyes. Besides being a spineless cheater, Ethan also had a flare for the melodramatic.

He turned to me, and I was surprised by the emotion on his face. He really did look miserable. Despite everything, a tiny part of me responded. I'd loved him once and trusted him with my whole heart. He'd been my world back then, and I hated to see him unhappy.

But then I remembered the horrible day I discovered he was cheating on me. The day I walked in to find Ethan on Ivy's couch with his pants around his ankles. She was on top fucking him. His hands gripped her hips as he groaned with pleasure. The pain was like ice water shooting through my veins. It froze my heart solid.

"I've already woken up from that dream," I said in a cold voice. "Welcome to reality."

NINE

~ Philip ~

"What the hell do you mean, you're not coming back today?" I held the phone to my ear in disbelief, listening to Doug's warbling voice tell me he was still in Seattle and that his mother still needed him.

"She's decided to... move. She wants me to stay here longer and help her fix up the house to sell."

"Have you explained that you have a job? That you run your own business?"

"I have... but she says she needs me here. What can I do?"

"You can tell your mother that she'll have to wait until you have more time." I just spent the last two days covering for him while putting my own work on hold. Initially, I'd intended to squeeze in both, but it turned out Doug's business was a mess. No wonder things were slow for him. When I stopped by the local hardware store to get flooring samples, I discovered Bradley Wood & Paint wasn't even listed as a contractor in their database. An oversight I immediately rectified.

"Oh." He sniffed. "I could never do that."

"What did Claire say when you told her?" Though we hadn't spoken to each other much, after two days in her house, it was obvious she was decent and hardworking and didn't deserve to be flaked out on like this.

I could hear Doug's heavy breathing on the line. "I haven't exactly told her yet."

"What do you mean?"

"I was hoping you could fill in for me on the job a little longer—just through next week!"

I was stunned into silence. Doug either had bigger balls than I'd ever given him credit for, or he was a bigger idiot than I imagined.

"I won't ask you for anything ever again—I promise!"

"I can't do it. You need to get back here right now or find somebody else."

"Come on, Philip. Please. Even for a few days."

"Just tell your mom you'll help her after this project is finished. It shouldn't take that long."

"But she doesn't want to wait." There was some kind of background noise. "Hang on, she wants to talk to you."

Great. The dragon lady herself—my dad's sister. It figured every connection to his family was a pain in the ass.

"Philip?" Aunt Linda barked at me. "Are you too good for us now? Is that it?"

"No, I—"

"Because that's what it sounds like. Have you forgotten your family? Have you forgotten who helped you in a time of crisis?"

My aunt once helped us many years ago, and she's never let us forget it either. Over the years, I've paid off all her debts, including her mortgage, and saw to it she had a new car regularly, yet it was never enough. "Of course, I haven't forgotten."

"Doug needs to stay here and be a responsible son."

"And I have a business to run with responsibilities of my own, so I'm sure you—"

"Don't interrupt me," she snapped. "I'm not finished. With my health the way it is, I can't manage this big house. He's going to stay and help me, and you're going to help him. That's all there is to it."

"That's not poss—"

"Stop being so damn selfish!" Her voice took on a disgusted tone. "You always were a selfish boy, and now it's no surprise you're a selfish man."

I clenched my jaw to stop from saying something I'd regret, knowing I was better than that.

"My poor Doug never had the same opportunities you had, and we both know it. But you don't think about anyone but yourself."

Ironically, the main difference between Doug and me was that he was raised by her—which, I had to admit, couldn't have been easy. She kept him on a short leash with all her imaginary ailments, demanding endless attention. I sighed, feeling a modicum of guilt that, despite everything that happened, I still had a better childhood.

"All right, fine. I'll cover for him one more day."

"Four days," she countered.

"No. And if you push me, it'll be zero again."

"Three days is the least you could do. You're acting just like that damn father of yours. What kind of man doesn't want to help his own family? Blood is thicker than water."

The muscle in my jaw clenched at the way I was being emotionally manipulated, though I couldn't deny it was working. "Two days and that's it. I have an important meeting on Wednesday."

"Done. See? Was that so difficult?"

I shook my head in disbelief.

"Thank you!" Doug exclaimed when he got back on the line. "I really appreciate it! I'm sure I can find somebody else to fill in if I have to stay longer."

"Sure, whatever." I was annoyed, but maybe the two days would give me a chance to see what else I could do to help improve his business.

"And about the, um, movie thing tomorrow tonight." Doug lowered his voice, speaking barely above a whisper. "Do you think you could fill in for me there too?"

I went still with amazement. "Did you just ask me to take Claire to the movies instead of you?"

"I had an idea," he said, still speaking low. I heard a door close behind him, and I suspected he'd locked himself in the bathroom. "Maybe you could take her out and then talk about me. What do you think?"

"Talk about you how?"

"Like build me up, you know? Tell her what a great guy I am. That I'm a real catch." He gave a dry chuckle.

I gripped my phone tighter. "That's a terrible idea. I doubt Claire would even go to the movies with me. She dislikes me, so I'm the last person you want speaking on your behalf."

"But you're *important*, Philip." His voice turned emphatic. "You're successful. Even if she doesn't like you, that's going to count for something."

How the hell was I getting roped into all this? "Look, Doug, when it comes to women, you need to step up and make the effort. Claire will never respect you otherwise."

"But that's why I need your help. If you tell her what a great guy I am, then it'll be easier when I see her next time." Doug went into his sad-sack routine, and I could almost see his hangdog face. "I know most women don't think much of me, but I'm a decent person worthy of respect. I get so nervous around her though. I'm worried she thinks I'm a dope."

"You have to show her what you're made of. I can't do that for you."

"How will I ever get her to fall in love with me though? I need help convincing her to give me a real chance."

"So you're really in love with this woman?"

"I am," he said eagerly. "She's the one for me. I just know it!"

I tried to imagine what my cousin's life must be like. Between his domineering mother and his low self-esteem, I was sure he seldom got laid. Then I flashed back to that pitiful display when he begged Claire to go out with him.

"All right." I sighed. "What exactly do you want me to say?"

"YOU BETTER BE NICE TO HER," my sister told me the next day after I explained how I was taking Claire to the movies that night as a favor for Doug. "She's not like those vapid women you're used to dating."

"I don't date vapid women."

She gave me a look.

Okay, so I sort of dated vapid women. Beautiful but vapid. Admittedly even I'd grown tired of not being able to have a conversation with them. "I'll have you know I'm currently seeing someone, and she's very interesting."

"What does she do?"

"She's a designer."

"What does she design? And please don't say purses."

I shrugged, feeling slightly uncomfortable. "What's wrong with purses?"

"Nothing, but everybody knows 'purse designer' isn't a real thing. I mean, have you ever *seen* an actual purse she's designed?"

I didn't reply. To be honest, this wasn't the first woman I'd dated who claimed to be a purse designer with nothing to show for it.

"How long have you been seeing her?" the pest wanted to know.

"I don't know. About a month."

"Have you ever taken her to a movie?"

"No."

My phone buzzed, and I checked my messages. There was a text from Gavin reminding me about the meeting on Wednesday with

Atlas, a commercial real estate group. He wanted to know if I'd looked over their portfolio.

Not yet, I told him. I let him know I was flying to Seattle tonight but had to be back here again on Monday.

After my phone conversation with Doug yesterday, I'd checked and discovered Truth Harbor had a small airfield, so I decided to make a short trip to the city this weekend. I figured I could grab my laptop and a few other things.

"Have you and this 'purse designer' ever had a meal with each other in a regular restaurant?" my sister asked. "Gone to see a football game? Done anything normal together whatsoever?"

"Not really." I glanced up at her. "Why are you asking all these questions?"

"Because I know you're not in an actual relationship. What's her name? When's the last time you even spoke to this woman?"

I smiled at my sister. "Yesterday." I'd called Madison yesterday to see when she was available. "I'm seeing her next weekend, and her name is Madison."

"So what's her favorite color?"

"I don't know."

"Favorite movie?"

I shrugged.

"Does she have any hobbies? What's her favorite vegetable?"

"Favorite vegetable?" I laughed. "Who cares?"

"For your information, that's exactly the kind of thing people in relationships know about each other."

I rolled my eyes.

"What's her best friend's first name?"

"Look, what does it matter if I know any of that stuff? We have a good time together. That's what matters."

The pest shook her head. "You've been dating this woman for a month and you don't even know her best friend's first name? It's just as I thought. Another one of your shallow relationships. You're still being a dog. It's nothing more than sex, is it?"

I chuckled. "Even if it is, I'm not discussing that with you."

The phone in my hand buzzed again. It was Gavin. *WTF? You're flying back out there on Monday?*

Long story.

Let me guess. It involves your hapless cousin. Did the dragon lady get to you?

I snorted. We'd been best friends since middle school, so he knew all about my family's sordid history.

"Who are you texting with?" my sister wanted to know, moving closer.

"Nobody, just Gavin."

"Oh, really?" Her voice changed slightly. "Tell him I said hi."

The pest says Hi.

Tell Eliza I said Hi too.

"What did he say?" She tried to peer over my shoulder.

"Nothing." I glanced at her. "He just said 'Hi' back."

She smiled, but I didn't like it. Every once in a while, I got the sense the two of them might be attracted to each other. I hoped that wasn't the case. In fact, it better not be the case. Gavin was my best friend, and I'd trust him with my life, but that didn't mean I wanted him going after my little sister.

BY THE TIME I arrived at Claire's gingerbread house, it was early evening. The house looked the same as the past couple of days—brown cookie dough siding with white frosting trim. Just like a fairy tale. *A naughty fairy tale*, I thought, remembering her bed that looked straight out of a seraglio.

I'd called earlier and left Claire a message about the movie but hadn't heard anything back. Unfortunately, that meant my only choice was to show up and hope for the best, because as far she knew, her date with Doug was still on.

The turquoise Kia with her business name on it was sitting in the driveway. The woods around her house smelled green and earthy.

I knocked on her front door and waited.

Nothing happened, so I knocked again.

I glanced back at her car in the driveway.

Was I being stood up? I paused to consider it. It had been years since I'd been stood up. Single, straight, and rich. Most women saw dating me as their chance to conquer Mount Everest.

Just as I got my phone out to try and call her again, I heard voices behind me. Turning, I saw Claire and her sister walking down the driveway.

Like the other day, it was difficult to believe the two of them were related. Claire's sister was tall and very slender. She was attractive, but I didn't find her nearly as appealing as Claire, who had curves in all the right places and a feisty temper to match.

But then I caught myself. I was here for Doug, to try and help him win this woman's heart. I wasn't supposed to be admiring her body or fantasizing about having explosive sex in that naughty bed of hers.

As usual, Claire didn't look pleased to see me. "What are you doing here?"

I chuckled. "Do you *ever* check your messages?"

"Of course I do." She seemed indignant. "I've been working all day."

Daphne smiled and said hello in her soft-spoken voice. "Where's Doug?" she asked. "I was hoping to talk to him. Is everything okay with his mom?"

"She's fine." The dragon lady would outlive us all. "He's tied up in Seattle though." I explained how Doug was helping his mom fix up her house to sell.

Daphne's eyes lit up. "He is? I could probably help. Maybe I should call him."

Claire opened her mouth. "Wait, so Doug and I aren't going to the movies tonight?" She wore jeans and a short-sleeved T-shirt that showed a nice bit of smooth cleavage. Instead of the usual severe style, her hair was soft and curly, flowing down around her shoulders. Her lips were a glossy pink.

"That's why I'm here." I'd already decided how to spin this whole thing. "Doug asked me to come by and tell you how sorry he was that he can't make it tonight."

I watched her closely, trying to see if she was disappointed. Was Claire romantically interested in my cousin? If so, it would make my job a lot easier.

"Anyway, what do you think of going to the movies with me instead?" I asked.

Her eyes widened. "With *you?*"

I shrugged. It was a delicate balancing act to appear indifferent and interested at the same time. Luckily, I'd had plenty of practice. Wooing touchy engineers at promising start-ups required a similar skill set.

"Why not?" I licked my bottom lip and sweetened the pot. "I'd like the chance to apologize to you for my recent... behavior." I gave her my most humble expression.

"You should go to the movies," Daphne told Claire. "There's no reason to stay home when you're dressed and ready. I'm going back to the house to see if I can get Doug on the phone."

She turned and headed up the driveway, leaving Claire and me alone.

"So what do you say?" I asked, still trying to appear humble. "Will you let me make it up to you?"

Her eyes were large and brown with flecks of gold that I remembered from the first time we met. Those flecks sparked now. "Does this mean you're admitting you took my phone?"

"I'm not admitting anything. Come to the movies with me though and all will be revealed."

She glanced over at her house. "I don't know."

"We can see whatever movie you like. I'll even spring for the tickets and popcorn."

She sighed with reluctance before turning back to me. "I guess, but just the movie. Nothing else."

I chuckled to myself. I couldn't remember the last time I had to talk a woman into going out with me. It was oddly refreshing. "Don't worry, I've chartered a flight back to Seattle later tonight."

Her brows rose. "You're leaving?"

"Just for a day. I'll be back on Monday to fill in for Doug again."

She nodded. "How long is that going to go on?"

"Only a couple more days."

On the drive to the movie theater, I did my best to put in a good word for my cousin. I told her how he was a nice guy and that she should give him a chance. "He gets kind of nervous around you, but don't hold that against him. I think it's because he likes you so much."

"I'm sure he is a nice guy, but I don't date." She was sitting with her head against the seat, eyes on the road. "You should tell Doug to quit asking me out. It won't get him anywhere."

I looked over to her as I drove. "You don't date ever?"

"No."

"Is there a reason for that?"

"None that I want to talk about. It's a long story and not one I want to share."

"I understand, but maybe it's time to change all that. Doug might be the new story in your life."

The theater was a multiplex, and judging by the poster, the movie she wanted to see was some kind of dramatic chick flick.

I groaned inwardly. Two hours long, though I was sure it would feel like ten by the time it was done.

Claire smiled. "You're the one who wanted to go to the movies."

"I'm not complaining."

"Your face is complaining for you."

"I happen to love deeply introspective movies about relationships told from the female point of view."

She snorted with laughter, and it turned out she had a dimple in her left cheek I'd never noticed.

I made a production of patting my jeans pockets. "Let me just make sure I have enough Kleenex for all the crying I'll be doing."

She laughed some more. "I take it you'd rather see something else?"

"And miss this tearjerker all the critics are in love with? Hell, no. I'd never forgive myself."

"Okay, but just so you know what you're getting into—" She paused for dramatic effect. "—there are no aliens or spaceships in this movie."

"I understand. As long as there are a few battle scenes with an explosion or two, I'm good."

She gave me a look. "Seriously, I should force you to watch this with me as punishment for stealing my phone."

I sighed. "That would be cruel and unusual, but if you're that coldhearted, I have no choice."

She considered me. The dimple appeared again while those brown eyes were calculating. Between her soft curls and soft curves, everything about her was turning me on. She even smelled good. Something feminine with a hint of spice.

"All right," she said. "We can watch a different movie, but I'm still choosing."

"I understand. I'm at your mercy."

Being it was Saturday, there were several films showing. In the end she chose a romantic comedy which, while not the epic sci-fi battle I'd hoped for, was better than that painful drama, so I didn't complain.

By the time we got our popcorn, candy, and soft drinks, the previews were already starting. The movie turned out to be surprisingly funny and had us both cracking up. Perfect first date movie. It had been years since I'd taken a date to the movies, and I realized it was because none of them would have wanted to go. The women I dated always wanted to be seen at the hot spots in town.

Claire wasn't like that, and obviously this wasn't an actual date, but I couldn't deny I was having a great time. We kept the tub of popcorn between us, and she kept moving it onto her lap.

"Damn, woman, you're a popcorn thief."

"I am not."

Our hands were bumping into each other in the bucket—not that I minded. "Is there any of that Kit Kat left?"

She turned to me. "I thought you got yourself a Hershey bar."

"I did." I lowered my voice. "But I'll share mine if you share yours."

Our faces were close, but she didn't move away. "I'll have you know I'm very possessive when it comes to my Kit Kat."

"Is that right?" My eyes went to her mouth. For a split second, I wished I could lean in even closer. I wanted to. I'd bet she tasted like popcorn and chocolate. Instead I turned my head back to the screen, feeling guilty.

A few moments later, she handed me a piece of her chocolate bar, and I was ridiculously pleased. I broke off a large chunk of my Hershey bar for her.

We continued to watch the movie, laughing at all the silly parts while sharing the rest of our candy. I couldn't remember the last time I'd gone out with a woman like this, just relaxing and having fun.

When it ended and we headed back to the car, I was genuinely sorry the evening was over. Glancing at my watch, I saw my flight wasn't scheduled for a couple more hours. I racked my brain for some way to continue things. Dinner seemed like too much, and I doubted she'd go for drinks.

"Would you like to get an ice cream cone?" I asked, remembering a place I saw in town.

"I don't know." Claire buckled herself into her seat. "I still haven't heard a confession or an apology from you yet."

"I promise you'll get both along with your ice cream."

"I *better*," she said, and I couldn't stop my grin.

As we drove back into town, we passed what looked like an abandoned factory. "What's that place?" I asked.

"It used to be a soda bottling plant, but they closed it down a few years ago." She told me how much it hurt the local economy. "It's busy here during the summer months because of the tourists, but it gets slow during the winter."

"Why was it closed?"

"The company moved its facility overseas. I guess the labor was cheaper."

I nodded. A familiar story.

After parking, we got out and headed toward the ice cream parlor. There were plenty of people out enjoying the warm summer evening. The air smelled like saltwater. Despite my earlier complaints about coming here, I couldn't deny the town had its charms. It was quaint and old-fashioned. Nothing like the city, but I could see how some people might enjoy the slower pace. It was like stepping back in time.

I tried to talk to her some more about Doug, mentioning how he would have liked that movie, that he had a good sense of humor.

"Really?" She tilted her head. "I can't picture that, but then I don't know him very well."

"You should get to know him," I encouraged her. "He's a decent guy."

"I'm sure he is. But like I said, I'm not interested in getting romantically involved with anyone."

After getting our cones, we walked down to the waterfront. It was balmy out near the harbor with a nice breeze. All the lampposts were lit, and there were tiny lights strung everywhere.

"So what flavor is that?" she asked as I bit into my ice cream.

"Coffee."

Her brows went up. "I thought you said you didn't like coffee."

"I don't like to drink it, but it's my favorite flavor of ice cream."

"Well, that makes no sense."

I chuckled. "I suppose not. How's your rum raisin?"

She considered me for a moment. "Would you like a taste?"

We stood by the wood rail that ran the length of the harbor. She offered her ice cream cone, and I put my hand over hers to hold it steady while I had a quick lick. It was sweet and creamy with a rich rum flavor.

"Not bad."

"It's my favorite."

"You know, I have an ancestor who used to smuggle rum. He's probably rolling in his grave that it's become so ubiquitous nowadays."

Her eyes widened. "You have an ancestor who smuggled rum?"

I nodded. "My grandfather, a few generations back, was a pirate. He smuggled all sorts of contraband up and down the East Coast and the West Indies. He stole ships too—one from the British Navy, apparently."

She seemed to have forgotten her ice cream and was staring at me. "How do you know all this?"

"My aunt Linda—Doug's mom—is into genealogy. She did our whole family tree a while back."

"What was his name?"

"Jonathan Quick. Though I guess everybody called him Quicksilver."

Her eyes widened. "Quicksilver?"

I took another bite of my ice cream and grinned. "Maybe I shouldn't be admitting all this. Kind of an infamous relative."

"Quicksilver was your distant grandfather?" She had a strange look on her face.

"He was. Why? Have you heard of him?"

She nodded and looked out at the water. "Pirates are part of the history here."

"Is that right?" I bit into my cone.

"They used the harbor as a refuge and a hiding place. We have a festival here every summer called Pirate Days."

"I never knew they came this far north."

"Oh, they did." She turned back to me again. "I guess from

growing up here, I've always been fascinated by pirates. I mean, I know they were bad guys," she amended.

"Yes, they were."

She didn't say anything more, just continued to stare at me with that strange expression.

"Your ice cream is melting," I pointed out.

"Oh?" She blinked down at it and then licked around the edges where it was dripping. I tried very hard not to let my mind go into the gutter.

I'm here to help Doug, I told myself. *My cousin is in love with this woman.*

The problem was I found her appealing. She was damn cute. I liked how she didn't put on airs and spoke her mind. I'd dealt with so many women over the years who wanted to play games. I hadn't realized how tired I'd grown of it all.

We both leaned against the wooden rail, gazing out at the harbor as we finished our ice cream. Boat lights glimmered in the distance. There were dozens of boats moored nearby, with some of the owners sitting on deck enjoying the warm evening.

I checked my watch again.

"Do you have to leave for your flight soon?"

"I've still got a little time."

"Good." She turned toward me and gave me her full attention. "Because I'm still waiting for a confession."

I chuckled to myself. It was clear she wasn't going to let me get away with anything. "You were right. I took your phone that day we first met."

Her eyes stayed on mine. The gold flecks in them burned. "I knew it. How could you do that?"

"I swear I was only trying to make a phone call. I was planning to give it back to you right afterward."

"And that's supposed to comfort me?"

"It was more like I borrowed it. In fact, I was going to drive out and return it to you that night, but then you showed up at the house."

"Do you know how much that stressed me out?" Those golden flecks were turning into a bonfire. "I have all my clients' info on there, all the stuff for my business. That phone is my life."

I frowned, taking this in. "Well, I hope you have backups for everything. If not, you should."

"I can't believe you hacked my phone," she ranted, her hands flying in the air. "What kind of person does that?"

"I didn't actually hack it," I admitted. Absurd as it was, I still felt irritated—embarrassed even—that I couldn't crack her phone. When I was younger, that would have been a no-brainer for me. I wondered if I was slipping.

That gave her pause. "You didn't?"

"No."

"Why not?"

I stared out at the harbor. "Some of the security loopholes have been fixed." I knew I should quit talking. Explaining my hacking inadequacies was nuts and obviously wasn't going to help my case.

She shook her head. "So you've hacked other people's phones?"

"Not as a habit. Only in an emergency, actually."

"Why would you even know how to do something like that?"

I shrugged, then rubbed my jaw uncomfortably. "It's just one of those weird things I know about. Look, I apologize for causing you distress. I realize it was an asshole thing to do. I'm sorry."

"You should be."

"I know. And I am."

She appeared to be taking my measure, and I found myself in the strange position of feeling genuinely lousy for something I'd done. I wasn't normally an asshole, but she didn't know that. *I guess we all have our moments.* I hoped she accepted my apology and this didn't ruin things between us.

I watched her thinking it over. "So that night, you figured out a way for Doug to find my phone on the beach?"

"Something like that." I lowered my voice and leaned toward her. "I thought I was doing a nice thing there since he likes you so much."

She shot me a look. "And I'm sure he'd never 'borrow' my phone."

"Probably not."

She was quiet again staring out at the water. I studied her a little. There were faint shadows beneath her eyes. Her jaw had a determined set, but there was something vulnerable there too. I wondered what had happened that she never dated.

From my time at her house the past couple days, I'd learned about her. I knew she left for work early and came home late. There were boxes of cleaning supplies and other items stacked in her living room. Sticky notes everywhere. Some of them had inspirational quotes on them while others were reminders for things she needed to do. From what I could tell, she was pouring her heart and soul into making her maid service a success.

It reminded me of my early days. The days before Gavin and I started NorthStone. I was a young entrepreneur back then, and I worked hard, even harder than I did now. Every day a hustle. I remembered putting sticky notes everywhere too. In truth, I felt a strong affinity toward her. I wanted her good opinion.

"I really am sorry," I said. "Sometimes I get so caught up in my own priorities that I don't take into account how I'm affecting other people."

She didn't reply.

"Do you think you could forgive me?"

"I guess so." She sighed. "But it's probably best if you take me home."

TEN

~ Claire ~

Despite my certainty that Philip had taken my phone, it was a disappointment to find out I was right. The problem was I was enjoying myself so much with him tonight, I'd forgotten he was an asshat.

An asshat with a pirate ancestor of all things.

His apology seemed sincere, and I could tell he felt bad. I believed him when he said he meant to return it to me that night.

But still.

I looked out the car window. Why were men so much trouble? More trouble than they were worth. I'd dealt with enough of their crap to last me a lifetime.

Neither of us spoke much on the ride back. As we pulled into the narrow driveway that led down to the carriage house, there was a car parked there I didn't recognize—a gray Toyota.

"Are you expecting company?" Philip asked, pulling up behind my Kia.

"No." I stared at the Toyota in bewilderment. "I have no idea who that car belongs to." I looked over toward my house, but bushes blocked the front porch.

He parked the SUV, and we both got out. I almost told him he didn't need to do that, that he could leave, then realized I was glad he'd gotten out with me. It was quiet outside in the woods. Dark too. I'd forgotten to leave my porch light on earlier. My little house always seemed straight out of a fairy tale, but tonight it looked ominous and more like a scary tale.

We walked up the stone pathway, but when we got to the front, nobody was there.

I looked around. "That's weird. I don't see anyone."

Philip was looking around too. "You have no idea whose car that is back there?"

"None."

He shook his head. "I don't like this. I'm coming inside with you."

Despite living in the woods alone, I'd never felt scared before. I mean, the main house wasn't that far away, and I enjoyed my privacy. Oftentimes I'd sit on my porch late at night, listening to the quiet or the occasional sounds made by the creatures that lived here.

When I got to the door, I tried to open it with my key but discovered it was already unlocked. Philip saw it too.

"Stay here," he whispered, putting his hand on my arm. "I'm going to check inside. Be ready to call the police."

I nodded, my pulse kicking up. "Okay."

He stepped in front of me to enter the house. I had my phone out, waiting and ready. I swallowed nervously. I could barely believe this was happening.

My heart raced as I tried to make sense of the situation. If someone wanted to rob me, would they really park their car right out front like that? I had nothing worth stealing anyway.

Suddenly the lights turned on, and I heard male voices shouting.

One of them was Philip's. My pulse skyrocketed, and I nearly dialed 911, but then I recognized the second voice.

I could barely contain my fury. *I don't believe this.*

I pushed through the front door. The first thing I saw was Philip standing in my living room, ready to brain my ex-husband with a chunk of plywood.

The two men were still shouting as I rushed over. "What the hell are you doing here?" I yelled at Ethan. "You broke into my *house?*"

Philip turned to me, eyes blazing. "You know this guy?"

"I didn't break into your house," Ethan huffed. He gripped the edge of my bed. His clothes were rumpled, and angrily, I realized he must have been lying on it. "I know where the spare key is kept."

"You have no right to enter my home! I don't care if you know where the key is." I made a mental note to move that stupid thing. "What are you even doing here?"

"I just wanted to talk to you," Ethan said, his voice slurred. "I *miss* you." He ran a hand through his hair before looking at me with a heartsick expression. "I think I'm still in love with you, Claire."

"Oh my God." I shook my head with disbelief. "Are you drunk?"

Philip was standing beside me, still holding that piece of plywood, and for an instant I wondered if I should let him give Ethan a good whack.

"Is this a friend of yours?" Philip asked me.

"Not exactly." I sighed. "We used to be married."

"I needed to see you," Ethan said in a pleading voice. "Don't you know what day it is today? It's our wedding anniversary."

I went completely still. *It is?* I'd been so busy having fun at the movies earlier that I'd forgotten all about it. And then I felt proud of myself. This was the first year since our divorce where I hadn't even noticed it.

"So what?" I said. "Go home to Ivy. I don't want you here."

"You don't mean that. I know you don't." He took a step toward me and tried to put his hand out, but Philip blocked him.

"You heard what she said." His voice was quiet but lethal. "You need to leave."

Ethan stared at him. "Who the hell *are* you?"

"I'm—"

"He's my boyfriend," I blurted out. I had no idea what lunacy possessed me to say such a thing. I just wanted Ethan to stop pestering me.

"Boyfriend?" Ethan blinked like he'd been slapped. "You have a *boyfriend?*"

"Yes, I do." I glanced at Philip to see how he was taking this new development, but his face was impassive, still staring at Ethan.

"I thought you never dated," Ethan said. "That's what Ivy told me. That's what *everyone* told me." His expression softened. "I figured it was because you still missed me." He looked at Philip, bleary-eyed, like he still couldn't believe it. "You're really her boyfriend?"

"I am." Philip turned to me, and there was the hint of a smile on his face. "As a matter of fact, Claire and I are crazy about each other."

I tried not to smile back.

"I can't believe it. How could you?" Ethan stumbled over and sat down on my bed. He let out a shaky breath and then glared at me. "How could you be with another man?"

I clenched my jaw in outrage. There were no words. None.

When I glanced at Philip, he was studying Ethan like he was an insect. But then I remembered he had a plane to catch tonight. "Listen, I can take care of this. You should leave. You're going to miss your flight."

Philip turned and looked at me like I was nuts. "Are you kidding? I'm not leaving you alone with this asshole."

"Don't worry, he's harmless. I can handle him." I glanced over at Ethan, who was still sitting on my bed, mumbling about wanting another drink. It was then I noticed the empty wine bottle on my nightstand.

Philip's eyes were on me. "I'm not going anywhere."

"I'll just call his wife to come pick him up." Though I wasn't looking forward to that conversation. I already knew somehow Ivy would make this my fault.

"Do you have any more... wine?" Ethan asked, hiccupping. "Let's open another... bottle. What do you say?"

I licked my lips, embarrassed about all this. "I'm sure you don't want to get involved in someone's pathetic family drama."

"Claire." Philip leaned closer. "I'm staying."

"But what about your flight to Seattle?"

He shook his head. "I don't care. I'll call and cancel it. I'm not leaving you alone with this guy."

I didn't mean to smile, but I couldn't stop myself. Ethan was still carrying on about wanting more wine. "Okay, thanks. I appreciate it."

Philip's eyes met mine, and when he saw me smiling, he smiled too. "I mean, come on." He lowered his voice. "What kind of boyfriend do you think I am?"

I CALLED and left three messages on Ivy's cell phone. "I don't know why she's not answering. It's Saturday night. Where could she be?"

Ethan sprawled out in my desk chair. "Oh, I'm sure she's out having a great... time. What's a little marital discord for Her Royal Highness?"

At least he wasn't lying on my bed anymore—Philip had forced him to get up and move to a chair. Ethan whined and complained, but Philip's stony expression left no room for argument. I was both grateful and relieved. The last thing I needed was my bed to stink like my drunken ex-husband.

To be honest, I was glad Philip had stayed. While I could probably handle things on my own, it didn't mean I wanted to.

I went over to check on my birds. All the shouting earlier had stressed them out, and they were huddled together. I felt terrible. At least they were still on their perch. When I first brought them home from the bird rescue, they'd been so stressed, they stayed on the bottom of the cage most of the time.

"I'm so sorry, my babies," I cooed at them. I wondered whether I should offer them some fruit, though I doubted they'd eat. I figured the best thing was to let them relax.

Philip came over to stand beside me. "Is everything okay?"

I explained how all the shouting had stressed out my parakeets.

"Damn." He seemed chagrined. "Sorry. I forgot all about the birds."

"Don't worry, it's not your fault." I glared over at Ethan.

Philip peered into the birdcage. "Hey, guys, that won't happen again. I promise. What are their names, anyway?" he asked. "I've been talking to them the past couple days but didn't know what to call them."

"Calico Jack and...." I paused, not sure how this would go over. "And Quicksilver."

"What?" He turned to me. "Did you say Quicksilver?"

I nodded. My eyes went back to watching my budgies. "Calico Jack was a ship's captain, and Quicksilver served on his crew. Apparently they were good friends."

"Which one is Quicksilver?"

I motioned toward the bird on the right. "The one with the blue and white markings."

"What a crazy coincidence." He chuckled. "I can't believe it. Why didn't you tell me this earlier?"

"I don't know." I bit my lip. "What was I supposed to say exactly? That I named one of my parakeets after your pirate grandfather?"

He laughed. "No wonder you had that look on your face."

Ethan snorted loudly, then leaned forward on his chair. "Are you fucking... serious? Did I just hear you say you're related to a *pirate*? Holy shit. That's why she's into you."

"Shut up, Ethan."

"You're like Claire's total wet dream."

Philip's eyes widened slightly as he glanced at my birds and then over to the pirate poster on my wall.

"You're not my wet dream," I said as my cheeks grew warm. I glared at Ethan. "Mind your own business. You don't know what you're talking about."

"I always hated your dumb pirate obsession," he went on. "Did I ever tell you that?"

"It's not an obsession. It's an interest." Such a jerk. He never could handle his liquor. Alcohol always turned him into a moron.

"Pirates are fucking *assholes*." Ethan flailed his arms so clumsily he nearly fell out of the chair. "Everybody knows that."

Philip was studying him like he was an insect again. He turned to me. "We should take him home. Do you know where he lives?"

I sighed. "Yeah, I do."

Between my cajoling and Philip's threats, we somehow got Ethan out the front door and into the back seat of Philip's SUV. He complained, though by that point he'd mostly gone maudlin and was declaring his love for me again.

"Tell me you don't still have feelings for him," Philip said once he shut Ethan inside the car.

"Definitely not."

"I know you were married, but that guy's a bonehead."

"That's why we're not married anymore." I glanced at the car. Ethan's face appeared in the window, his forehead pressed against the glass. He mouthed the words "I love you."

I rolled my eyes. It was terrible to admit, but I felt a malicious pleasure at the hangover he was going to have tomorrow.

We decided that I'd drive Ethan's car and Philip would follow me in his. I could only imagine the conversation the two of them were having as I drove, glancing in the rearview mirror frequently to make sure he was still behind me. At least I knew Philip could handle it. I didn't know him very well, but I'd seen enough that it was obvious he could handle anything.

I pulled into the driveway of Ivy and Ethan's large house next to their red BMW, with Philip's SUV right behind me.

As we all got out of our cars, Ivy came out the front door. She was wearing jeans, heels, and a tight crimson tank top. The little demon dogs trailed behind her. They began to yip as soon as they saw us.

"Hush," Ivy told them, glancing down.

"I've been trying to call you for the last hour," I said. "Did you get my messages?"

"I got them." Her eyes went from Ethan to Philip, lingering on the latter before coming back to me. "What's going on here?"

"Ethan showed up drunk at my house."

She frowned at Ethan, who was leaning against the SUV looking miserable. "What's wrong with you?" she said, obviously irritated.

He shook his head. "Go to hell, Ivy."

"He drank a whole bottle of wine and who knows what else. I think he just needs to sleep it off," I told her.

"Don't tell me what he *needs*," she snapped. "I know what he needs more than *you*. He's my husband. Something you'd do well to remember."

I was taken aback. "Excuse me?"

"You're pathetic. You'll do anything to hang on to him, won't you?"

"Are you *crazy*?" My voice rose an octave. "I want nothing to do with him."

Ivy smirked. "We both know that's not true."

Philip spoke in a stern voice. "This guy broke into Claire's house tonight. We're only bringing him home because he was too drunk to drive. You're lucky she didn't call the police."

Ivy's jaw tensed as she studied Philip, trying to size him up. She seemed uncomfortable. "Who the fuck are you?"

"That's Claire's boyfriend," Ethan offered. "It turns out you were wrong, and she *does* date."

"Boyfriend?" Ivy's mouth opened in surprise. "Since when do you have a boyfriend?" Her eyes roamed over Philip, and I had to admit her expression was priceless. I couldn't have chosen a better fake boyfriend. Philip was seriously hot, and between his stony expression and unyielding body language, he was also someone you didn't want to mess with.

But then Ivy's mouth changed to a smirk again. "I guess you didn't know Claire was two-timing you, then," she said to him.

"What are you talking about?" Only Ivy could turn my barren love life into something scandalous.

"Don't play dumb." She was still smirking, but her expression changed when she looked at me. "You were *seen*, Claire." She crossed her arms. "A friend of mine saw you and Ethan together at the park the other day."

"What?" I blinked at her in confusion.

"My friend Mona saw you two sitting together inside that hideous car of yours. I know Ethan left you, but get over it. Can't you just stay away from him?"

I opened my mouth, flabbergasted. "Are you kidding me? He got into my car uninvited!"

She scoffed. "How stupid do you think I am? And after everything I've done for you."

"Done for me? You've never done anything for me." Except destroy my life, but I was past that. Ethan was a cheater, and she was welcome to him.

"I've been recommending your maid service to all my friends. Have you forgotten? You can bet I won't be doing that anymore."

"Good! I'm glad to hear it, because your friends are horrible." I knew I shouldn't have said that. Those were customers, and insulting them was no way to grow my business. But then I realized Ivy would probably tell them all to leave now anyway. *At least I won't have to deal with fish-face Mona anymore.* "And Ethan *did* get into my car uninvited." I looked over at where he was still leaning against the SUV. "Tell her the truth!" I demanded.

But Ethan only shrugged.

I shook with rage, wanting to scream. *When will I ever be free of these two? Will I be tortured forever?*

But then I felt a hand on my arm. It was warm and firm, steadying me. Philip's hand.

I turned with surprise. Our eyes met. The clear blue of his was like gazing into a calm sea. I couldn't explain it, but I got the sense he understood me. He understood me better than I would have ever guessed.

"Come on, let's go," he said quietly. He leaned closer and put his mouth to my ear. "You're better than this."

He was right. I *was* better than this.

"I don't know why I bothered to help you at all," Ivy went on in a vindictive voice. "Your business is a complete joke, and so are *you*."

Philip's hand was still on me.

"Let's leave," he urged.

He stepped toward his car, but then something distracted him. He was focused on the ground at his feet. The demon dogs were there all lined up. Their foxy faces tilted at an angle. They appeared happy to see him.

"I recognize these dogs." He seemed puzzled.

"They're Ivy's. I was walking them when we first met."

He nodded. His hand went to the driver door of the SUV, and the dogs all followed it with interest. One of them yipped.

"I think they want another car ride." I couldn't help smiling.

Ivy called her dogs, telling them to heel, but they ignored her, still focused on Philip.

His mouth twitched. "Maybe we should take them with us."

"No," I said. "Trust me." Those dogs were seriously high maintenance. He had no idea.

"I wish you would take them." Ethan pushed away from the car. "She loves those damn dogs more than she loves me."

Ivy's face darkened upon hearing that, but there was something else too. She was wounded. She watched Ethan move past her, unsteady on his feet, and I knew from experience how a wounded Ivy could be a dangerous thing.

She flashed back to me. "This is *your* fault."

I shook my head. "You created this mess yourself."

"You betrayed me."

My eyes widened. "I betrayed *you*?" An ironic laugh escaped me. "I haven't betrayed anyone. You need to look in a mirror."

Her jaw tensed. Her gaze flickered over to Philip before settling on me again. "No, you started it years ago, and I'll never forgive you for what you did."

I stared at her in bewilderment.

Ivy turned and called for her dogs to follow, but they didn't budge, still too enamored with Philip.

"Heel!" she insisted, but the dogs only glanced at her.

Philip seemed bemused. "Go on," he told them lightly. Two of them yipped. Finally, he waved his hand toward Ivy, and all three dogs trotted after her.

Once we were in the car driving away, he turned to me. "Is she your sister?"

"Yes." I sighed. "Stepsister."

"I remember you mentioning those dogs were hers."

"Daphne is also my stepsister. Their mom, Violet, married my dad when I was in middle school." I figured he'd seen enough dirty laundry tonight that he might as well know who the players were. "Ivy married Ethan about two years ago. He left me for her. I caught them together."

"Damn, really?" He glanced at me, incredulous. "That guy's an even bigger bonehead than I thought."

His eyes went back to the road, his profile straight and true. I could tell he meant it. His comment made me warm all over. Warm in a good way.

"I'm guessing he's the reason you don't date, huh?"

"Basically."

"Not all men are cut from the same cloth."

I looked out the window and sighed. "I know."

"So your stepsister married your ex-husband." He shook his head. "Jesus, what a clusterfuck."

I snorted with laughter. Maybe it was the stress of the evening or seeing the absurdity of all this through someone else's eyes. "It *is* a clusterfuck," I said, then laughed.

"I'm surprised you still talk to any of these people."

"I don't have much choice. They're the only family I have."

He seemed to consider this. "I know your dad passed away, but what about your mom?"

"Oh." I looked out the window again. "She left when I was a baby. I guess you could say she's a... free spirit."

His gaze went to mine again. "Your mom left when you were a baby?"

I nodded. "She left both me and my dad. Just picked up one day and was gone. He raised me on his own until he married Violet."

Philip's eyes stayed on me until he was forced to turn back to the road.

We drove through the gate past Sullivan House and then down the dirt driveway. I'd left the house light off for my birds, but the porch was lit. After parking, we both got out. It was nearly midnight. Philip followed me up the narrow path to my front door.

"Thank you for your help," I said. "I really appreciate it, and I'm sorry you missed your flight."

"Don't worry about it."

We both grew quiet, and I wasn't sure what else to say. I was still embarrassed about everything. The whole evening was like an episode from a bad soap opera.

"I had a nice time at the movies earlier," I offered. Hard to believe that was only a few hours ago. It felt like days.

"I did too. And I apologize again for the way I took your phone. I hope you can forgive me."

I decided to let him off the hook. "I suppose it's all that pirate blood in your veins."

"Must be," he said with a grin, stepping closer. Close enough that I could smell him. Clean like soap. Like a guy.

His eyes were on me, but I felt shy. I looked down at the cobblestones as if they were interesting.

"Claire." His voice softened.

I bit my lip, still studying the ground.

"Look at me."

I forced my eyes up. With the porch light on, I could easily see his handsome features.

It was a warm summer night, the air dancing with energy.

We gazed at each other, but then his eyes dropped to my mouth.

My stomach went tense with alarm. I could barely catch my breath, and it wasn't because I didn't want him to kiss me.

It was because I *did*.

ELEVEN

~ Claire ~

I knew I should back away from Philip, should go inside the house and call it a night. I wanted to, except my feet weren't listening.

He seemed to be struggling with something too. "I should go," he said, though it sounded more like he was talking to himself than me. His gaze shifted from my mouth back to my eyes. "I should leave."

We watched each other, neither of us making a move to go anywhere.

I realized it had been a long time since I'd felt desire like this.

He brought his hand up and took a strand of my hair between his fingers. It seemed a sweet gesture, familiar, as if he were my real boyfriend. He wrapped a curl around his thumb.

I remained still, too aware of his nearness and of the effect it was having on me.

I could hear Philip breathing. It warmed me. Just like his words in the car had earlier. My heart was frozen, inaccessible, but this was the first inkling I'd had that a thaw was possible.

He played with my hair while his expression looked like he was trying to solve an algebra problem.

"What is it?"

He shook his head. "Nothing." But then he hesitated and seemed to think better of it. "Can I ask you something?"

"Okay."

He licked his lips, opened his mouth to speak, but spaghetti western music blared from out of nowhere. A twangy lonesome whistling that didn't stop until Philip pulled his phone out of his front pocket. He glanced down and snorted softly when he saw who the caller was before declining it. I saw it too.

"Was that Doug?"

Philip sighed. "Yeah, it was."

"Does he always call you this late?"

He chuckled, and there was a dry sound to it. "No, I can't say that he ever has."

He slipped his phone back into his pocket. Whatever the problem was, he appeared to have found a solution, because he stepped away from me.

"I should go."

I nodded. "Thanks again for your help."

"Sure." He turned to leave, but then paused. "Maybe we should do it again sometime."

My brows creased with confusion. "Do what?"

"See another movie."

A tingle of excitement ran through me at his words. "Maybe we should."

He grinned, and it did all sorts of things to me. My stomach flipped like it was doing cartwheels.

Philip tilted his head toward the driveway. "Okay, I'm leaving."

"I'll see you later."

He didn't leave though, just stood there watching me. Finally, he gave a short nod.

As he walked away, I didn't move from the spot. I listened as he got into his car, as the engine started. I couldn't explain it, but there was a spark ignited inside of me. Somehow this night had been momentous in a way I couldn't quite put into words.

I heard his car backing out of the driveway and realized I didn't want to be caught still standing on the front porch. I fumbled to get the door unlocked. Once inside, I slid the curtain back and watched his headlights until they were gone.

Then I checked on my birds.

"Hi, sweeties," I said, going over to them. Happily, they both looked relaxed and weren't huddling together anymore.

"Kiss, kiss," squawked Calico Jack.

"I bet you're hungry. I'll be right back with dinner." I went into the kitchen to make a plate of food for them—steamed veggies and grains with some fruit on the side.

I hummed to myself as I prepared their meal. It was crazy late. I should have been exhausted, especially after the night I'd just had. Instead I felt like dancing.

I went back and opened the cage door, setting the plate on the bottom. Both birds hopped down for their meal. I sat nearby and watched them eat, relieved they weren't stressed anymore. When they were done, Calico Jack came to the open door, and I put my hand out for him to step up.

We sat together as I stroked his green feathers. "Guess what?" I whispered to him. "I met a guy."

His dark eyes appeared to contemplate me. Apparently he was as confused as I was about what to do with this.

"I didn't like him at first," I admitted, "but it turns out he's okay. He's even related to a pirate."

Calico ruffled his feathers.

"Don't worry, nothing romantic is going to happen. I'm miles from being ready for that."

He cocked his head to the side.

"But maybe someday," I murmured, still stroking him. "Maybe someday I will be ready."

I WOKE up the next morning to the sound of my phone buzzing with a text from Violet. This was strange for a number of reasons. First of all, Violet never texted anyone as far I knew. In fact, I was surprised she knew how to text. Second of all was the message itself.

Your presence is requested at the house for breakfast.

It was Sunday. The unspoken rule around here was that I never went to the house on Sundays because that was the day Ivy and Ethan came over.

I stared at my phone and knew this was about last night. It had to be. There was no way I wanted to deal with that right now.

I'm sorry, but I'll have to decline.

Do you have company? If so, you may bring your guest.

My eyes widened. Seriously? I checked the time. It was barely eight o'clock. If I had "company," it could only be of the male variety. I was immediately suspicious. It wasn't like Violet to be so modern.

I put my phone down on the bed. Ivy had obviously called her mom, most likely ranting and raving about me. She also apparently told her I had a boyfriend.

Crap.

Philip was right. Total clusterfuck.

I rolled onto my side, hugging my pillow, as I thought about him on my porch last night. That tingle of excitement was still there. I smiled, because it was real. The first sign of a thaw.

My phone buzzed. It was Violet again.

I'll expect you and your guest in thirty minutes.

I closed my eyes. She'd always been pushy, and if I didn't go to the house, she'd start calling and probably show up down here.

I sighed and got out of bed. *Might as well get it over with.* If Ivy and Ethan started in on me though, I was leaving immediately. Not bothering with a shower, I threw on a green hoodie and jean shorts, then pulled my hair into a messy bun. After giving my birds some fresh pellets for their breakfast, I trudged up to the house.

It was an overcast morning, and the woods smelled like damp earth. Things were quiet outside as I braced myself for the battle ahead. The only sound came from my flip-flops against the dirt and gravel road.

To my surprise, there was no sign of Ivy's red BMW out front, and when I entered the dining room, only Violet and Daphne were at the table.

"Good morning," Daphne said in her soft voice.

"Good morning," I murmured in return, relieved that Ivy and Ethan weren't here.

Violet, who was reading the paper, looked over her glasses. She didn't say anything at first, merely studied me. "Are you alone?" she asked finally.

I made a show of peering to my left and right. "Gosh, it sure looks that way."

She frowned. "I thought you might have brought your *boyfriend* with you."

"Nope."

She continued to frown and was obvious waiting for me to elaborate.

I'd always heard if you were going to lie, it was best to say as little as possible, so I ignored her and went over to the breakfast buffet to pour myself coffee.

Violet was still quietly assessing me when I sat down at the table. "Did he stay with you last night?"

I slowly stirred cream into my mug. "That's none of your business."

"As a matter of fact, it *is* my business." She put her newspaper down. "This is my house and property, and I expect to know what's going on within its bounds."

I took a sip of coffee and smacked my lips loudly. "It's half mine too."

Her frown deepened. I could tell she wasn't enjoying my attitude, but I really didn't care.

"Yes, of course it's half yours." She took off her reading glasses. "What's going on here, Claire? I've always thought we were close."

Close? This was news to me. I'd never considered us close, but in her own formal way, Violet probably did think we were.

Her expression turned incredulous. "I could barely believe my ears when Ivy called me this morning and told me you had a boyfriend. A boyfriend that none of us have ever even met!"

"I've met him," Daphne piped up.

Violet turned to her with raised brows. "You *have*?"

Daphne nodded with enthusiasm. "I've met Claire's boyfriend, Philip, a couple of times now."

I stared at Daphne in amazement. She knew Philip wasn't my boyfriend.

"He's super nice," Daphne continued. "And very handsome."

Violet appeared too stunned to speak. "Is that so?" she finally said. "Well, I'm surprised you never mentioned this."

Daphne shrugged. "He's Doug's cousin, and I figured Claire would tell you about him when she was ready." She smiled and gave me a conspiratorial look. I didn't know why she was doing this, but I returned her smile.

"Doug's cousin?" Violet leaned back in her chair. She seemed relieved for some reason. "Are you certain? That's not how Ivy described him."

"What did Ivy say?" I had to admit, I was curious how she would have described Philip to her mother.

Violet waved her hand. "It doesn't matter." She looked at me again. "I'm disappointed you didn't share this with me. I consider you my daughter as much as Ivy and Daphne, and I'd like to meet this young man of yours."

I'd been fiddling with my coffee mug but froze at her words. Meet him? "Sure, whatever." There was no way I could ask Philip to come here and pretend to be my boyfriend again. That would be too humiliating. "So where are Ivy and Ethan this morning?" I picked up my coffee, purposefully changing the subject. "I assume you heard what happened last night."

Violet pursed her lips. The pink color on them seemed too garish for her pale skin. She was only in her early sixties, but the lines around her eyes and mouth had deepened of late. When my father was alive, she used to get Botox and facial fillers and always looked younger than her age, but once he passed away, she stopped all that.

"You girls and all this ridiculous business with Ethan." She sounded annoyed, and her southern accent grew stronger. "How that boy can invoke such passion, I'll never understand."

"The only passion he invokes in me is the negative kind," I told her. "I want nothing to do with him."

"Then why, may I ask, was he at your house last night?"

"I have no idea. He let himself in without my knowledge and then drank a bottle of wine." It was obvious he and Ivy had been fighting, but I figured there was no point going into that.

Violet considered my words. I got the sense she thought I wasn't being truthful. Not only was Ivy a beauty who could get any man she wanted, but she was also her real daughter, so naturally, Violet would take her side in anything to do with Ethan.

"Poor Claire." She leaned toward me. "You've been through so much. I worry for you. You aren't still hoping for a reconciliation with him, are you?"

I gripped my mug in frustration. I hated being called "poor Claire." And no matter how many times I told them I wasn't in love with Ethan anymore, they didn't believe me. What was I supposed to do? File a restraining order against him just to shut them up? I could only imagine the fuss Ivy would make. She and Violet would probably turn it around on me, claiming I did it for the attention.

"Look, I have a boyfriend," I said emphatically. "I've moved on. In fact, we're crazy about each other." I threw in Philip's words.

"I want to believe that, Claire. I truly do."

Somehow Violet couldn't see how insulting all this was. It was like she thought I couldn't possibly do any better than Ethan, that my marriage to him was the pinnacle of my life.

Daphne put her glass of water down and spoke up with enthusiasm. "Oh, I could definitely see how crazy you and Philip are about each other. You guys seemed *totally* in love."

She smiled at me, and I forced myself to smile back. I knew she was only trying to be helpful, but saying we were in love was a little more than I intended.

Violet's brows went up. "Is that right? Well, then I'm happy for you. Maybe this whole thing with Ethan really is a misunderstanding." She shook her head and sighed. "I don't know what's gotten into him lately."

"I guess karma is a bitch," I muttered into my coffee. *A bitch named Ivy.*

"What's that?" She gave me a sharp look.

"Nothing." I smiled sweetly. "I said this coffee is rich."

Her gaze drifted down to my body. "Maybe you should add less cream next time." She leaned closer, and her voice took on a confiding tone. "Men don't like it when women are too... plump."

I ground my teeth together, trying to ignore her insult. *I'm better than this*, I reminded myself. At least I knew she was critical with Ivy and Daphne too.

"Now, let's see." Violet tapped her bottom lip. She appeared to be deep in thought. "We'll need to invite this Philip of yours over for dinner soon. Is he very much like Doug? I'm curious to meet him."

I shifted in my chair. "Well, actually, he lives in Seattle, so it might be a while before he can make it for dinner."

"Seattle? How did you two meet each other?"

"He's been here helping finish my new room."

"Oh, he works for Doug?" Violet picked up her spoon to stir her tea. "I didn't realize Doug had employees."

I opened my mouth to explain that Philip wasn't Doug's employee. In fact, I doubt he was being paid to help him at all.

"That reminds me," Daphne said to her mother in a light tone. "I'll be taking the ferry to Seattle on Tuesday. I might be gone for a few days."

"What's this?" Violet paused with her teacup in midair. "Why on earth would you be going to Seattle? And for a few *days*?"

"Oh, it's just work. I'm helping one of Claire's customers sell her house there." Daphne's demeanor was casual, though she gave me a quick glance.

I had no idea what she was talking about.

"How strange," Violet said, putting her teacup down. "You've never done that before."

"I know, but Claire asked me if I could help. Her customer is elderly and didn't know where else to find a realtor." Daphne turned to me. "Isn't that right?"

I nodded, catching on now. So this was the reason Daphne had been so willing to go along with my fake boyfriend.

"Um... yes. That's right," I said, leaning forward. "My customer Mrs. Lamb has an older brick home in Seattle that she's desperate to sell. It's a four bedroom house with hardwood floors, a nice set of windows—and a good-looking roof." I chuckled at my little joke. "In fact, that house is a real hottie."

Both Daphne and Violet stared at me. Neither of them had a sense of humor.

"Mrs. Lamb used to teach history," I added for no reason except I thought it was awesome.

Violet ignored me and turned toward Daphne again. "Exactly how long do you plan to be gone? Where will you be staying?"

Daphne answered all her mother's questions in her usual mild-mannered way. It struck me how we were both grown women, yet Violet managed to turn us into a couple of teenagers.

When I announced I was headed back to the carriage house, it was no surprise when Daphne said she'd walk down there with me.

"Why are you really going to Seattle?" I asked once we were outside. I had to admit I was curious. I'd never seen Daphne lie so boldly.

"I'm going to help Doug and his mother put her house on the market and find her a new place to live."

"Why not just tell your mom the truth?"

"Oh." Daphne grew quiet. "I know she'd disapprove. She'd say I was interfering."

"That's silly. I'm sure they'll be glad for your help." I turned to her. "And thank you for backing me up with Violet in there. You seem to be the only one who understands I'm not hung up on Ethan."

Daphne stopped walking. We were halfway down the driveway. "Listen, Claire, I wanted to ask you something." Her face grew serious. "Are you... do you have any interest in Doug?"

"Doug? Not at all. You know I don't date."

"I know that," she said quickly. "But I wondered because you agreed to go to the movies with him."

That familiar pang of guilt arose. "To be honest, I really didn't want to go. He asked me in a way that I couldn't say no."

She remained silent.

"When I see him again, I plan to straighten things out. I just didn't want to hurt his feelings."

"So you don't have any problem with me going to Seattle to help him and his mom?"

"Not at all." And that's when a lightbulb finally lit up in my head. "Are you interested in Doug?"

She bit her lip and gave me a shy smile. With her dark blue eyes, dusting of freckles across her nose and cheeks, and strawberry blonde hair, Daphne was strikingly pretty. "He seems like such a nice guy, don't you think?" She giggled. "And he's sort of great-looking too."

I could see now why she'd lied to her mom. Violet would never approve of her dating Doug.

"Does he share your feelings?"

She sighed. "I don't think he's interested in me that way."

"Well, maybe he will be after you spend more time with him."

She perked up a little. "Do you think so?"

"I do." Doug should be thrilled by Daphne's interest. "He just needs to get to know you better."

———

A COUPLE HOURS LATER, I was in front of the house, cleaning Quicksilver and Calico Jack's large cage. I kept trying to figure out what Ivy meant last night when she said I'd started the problems between the two of us and that she'd never forgive me.

Forgive me for what? What betrayal? If anybody should be begging for forgiveness, it was her. It made no sense.

My thoughts were interrupted when a familiar silver SUV came rolling down the driveway. Nervous excitement shot through me until I realized I was dressed in grungy clothes and covered in bird poop.

I nearly ran inside the house, then noticed Eliza was driving the car, and she appeared to be alone. She waved at me through the windshield before parking behind my Kia.

"Happy Sunday," she called out, walking over in her jaunty way. Her dark hair was pulled into its usual topknot. She wore a striped T-shirt and flowered shorts that emphasized her lanky frame. Stripes and flowers seemed an incongruous match, but somehow she made it work.

"Hi, Eliza." I turned off the hose I'd been using to rinse out the cage. "How's it going?"

She grinned, pushing her giant sunglasses on top of her head. "Philip told me about your pirate birds and how one of them is named after Quicksilver! I just had to meet them."

I laughed. "Well, I'm cleaning out their cage right now."

"Really? Can I help?" She looked around at my cleaning supplies.

"I'm almost done, but you can help me dry it if you want. Just give me a second."

I finished hosing away the rest of the soap, and soon Eliza and I were busy drying the large cage with a pile of cleaning cloths from Your House Sparkles.

She took on the task with great exuberance, her topknot bouncing vigorously. I suspected it was the way she approached everything in life.

"Did I tell you my mom and I are both staying for the rest of the summer?" she asked.

"You are?"

She nodded. "My mom's writing a cozy mystery novel—isn't that too cool? She retired from teaching recently and has been trying to decide what she wants to do next. It turns out she's always wanted to write."

"That is cool," I agreed.

"And remember that play I told you I was trying out for? Well, I got the part!"

"Wow, that's wonderful. Congratulations."

"Thank you. I'm really excited. This is my first time working with a professional theater." She smiled sheepishly. "I have to admit, I'm nervous."

"I'm sure you'll be great. Obviously they saw something in you. Just remember, stay positive even when you don't feel it." It was a motivational quote from one of the many sticky notes I had plastered all over my house.

"I'm trying to, believe me. Unfortunately, my brother is being a total freak about it." She huffed in frustration. "I wish he'd just chill."

I felt a surge of excitement at the mere mention of Philip. "What do you mean?"

"I'm taking fall semester off from school so I can be in the play, and he's having a conniption."

I reached for a fresh cloth to dry the top of the cage.

"I just need a break," she continued. "You know? I mean, I've been in college for seven years now. I'm exhausted. He insists I should finish my degree this year though."

I stopped drying. "You've been in college for seven years and still don't have a degree?"

She seemed embarrassed. "I know it sounds bad, but I just wasn't sure what I wanted to do. But now I finally do!"

"So, he wants you to quit the play?"

She nodded. "Quit the play and go back to school. What's even more ridiculous is he never finished college himself. He dropped out during his second year, so where does he get off acting like a dictator?"

I listened, taking in this new information about Philip.

"Talk about a hypocrite," she grumbled, still drying. "He needs to get a life."

"Why did he drop out?" I was a college dropout too. Right after I got married, I quit and took a job to help support us. Ethan, of course, did get his degree. My dad tried to talk me out of it at the time, and I sure wish I'd listened to him.

Eliza stepped away from the cage and used the back of her hand to brush hair off her face. "Apparently he was running a couple businesses while he was in school, and it all got to be too much, so he quit."

"Maybe he regrets it," I offered. "Maybe that's why he's pushing so hard for you to finish."

"Regrets it? Are you kidding?" She rolled her eyes. "You don't know my brother. Trust me, he never regrets anything."

"I don't mean to interfere, but he *is* only your brother," I pointed out. "You're an adult. You can do whatever you want."

"That's what I said! He may be eleven years older than me, but so what."

"What does your mom think of all this?"

"She's worried I'll quit school too. But at least she's agreed to support me. She says as long as I promise it's only for one semester."

"Well, that's sounds reasonable."

"It is, if only I can get Philip to stop complaining." She bit her bottom lip. "Don't get me wrong. He's helped me a lot, and I don't want to give you the wrong impression. He's normally pretty cool."

I nodded. I got the impression Philip would do anything for his mom and sister.

"But I really want to do this play. They're paying me too. It might not be that much, but it's something, you know? It's very satisfying to get paid."

"I understand." In fact, I understood completely.

We finished drying the cage, and Eliza helped me move it back into the house. My birds were inside their small travel cage, waiting to be let out. I could hear them chirping with impatience.

"Oh my gosh, your house is adorable on the inside too." She spun around with delight. "I love it!"

"Thank you. I'll love it a lot more when my spare room is finished and I can finally move all these supplies out of here." I motioned toward the large stack of boxes piled opposite my bed.

"It's like you're living in a little jewelry box."

I laughed. "I guess that's one way of describing it."

I set up the cage for my birds again, replacing their ladders and toys, along with fresh pellets and water. When I let them out of the travel cage, they both flew over and hopped inside the larger one, inspecting it to make sure everything was as it should be.

"They're amazing," Eliza said, coming closer. "I've never known anyone who had birds before." She was still watching them when she turned toward me. "So I just have to ask—what happened between you and my brother last night?"

"What do you mean?"

"He came home late, and this morning when I asked him how things went, he wouldn't tell me."

I shook my head. "It was a crazy night." For some reason, I decided to share the whole story about finding Ethan here. I wasn't sure why, but I had a good sense about Eliza.

She listened, but didn't say much until I was done. "I'm glad

Philip stayed to help. He's good in a crisis." I felt her eyes lingering on me. "Did anything else happen between you two?"

"Not really." I smiled a little, remembering the way I felt standing outside with him. That tingle of excitement. "Why? Did he say something?"

"No, but he was acting funny this morning." She watched my birds again and appeared to be ruminating. Finally she turned toward me. "You know what? I think you should come over for dinner tomorrow night."

"That's a nice offer, but I have to work." I had my monthly staff meeting with Laurie and Kyle.

"Tuesday, then. Please say yes."

"I guess I could do that."

"Really? That's wonderful!" She swooped in and gave me a hug. "I can't wait to tell my mom. She'll be excited to have someone local over as a guest."

"Thanks for the invitation," I said, still wrapped in the hug.

She pulled back. There was a grin on her face, and just under her breath, I heard her mutter what sounded like "And I can't wait to tell my brother too."

TWELVE

~ Philip ~

"Look, I've already explained it to you three times," I said in frustration to Doug over the phone. "Claire and I went to the movies, walked along the waterfront, and then I brought her home." I didn't explain what happened with her boneheaded ex-husband, since I figured that was nobody's business but Claire's.

"Did you talk about me? Do you think she could fall in love with me?"

"She barely even knows you."

"But you told her about me, right? That I'm a great guy?"

I rolled my eyes. "Yes, I said nice things about you."

"Did anything else happen?"

"Like what?"

"I don't know. I tried calling you at midnight on Saturday, but you didn't pick up." Doug sounded worried and, to be honest, for once he had good reason to be.

"Nothing else happened," I assured him.

Except I nearly kissed Claire.

I felt guilty as hell for my attraction to her. And after giving it some thought, I'd decided the best thing was to stay away from her. Far away. There were a lot of women in the world, and I didn't need to go after the one my cousin happened to be in love with. Luckily I'd timed things the last two days so she'd already left for work when I arrived at her house.

"Okay." He sighed with relief. "I'm glad. Real glad! And believe me, I appreciate what you're doing for me."

"So when do you think you'll be coming back?" I took a sip from the lemonade my mom made earlier. She'd also made a devil's food cake—my favorite, so I'd helped myself to a large slice. "I may have more work lined up for you."

"You do? Well, gee, that's great... only there's a problem." He sighed, and I could already predict what he was going to say. "I haven't found anyone else to fill in for me yet, and my mom still needs my help."

I swallowed a bite of cake. Fortunately, I was two steps ahead of him. "That's okay. I've decided to stay longer."

"You have?" I could hear the surprise in his voice.

"Yes." I'd decided recently that I wanted to stay and make sure Claire's room got finished properly. Not to mention there was a lot more I could do to help Doug whip things into shape. I had his business voice mail forwarded to my phone, and it turned out he had a few calls waiting from people trying to hire him. I checked out two of them yesterday and had another one lined up for later in the week. Not to mention the one that came from Claire's sister. I took photos of each site and sent them to Martin, Gavin's dad. I knew he could tell me what kind of bid we should offer in case Doug didn't get back to me soon enough.

"Gosh, are you sure? What about your work? I can't believe you'd have time to run more than one business."

I smirked, using my fork to cut off another large piece of cake.

"Trust me, I've done it before. Besides, I don't need to be in the office for most of what I do." I contacted my assistant, Sam, yesterday with a list of things I needed, and he was flying out with them this afternoon. I'd also texted Gavin and told him I'd be videoconferencing for the meeting with the real estate group tomorrow.

"Well, if you're... if you're really sure," Doug stammered.

"No problem." I reached over for his iPad on the counter. "So, let me tell you about these jobs." I brought the info up on screen and briefly described each one to him. "I also sent you an email with photos. When you have a chance, take a look and give me your opinion on cost."

"Sure, sure...." Doug sounded distracted. "Say, listen." He breathed into the phone. "You staying out there longer has got me thinking."

I picked up my lemonade—another favorite. My mom had been spoiling me lately.

"Maybe this is a perfect opportunity for you to really help me get things settled, if that's okay?"

I nodded. "No problem. That's exactly what I was thinking." It was a relief to discover we were finally on the same page about something. "I don't think it'll even take me that long."

"You don't?"

"No. A couple of weeks should do it." Hell, by then I'd probably have enough work lined up to last him the rest of the year. He'd be too busy to complain about anything.

"Wow." Doug sounded in awe. "I can't thank you enough. I'm really impressed!"

I shrugged. "Don't sweat it. It's what I do." I took another bite of cake.

"But next time I think you should take her out for dinner and not a movie."

I stopped chewing and swallowed. "What?"

"If you take her out for dinner, it'll give you more of a chance to talk about me."

"Do you mean Claire?" I put my fork down. "I'm not taking her out again."

"Just make sure you tell her about all my redeeming qualities," he continued. "Don't forget to mention how much I like baking those health muffins. That will for sure impress her—if it hasn't already."

Suddenly there was a loud noise in the background. It sounded like the dragon lady bellowing at Doug.

"I've got to go," he said quickly. "My mom needs me to take her to the groomer's—I mean the salon." He lowered his voice so it was almost a whisper. "And I appreciate everything you're doing to help me win Claire. Hey, maybe you can be the best man at our wedding!"

And with that, he hung up.

I stared at the phone.

What the fuck?

Did he really just tell me to take Claire out for dinner?

My first thought was I'd love to take her out for dinner. Someplace with great ambience and great food. Someplace romantic but still relaxed and comfortable. Someplace where we could get to know each other a little better.

I shook my head. This was crazy. I couldn't take her anywhere. I was way too attracted to her.

What the hell was Doug thinking pushing us together?

Of course, he didn't know any better. He didn't know he wasn't the only one having thoughts about Claire—and I was sure mine were a lot dirtier than his. Although I had to admit I liked her.

I liked her a lot.

Well, I wouldn't do it. It was as simple as that. *It should be enough that I'm straightening out his business problems for him. If he wants Claire, he needs to man up and go after her himself.*

I checked the time on my phone and realized I should get to the airfield soon to meet Sam. I also noticed a missed call from the CEO of a tech start-up in Vancouver that Gavin and I had been in talks with. He was looking for capital to expand into the States.

Just as I was putting my plate in the sink, there were voices at the front door. I thought it was my mom coming back from town—which was just as well, since I'd rather take the car than Doug's truck—but to my amazement it was my sister followed by the other half of NorthStone, my best friend Gavin.

They were both laughing at something as they came into the main living area, and when Gavin saw me, I could have sworn he flashed a guilty look at Eliza.

"Surprise," he said, grinning at me.

"Hey, what are you doing here?"

"I figured I'd come and check out the summer beach house you guys are all holed up in." He glanced around, nodding with approval. "Very nice."

"What was so funny?" My eyes went from Gavin to my sister. "You guys were laughing when you came in the door."

"It was nothing. Eliza was telling me about some people she worked with on that commercial." He came closer and set a travel bag on one of the kitchen chairs next to the center island. "And by the way, here's all your shit."

My eyes went to the bag.

"Sam packed it for you. When I heard he was flying out here to bring it, I told him not to bother, that I'd do it instead."

"Thanks. I appreciate it—though I'm surprised to see you here at all."

Eliza walked to the fridge and opened the door. "Do you want anything to drink?" she asked Gavin over her shoulder.

"Sure." He placed another bag on the ground and took the nearest kitchen stool. "What are you offering?"

"Well, there are these gross wine coolers."

"The healthy ones?" He chuckled. "Pass."

I picked up my glass of lemonade, which was mostly ice now. "The polling numbers on those are excellent though. Have you seen them? Also, have you spoken to them about changing the taste yet?"

"Yeah, those numbers are great. And I talked to them yesterday.

They said they're working on some new flavors and will get back to us in a few weeks."

I crunched on an ice cube. "That name has to go too."

He nodded in agreement. "Totally. That name is a joke."

"How about some lemonade?" Eliza asked him. "My mom made a pitcher for everyone tonight."

"Sounds good."

"Everyone tonight?" I looked at Gavin. "You told my mom you were flying up here?"

He shook his head. "Nah. It was sort of a last-minute thing. I figured I'd surprise all of you."

"'Everyone' means Claire," the pest announced casually as she poured him a glass.

I was crunching on another ice cube and almost bit my tongue. "Claire?"

"I invited her for dinner tonight. Didn't I mention that?" She turned to me, and there was a tone in her voice I couldn't quite place.

"No, you didn't."

"I guess it must have slipped my mind." She smiled sweetly at me.

"Who's Claire?" Gavin asked.

"She's one of our neighbors here." She handed him his lemonade and explained how I was filling in for Doug.

"Ah." Gavin grinned at me. "Now it all makes sense. So that's why you stayed longer. I couldn't figure it out. I should have guessed there was a woman involved."

"My staying here has nothing to do with Claire." I put my glass down. That wasn't entirely true, since I wanted to make sure her room got finished, but I already knew that would be misinterpreted. "The only reason I'm staying here is to help my cousin," I said, feeling inexplicably grouchy.

"Really? So what does Claire look like?" Gavin rested his arms on the island's counter. "If you're not interested in her, maybe I am." He winked at the pest, who laughed.

"She's very pretty," my sister said, coming over to the opposite side of the island. "She's also super nice and fun to talk to. I went over there on Sunday to meet her birds." Eliza told him about Claire's pirate parakeets and how one of them was named after our ancestor.

Gavin listened with interest, and even though I knew he was only joking about going after her, I didn't like it. Not at all.

"Doug's in love with Claire," I told him. "She's off-limits."

"Is that right?" He made a show of looking around the room. "Well, unless I'm mistaken, I don't see Doug here anywhere."

Exactly, I thought. *Where the fuck is Doug? If he wants Claire, he should be here making the effort and not having me do it for him.* The whole situation was ridiculous. I didn't want to spend another evening singing the praises of my cousin to a woman I was interested in myself.

"That's true," Eliza said. "Doug's in love with Claire. Philip's been trying to help him win her over."

"Really?" Gavin's eyes widened. "And how has he been doing that?"

Eliza explained how I took Claire to the movies on Saturday and that I'd been talking up Doug every chance I got, telling her how great he was.

"You've got to be kidding." Gavin laughed and turned to me. "Is that true?"

"I was trying to help him out," I said, feeling even grouchier.

He laughed some more. "Whatever you say."

I went over to grab my bag off the kitchen chair. "I should probably get some work done. I assume my laptop is in here?"

He shrugged. "I have no idea."

"Why don't you put yourself to good use and explain some of those figures from the Atlas portfolio to me."

"What? Right now?" He glanced toward the large living room window. "I was thinking I'd go for a walk on the beach. Unlike you, I haven't had a vacation all year."

I scowled. "This is *not* a vacation."

"Damn. What bug crawled up your ass?"

"Nothing. We're talking to them tomorrow, and I want to make sure everything is clear." I was good with numbers, but commercial real estate was not my area of expertise. I dealt primarily with technology companies, though I was also familiar with food and beverage industries.

"Fine." He rolled his eyes. "Let's go over it. But I'm definitely walking on the beach while I'm here."

"We should rent bikes!" The pest bounced up and down. "I've been wanting to do that since we arrived."

"Sounds awesome," Gavin agreed.

We spent the rest of the afternoon going over the real estate group's holdings and plans. To my surprise, it turned out a chunk of Truth Harbor's downtown and waterfront was part of the large land package they were trying to acquire. Gavin explained how several entities were bidding against Atlas. It was one of the reasons they wanted NorthStone involved—our investors had deep pockets. I listened but didn't comment much, mostly thinking things over.

As it grew closer to six, I could smell food cooking. My mom and sister were in the kitchen preparing dinner. By the time Claire arrived, I was sitting on the living room couch with Gavin, both of us drinking a beer while we watched golf on TV.

It was her voice I heard first. That pretty voice. I tried to ignore the way my pulse kicked up at the sound of it. Before I knew it, she was right in front of me, as pretty as a picture.

"Hi," she said.

"Hi." I grinned back. We hadn't seen each other since Saturday, and I had to admit I was pleased at the sight of her. More pleased than I ought to be.

Like the other night, her hair was flowing down her back, though she'd pulled some off her face with a few loose curls. It suited her. Best of all, she wore a dress. I'd never seen her in a dress, and I approved one hundred percent. It was a pink-flowered sundress with short sleeves and came to just above the knees. It fell over her breasts and hips in a way that flattered every curve.

Unfortunately, I could feel Gavin checking her out too.

"It's nice to meet you," he said, leaning forward to shake her hand. "I've heard nothing but good things about you and your birds."

Her brows went up. "I didn't know my birds were so famous."

"Eliza told me all about them. I enjoy birds myself." Gavin told her a story about how he owned a parakeet as a kid, a story I was almost certain he was making up.

"Really? Well, it's nice to meet a fellow bird lover."

"Hopefully I'll get another bird someday when I'm not traveling so much for work." Gavin sighed and leaned back on the couch. "I sure do miss old Napoleon."

"Napoleon?"

"That was his name. Napoleon Bonapartridge."

Claire laughed. "Oh my gosh, that's so cute. I love it!"

I tried not to roll my eyes at his ridiculous story. "Would you like me to get you anything?" I asked. "There's beer, or my mom made lemonade."

"Napoleon was one of a kind," Gavin continued. "I loved that bird. At least we gave him a good life."

"That's so nice," Claire said before turning to me. "Thanks, your mom already got me some lemonade. I'm helping them with dinner, but I wanted to come over and say hi." She smiled, and I couldn't help grinning back like an idiot.

When she left for the kitchen, I turned to Gavin. "You are so full of shit. When did you ever own a parakeet?"

"What do you mean? I had one as a kid."

"And that name?" I chuckled. "Let me guess, you were googling bird names earlier."

Gavin smiled and picked up his beer. "I don't know what you're talking about. I loved that parakeet."

"Napoleon Bonapartridge?" I laughed some more. "Very creative." I'd been best friends with Gavin for a long time, so I knew exactly how he operated. He came across as laid-back and casual, except it was all an act. He plotted his whole life three moves ahead like a chess game.

"Now don't go disparaging little Napoleon," he said in mock injury. "That bird was practically a fixture in my childhood."

"I'm sure he was." I took a swig of beer.

Gavin looked over his shoulder toward the kitchen and then grinned at me. "I have to agree, she's cute. Nice body too."

I didn't say anything. My eyes went back to the golf game on television. I normally didn't care if Gavin made comments about women, but I wasn't happy listening to him talk about Claire.

"Just remember she's off-limits."

"That's right." He chuckled softly. "Off-limits to whom, I wonder."

DINNER WAS SPAGHETTI WITH MEATBALLS, garlic bread, and a Caesar salad. One of my all-time favorite meals. My mom made the meatballs just the way I liked them with sausage and lots of spicy oregano.

"I feel like you're spoiling me," I said as we all dug into our food. "Thanks for making that chocolate cake too."

She smiled. "I feel like I don't get to spoil you enough."

"Hey, I'm not complaining."

"How did the writing go today?" Eliza asked her. "I can't wait to read your book when it's done."

"You're writing a book?" Gavin looked over. "I didn't know that."

My mom nodded. "A cozy mystery. I've always wanted to write one, so I'm finally doing it."

He tore off a chunk of garlic bread. "That sounds pretty great."

"I think it sounds great too," I agreed. "I remember all those stories you used to make up about Bailey when we were kids."

My sister sighed. "I still miss Bailey."

"Who's Bailey?" Claire asked, cutting one of the large meatballs in half. She was sitting next to me at the table, and I was all too aware of her proximity.

"Our dog when we were growing up." I explained how my mom used to make up stories about him and his whole extended dog family.

"The book's going okay," Mom told us. "I need to do more research. I've decided to set it here in Truth Harbor and possibly even turn it into a series."

Claire looked up from her plate. "Really? What a perfect idea. I don't think anyone's ever based a book series here before."

Eliza's eyes lit up. "See? I love this town. The culture here has everything."

"What made you decide to set your book here?" Claire asked.

My mom tilted her head and thought about it. "I guess it's because I've always enjoyed harbor towns. There's an old-fashioned feeling here that I thought lended itself well to a cozy mystery."

Claire nodded but then sighed. "Though that might all be changing soon."

"What do you mean?" Eliza asked.

"Apparently some big real estate group is buying part of the land downtown, including the waterfront. They plan to build condos and turn the whole area into a shopping mall."

My sister's eyes widened. "Are you kidding?"

"I wish I was."

Gavin and I glanced at each other.

"That would be a shame," my mom said, frowning. "Why would anyone want to destroy the flavor of this lovely town?"

Claire shrugged. "Profit, I guess."

My mom picked up her glass, still frowning. "Well, I hope that doesn't happen."

Gavin and I both stayed quiet. Neither of us were sentimental when it came to making money. It might sound cold, but I didn't get successful by ignoring opportunities.

"What kind of research do you still need to do for your book?" Claire asked my mom.

"Oh, mostly just information about the town's history. I was thinking I'd swing by the local library and see what I could find."

She sat up straight. "Really? You know, I have a client who'd be the perfect person for you to talk to."

"You do?"

Claire told us about a client of hers who used to be a history teacher and knew everything there was to know about Truth Harbor. "Let me ask her, but I'm sure she'd be more than happy to meet with you."

"That would be wonderful." My mom was obviously thrilled. "Thank you."

The rest of the dinner conversation continued along just fine until my sister started talking about the play and how she was still planning to quit school.

"It's a mistake," I said for the hundredth time since she'd made this absurd announcement two days ago. "Just get your degree and be done with it. Then you can act in all the plays you want."

"But not this one," she countered. "This one will be finished by then."

"Who cares? There are a million plays in the world. Your top priority should be finishing college."

"You didn't even finish, so why are you being so pushy about this?"

I shook my head. "Because it's not the same situation. You've been in school forever. It's time to quit screwing around."

"Oh, I see. So you get to live however you choose while I'm dictated to by my own brother?"

"I'm offering you good advice. You should take it."

My sister glared at me. "Let me offer you some advice. Get a life and stop trying to run mine."

"I'm not trying to run your life, and I happen to have a great life."

"Puh-lease." She snorted. "All you care about is work."

My mom held her hand up. "Let's continue this discussion another time, shall we?" She looked at us both. "We have a guest tonight, who I'm sure would rather not listen to you two squabbling."

Gavin shrugged and grinned. "I don't mind. Actually, I think it's entertaining."

I snorted. "That's because she's not talking about you." Gavin was basically family, and he knew it.

"Claire is our guest," my mom reminded us, then turned to her. "I'm sorry you have to listen to these two arguing."

"It's okay. Your family is great. Even when you guys argue, I can tell it's only because you care about each other."

I nodded to myself, and I could see Eliza taking in her words.

After dinner, Gavin and I cleared the table and loaded the dishwasher. It was a tradition that whoever didn't prepare the meal had to at least help clean up afterward.

"What now?" my sister asked as we were finishing. "Do you guys want to play cards or a board game?"

"Sure," Gavin said. "What do you have in mind?"

"How about we let Claire decide?" my mom suggested. She motioned toward the bookcase in the other room. "There's a number of games. Would you like to go pick something out?"

"Okay." Claire got up and went into the living room. When she returned with her choice of board game, I could barely believe it.

"Oh no," the pest groaned. "Not that. Are you sure that's what you want to play?"

Meanwhile Gavin and I were laughing and fist-bumping. "All right!"

My mother hesitated but then smiled at Claire. "Isn't there perhaps another game you'd like to choose instead?"

THIRTEEN

~ Claire ~

"I s there something wrong with Monopoly?" I asked.

Philip and Gavin were obviously happy, but Eliza and Sylvia looked apprehensive.

Sylvia sighed. "It's just that Monopoly brings out the worst in these two." She motioned toward her son and Gavin, who were cheering and giving each other complicated handshakes.

Eliza leaned forward in her chair. "What she's trying to say is it turns them into assholes."

"It does?"

She turned to her mom. "Didn't we already ban these two from playing Monopoly ever again?"

"It does *not* turn us into assholes," Philip said matter-of-factly as he took a seat at the table. "The pest doesn't know what she's talking about."

"Yeah, that's silly," Gavin said, taking a seat too. He leaned in toward Philip and spoke in a loud stage whisper. "I think your mom and sister are having a false memory."

Philip reached for the box. "Monopoly happens to be one of the greatest games ever invented."

Eliza looked up at the ceiling. "God help us."

"I can pick a different game," I offered.

"That won't be necessary." Philip patted the chair beside him and grinned. "Have a seat, Claire. You're in for the most exciting Monopoly game of your life."

Sylvia got up. "Would anybody like anything from the kitchen? I think I might need a beer for this."

"Me too," Eliza said in a desperate voice. "Maybe bring the whole six-pack with you."

"Nah, I'm good." Philip was rubbing his hands together, glancing around the table. There was a gleam in his eye. "Now, who gets to be the banker?"

"I'll do it," Gavin said.

Philip scoffed. "Like I trust you."

"What do you mean? I'm as trustworthy as they come."

"Let's just keep things simple and *I'll* be the banker." He opened the lid on the box and started setting things up.

"Like hell you will." Gavin reached for the stack of Monopoly money. "There's no way I'm letting you be the banker."

Eliza accepted a beer from her mom. "What does it matter? You guys both cheat like crazy anyway."

"No we don't!"

"That's ridiculous!"

The men seemed comically indignant.

"You should let Mom be the banker," Eliza said. "She's best at thwarting you two."

"Or maybe Claire should do it." Gavin turned to me with a flirtatious smile. "Would you like to be the banker?"

"I don't know." I glanced over at the pieces Philip was setting up. "It's been a while since I've played."

Sylvia sat down. "It's best if I do it. At least there's a chance this won't turn into a circus."

As she organized the bank and gave everyone their money, Philip and Gavin argued over who got to be the car.

"You were the car last time," Philip said, keeping all the game pieces in front of him. "It's my turn."

"What?" Gavin threw up his hands. "That was a year ago. Who remembers that?"

"I do." Philip handed him a game piece. "Here, you can be the shoe."

"The shoe? That's for girls. I want the car."

Philip steepled his fingers and eyed Gavin in a calculated way. "Exactly how much money are you willing to pay?"

"And so it begins." Eliza rolled her eyes.

I took a sip from my beer, watching the two men with interest. "You guys are kind of crazy with this game, aren't you?"

"Trust me," she muttered, "you haven't even begun to see crazy."

After some heavy negotiating, Philip agreed to sell the car to Gavin for a hundred dollars.

Philip took the dog for himself, and when Eliza stuck the hat on it, he immediately removed it.

"Anybody who puts the hat on this dog again will be fined ten dollars," he said in a starchy tone.

Eliza picked up the dog and held the hat in place for everyone to see. "Just look at him though. He's so cute."

Indignant, Philip reached over and took his game piece back from her. "I'll have you know this dog deserves respect."

Once we began to play, the game grew even more entertaining. It turned out Philip and Gavin competed against each other with a maniacal intensity. As soon as anybody bought a property, they jumped in and bought it off the person in a bidding war. It wasn't long before everything they owned was crammed with hotels and houses.

"You guys are cheating," Eliza accused them about an hour or so into the game. "In fact, I saw Philip's hand right next to Claire's money."

He turned incredulous. "Are you nuts? I wouldn't steal from Claire."

I glanced down at my pile of money. If anything, it seemed to be growing on its own, which made no sense. "Philip hasn't taken anything from me. I've got more money than I even thought I had."

"All right." Eliza sniffed. "I apologize. Maybe I'm wrong. But something strange is happening. There's no way you guys could be this rich."

"We're good with money." Gavin smiled at her. "Haven't we already proven that?"

"Whenever any of us turn our heads for a second, you're robbing the bank."

"You need to learn how to strategize better," Philip said. "Stop losing your cool, and stop selling all your properties to Gavin."

"Hey, I'm doing just fine. Look how much money I have."

"I thought Monopoly was a game of luck," I said.

Philip grinned. "It is, but it's also strategy and knowing your opponents."

I had to agree with Eliza though. There was something peculiar going on. Both guys kept dropping things on the floor and asking everybody to bend down and find their missing item. Another time, Gavin yelled there was something in his eye and made a comical show of leaning over the table, asking us to look at it. The most bizarre point in the game was when Philip had us all craning our necks at the ceiling when he claimed he saw a bat flying through the house.

"Are you trying to tell me you actually saw a *bat* hanging from the ceiling?" Eliza asked.

"It wasn't hanging," he corrected her as he counted his cash. "It was flying."

"It could have been a flying squirrel," Gavin interjected. "I saw it too."

"A flying squirrel?" Eliza started laughing. "You guys are completely full of it."

By that point both Sylvia and I were in stitches. It was the craziest game of Monopoly I'd ever played.

When it was my turn, and I landed on one of Gavin's heavily improved properties, he turned to me with a flirtatious grin. "Don't worry. You're a fellow bird lover, so I'm not going to charge you rent."

"Really? Um... thanks."

"I'm a gentleman like that. In fact, none of you ladies will be charged rent from now on."

"Isn't that against the rules?"

"Darlin', I make up my own rules."

"Of course it's against the rules," Philip growled. "But he'll be bankrupt soon, so I wouldn't put much stock in his 'free' rent."

"In your dreams," Gavin countered. "I'm looking forward to your complete annihilation."

The two guys were battling each other like titans of industry. Throughout the game, a peculiar excitement grew in me. Philip's eyes kept finding mine. Even the crazy way he played Monopoly was exhilarating. There was a boyishly bold quality to it. Ethan had never been bold like that.

Eventually the bank was empty, and the men were doing trades so complicated I couldn't even keep track of what was happening.

In the middle of all the chaos, Sylvia's phone rang. It had been ringing and then buzzing throughout the game, but she'd ignored it.

"Who keeps calling you?" Philip asked her. "Maybe you should answer it."

Sylvia picked up her phone. "Maybe you're right." There was an odd note in her voice. "I need to take this outside," she told everyone, getting up from the table and leaving.

"Do you have any idea who that is?" Philip asked his sister before rolling the dice.

Eliza's eyes followed her mom onto the back deck. "No clue."

We played until it was Sylvia's turn and then waited for her to come back. Philip and Gavin used up the time cracking jokes about the creature they claimed was living in the ceiling rafters. They named him Jocko the flying squirrel-bat. When Sylvia returned, she seemed more subdued than earlier.

"Is everything okay?" Philip asked her. "Who was that on the phone?"

She took a deep breath. "I'll tell you, but don't get upset." She hesitated. "It was your father."

Philip froze beside me.

Eliza's eyes grew wide. "That was... our father?"

"Why would he be calling you?" Philip's voice grew deeper. Obviously he *was* upset. He and Gavin had been competing against each other throughout the game, but there'd been no doubt it was all in fun. The tone in Philip's voice made it clear the fun was over.

Sylvia licked her lips. "He wanted to talk to me. He's been asking about you two."

"Why would you speak to him? He has no business calling here and asking anything."

"To be honest, I feel sorry for him."

Philip stared at his mom, and I sensed he was trying to control his anger. "Sorry for *him*?"

"I know." She laid her hands on the table in front of her. "I understand your animosity, but a nurse called me this morning from a hospital emergency room. She was calling because he couldn't."

"He's in the hospital?" Eliza's voice was small. "Is he okay?"

She nodded toward her daughter. "He's fine. At first they thought he was having a heart attack, but it was only stress."

I glanced at Philip, his expression one of contained fury. "You think I care if he's in the goddamn hospital? I don't want you speaking to him again. Do you hear me?"

Sylvia looked up at her son. "I'm not defending what he did."

"You and I both know he made his choice years ago. Now he can live or die with it." Philip shoved his chair back from the table and abruptly left through the sliding doors onto the back deck. We all remained silent, listening as his heavy footsteps traveled down the stairs that led to the beach.

Sylvia gave me a wry smile. "Sorry, Claire. We're not usually this dramatic."

"It's okay." I smiled back.

"Please don't hold this against my brother," Eliza said to me with concern. "Our father is a touchy subject for him."

I wondered what Philip's dad had done that was so terrible.

The four of us put away all the game pieces. Philip's abrupt departure was still jarring, and things felt kind of awkward, but then Gavin spoke up. "At least there's one silver lining to all this. I'm the winner by default."

We all smiled.

Eliza turned to me. "My brother hates to lose money, even if it's only pretend. And as you might have also noticed, he's very competitive."

"Yeah, he is." Gavin grinned. "But that's what he gets for running out of here like a prima donna."

I figured it was time for me to leave and go home. I picked up my small cross-body purse, thanking Sylvia and Eliza for having me over. I told them I was going to find Philip outside. "I just want to talk to him and see if he's okay."

"Make sure you tell him I won the game," Gavin called after me. "Let him know I'm the winner and he's the l-o-s-e-r."

I could still hear him chuckling before I shut the sliding glass door.

Glancing around the deck, I let my eyes adjust to the dark. The night was warm and breezy. I took a deep breath, inhaling the rich salty air. So familiar. Everything about Truth Harbor was a comfort to me. I didn't even want to think about all those rumors going around town, all the changes that might be coming.

To be honest, I wasn't sure why I was going after Philip. I knew I should go home. Go back to my cozy house, my birds, and my safe life.

But something compelled me forward.

The night sky was clear and the moon bright, so I had little trouble making my way down to the water. It didn't take long to find him, the lone figure on the beach.

As I approached him from behind, I hoped this wasn't a mistake.

He stood with his hands shoved into his front pockets, his broad shoulders tapered down. There was something unforgiving in his posture, and it struck me how formidable Philip was. Clearly he was loyal to those he loved, probably to a fault, but I wouldn't want to be on his bad side.

He must have heard my footsteps, because he turned to face me.

Neither of us spoke. Under the moonlight, his eyes appeared silver beneath those black brows.

"Gavin wanted me to deliver a message," I said, coming up to stand beside him.

"What's that?"

"He said to tell you he's the winner and you're the l-o-s-e-r."

Philip smiled, shaking his head. "That asshole."

"Apparently you hate to lose money, and you're very competitive."

"So I've been told."

I shifted around on the beach, which was a mixture of sand and rocks. "That was an interesting Monopoly game." I turned to him. "I have to ask—were you sneaking extra money into my stack of cash?"

He glanced at me and then looked away. "Yeah, I was."

"Really? Why would you do that?"

"Gavin and I have been doing it for years. My mom and Eliza always sell their properties too easily. And we're both so aggressive that if we don't add to everyone's bankroll, the game ends."

"That's crazy. I've never heard of such a thing. I guess it explains Jocko the flying squirrel-bat."

"My mom and Eliza are both terrible with money and have no strategy. They miss every opportunity."

"It's still cheating though," I pointed out. "Reverse cheating, I guess. You're controlling the game."

He seemed embarrassed. "Maybe I shouldn't have admitted it to you. Between this and your phone, you probably think I'm a dick."

I thought about Saturday night, about the way he insisted on staying to help me with my drunken ex-husband. The way he reminded me I was better than all the crap Ivy and Ethan had put me through. "I don't think that."

"Because, I swear, I'm normally an upstanding and law-abiding citizen."

I rolled my eyes. "I don't know if I'd go *that* far."

"It's true."

The breeze blew my dress around, and I tried to tame it. Excitement flamed through me, and I tried to tame that too. Out here, under the night sky, there was an air of danger about Philip, and it was easy to imagine he had an ancestor who was a pirate.

"I should go," I said, motioning in the direction of Sullivan House. Part of me wanted to stay, to see what might happen between us, but the other part knew that was a bad idea.

"It's late. Let me walk you home."

I glanced around. It *was* late. "All right. I guess you can try and convince me about what an upstanding citizen you are."

He chuckled. "I'm a regular Boy Scout."

We started down the beach together toward Sullivan House, neither of us speaking at first.

Eventually I broke the silence and asked him about the phone call upstairs. "It seemed to really upset you. Are you okay?"

"It was nothing."

"Are you sure?" I didn't know why I was prying. I wasn't normally like that, but I figured he'd already seen all my dirty laundry up close and personal on Saturday.

"Let's just say I don't have the greatest relationship with my father."

"I'm sorry. That sucks."

"Yeah." He gazed out at the water. "I suppose it does."

Philip seemed so vibrantly male that I would have guessed he'd had a strong father figure, but then I didn't know a lot about men. Besides my dad, I hadn't grown up with any males, and I'd only had two lovers my whole life—the second of which was a blur since I had to drink two shots of tequila and half a bottle of wine to even get the deed done.

I was wearing sandals with my sundress, and as we walked, tiny pebbles kept getting caught in them, so I stopped to slip them off.

"Do you really think it's such a bad idea if the downtown and waterfront are built up?" he asked, changing the subject. "It could be an improvement. It would bring in new jobs. In fact, it would probably help your maid service."

I considered his words as we walked again. "Maybe, but at what cost? I hardly think turning everything into condos with a big mall in the middle of town is an improvement."

He seemed to mull this over.

"I don't want to see our town destroyed," I continued. "Eliza's right. We have a lot of culture here, and it's a great place to live."

"Culture, huh?" There was a subtle criticism in his tone, and I sensed he was thinking about his sister and that play.

"I know it's none of my business, but maybe you should stop giving her such a hard time. She can still finish college. It sounds like being an actress is what she wants to do with her life."

He snorted. "That's because you don't know about all the other careers."

"Other careers?"

"Yes, let's see... graphic designer, interior decorator, fashion designer, children's book illustrator." He paused. "There are so many, it would probably be easier if I alphabetized them."

"It sounds like she's been searching for the right fit."

"Give me a break. She's been searching for almost eight years. She could have two degrees by now."

"Maybe she—ow!" I yelped as I stepped on something sharp.

"Hey, are you all right?"

We both stopped, and I lifted my foot in pain, trying to see the bottom. "I don't know. It feels like something sharp pierced my heel."

"Here." He put his arm out. I switched my sandals to the opposite hand and grabbed a hold of his muscular forearm.

Philip led me limping over to a group of fallen logs, where we both sat down.

"Give me your foot," he said. "Let me see it."

I scooted back a little and put my foot in his lap. "I hope it's not bleeding," I whined. All I could picture was blood flowing. "I wonder what I stepped on."

He pulled his phone out and turned on the flashlight. I watched his handsome profile as he gently brushed the sand off the bottom of my foot, examining it. I was in pain, but I couldn't deny it felt nice the way he was touching me. His hand was warm. I tried to focus on that instead of the pain, which was diminishing.

"Is it bad?"

"No," he murmured. "I don't see anything."

"What do you mean?" I tilted my foot on his lap so I could see it too. To my relief there was no blood.

"It looks fine. It's red on your heel, but the skin isn't broken."

"Gosh, that really hurt. I'm glad it's nothing."

"Me too." Philip turned his phone off, and we were thrust into darkness again.

Moonlight shone above us, creating a silky glow. I could hear water lapping against the shore.

My foot was still in Philip's lap with his hand resting on top. He didn't seem inclined for me to move it, so I kept it there.

He looked down at my toes. "You have pretty feet."

"Thank you." I was glad I'd painted my nails a frosty pink earlier.

His hand slid over my skin, the warmth of his palm moving farther upward. "Pretty ankles too." His voice sounded deep, an intimate rumble.

I tried to steady my breath, to calm myself. I knew I should pull my foot away, should put my sandals back on and leave.

"I should get going," I said.

"Probably," he murmured.

His hand encircled my ankle. I couldn't believe how sensual his touch was. Strong hands. Masculine fingers. It had been a long time since a guy touched me like this. A long time since I wanted anyone to touch me at all.

His palm slid farther up my leg, over my calf, until his fingers brushed the back of my knee. His eyes met mine under the moonlight, watching my reaction.

A riot of emotions tumbled through me. I licked my lips, trying to steady myself. His fingers continued to caress my skin. The sensation sent shock waves through every limb.

When a breeze blew my dress up so it covered only half of my thigh, I wondered if he'd try to slide his hand up even farther. I wondered if I'd let him. But then his thumb ran over the front of my knee, smoothing my recent calluses.

"How did you get these?" he asked.

It took me a second to compose myself. "Sometimes I forget to bring knee pads... when I'm cleaning a floor or a bathtub."

He ran his thumb over them again, and sparks shivered through me. "You work a lot," he stated.

"I'm trying to grow my maid business."

He nodded. I'd already noticed how he didn't seem to think any less of me for being a maid. Unlike Ethan's irritating pity, Philip seemed unfazed.

"You need to pace yourself better. You don't want to burn out."

"I can't slow down," I said stubbornly. "This is too important to me."

"How many days a week are you working?"

"I don't know."

"Yes, you do." His voice was warm, as was his hand stroking my skin.

I didn't want to admit to him that I'd been working seven days a week for months. "You're going to give me a hard time about this? The man who works so much his mother and sister had to trick him into taking a vacation?"

He grinned a little. "All the more reason you should listen to me." He ran his fingers gently over my calluses. "You don't want to over-work yourself to the point of failure or an injury."

"I suppose not." I could tell he was only looking out for me. I got the sense he understood what I was trying to do—probably better than anyone I knew.

"So slow down a little, okay?"

I nodded but didn't say anything. The problem was the last guy who'd looked out for me was Ethan, and we all knew how that ended.

He was still caressing my leg, and despite how pleasurable it was, I pulled away.

In truth, I was scared.

Not of Philip but of what I might be opening myself up to with him. That was why he was dangerous. It had nothing to do with pirates. He'd shown up here out of nowhere, but somehow he'd sparked something in me, and while a part of me was excited, the other part was scared.

"I really should go," I said. "It's getting late."

He released me, and I put my foot back on the ground.

I pulled my skirt down so it covered my thighs. "Will you thank your mom and Eliza again for me? It was nice of them to invite me for dinner."

"Sure."

I sensed his eyes as I bent over to put my sandals back on. "Doug called earlier today," I said as I fastened the straps.

Philip stiffened beside me. "He did?"

I nodded, sitting upright again. "He was checking on the room. It's almost done, isn't it?"

"Yes, the flooring just needs to be laid."

"Good. That's what I thought."

"Is that the only reason he called?"

"No." I gazed out at the water. There was a lighthouse in the distance. "He wanted to make sure he still had a rain check on our movie date."

"What did you tell him?"

I shook my head. "I tried to tell him I don't date, but he started begging me again." I thought of Daphne and wished he was begging her instead.

"And?"

"I didn't really give him an answer. For some reason he kept going on about how I should listen to *you*. Does that make any sense?"

Philip went quiet for a long moment. "You should give Doug a chance."

"What?" I stared at him in surprise. "You really think I should date Doug?"

"He's a decent guy."

I couldn't believe I was hearing this. What did he take me for? Caressing my leg one moment and telling me I should date his cousin the next? "Really? Well, gee, maybe I *should* go out with him."

"That's what I said, isn't it?"

"I'll just call Doug back and tell him yes."

"Good," he growled.

"Especially since you keep telling me he's so *decent*."

Philip scowled as he glanced around at the empty beach. "Come on, let's go. I'll walk you the rest of the way home."

We both stood up. I was so angry I wanted to get away from him as fast as I could, but before I could take two steps, he grabbed my arm.

"Let go of me!" I turned around, furious.

His only response was to drag me closer. My pulse shot up. I could just make out his intense expression, those black brows drawn together over silvery eyes.

"I lied." His voice was low and fierce. "I don't want you with Doug."

And before I could say another word, his mouth was on mine, kissing me.

For a split second, I was too stunned to move or do anything. He tasted hot and delicious. Electricity skittered down my spine. His hands were on my lower back, pressing me into him while I grabbed his muscular forearms, his whole body hard and rock solid against me.

I kissed him with abandon. I knew I shouldn't, and I kept telling myself to stop, but it had been so long, and he felt so good.

He broke the kiss. "Dammit."

My arms were around his neck. "What's wrong?"

He was breathing hard. Both of us were panting from this single kiss.

"Nothing." He shook his head.

I brought my fingers down to stroke his jaw, his skin rough with stubble. "Aren't you a decent guy too?" I asked.

He blinked at that, his eyes roaming my face with intensity. "No... I'm not."

And then his mouth came crashing onto mine again.

FOURTEEN

~ Philip ~

I wasn't a decent guy. In fact, I was an asshole.

There was no other explanation for stealing my cousin's girl. Okay, I knew Claire wasn't actually Doug's, but he was in love with her, which was close enough.

When he'd asked me to help him win her heart, kissing her senseless probably wasn't what he had in mind.

Of all people, I never thought I'd be in competition for a woman with Doug.

Claire moaned softly in my arms. Warm like the night around us, she tasted sweet and sensual. A small, curvaceous package. I wanted to take her back to that little fairy-tale house of hers, to that wicked bed, and do wicked things.

Except she was already coming to her senses. Hot kisses were one thing, but she wasn't offering more.

"I should go," she whispered.

"You should." My voice was low, rumbling, as I slid one hand down to her voluptuous ass. "But stay here and be bad with me." I put my lips to her throat and heard her intake of breath. I liked that sound. The hard-on pushing against my zipper liked it too. I remembered that fantasy I'd had the first day I met her. The one with the white string bikini.

I groaned. *God, I'd love to see that.*

Her fingers were on my scalp while I lightly bit her neck. I wondered if there was some way to make that fantasy and all the other ones I'd had about her a reality.

"Philip." She sighed, and I could tell it wasn't so much a 'take me home and let's get naked' sigh as a regretful, 'we should stop now' one.

So I pulled my mouth away from her skin, away from her feminine scent, and away from her soft body. As I tried to catch my breath, it became clear my hard-on wasn't going anywhere, so I started thinking about the numbers from that real estate portfolio, the meeting tomorrow—anything but Claire.

Her arms unwound from me, and she slid her hand down to my chest with her palm directly over my heart.

"I can't take this any further between us," she said softly. Her eyes met mine. "I'm sorry."

And even though her words weren't the ones I wanted to hear, I liked that she was straight with me. No games.

"Okay." I nodded, then grinned. "Rain check?"

A snort of laughter escaped her, and I felt inordinately pleased. I was like a high school kid trying to impress a girl. Every joke I cracked during that Monopoly game had been for her benefit.

I knew her ex-husband had done a number on her. The guy was obviously an ass. I honestly couldn't imagine how he'd married a woman like Claire to begin with. The fact that he was stupid enough to lose her said it all.

A wave of protectiveness came over me. She deserved far better than what she'd had to deal with. I knew quality, and Claire was quality all the way through.

As we walked along the water toward her house, I wished I could reach for her hand but sensed it would scare her off even more.

"You must know this beach pretty well," I said, making conversation.

"I do. I've lived on it my whole life. I have a lot of good memories." I listened to her lilting voice, the way it carried into the night as she told me how her dad and stepmother used to throw a big beach party every summer. "It coincided with the Pirate Days celebration the town puts on. There were games, a barbecue, big bonfires all along the water."

"Sounds like fun." It reminded me of Gavin's family. They liked to throw big crazy parties too.

"My dad used to be mayor, so everybody came."

I glanced at her. "Your dad used to be the town mayor?"

"For a number of years."

I took in this new information with interest. "I didn't know that."

"He was popular. The whole town came to his funeral."

"It sounds like you two were close."

"Yes," she murmured softly.

"I'm sorry I didn't get to meet him."

She nodded, and then we were both silent.

My gaze went out to the harbor, to the way the moonlight reflected on the water. I tried to imagine what it was like for her living here her whole life. So different from my childhood.

"I grew up in the city," I told her. "Nothing like this. Just a small house, but I had some good memories there too." It was strange to think back to that old house, the one my mom moved us into after my dad left. She made it a real home, despite everything that happened.

"It's the people that make a place, don't you think?" she said.

"Definitely."

"I have to admit I loved growing up on the water. I know every secret spot on this beach. I used to pretend there was buried treasure in each one."

"Yeah? You should show me some of them."

She glanced over. "Aren't you leaving soon?"

"No, I've decided to stay and help Doug a little longer."

"Oh?" She sounded surprised. "I didn't know that."

We reached what appeared to be the gate behind the main property of her house, within a tall white fence that ran along the edge.

"Well, thanks for walking me home." She searched through the small purse she wore at her side. "I know I have my key in here."

"I take it the gate's kept locked."

She nodded, still searching through her bag.

Meanwhile, I was standing there feeling guilty as hell again. Not that it was going to stop me.

"Claire," I said, my voice low.

Her head was still down as she rummaged through her purse. I sensed she was purposefully avoiding my eyes. "It has to be here somewhere."

"Look at me."

"I found it." She pulled it out in triumph, and I wondered if she would unlock the gate and disappear inside without a backward glance.

I didn't want that. "Don't go yet."

The urgency in my voice must have given her pause, because she finally looked at me. "I'm sorry, but I have to get up early. My first cli—"

I stole another kiss. I couldn't help myself. I meant it to be a short one, but then I lingered. Her lips were so lush.

"Good night," I whispered, gently stroking along her cheek with my thumb. There was a surprising rush of emotion in me, a mix of desire and tenderness.

I stood there as she unlocked the gate, waiting to make sure she got inside safely because, despite that stolen kiss, I was still a gentleman. Just before she went in, her eyes found mine. It was dark, but I still saw her smile, and a thrill went through me because I knew she felt something too.

That little dimple gave her away.

SMITTEN. I was officially smitten.

Seriously though. Was that a word I've ever used in my entire life?

It sure as hell wasn't something I'd repeat out loud and could only imagine the shit Gavin would give me if he heard me describe myself that way. I sounded just like Doug.

Fuck it.

I was smitten.

I couldn't stop thinking about Claire. Retracing our steps on the beach a thousand times. Sitting on that log stroking her leg, her skin so soft. I imagined stroking up her thigh. I could picture the two of us out there under the moonlight in a lot of ways, all of them erotic, and all of them ending with her cries of ecstasy.

Damn.

I needed a cold shower.

I needed to pull myself together and stop this torture.

And then there were those hot kisses. We had chemistry. That curvy little body pressed right into mine. She felt fantastic through the fabric of that dress. I wished I could have slipped it off of her, or better yet, I wished she'd slipped it over her head and offered herself to me under the night sky.

I groaned inwardly. That fantasy would be my new favorite.

This attraction wasn't just physical either. That was why it was so powerful. It was because I understood her. She was tough. All the crazy shit with her family, and the way she was trying to build her business, giving it her all—I totally got it. I'd been there myself. When I looked at the women I'd dated over the years, it was like I was finally waking up. This was the missing element all along. I never understood those women. They were like Martians.

Unfortunately, there was a big problem.

What the hell did I say to Doug?

Not to mention Claire herself, who had made it plain that she wasn't offering more. Somehow, I needed to convince her to go out with me again.

"Ow!" There was a stinging sensation on the side of my face. "What the hell are you doing?" I rubbed my skin where Gavin had just flicked me with a rubber band.

"I'm trying to get your attention. I said your name three times."

"What do you want?"

"I just got an email from the CEO of Drink Virtue. They're still working on a few of the flavors but have come up with some new names. I forwarded the list to you."

I opened the email and quickly scanned through it. Every single name had the word fizz in it. "This whole fizz beverage trend is over-done. They'll be lost in a sea of them."

"Yeah, I agree. It needs something else."

I leaned back in my chair and thought it over. We were both set up at the dining room table with our laptops in preparation to tele-conference with the real estate group later. "What about a play on the word doctor? Since their drinks are infused with minerals and herbs."

"That's not a bad idea."

We tossed some phrases back and forth for a while, with Gavin googling each one of them to see if they were taken. As usual, a surprising number were already in play. He started a list of the ones we liked and were available. Gavin and I always worked great together like this, just spitballing ideas.

Eliza came into the dining area, watching us as she munched on an apple. "What are you guys doing?"

"An apple a day," I said, motioning to the fruit in her hand, "keeps the doctor away."

"Dr. Apple?" Gavin asked.

"Dr. Apple's Ale."

Gavin grinned and typed into his computer. "It's not in use. Maybe it could change with each flavor. Cherry and plum, et cetera, but keep the ale."

I nodded, envisioning ideas for the ad campaign. Something fresh but with a hint of nostalgia. "I agree. Definitely add those to the list."

"What do you think?" Gavin asked my sister. "We're trying to come up with ideas for those fizz drinks."

She nodded. "I like that a lot better, but doesn't the company choose the name?"

I started an email to a market analyst we worked with about setting up a consumer survey to test some of the ideas. "Not if we're investing large amounts of money and don't like it."

"It seems weird that you can just change it like that." She bit into her apple and chewed. "How much money are you guys giving them?"

"Enough to bring their little company out of obscurity and into every grocery store chain in the country."

"There's always a risk," Gavin told her. "If we back an entrepreneur and they go under, we take a financial hit and so do our investors. As a result, we do everything we can to help them be successful."

"But there are also ways to evaluate a company that help us determine which risks are worth it." I explained some of the math to her, the way we used a scorecard method to calculate the variables, but I could already see her eyes glazing over.

"Enough. Please." Her face took on a dramatic expression. "This is starting to *hurt*."

I shrugged. "It's fun if you really get into the numbers."

"Speaking of fun"—she turned to Gavin and smiled—"I rented us bikes for this weekend. Is that cool?"

I watched the way Gavin smiled back and told her that was great. Did I imagine their eyes lingering on each other? "Hey, why wasn't I invited bike riding?" I liked to ride and went biking often in the city.

The pest looked at me. "You want to come with us? Mom told me you were headed back to Seattle."

"I've decided to stay longer." The perfect notion came to me then. Solid gold. "In fact, we should probably invite Claire biking."

"Awesome idea." She paused, considering me. "Are you still trying to help Doug?"

"Of course."

What the hell else could I say? That I was a devious asshole? That I'd already decided my cousin wasn't good enough for Claire? That if anyone was going to have her, it would be me?

No, I wasn't going to say all that.

After she left, I could feel Gavin's eyes on me. Ignoring him, I answered an email from that firm in Canada. There was another message from a guy I was in frequent contact with, an angel investor for tech start-ups who regularly sent me info about ones that were doing well and were looking for venture capital.

"What?" I finally asked.

"You were out on the beach awfully late last night."

"So?"

"So what the hell happened? Did you and Claire get together?" He grinned at me. "Some midnight wango tango?"

I chuckled and shook my head.

"Come on, spill it."

"Why do you think something happened?"

"Because, dude, you were staring at her all night. You're obviously into her."

"No, I wasn't."

Gavin snorted. He went silent then, studying me. "You must really like this woman."

I didn't respond right away, still typing. "Yeah, I like her."

"And?"

"My cousin's in love with her."

"So that's going to stop you?"

"Shouldn't it? Doug's family."

Gavin went quiet. He knew all about family obligations. His family wasn't screwed up like mine, but they were intense and always in each other's business. It wouldn't exactly go over well if he dated a woman one of his brothers was interested in.

But I didn't have any brothers. Just this one pathetic cousin who was almost like a brother, and I'd promised to help him, not stab him in the back.

"Maybe you should let this one go." Gavin sighed. "I mean, you only just met her."

I nodded, knowing he was right. I should let her go.

We started our meeting with Atlas, the commercial real estate group we were considering partnering with. They laid out all their ideas and how much money they needed, which was a sizable amount. I could see there was money to be made, possibly a lot, but I couldn't help thinking about Claire and everything she'd said about her hometown. How the changes wouldn't be for the better. After hearing the group's proposals, I honestly couldn't say whether she was right or wrong.

Afterward, I told Gavin I was out. We both agreed from the moment we'd started NorthStone Capital that if either of us didn't green-light a project, we'd move on.

"Are you sure?" he asked. "We could table it for now and come back to it in a couple weeks. There's still time."

"It doesn't sit right."

He held a pen in his right hand, clicking it as he studied me. "This isn't about the dinner conversation last night, is it? The one where all the women talked about how this town is so cute?"

"Of course not." I closed my laptop. "We've never invested in real estate on this scale. This project is massive. I think we're out of our depth."

Gavin shrugged. "It could be a new area for us."

"I prefer to stick with what I know and understand."

He stopped clicking and put his pen down. "I do think there's money to be made. We could always look at a smaller opportunity, something to get our feet wet."

I nodded. "Maybe."

LATER THAT AFTERNOON, I got a phone call from Doug. I was tempted not to answer it, but instead I stepped out onto the back deck so I could talk in private.

"How's it going with everything?" he asked. His voice was low, and I suspected he was hiding in the bathroom the same way I was hiding out on the deck. What a pair we'd become.

I described another job I might have lined up for him and how two of the recent bids came back with a thumbs-up. "I've put them on the schedule. The first one starts next week." I told him about the individual contractors I'd hired to step in and do the actual work.

"Gosh," he said. "That's... really great. Except that's not why I was calling."

A flash of irritation ran through me that I was making money for Doug, yet he barely seemed to care.

He lowered his voice. "I was calling about Claire."

I took a seat in one of the deck chairs. The sun was setting, and the sky was a stunning mix of orange, blue, and gold. To be honest, I already knew why he was calling.

"It's going fine with Claire," I said.

"It is?"

"Sure." I studied the kaleidoscope of colors above me.

"Because when I talked to her yesterday, it sounded like she was trying to back out of our movie date."

"Was she?" My mind drifted back to last night, to the way she felt in my arms. To that kiss that left us breathless.

"Have you been telling her all the great things about me?"

And then there was that stolen kiss. How that dimple appeared when she smiled at me before closing the gate.

I could hear Doug breathing into the phone. Could feel his expectation of me. The weight of it. He didn't doubt I would come through for him like I did for everyone in my life.

Gavin was right. I should let this whole thing go. I should step aside and give Doug a great piece of advice. I should tell him if he wanted Claire, he needed to get back here and make the effort, because that was how you grabbed a woman's attention. I should tell him I was done helping, that I was out, the same way I was out with that real estate investment.

But I didn't say anything.

I didn't say anything because I was a greedy bastard and wanted her for myself.

"Philip? Are you still there?"

"Yeah, I'm here," I muttered, rubbing my forehead.

"Geez, I hope she's not interested in someone else. Do you think that's why she tried to back out of our movie date?"

I paused. "Why would you say that?"

"I just worry, that's all." I could picture his hangdog expression as clear as day. Those big doe-like eyes. "That some other guy will come along, someone more flashy than me, and steal her away."

"Well, maybe you should get back here, then," I said irritably.

"I'm trying!" Doug let out a shaky breath. "At least Daphne came out to help us find a new house."

"Daphne?" That name was familiar. "Wait a minute, Claire's sister is there in Seattle?"

"My mom wasn't too happy about her showing up here, I can tell you that. But now the two of them seem to get along great. Daphne's been driving her everywhere and even taking her to her doctor's appointments."

"Is that right," I murmured.

"She's been a big help. Hopefully I'll be done here soon." He sighed, sounding as beleaguered as always.

Eventually we ended our conversation with my agreeing to tell Claire about the time he won a fourth grade essay contest for writing about his cat. "See? That way she'll know I'm an animal lover."

"Sure," I said, feeling guilty. "I'll tell her."

After we hung up, I kept the phone in my hand. I brought up Claire's number. She answered on the third ring.

"Hi, it's me, Philip."

"Yes, hi...." Her voice drifted off, and I sensed awkwardness.

"I just wanted to let you know I'll be by tomorrow morning." I told her how I had a guy scheduled to come and lay down the laminate.

"Oh, that's great."

We both went quiet. I could hear her birds twittering in the background.

"So how are the little pirates doing?"

"They're fine, though Quicksilver is causing trouble as usual."

"What do you mean?"

"He likes to chew. He just chewed through a wooden perch I got him. That bird has a wild streak."

I grinned. "You have to understand that's a good trait."

"It is?"

"Sure. It means he's strong-willed. He can't help going after what he wants."

"Hmm... maybe."

She quieted again, and I tried to think of something else to say. I knew she'd built this wall around herself and wasn't planning to let anyone in. I'd never been someone who gave up easily though.

"I'll see you tomorrow," Claire said, like she was ready to hang up.

"Wait, listen... do you know how to ride a bike?"

She paused. "Yes."

"Great. Look, I need your help on Saturday. We've been approached by a business looking for growth funds, and we need someone who can ride."

"I don't know. I'm not really interested."

"Come on, it'll be fun. Gavin and Eliza will be there. You can see what a young company does when they're trying to expand." It was low-hanging fruit, but I also knew it would get her attention.

"Oh?" Her voice lifted. "What kind of business is it?"

"It's a...." I racked my brain for something that sounded legit. "A bike company that's selling a new safety feature. It's hard to explain exactly. It has to do with the gearing system."

"How long do you think it will take?"

"Not long. Maybe an hour of us riding together." I couldn't believe I was making up this preposterous story, but what choice did I have? I wanted her to come bike riding with us, and I knew she'd say no if I asked her outright. "Just keep Saturday available. Believe me, it'll be worth your while."

FIFTEEN

~ Claire ~

"What?" Leah screeched. "You kissed Philip North!"

"Technically he kissed *me*," I said primly, picking up my glass. I didn't know why I was being so prim because, let's face it, I'd kissed him like there was no tomorrow.

"Holy cow," Theo said. "I think my ears just caught fire."

I laughed. The three of us were sitting at Bijou's for our regular dinner, and I was the hot topic of conversation.

"Wow." Leah seemed both dazed and impressed. "I always thought Philip North was so cool. A little more brooding and serious than Gavin—though, don't get me wrong, he's hot too."

I took a sip from my water and put it down. "Gavin seemed nice enough, but he's not really my type."

Leah's eyes bugged out. "Are you telling me you *met* the other half of NorthStone?"

I told her how Eliza had invited me over for dinner and game night a couple days ago, and they were both there.

"I don't believe this. You were actually playing Monopoly with Philip North and Gavin Stone?" Leah sounded incredulous.

"You'd think they were rock stars or something," Theo said, turning to me. "They're just some boring business guys, aren't they?"

Leah shook her head at our apparent ignorance. "They're *better* than rock stars. I may not be involved in finance anymore, but those two are geniuses." She leaned forward. "What was it like to hang out with them?"

"Pretty crazy," I admitted. "Fun too though."

Leah studied me. "I can't believe it. You and Philip North. This is *so* freaking cool!"

I shook my head and laughed. "Are they really that big of a deal?" I thought about Jocko the flying squirrel-bat and the way they were cracking jokes all night. Admittedly they were intense, but mostly they seemed like normal guys.

"Yeah, they're a pretty big deal." She sighed. "This is amazing. I haven't talked to you in a week, and it turns out you're living the glamorous life."

"I wouldn't say it was glamorous. It's actually been kind of stressful." I told them both about what happened on Saturday and finding Ethan drunk in my house.

Leah's eyes sparked with anger. "That asshole! Why didn't you call me? I would have come over and helped. I'm sure Theo would have come too."

"Sure, I would have." Theo nibbled a french fry and raised an eyebrow. "If it happens again, I say we alibi each other and bury the body."

Leah laughed, nodding in agreement. "Sounds good to me."

"It's okay. Philip was there, and he helped me get Ethan back home." I explained the rest of the story, the way Ivy and Violet acted like I was still in love with him. "I didn't know what to do, so I lied and told them Philip was my boyfriend."

"I wish I could have seen their faces." Leah grinned. She knew the way they were always calling me "poor Claire" and how much I hated it. "Do they know who he is?"

"No. Why would they? They think he works for Doug."

"You're kidding." She burst out laughing. "Really?"

"Well, he's been coming over making sure my room gets finished. So it's like he sort of is working for Doug."

"He's doing all that?" Her brows went up. "Damn, he must really like you."

"He's not doing it for me. He's doing it for his cousin."

"And that's why he kissed you? For his cousin?"

"No." It was actually quite strange the way Philip went from telling me I should date Doug one minute to kissing me the next.

"This is so exciting." Leah dug into her plate of food. "I can't wait to hear what happens next between you two."

I glanced down at my left hand. After two years, I'd finally gotten used to my bare ring finger. "Nothing is going to happen between us. I can't get involved with him." I thought about the bike riding thing on Saturday, but that wasn't a date.

Leah looked up at me from her plate. "What? Why not?"

"You know why."

Her expression grew panicked. "Now let's not be hasty. At the risk of sounding like a gold-digging mama, I should inform you that Philip North is what's commonly known as a *catch*."

I shrugged. "So what? I don't care about that."

"So what?" Leah rolled her eyes. "He's super hot, super rich, and from everything I've heard, he and Gavin are actually nice guys. He's basically perfect."

"Maybe you could just have some fun with him," Theo said. "It doesn't have to be serious."

How did I explain my fear to them? That when I imagined spending more time with Philip, giving him my trust, it scared the crap out of me.

"This is Philip North we're talking about." Leah put her fork down. "Think before you say another word."

"Why don't you just use him for sex?" Theo chimed in. "Would that be so bad?"

"Yeah," Leah agreed adamantly. "At least do that!"

While the thought was tempting, I also knew it was impossible.

THE NEXT MORNING I went up to the house for breakfast. I wasn't sure why, since it was only Violet and me, as Daphne was still in Seattle. But Violet texted me about joining her, and I got the sense maybe she was lonely. I knew it had been hard for her without my dad.

Only two seconds into the meal, I realized my mistake.

"I've been thinking about you and your new boyfriend. Why don't you invite him over for dinner tonight?" She sat serenely with her newspaper and plate of food.

"Um... *tonight?*" Panic shot through me. "Sorry, he can't. He's going back to Seattle tonight."

She paused, considering me. "You two haven't broken up, have you?"

"No, of course not." I waved my hand like that was the silliest thing in the world. "Everything is fine."

"Good." She nodded. "I want to set up something with Ethan and Ivy soon. I thought it would be nice for you to patch things up."

The last thing I wanted was to spend time with Ethan and Ivy. "Unfortunately I have a really busy week ahead."

Violet's dark blue eyes contemplated me.

"In fact, I should probably get going." I took a large swallow of coffee that burned the roof of my mouth. There were blackberry scones laid out on a plate nearby, and I grabbed one. Paused. Grabbed a second one. I wrapped them both in a napkin as Violet watched me.

I nearly made it to the dining room door when she started talking again. "I've been approached by a couple of civics groups I'm involved with. They want to know if I'd consider hosting a summer party here at the house for Pirate Days."

I knew Violet was on the town council. I stopped and turned around. "Are you serious?"

She nodded. "I told them I needed to consult with you, since you're half owner."

A sharp longing pierced my heart, remembering all those parties I grew up with, the ones my dad hosted. "Gosh," I said, finding my voice. "I can't afford something like that."

"You wouldn't have to pay for it. It would be a fundraiser with local businesses sponsoring it."

"A fundraiser for what?"

"They're trying to raise money to have the downtown area declared a historic district."

"Wow, really?"

"Hopefully it will prevent any real estate deal from disturbing the area. It takes time and money though. However, I believe your father would have approved."

I nodded. He would have definitely approved. "Okay, I'm fine with it. I'd like Your House Sparkles to be listed as one of the sponsors."

"Certainly." Violet nodded. I was ready to leave, but I got the sense she had more to say. Her voice softened. "I have to tell you, Claire, I've been thinking about selling the house."

My stomach dropped. "What do you mean?"

"Just what I said. I'm getting older, and this house is too large for one person. Daphne is only living here temporarily." She fiddled with her teacup. "A sale could benefit you too. I know you've been struggling to pay the taxes and insurance every year."

My throat went tight. This was my home. Except for my time being married, I'd lived in this house or on this property my whole life.

"I can see by your face this upsets you. I'm not planning anything right away, but I thought it only fair to mention it."

"Okay." I tried to catch my breath. "Thanks for telling me."

By the time I made it outside, my head was spinning. *Violet might sell the house?* I stopped at the mailbox out front. If she decided to sell, I'd have no choice but to go along with it. There was no way I could buy her out.

My phone buzzed, and I glanced down. There were a few voice messages waiting. I listened to them as I made my way down toward the carriage house, glancing through the mail, still in a daze about what Violet just told me. One of the envelopes caught my attention as its return address was an attorney's office.

The first voice message turned out to be one of our clients telling us she'd no longer be using our maid service. I didn't enjoy hearing that, and she didn't give a reason, but sometimes people canceled if their situation changed. The second message was from another client calling to cancel too. By the time I heard the third message from a client canceling, I knew something was wrong.

I stopped walking. Three people canceling in one morning?

The fourth message began, and it was Ivy using her sugary voice, telling me she'd no longer be requiring our maid services. She ended her message with "Have a nice day."

I realized then that the people who'd canceled were all ones she'd recommended. I shook my head, angry that she'd be so petty.

"To hell with her," I said. At least I wouldn't have to deal with her and her snotty friends anymore.

I continued down the driveway, opening the letter from the attorney with curiosity. It was addressed to me by name and was from a law office in Bellingham. To my shock, the letter informed me I was being sued by one Mona Hendricks for extensive damages to her floors and carpeting. She wanted them replaced, and their estimated worth was over twenty grand.

I stopped and stared at the letter in shock.

Mona Hendricks was fish-face Mona.

What the hell? I read it again. Ivy had obviously put her up to this. I couldn't afford to replace Mona's floors and carpeting. And of course, I'd never damaged them in the first place. All I did was clean her stupid house. And she never even paid me for it. In fact, *I* should be the one suing *her*.

My stomach clenched with fury. What was I supposed to do? I'd have to get a lawyer, not that I could afford one. My mind raced. I didn't have the money for any of this. It could put me out of business. It was as simple as that.

"Is everything all right?"

My head whipped up. It was Philip. He was standing next to the back of Doug's truck. I hadn't even noticed him there. He must have arrived while I was up at the house with Violet.

Immediately, I burst into tears.

It was mortifying, but I couldn't seem to control myself. Between Violet's talk of selling the house and now all this, it was too much.

His brows slammed together as he came to my side. "Hey, sweetheart." He put his arm around my shoulder. "What is it? What's wrong?"

I only shook my head and continued to cry.

He searched my face. "Tell me what's going on?"

I struggled to speak as he waited patiently.

"I'm being sued," I said between sobbing breaths. I hated that I'd lost control, but the tears kept flowing. After everything I'd gone through with Ethan, I was finally turning my life around, and now Ivy was trying to destroy it again. How could she? Why did she hate me so much?

Philip took the letter from my hand. I watched as his eyes scanned the paper, the muscles in his jaw tight.

"I never ruined her floors or carpet," I croaked. "It's a lie. Mona never even paid me for the work I did. She's a friend of Ivy's. They're trying to ruin me." I told him about all the voice messages.

"Do you have liability insurance?"

"No. I had to cancel it because I couldn't afford it."

"Claire," he murmured, glancing at me. "That wasn't smart."

"I know." My voice shook. "But I didn't have a choice. Between all the licensing fees and workers' comp the state required, I had to drop it. I was planning to reinstate it as soon as I could." I shook my head, feeling stupid and angry at myself. "I've worked so hard!"

"I know you have," he said quietly. He studied me, and I realized he completely got it. He understood.

I burst into tears again.

Philip pulled me in, wrapping his arms around me. It felt so good to be held. To have someone take care of me. He smelled amazing too —like soap, along with his own guy scent.

"It's going to be okay."

I didn't respond, resting my head against his shoulder as he stroked my back. I felt sheltered and safe. It was only an illusion, but I didn't care. I wanted it. Just for now. Just for this moment. I let myself enjoy it until my crying slowed.

"Oh no, what time is it?" I pulled back with alarm. My nose was running, and I sniffed, wiping it with the back of my hand. "I have to clean Mrs. Lamb's house this morning, and I'm picking up your mom on the way."

"My mom?"

I told him how I was taking his mom over to meet Mrs. Lamb, who knew all about the history of Truth Harbor. "Remember she wanted to get some background on the town for her book series?"

He nodded. "I do remember."

"Sorry." I sniffed again and quickly wiped the tears from my cheek. "I have to get going."

"Sure. I'll let you know how things progress with the floor today."

We stood there staring at one another. His face had a day's worth of beard growth, and his black hair needed a cut. He looked more like a pirate than ever. A handsome, roguish one.

"It's all going to be okay," he repeated as he looked down at me and stroked my hair, his face solemn. "I promise you."

I nodded and bit my lip, trying not to cry again. I didn't believe him. I knew he was only trying to comfort me. I also knew how easily businesses like mine went under. I'd read online how the first year was the hardest for any new company.

After I left in my car, I kept thinking about what I could do to solve this mess. I'd come so far. I couldn't give up.

I tried calling Ivy, but of course she didn't answer. I left a voice message asking her why she was doing this to me. I sounded hysterical, but I didn't care. She already had Ethan. What more did she want? I considered calling Violet, even Daphne, but then realized there was nothing they could do.

In the end, I only had myself to rely on.

It was a lesson I'd learned the hard way, and I wasn't going to forget it now.

I took a deep breath. I had to toughen up.

First, I needed a lawyer. I figured I'd call my dad's old law partner. He was retired now, but hopefully he could steer me toward someone reasonable—though I had no idea how I'd pay for it. I could dip into my trust, though it pained me to do it, since I needed every penny for Sullivan House. But what other choice did I have?

Violet wanted to sell anyway. My stomach ached at the thought. If she sold the house, I'd get some money, but I'd lose my home. I'd be forced to move into an apartment in town, some generic place I'd hate. My birds would hate it too. Every morning, I opened the windows so they could chirp and twitter with all the other birds in the woods. They loved it.

My heart was heavy. It became even heavier knowing I might lose my business.

I'd be back to zero again.

I didn't mention any of this to Sylvia when I picked her up. As usual, she was friendly, chatting about her book and her visit yesterday to the local library. In some ways she reminded me of Eliza, always looking at the bright side of life.

When we arrived at Mrs. Lamb's house, it turned out her son,

Elliot, was there. Like his mother, he was a teacher—an archeology professor at the University of Washington.

As I cleaned the house, Sylvia sat with Mrs. Lamb, asking her questions about the town and taking notes.

To my surprise, Elliot joined the discussion. He seemed genuinely interested in the mystery books Sylvia planned to write.

I liked Elliot. Right after he hired me, I could tell he was a thoughtful son who always made sure his mom had everything she needed. I had a number of elderly clients, and unfortunately, some of their kids were real jerks. Elliot wasn't one of them. He was in his mid-fifties, handsome, divorced, with a couple of grown children. He seemed like your classic professor type. He was also quite adventurous and traveled to some pretty out-of-the-way places.

"Pirates *here?*" Sylvia questioned. "I always think more of the Caribbean when I think of pirates."

"There was definitely activity here," Elliot said. "Plenty of maritime stories about the Pacific Northwest involved pirates, rum running, and even ghost ships. You'd be surprised."

He and his mom told her about the legend of Iron Jim Sallow, a pirate who had buried treasure in the Seattle area. I already knew the story but listened for a while anyway before I left to go do Mrs. Lamb's weekly shopping. Just as I was headed for the door, I heard Elliot suggest that he and Sylvia meet for coffee, that he'd like to hear more about her book series. I smiled to myself as Sylvia laughed lightly, saying she'd like that.

LATER, when I was done cleaning for the day and arrived home, I was surprised to discover Doug's truck still sitting in my driveway. I was even more surprised when I went inside the house and found Philip in my spare room, laying down the laminate himself.

"What are you doing?" I asked. "I thought someone was coming in for this today?"

He reached over to turn down the radio. It was playing the same alternative rock station I listened to. "The guy never showed."

I opened my mouth. "You're kidding."

"When I finally got a hold of him, he was drunk, so I fired him."

"You didn't have to do this yourself though."

He shrugged. "Sometimes doing a job yourself is the best way to get it done." He glanced up at me. "I know how badly you want this room finished."

I realized then that he was doing it for *me*. After the emotional morning I'd just had, between all the tears and worry, I was touched by the gesture. "Thank you."

He gave a nod.

I looked around at the tools and stack of cut boards. "How do you even know how to do all this?"

Philip explained that as a teenager, he'd worked for Gavin's dad's construction company doing whatever odd jobs needed an extra pair of hands. "We both worked for him. In fact, he'll be here in a few minutes to help."

"Gavin's coming here to help with my flooring?"

He nodded, pointing at the doorjamb. "I've forgotten how to lay the end pieces, but Gavin says he remembers."

My phone buzzed, and I glanced down to see it was Leah. "It's my best friend. I need to answer it."

"Sure." Philip tilted his head. "What's your best friend's name?"

"Leah."

When I answered the phone, Leah was already ranting. "That bitch is suing you? Unbelievable." I'd left both her and Theo a voice mail earlier relaying what had happened. She agreed that Ivy had to be behind the whole thing. "You should countersue them for harassment. Countersue them for everything they've got."

I listened, but I couldn't resist lingering in the doorway and getting an eyeful of Philip as he reached over to turn the radio up. His muscular shoulders looked powerful measuring out the floor. Despite my attempt to squelch the memory of us kissing the other night, it kept replaying in my mind.

I forced myself to turn away. I shouldn't be allowing these indulgences. It wasn't like I could act on them. That kiss was a onetime thing.

Leah wanted to know exactly what the letter from the lawyer said, so I found it on the kitchen counter, then went outside. I had a seat in one of my plastic Adirondack chairs and read the whole thing to her.

She huffed. "You know she has to prove damages. That bitch can't just make this up and expect you to pay."

"I'm worried though. What if she damages her own floors and then claims I did it?" I'd been analyzing the situation all day and was seeing all sorts of terrible ways it could go down.

"There has to be some way to prove she's lying."

I thought about it and remembered something. "You know what? Mona's nanny was there that night I cleaned. She would know I didn't damage her floors."

"So you have a witness?"

Amazingly, I did. "I can't believe I forgot about her being there. How do I get a hold of her though?"

"Do you know her name?"

"Only her first name. It's Taylor."

Leah suggested I call the different nanny services in town.

"It's a long shot though," I pointed out. "I mean, she might not want to get involved, especially if Mona is her employer."

"True."

"This whole thing is crazy. All I did was clean her stupid house." A wave of anger came over me. "Between Mona and Ivy, they're going to put me out of business."

"No they're not. Don't talk like that."

There was a sick feeling in my gut. It reminded me of the days and weeks after I'd found out Ethan was cheating on me. The terrible sense that my life had spun out of control, that I had no way to stop it.

"We'll figure something out," Leah said. "I'll help you hire a lawyer if that's what it takes. Don't worry."

I sighed. I appreciated the support, but I couldn't take money from Leah. She had her small yarn business and her farm. I knew she'd sunk everything she owned into them and was barely getting by.

"You should have taken Theo up on her offer to infest Mona's house with those flying tarantulas."

I laughed despite myself. "I thought they were cockroaches."

"Whatever. I say we have her do both Mona's *and* Ivy's houses."

A blue sedan I didn't recognize made its way down my driveway. I could see Gavin behind the wheel as he parked right behind Doug's truck.

"I don't want to generate bad karma."

"Bad karma?" Leah sounded incredulous. "The only bad karma is the tsunami of flying spiders coming Ivy's way. In fact, I'm going to video the whole thing and watch it with a bowl of popcorn."

I laughed some more. In some ways, Leah was more vindictive toward Ivy than I could ever be.

I waved to Gavin. "I appreciate you coming by to help," I called out to him as he came closer.

He grinned and waved back. His eyes roamed over the outside of my house. "Damn, Eliza told me it looked like something out of a fairy tale, but I guess I didn't believe her."

I got up from my chair. "I hear that a lot." He followed me as I went to open the front door. "I'll take you to Philip. Can I get you anything to drink?"

"Who are you talking to?" Leah wanted to know.

"Nah, I'm good."

"Gavin is here to help with the flooring," I told her.

"*What?*"

He glanced around. "This is really... cute." His brown eyes seemed to stop on my bed, but then they found the large cage, and he grinned. "Your pirate birds?"

"That's them. They're being quiet at the moment."

Meanwhile, Leah was squawking louder than any parrot I'd ever heard. "He's there right *now*? Gavin Stone is in your house right *now*?"

"Yes," I said to her, watching as he went over to the cage.

Philip poked his head out from the spare room. He grinned when he saw me, and I couldn't help grinning back. He was so handsome. My stomach dipped.

"What *exactly* is he doing there?" Leah wanted to know.

"Well, he's talking to my birds right now."

It occurred to me that I rarely had visitors, and yet there were two hot guys in my house. When had my life taken this crazy turn?

"He's here to help Philip lay the laminate in my spare room," I explained as I walked back outside, realizing I'd left the letter from the lawyer out there.

"Are you *freaking* kidding me? Philip's there too?"

I reached down for the paper. "Yeah, they're both helping."

"So let me get this straight. You have a couple of billionaires laying down the new floor in your spare room?"

"Billionaires?" I was taken aback. "What do you mean?"

Leah didn't answer because she was too busy laughing.

I knew Philip was successful, but Leah had to be wrong. "Are those two really billionaires? That can't be true."

She caught her breath. "I don't know their individual net worth, but NorthStone is worth a fortune. They've invested in nearly every major tech start-up from the last decade."

I glanced over at Doug's dented late-model pickup truck. The one Philip had been driving around town. Then there was Gavin's plain blue sedan parked right behind it. Granted, it was a rental, but it wasn't exactly glamorous.

Wouldn't a billionaire have at least rented a sports car or something? The only thing I knew about billionaires was what I'd seen on television and movies.

"No way," I said. "You're wrong."

"I'm not wrong."

"They don't seem anything like that guy."

"What guy?"

"You know, the billionaire guy from those sexy movies."

Leah snorted. "Don't be silly. That's just fiction."

I thought more about those movies. Some parts were hot, but other parts weren't my style. "Do you think Philip's into all that bondage stuff?"

"How should I know?" Her voice took on a sultry tone. "Has he mentioned his 'special red room' or how he wants you to sign a contract?"

"Very funny." I thought about Philip's beat-up sneakers. He was wearing them right now. "Unless he's a billionaire on hard times, I don't think you're right."

"Trust me, he's loaded. Not all billionaires are living on private islands. Think about Warren Buffett."

I headed back to the house, still doubtful. Leah continued to gush about Philip and Gavin. "They're badass, but they're not ostentatious. That's why I always thought they were so cool."

"I have an idea. Why don't you come over and meet them?"

I heard her sharp intake of breath. "What do you mean, like right now?"

"Yeah, right now." I walked back into the house. The radio was playing a Pearl Jam song, and I peeked inside the door of my spare room. Sure enough, both men were laying down the floor. It looked like they were almost done too. My room would finally be finished.

"I don't know." Leah sounded excited but nervous. "Do you think I should?"

"Looks great," I said to them, stepping inside the doorway. "My friend Leah is coming over to celebrate the room's completion. Do you guys want her to get anything?"

"Sure," Philip said. "Maybe have her pick up a pizza. I'll pay for it."

"No, I'll pay," I said quickly. "I owe you guys for doing all this work."

I could hear Leah shouting, "For God's sake, let him pay!"

"Yeah, I'm starved," Gavin agreed. "Have her get two pizzas. One of them pepperoni and mushroom. And maybe some cold beer."

"Did you hear that?" I said to her. "Two pizzas. Cold beer."

There was silence on her end of the phone, and I suspected she was lying flat on her back on her living room floor.

"Are you okay?"

"Yes," she muttered. "I'll be there as soon as I can."

SIXTEEN

~ Claire ~

"I think I'll call Theo too," I said, still standing in the doorway with the phone in my hand after hanging up with Leah.

Philip looked over at me. "Theo?"

Even Gavin had stopped what he was doing and seemed interested.

"My other best friend."

Philip's mouth gaped. "Your *other* best friend?"

I dialed Theo's number. Happily, she picked up right away. She wanted to know about Mona suing me, but I said I'd explain it all to her later. I told her about Philip and Gavin working on the room. "It's nearly finished, and we're going to celebrate with pizza and beer. Do you want to come over? Leah's already on her way."

"Sure." She paused. "Have you kissed Philip again since last time?"

"No." I felt embarrassed since he was standing right there watching me.

"Why? Come on, he's hot. I think you owe it to yourself to use him for sex."

"Um...." My face grew warm. I hoped Philip couldn't hear any of this conversation. "Let's talk more later," I mumbled.

"All right, fine." She told me she'd be over after she wrapped up a few things.

Philip's eyes were still on me as I hung up. I got the impression he was trying to decipher my phone call.

"She'll be here soon," I told him.

"*She?*" His brows went up. "Theo is a female?"

"Theo is short for Theodora. You met her briefly—Leah too—when we ran into each other at Bijou's. She's tall with red hair. Don't you remember?"

"I did?"

I nodded.

Gavin smirked. "I think Theo's name nearly gave Philip a heart attack."

Philip rolled his eyes and looked at me. "Ignore him. He always likes to make trouble."

While the guys finished up the floor, I made sure my birds were fed and had fresh water. My house was too small for everyone, so I put a blanket outside and then moved the two Adirondack chairs in closer. I brought in a couple more lawn chairs from the back so my guests would have a place to sit.

By the time Leah arrived, Philip was in the kitchen washing his hands.

Gavin moved my boom box radio outside. "It's nice out," he said as he came back into the kitchen and snagged a beer from one of the packs Leah had brought. He put his hand out to her and introduced himself. "I'm Gavin."

She nodded with wide eyes and shook his hand, though she didn't speak.

Philip grabbed a beer and shook hands with her too. "Apparently we've met already. Thanks for picking up beer and pizza. What do I owe you?"

"Nothing," I interjected. "I'm paying as a thank-you, remember?"

Philip gave me a funny look before the guys helped carry the pizza outside along with plates and napkins.

"Should we invite Eliza and your mom?" I asked Philip after we took a seat.

"Eliza has rehearsals tonight," Gavin said, popping a slice of pepperoni into his mouth. "Sylvia wasn't around. I think she said she was meeting someone for coffee."

Philip brows drew together. "Meeting someone?"

"Oh, I think it's Elliot." I turned the cap off my beer. "He invited her out earlier."

Philip considered me. "Who is Elliot?"

I explained about Mrs. Lamb's son, though I could see right away that Philip wasn't thrilled.

"What do we know about this guy? Is he okay?" he asked.

"He's okay. He's great, actually," I told him.

When Theo showed up, we were all still on our first beer, though the guys had already devoured a few slices of pizza. More introductions were made. I got up to give her my lawn chair and moved to the blanket.

To my surprise, Philip came over with his plate and beer and sat next to me. "I wouldn't want you to get lonely over here," he said with a grin.

My pulse jumped at having him so close.

Leah was asking the men questions about themselves. "So I've always wanted to know." She fiddled with her beer bottle. "Which of you is Butch and which is Sundance?"

Both guys burst out laughing.

"Damn, I haven't heard that one in ages," Gavin said. "It takes me back."

"Me too," Philip agreed. "That magazine article is still one of my favorites."

Gavin leaned toward Leah and affected a southern drawl. "Well, if you must know, little lady, *he's* Butch and I'm Sundance. After all, I'm younger and more handsome."

Philip scoffed. "Get out of here. You're two months younger than me."

"And Butch here, being older, is more ornery."

Philip chuckled and sipped his beer.

"Do you ever mind it when people call you guys the Wild Bunch?" Leah asked.

Gavin shook his head. "Not at all. I call us that myself. Hell, we are a wild bunch."

"I still have a western ringtone on my phone," Philip admitted.

"How do you even know about that article?" Gavin asked, eyeing Leah with curiosity.

"I used to work for NorthStone."

"What?" Gavin was clearly taken aback. "Are you kidding me?"

"I'm not. I worked in Seattle at the main office downtown for a year."

Philip seemed astonished too. "What was your job?"

"Financial analyst." Leah listed the names of people she used to work with, and both men nodded.

"So we never met before?" Gavin took a swig from his beer.

"No." She shrugged. "I was just a lowly analyst, and I was only there a year—less than a year, actually."

"Are you still in finance?" Philip asked, reaching for another slice of pizza. "Where do you work now?"

"No, I quit altogether." Leah told them how she left the industry recently, moved back to Truth Harbor, and bought a small farm with llamas, alpacas, and sheep. "I sell raw fleece and the yarn I spin."

"Quite a change," Philip commented.

"Leah's the one who told me about you guys," I said. "I had no idea you were so famous."

"More like *infamous*." Gavin grinned at me.

I was glad to see Leah had finally relaxed around the two men and seemed to be enjoying herself. Theo was totally mellow. To her they were just a couple of business guys. It was fun when she told them what she did for a living. It wasn't every day you met a bee entomologist.

Ironically, I was the only one feeling nervous. It was Philip's fault. With him sitting beside me, it was difficult to ignore his proximity. I wished I wasn't so attracted to him, but every time I looked at him, I felt a zap of excitement.

I leaned back and took a deep breath. The sky was turning a darker shade of blue, and the air smelled green and rich. With the radio playing in the background, it was the perfect summer evening. Despite the hour, no one seemed in any hurry to leave.

Gavin sat between Theo and Leah, the three of them discussing the merits of the show *Shark Tank* and whether it was realistic. Philip joined the discussion for a while, but our eyes kept finding each other.

"How are you?" he asked, leaning toward me, his voice low. "After this morning."

"Worried. But there's not much I can do—except get a lawyer. I tried calling Ivy, but she won't return my calls."

"Do you really think she's behind the whole thing?"

"She's friends with Mona, and I think the two of them cooked it up. Ivy has it in for me."

He paused for a moment. "Because of your ex?"

"I guess." I shrugged. "I don't really know. She seems to have a grudge about something." It was ridiculous. If anyone should have a grudge, it's me.

"I got the impression your ex-husband is still carrying a torch for you."

"Believe me, I want nothing to do with him. He's Ivy's problem now. I wish they'd just leave me alone."

Philip took this in with a frown. "So these women are bullying you?"

I nodded. "Basically."

His frown grew deeper.

I reached over for my beer and took a sip. "So, what is it with you and all these outlaw associations?" My voice had a teasing note. "First pirates and now western gunslingers?"

His expression changed, and he chuckled a little. "It is kind of strange, isn't it?"

"I already know about you and cell phones. But is there something else you haven't told me?"

"Nope. Like I said, I'm a straightforward guy."

I raised an eyebrow. "Is that so?"

"It is."

"Hmm... why don't I believe you?"

"You should get to know me better and you'll see."

Our eyes lingered on each other, and a slow warmth glided through me. "I'll bet you say that to all the girls."

He leaned closer. "Only you."

We were still gazing at each other. I knew I should pull back, look away—anything to break this growing intimacy. I needed to protect myself. The problem was that little part of me he'd ignited didn't want protection.

There was a peal of laughter from Leah, Theo, and Gavin, who were all cracking up at some joke.

"You have unusual friends." Philip glanced over to them.

"Do I?" I glanced at Leah and Theo again.

Theo was grilling Gavin, questioning him about whether he was one of those capitalists who didn't care one whit about the environment. "Are you kidding?" Gavin seemed indignant. "I'm a tree hugger all the way."

"A yarn spinner and a bee entomologist?" Philip gave me a look. "I'd say so. How did the three of you meet?"

"Leah and I were best friends growing up." I leaned back on the blanket to get more comfortable. Philip watched me, his gaze following my body. "And I met Theo at a yoga class two years ago."

Out of nowhere, I heard a familiar voice with a southern accent. "I didn't realize you were throwing a party tonight, Claire."

I jerked up into a sitting position. It was Violet. I hadn't even heard her coming down the driveway. She stood there on the edge of the grass wearing one of her endless twin sets.

"Are we being too loud?" I asked, though I didn't think we were being loud at all.

"I figured I'd come down here and meet your new friends." Her accent was strong, which usually meant she was upset. "Perhaps you could introduce me?"

"Um, sure."

Instead of waiting for me though, she marched right up to Philip —a heat-seeking missile finding its target. "I assume you're Claire's new boyfriend?"

Everyone fell silent. All I could hear was the radio playing "Trouble" by Cage The Elephant.

I glanced at Leah and Theo, who both looked worried. Gavin's brows shot up.

But Philip caught on fast. Unfazed, he immediately stood up from the blanket and put his hand out to Violet. "That's right, ma'am. I'm Philip North."

"Well, it's good to meet you finally." She wore a polite smile as she shook his hand, but as she studied him, her smile wavered. "And you are... Doug's cousin?"

"I am."

She nodded, but I could see she was uncomfortable. Violet liked it when people met her expectations, when everyone fit into their proper box, and she was obviously having trouble deciding which box Philip should go into.

"And you work for Doug?" she asked.

I heard Gavin chuckle.

Philip grinned a little. "Not exactly. I'm just here helping him out."

"I see." Violet studied him some more. "Who exactly *is* your employer, if I may ask?"

"My employer?"

"I just want to be sure my stepdaughter isn't dating someone who might try to take advantage of her. People see a house like this"—she motioned back toward Sullivan House—"and they get all sorts of ideas."

"Violet!" I couldn't believe she'd said that.

She turned in my direction. "I'm only looking out for you, Claire. Since you haven't brought this young man up to the house, I'm forced to come down here and meet him myself."

This was unbelievable. I wanted to die of embarrassment. It was bad enough Philip was going along pretending to be my boyfriend, but now Violet was accusing him of being a gold digger?

"That's all right," Philip said, trying to hide his smile. "I guess you could say I'm self-employed."

Violet studied him. She didn't seem to like this answer.

He motioned behind him. "Gavin and I are in business together."

Gavin immediately got up from his chair, came over, and put his hand out to Violet. "I'm Gavin Stone. It's nice to meet you."

"And what exactly is it that you two boys do?"

"We're VCs." Gavin grinned at her. I got the sense he was enjoying this exchange immensely.

"I'm sorry?" Violet blinked at him. "What is a VC?"

"Venture capitalists," Philip explained. "We own NorthStone Capital."

Violet frowned, her gaze traveling over both men with a critical eye. She didn't seem impressed with either of them.

Between Philip's shaggy hair, dark stubble, and those beat-up sneakers, he didn't exactly look like someone who'd invested in nearly every successful tech start-up of the last decade. Gavin wasn't any better in his faded T-shirt and ripped jeans. Neither of them were what you'd expect a couple of guys who ran a billion-dollar company to look like.

"Let me offer you boys some advice." Violet was still studying them. "If you want to make it in this world, you've got to remember that appearances matter."

"Violet, please leave them alone," I said, exasperated. "Their appearance is fine. They were just laying down the floor in my new room today."

"I understand, but if they want to be successful, this is important." She turned to them again. "Would you like to hear the rest of my advice?"

"Yes," Philip said, nodding.

"Absolutely!" Gavin's grin was a mile wide.

Violet paused. "At least you both have good manners, so you must have been raised well." She smiled at them. "Something my father always told me is that you mustn't let your guard down in public for even one minute. I'm sure you two boys are just starting out, but if you want to be successful, you've got to be mindful of how you present yourself—and think big. Do you understand?"

"I do," Philip said.

"I'm always thinking big," Gavin agreed. "The bigger the better!"

"Good." Violet nodded. "I'm glad I came down here." Her eyes went to Philip. "That means you might want to get yourself a haircut. I'm only saying it wouldn't hurt." She looked down at his feet. "And new shoes don't have to be expensive."

"Oh my God," I groaned.

"I'll keep that in mind," Philip said, his lip twitching with a smile.

"Yeah, really," Gavin scoffed at him. "You need to pull yourself together. I'm almost embarrassed to be seen with you."

"And you could do with some new blue jeans, young man," Violet said to Gavin. "Those holes are unseemly. No one is going to take you seriously in those."

"I understand," he said gravely.

She smiled at them both. "Once you're cleaned up, I believe you two boys have a lot of potential."

After she left and went back up to the house, I groaned again. "I'm *so* sorry. If it's any consolation, she insults everybody."

"That was fun," Gavin said with a grin. "I can't remember the last time I had a good talking-to like that."

Philip chuckled. "Me either."

———

DESPITE BOTH MEN being good-natured about Violet and her advice, our little party wrapped up soon after she left. Both Leah and Theo had to get up early the next morning, and Gavin said he still needed to get some work done tonight.

Before I knew it, there was just Philip and me.

Alone.

He helped me throw the empty pizza boxes away and put the leftovers in the fridge.

The whole time I was torn between wanting him to leave and wanting him to stay. There was this feeling in the air between us. Something unspoken.

We went back outside and had just finished folding up the two extra lawn chairs when the radio played a Daughtry song, "Start of Something Good."

To my surprise, Philip took the lawn chair from my hand and placed it against the porch rail.

"Would you dance with me, Claire?" He held his hand out.

My pulse sped up. It'd been a long time since a guy asked me to dance. I glanced up at him, uncertain, but his gaze was straight and true.

I took his hand, and my breath caught when he pulled me in close.

"I like this song," I managed to say.

"Me too." His voice was low.

We both went quiet as we slow danced.

I tried to ignore the excitement building in me. "I'm sorry about Violet. She can be kind of forceful sometimes."

"Don't worry about it. I like her."

"You do?"

"She thinks I have potential."

I couldn't help my laughter.

"Seriously, she was just looking out for you. I get that."

I considered his words. I always saw Violet as Ivy and Daphne's mother, someone in their corner, not mine. It occurred to me Philip was right. She was looking out for me tonight.

"Thank you for pretending to be my boyfriend again." I bit my lip, embarrassed how he kept getting pulled into my family dramas.

He grinned. "I didn't mind that either."

"You didn't?"

"No," he whispered. "Not at all."

Our eyes stayed on each other.

My excitement grew even more. I tried to say something, but when I opened my mouth, he leaned down and kissed me. Just like the song, we were caught up in the start of something. I knew I should stop, but the pull of him was strong—irresistible. His body felt so good pressed into mine.

When we broke the kiss, he didn't move away. His eyes roamed my face. "I can't believe this," he said. "Where did you come from?"

I wasn't sure how to respond.

"A fairy tale." He tilted his head toward my house. "Or maybe a pumpkin."

I laughed nervously. "Maybe."

The song ended with a commercial. Still holding my hand, he led me over to the blanket on the ground. I pulled back because I knew what he wanted. I wasn't born yesterday.

"I can't," I said. "I'm sorry, but I'm just not ready for this."

He turned to me. "Ready for what?"

"I probably shouldn't have kissed you again. I don't want to lead you on."

That seemed to give him pause. "You're not leading me on. I just want to hang out and talk."

"You just want to talk?" I gave him a skeptical look.

He chuckled. "I swear I'll keep my hands to myself. I only want to get to know you better."

I didn't reply right away, thinking it over. I'd grown to like Philip. I liked how he was so protective over his mom and sister. The way he stayed and helped me with Ethan, and then tonight with my room.

I thought about how he held me this morning when I cried. He didn't act like I was 'being a girl' or that I should have been tougher.

"Do you want me to go?" His voice was low. He'd obviously misinterpreted my silence. "I don't mean to push you."

"You don't?" I smiled a little, because I'd bet he was pushy and bold in every area of his life.

"No." His expression was serious, and I could tell he meant it.

"Okay, we can hang out. But you have to keep your hands to yourself."

He grinned. "All right, but I won't be responsible for you." He gestured to his body and waggled his brows. "You might not be able to resist all *this*."

I laughed and we sat next to each other, Philip with his knees up while I crossed my legs.

He grinned at me once we were settled in. "So let's start with food," he said. "What's your favorite meal?"

"My favorite meal?" I didn't have to even think about it. "Pad Thai."

"Really?" He seemed delighted by that. "A Thai food lover."

"My favorite restaurant is right here in town."

"I like Thai food too. We should go there sometime."

I nodded but didn't commit to anything.

His eyes stayed on me. "Okay, what's your favorite movie?"

"*Pirates of the Caribbean.*"

He shook his head and chuckled. "Damn, I should have guessed that one. It's probably because I've never seen it."

"Really? I can't believe that, especially with your family history."

"Eliza's seen all the movies. I just haven't had time."

"Well, you should make time."

He grinned and pointed to my car. "I'll bet your favorite color is turquoise."

I shook my head. "No, it's sky blue."

"It is?" I knew what he was thinking. His eyes were sky blue.

"What about you?" I asked. "What's your favorite movie, meal, and color?"

He grinned. "That's easy. My favorite movie is *The Godfather*. My favorite meal is the spaghetti with spicy meatballs my mom makes, and my favorite color is green."

"I've seen *The Godfather*, but I really didn't think much of it."

"*The Godfather* is the greatest movie ever made."

I shrugged. "That's debatable."

"There's no debate. It's got everything—duty, honor, courage—even romance."

"So do other movies. I don't see why a Mafia movie is considered that great." I leaned back on my elbows, stretching my legs out to get more comfortable. "To be honest, I thought it was boring."

He blinked at me. "*Boring?*"

I laughed at his expression. "Okay, I have to admit I barely remember it. I saw it years ago when I was a teenager."

"Ah." He nodded. "That's your problem right there. We need to fix that."

I shrugged, still smiling.

"All right," he said. "Let's move on. What's your favorite vegetable?"

"My favorite vegetable?" I laughed again.

"What's wrong?"

"You seriously want to know my favorite vegetable?"

"I'll have you know this is highly important information. A lot can be determined about a person's character from their favorite vegetable."

"Gosh, I'm really sorry." I tried to look apologetic. "But that's way too personal for me to divulge."

His expression turned sly as he scanned down the length of my body. "Maybe I should try and torture it out of you."

A tingling sensation ran through me. "You promised you'd keep your hands to yourself, remember?"

He leaned in and lowered his voice. "Trust me, you'd enjoy it."

My breath caught. He was so close. I imagined myself reaching out for him and pulling him onto me. How good he'd feel. His taste and smell. The weight of him.

"Sorry." I forced myself to turn away, catching my breath. "My favorite vegetable will have to remain classified."

"I suppose I'll let this one go." He sighed. "But only for now."

I peeked at him, watching as he changed position on the blanket to get more comfortable. He lay down on his back with one arm tucked under his head as he gazed up at the sky.

"What is it with all these questions anyway?" I asked. "It sounds like you're going down a list."

His eyes flashed to mine. "I'm just trying to get to know you. Isn't that what boyfriends do?"

I didn't reply, not sure what to say. I hadn't had a boyfriend since my senior year of high school, and it was Ethan. I didn't remember him ever being this interested in me.

We both remained silent, though it was a comfortable silence. The grass smelled cool and green around us. Crickets chirped. Usually I was alone when I sat outside like this.

Philip was still lying on his back, gazing up at the sky. "I can't remember the last time I've seen this many stars."

I turned upward. "It's because there's no city nearby to cause light pollution."

"It's incredible." He took a deep breath. "I think this town is growing on me."

"I'm not surprised. I love it here."

"It does have its charms."

Our eyes met. It was dark, but we could still see each other.

"So tell me," he said, his voice quiet. "What are your hobbies?"

"We're back to this again? You're relentless."

"Yes, I am. So tell me."

I lay on my side next to him, propped up on one elbow. "Well, there are my birds. I enjoy taking care of them. I also like to garden and plant flowers around my house." I smoothed my hand over a lump of grass beneath the blanket. "I grew up sailing but haven't done it for a long time."

"You sail?"

"Not anymore, but I miss it. My dad and I used to sail together. We went all over the San Juan Islands. We even sailed up to Victoria a few times."

"You two were really close, huh?"

I nodded, remembering the fun we used to have on the boat when I was growing up. All the talks we had. "My dad always told me happiness takes work. If you want your life to be something special, you have to make it that way. He was a great believer in action."

Philip nodded. "I agree with him." He glanced over at me. "So why did you stop sailing?"

I shook my head, picking at a blade of grass poking through the blanket's rough fabric. "It's a long story." I didn't want to get into how my dad had given Ethan and me the boat as a gift after our wedding, how we had to sell it as part of our divorce, how I used my half to pay for attorney's fees.

He studied me, and I could tell he wanted to hear the long story.

"What about you?" I asked, genuinely curious. "What are your hobbies?"

His eyes went back to the sky. "I don't know." He shrugged. "I like to make money."

I laughed. "That's not a hobby."

"Sure it is."

"What else?"

His brow creased. He appeared to be thinking it over. "I like to follow the news and keep up on current events."

"A news junkie," I groaned. "I should have known."

"Why? What's wrong with that?"

"Nothing. My dad was a news junkie. I grew up with C-SPAN playing in the background like other people listen to music."

He grinned. "I've been known to watch C-SPAN."

"And do people around you complain?"

"Yes." He chuckled. "All the time."

It occurred to me that my dad would have approved of Philip. He was industrious and hardworking. He took care of his family. It wasn't that my dad disliked Ethan, but he thought less of him after Ethan encouraged me to quit college to support us. I couldn't even imagine Philip allowing a woman to do that for him.

We both went quiet. It had grown late. The witching hour, to be exact, the time of night where it felt like we were the only two people left in the world. I thought about how I needed to get up early in the morning.

I should send him home. It was the smart thing to do.

Instead, I moved closer, rising so I rested on one arm. Nervous energy fluttered through me. I felt him go still at my nearness, saw the way his eyes took in my face. I sensed he wanted to reach for me but didn't want to break his promise.

"You're very pretty." He licked his lips. "Hard to resist."

I blinked with surprise. And then I did something that surprised me even more.

I bent down, and I kissed him.

SEVENTEEN

~ Claire ~

Philip tasted like a wonderful dream I once had a long time ago. A dream I'd forgotten but wanted to remember. I drew back from the kiss and gazed down at him.

He smiled. "Do that again."

"I guess you were right after all."

His fingers moved gently across my forehead to brush my hair back. "About what?"

"It turns out I couldn't resist you."

"I told you."

Our eyes stayed on each other, both of us smiling. Then I watched as his face grew serious. "Come here," he whispered. "Kiss me again."

And so I did. His mouth opened to me, his taste and smell permeating my senses. Nervous energy still vibrated through me, but I didn't fight it anymore. I let myself enjoy it.

"Lie on top of me," he murmured after a few more kisses, shifting position so his hands were free to help.

I did as he asked, lying over him so our bodies pressed together.

His hands slid down to my ass. "Damn, you feel incredible."

My insides were a jumble of nerves.

He moved his hands everywhere, exploring my body, and we went at it for a while, kissing and rubbing against each other. It was sexy, even though we still had our clothes on. I could taste a hint of beer, but mostly he tasted like himself. It struck me that I'd kissed him enough that he was becoming familiar.

Eventually his hands slid under the back of my shirt, caressing my skin. They went to my bra. I squirmed against him as his fingers deftly undid the hooks.

I broke away. Sitting up, I balanced myself on my forearms, hovering over him.

Philip's eyes were on me with concern. "Is something wrong, sweetheart?"

"I don't know." I licked my lips, still nervous. "It's been a while for me. I'm not sure if I want to do this."

"Do you want to stop?"

He was breathing hard, and I knew he was turned on. "No, but I can't have sex with you." I sat up some more, embarrassed. I was a grown woman in my thirties. This shouldn't be a problem.

"It's all right."

My eyes went back to him. "It is?"

"Of course."

His expression was sincere, but I could feel his hard-on. "I almost believe you."

"I wasn't expecting sex."

"You weren't?" I studied him. For the first time, it occurred to me that maybe my assumptions were wrong. It'd been so long since I dated that I wasn't even sure about the etiquette anymore. I figured guys wanted sex right away.

Philip considered me too. "How about this—you tell me when something is too much, and I'll stop."

"Really?"

"I like you. I don't want to rush things between us. Let's take it slow."

I thought it over. "Okay, I guess that's fine. I could do that."

"You sure?"

I smiled. "I'm sure."

His hands rested on my hips, but then he tugged me toward him with a devilish grin. "Then bring thyself closer, my pirate princess. I've a hankerin' to taste yer sweet lips."

"Oh my gosh." I laughed at his pirate impression.

"Aye, you're a ripe treat." One hand slid over my bottom and squeezed. "*Very* ripe indeed."

I raised an eyebrow. "Ye best watch that hand, ye salty dog, lest ye lose it in a quick way."

Philip's eyes widened with fake terror. "Shiver me timbers. Me lady has a tongue as sharp as a razor!"

"And a sharp sword too!"

His other hand moved down to my ass, both squeezing me now. "Alas, she is too ripe to resist." He grinned at me, looking every inch a real pirate. "I'll have to take me chances."

Our eyes stayed on each other, both of us grinning and being silly. And it was in that moment that something changed in me. I relaxed in a way I hadn't for a long time.

A crazy thought came out of nowhere.

He's the one you've been waiting for.

Philip must have felt it too, because his gaze softened. His hand moved up to stroke my back.

"Claire," he whispered. "My sweet Claire."

He drew me close, and we kissed again. Tenderly at first, our tongues and lips lightly exploring each other. But then the kiss grew deeper. Purposeful. Like sinking into a slow burn.

Philip flipped me onto my back. My bra was still unlatched from earlier, and he slid his hand under it, kneading and fondling me. He pushed my shirt up, and when his mouth went to my right breast, suckling, I gasped.

His eyes flashed to mine. "Too much?" he asked. "Should I stop?"

"N-No," I managed to say, excitement barreling through me.

He tried to catch his breath. "Are you sure?"

"Yes." I nodded and smiled.

"All right," he murmured. He rolled his thumb over my nipple, which sent more sparks through me. I swallowed. He was gazing down. "Look at you. So much treasure to plunder."

I tried to pull him close, to kiss him again.

"I want to see more of you," he said. "Can we take your shirt off?"

"Geez," I joked. "Give you an inch...."

But I sat up partway to help him remove my shirt and bra. I glanced around, grateful for the darkness. Luckily the carriage house was pretty much invisible from the main house during the summer months.

Philip caressed my breasts. "You're beautiful," he whispered. His hands were warm as they slid down my body before his eyes met mine. "I can't believe how much you've affected me."

I reached out and stroked his jaw. He'd had a big effect on me too, but I didn't want to admit it. "Kiss me some more."

And so he captured my mouth, wrapped his arm around my waist, and laid me down under him again. When he slid lower and went back to teasing and suckling my breasts, I sighed with pleasure. I tangled my hands in his dark hair before moving down to his muscular back, grabbing at his T-shirt.

He took the hint and reached behind himself to pull it off.

I could just make out his body in the moonlight, and he was exactly as I'd pictured. Better even. Smooth skin over solid muscle. Philip was strong and well-made.

"You're going to have to stop eyeing me like that," he said.

"Or what?" I answered, slipping my arms around him.

He didn't reply, only lay over me so we were skin to skin. I felt turned on in a way that I hadn't in ages and squirmed against him. Our tongues slid over each other, our bodies moving to a silent beat.

After a while, he slipped his hand between us to unzip my jeans. "Can I touch you here?" he asked, his voice husky.

I nodded, and he tugged my jeans off so I was just wearing panties. As soon as his fingers slid over the outside of them, I closed my eyes. It had been so long since I'd wanted a guy to touch me like this.

Philip was gentle, though his breathing was harsh. When he slipped his fingers inside the fabric and stroked me directly, he groaned. "You're perfect," he said in a low rumble, his mouth at my throat. "So damn perfect."

My breathing was harsh too. I decided to forget about our deal, about taking it slow. I reached down for him and put my hand over his erection, squeezing him through his jeans. He grunted at the contact. I tried to unzip him, but he stopped me.

"I want to touch you too," I said.

His eyes weren't silver anymore. They were solid black, his pupils huge. I could feel his heart pounding. "That's not a good idea."

"Why?" I wanted him. Badly. "Do you have any kind of protection?"

I sensed he was trying to calm himself, though he was struggling. He shook his head. "You don't know what you're asking."

"I do," I insisted. I put my mouth to his ear and whispered, "I want you. Let me be with you."

Philip sucked in his breath. "God, Claire... don't do this to me. Just moments ago you told me you weren't ready."

"Come on." I slid my leg around his hip and rubbed my body against his, trying to convince him.

"I can't," he said. He licked his lips, and I sensed him warring with himself.

"Why?"

"Because I don't want you to regret your decision."

"I won't. I swear."

But he shook his head. "No."

I moaned with frustration, still pulling on him, trying to assuage my need.

"It's okay, sweetheart," he whispered. "I'm going to take care of you."

At first I didn't know what he meant, but then his fingers were on the outside of my panties. He slipped them beneath the elastic so he was gently stroking me.

My breath trembled. I reached for him, pulling him even closer. His lips brushed over mine as he played with me, and I wrapped my arms around him.

He knew what he was doing—I couldn't deny that. His fingers were experienced as they gently circled and rubbed before sliding inside me. I tried to hold out but failed miserably. It had been so long. Too long. How could I have forgotten this? Before I knew it, I was grabbing his forearm, moaning with abandon as he brought me to a shattering climax.

When I came down, I was still wrapped around him, his heart hammering against my chest. His skin was covered in a sheen of sweat, his body tense, trembling—like kindling ready to flame.

"Let me do you too," I said softly.

I thought he might argue or try to stop me, but he didn't. He was too far gone.

I pulled the zipper on his jeans down and slipped my hand inside his boxers, moving my fingers over him and squeezing at the same time. Immediately he groaned, dragging me close, his mouth hot and needy on mine.

It didn't take long before his whole body went tight against me. "God... Claire," he growled, panting. His muscles tensed for a long moment, and then I felt something warm.

Philip was quiet afterward. We both were. I wiped my hand on the blanket, then moved up and laid my head on his shoulder. We stayed that way for a while as he lightly grazed his fingertips down my spine, the night quiet and still around us.

"Thank you," he said in a low voice.

I kissed his chest and then looked up at him. "You don't have to thank me."

"I broke our agreement."

"No you didn't. That's silly."

"We were supposed to take it slow. You getting me off is not taking it slow."

I rolled my eyes. "So what? Clearly I changed my mind."

I could see his face well enough, and his expression was serious. "I meant what I said. I don't want to rush things between us."

"Don't worry." I stroked his cheek. "This is fine. Trust me."

He stared at me and then began to laugh.

"What is it?" I asked, enjoying his good humor.

He shook his head, still laughing. "I sound just like the girl."

———

I SPENT the whole next day thinking about Philip. As I scrubbed and vacuumed other people's houses, as I loaded their dishwashers and mopped their floors, as I folded laundry and dusted family photos, he was there. A great diversion from Mona and her lawsuit, which was just as well, because I needed one. I relived every single detail of last night. It was like I was Cinderella and had found my prince.

But I knew that wasn't true. No illusions there. I didn't believe in fairy tales.

And I certainly wasn't in love. No illusions there either. My heart wasn't ready for that, but at least I'd met a guy I could be myself with. And I decided to be happy about it, even if it was only temporary.

During one of my breaks, I called Jim, my dad's old law partner, and left a message. I told him my business was being sued and asked if he could recommend a good lawyer, one who wasn't too expensive. He got back to me right away and gave me a couple of names to try.

I also called a few of the nanny services in town and asked if they had an employee named Taylor. They wouldn't give out names, but I left a message with my phone number for each one just in case.

For lunch, I went out to the harbor. My usual spot with a view of the sailboats. I watched them as I sipped coffee and ate my peanut butter sandwich.

I thought about my dad. We went sailing every weekend when I was a kid. Our first boat was a dinghy, but eventually we moved up to a twenty-eight-foot Ericson. There was one almost like it on the water right now. The weather had been good this summer too. Warm with just enough wind.

When my phone rang, I glanced down at the number. It was unfamiliar, but then I thought it might be one of the lawyers calling.

Unfortunately, I was wrong.

"It's Ethan—don't hang up!"

This was not a voice I wanted to hear. "Leave me alone. I can't believe you have the nerve to call me." It figured he'd call today. He must have psychically sensed I was having a good day and decided to ruin it.

"I'm only calling to apologize."

"Great. Goodbye."

"Wait! Ivy and I are seeing a marriage counselor."

"So? What does that have to do with me?"

"I just wanted to explain my behavior that night at your house. Ivy and I were fighting."

I bit my tongue. There was no point in talking about karma.

"Marriage with her is so different than it was with you," he continued, sounding unsure of himself. "It's been an adjustment."

"Whatever. I hope the counseling works and you're both happy."

Or it fails and you're both exceedingly miserable.

"Do you really feel that way? That you want us to be happy?"

I sighed. "If you'd asked me two years ago, I would have said no, but now, to be honest, I just don't care either way."

He was quiet. "I guess you've moved on, huh?"

"Yes, I have."

"With Philip?"

I should have been honest and said Philip had nothing to do with it, but I didn't. I'd discovered I liked having a fake boyfriend. I should have made one up sooner. "Yes, if you must know, with Philip."

"Are you in love with him?"

"We're crazy about each other."

There was a moment's pause. "Well, then I'm glad for you."

"Thanks. I'm hanging up now."

"Again, I'm sorry. I know I made an ass out of myself. Let me know if there's any way I can make it up to you."

I almost said there wasn't, but then something occurred to me. "Actually there *is* something you could do. You could tell Ivy to call off her lackey. Did you know Mona is suing me?"

He hesitated. "I did hear something about that."

"The two of them are trying to put me out of business."

"Oh no," Ethan said quickly. "I doubt that. Mona just wants you to pay for the damage you did to her floors."

"I didn't damage her floors!" I gripped my phone in frustration. Ethan could be so naive sometimes. It was annoying when we were married, and it was still annoying. "They're making this whole thing up."

"But why would they do that?"

"Because Ivy hates me."

He went quiet. The interesting thing was Ethan didn't deny it. "I could talk to her about it," he said finally, "but I doubt it will do any good."

"Try."

"She's jealous of you. I think she's even jealous of your maid business. And she's still angry at me for forcing her to quit her job and move back here. I wish now I'd listened to her."

I wished he had too. But then what he said sank in. "Wait, it was *your* idea to move back to town, not Ivy's?"

"She didn't want to quit her job, but I agreed to open a satellite office for work. And it's doing really well," he added. "Ivy's miserable though."

"What was her job?" It occurred to me that I knew practically nothing about her life.

"She was a buyer for a clothing store."

"And she can't do that here?"

"Apparently not. It was very high-end. She claims there isn't anything equivalent."

I thought about all the different shops in Truth Harbor. There were a few nice ones, especially along the water. It figured they weren't good enough for Ivy.

Later, after work, I considered driving by their house and confronting Ivy myself. I knew it wouldn't make any difference though. I'd called her twice now, and she hadn't returned either call, freezing me out. She did the same thing in high school.

I was even tempted to go by Mona's to try and reason with her, but I knew better than that. Growing up with a father who was an attorney, I'd learned the number one rule to follow if you had legal trouble was to keep your mouth shut. He always said to let your lawyer do the talking. Innocent or guilty, it didn't matter.

So instead I went home to my birds.

I fed them dinner, then heated up some leftover soup for myself. As I was toasting a bagel to go with it, I got another call, this one from Daphne.

"Hey," I said, stirring the soup as I waited for it to boil. "How's it going in Seattle?"

"Things are fine. We're still trying to find a house for Linda— Doug's mom. She's very particular."

"And how are things with Doug? Any progress?"

"Actually...." She giggled. "That's going fine too."

My brows went up. "Oh, *really*? Let's hear it."

"Well, we've been taking these long walks through the neighborhood after dinner every night. We're really getting to know each other."

"That sounds promising."

She sighed. "I hope so. He's such a neat guy. He never tries to show off or act cocky like so many of them do, you know? And you should see how nice he is to his mother." She lowered her voice confidingly. "People always say you can tell a lot about a man by the way he treats his mother."

"I've heard that too," I murmured. I thought of Philip, who respected his mom and treated her well. "How are you getting along with Doug's mom? Is she nice?"

"I have to admit she's demanding," Daphne said in her soft-spoken voice. "But the more time I spend with her, the more I think she's also lonely. I've been encouraging her to get out more. She recently joined a book club, and I found a knitting group she likes."

I turned the heat off on the soup and removed it from the burner. It sounded like Daphne knew what she was doing.

"Oh, and I brought a few jars of my homemade jam," she went on. "Did you know Doug likes to bake? He makes these incredible muffins."

"Oh yeah?" I didn't want to be unkind, but those muffins were horrible.

"They're delicious with my jam on them. We served them to the book club, and people were gobbling them down." She laughed. "Doug said he'd never had that reaction to his muffins before."

"That's great," I murmured, opening the drawer for a butter knife. "How are things otherwise? Are you still staying at a hotel? It must be getting expensive. What about work?"

"No, it's fine. Linda invited me to stay in her guest bedroom. And I've been helping one of the knitting group members buy a new condo." The tone of her voice changed. "Please don't tell my mom or

Ivy about this. I'll tell them eventually, but first I want to see how things turn out here."

I spread some cream cheese on my bagel, thinking about how different Daphne was from her sister. She was kind and generous. I hoped Doug was smart enough to see it. "Don't worry, I won't say a word."

EIGHTEEN

~ Philip ~

I arrived at the trailhead twenty minutes early on Saturday morning. Eliza and Gavin would be along shortly, but I wanted to get here first so I could tell Claire how the fake bike company wasn't going to be here today.

I felt ridiculous for making up that story, but I was still glad I did it, because it meant I got to see her today. The other night had been playing on repeat in my mind. How beautiful she looked under the stars.

As I waited, I checked social media for some of the companies we invested in. It was a quick way to keep an eye on everyone. I also had a large following of my own and posted regularly on topics I felt were newsworthy.

I noticed a voice mail from Madison and shook my head. I'd deal with that later. She was angry when I canceled our date for this weekend, but I had no intention of going out with her again. A few other women had also left messages, but I deleted those without even listening to them. There was a voice mail from one of our office managers and two from my assistant, Sam. I texted them both back. There was also an email about a new job for Doug. I'd struck gold recently with a group of homeowners in the same neighborhood who were all looking to remodel.

There was movement from the corner of my eye, and I glanced up to see it was Claire. She wasn't riding but rather pushing her bike up onto the trail.

Even from this distance, my pulse quickened watching her. She wore tight black bike shorts and a blue Lycra top that showed off her curves. My mind flashed back to the way they'd felt beneath my hands and mouth the other night. Incredible.

Hot and incredible.

I kept watching. She waved, and I waved back.

"Hey, I'm glad you could make it," I said as she drew near.

"Sure, that's fine." She wore her hair in braids, one hanging down each shoulder, and I could barely believe it. I *loved* women in braids. It was practically a thing with me. I wanted to lean over and kiss her, but she wasn't standing close enough, and I figured it was a sign. Her wall was still up.

"Where is everyone?" she asked, looking around. "Are we meeting them someplace else?"

"Well, unfortunately, I have bad news." I sighed, trying to look contrite. "It's been canceled."

"What?" Her face fell.

"But the good news," I said quickly, "is the bike ride is still happening. Eliza and Gavin should be here any second. In fact, they were psyched when I told them you were riding with us today."

Her mouth opened, and I could see the wheels turning. I hoped she didn't bail.

"So how far does this bike path go?" I asked, trying to keep her engaged. "It's a good thing we have you here as our guide."

She blinked up at me. The gold in her brown eyes made me think of sunshine, of all the summer days I hoped to spend with her. "It goes for about twenty miles, though we don't have to do the whole thing. Part of it is along the water. It's a really pretty ride."

"Sounds great."

She looked down at my bike. "Did you bring that with you from Seattle?"

"No, I picked it up at a shop here in town." Luckily, I noticed a bike shop when I was driving home from a meeting with one of the local contractors last night. "It's an Alchemy Eros with a titanium frame. It gives an excellent ride. I have a similar bike at home," I explained.

"So you bought a second one?"

"Yeah, Gavin and my sister are renting theirs, but I prefer riding my own." I glanced down at her bike, which was an older generic brand. "We could get you fitted for a new bike, if you're interested."

"Get *me* a new bike?"

"Sure, if you're interested."

"That's okay."

I picked up my helmet. "Are you sure? I'd be happy to get you one. The shop had a number of high-quality options if titanium doesn't appeal to you."

"My bike is perfectly *fine*." She wore a strange expression.

"All right." I shrugged. "Let me know if you change your mind."

The pest and Gavin arrived, and there were greetings all around, with my sister hugging Claire like they were long-lost friends.

After a bit of discussion, we agreed to take the trail down to the harbor. Eliza and Claire were busy chatting, so Gavin and I rode ahead. We raced each other, but it was pointless, as my bike was way faster than his rental.

"That's a sweet ride," Gavin said, admiring it when we stopped. "You picked that up in town? Maybe I should upgrade while I'm here."

"You should check it out." I told him about the shop, and we discussed the merits of titanium versus carbon fiber as we waited for the women.

When they finally caught up, we rode together for a while, but eventually Claire and I paired off while Gavin and Eliza rode ahead. They must have been joking about something, because I could hear my sister's squeals of laughter even from a distance.

I frowned, still trying not to read anything into the two of them.

Claire and I talked a little as we rode, but mostly we just biked and took in the scenery. She seemed noticeably subdued, and I wasn't sure what was going through her mind. I hoped she wasn't regretting the other night, because I sure wasn't.

"Is everything okay?" I asked, riding up alongside her.

She nodded. "I'm fine."

"I had a great time the other night. I hope you did too."

"Oh, I... did." I could see that dimple in her cheek as she gave me a sideways glance.

"I'm glad to hear it. Because I'd like to see more of you." *A lot more of you.*

I was hoping she'd tell me she felt the same way. Instead, she murmured something incomprehensible and rode farther up the path.

Never one to give up easily, I rode alongside her again. "Look, did I do something wrong?"

"Of course not." Her eyes stayed on the trail, avoiding mine altogether.

"Are you upset that I didn't call you yesterday? Because I wanted to, but I worried you might think I was coming on too strong."

She shook her head. "No, it's fine."

"Then what is it?"

Claire seemed to deliberate something. Finally, she gave me a look. "I don't want you offering to buy me expensive gifts like that."

I was genuinely confused. "What?"

"That bike must have cost you at least a thousand dollars, and you were going to buy me one totally out of the blue?"

My brows shot up with surprise. That was the last thing I'd expected, though I now understood that strange expression.

"It made me uncomfortable," she went on. "I don't want you buying me anything or even offering to."

This bike cost triple what she thought it had, though I didn't see any point in correcting her. "I thought you might like an upgrade to something better, that's all. I didn't mean to offend you."

"I'm not offended. I'd just prefer you didn't do it again."

I mulled over her words. Maybe I shouldn't have offered to get her a new bike. Was it too much? Most women were fine with me buying them things. In fact, they all seemed to expect it.

Claire obviously wasn't most women.

"Okay," I said. "I understand. It was too much."

"Not that you weren't being generous, but it was weird."

"Sure, I'll cool it."

"Thanks." She nodded. "And I appreciate you not taking it the wrong way."

"No problem. Though I guess this means I'll need to get back the deposit I put down on that sailboat for you."

Her eyes widened, but then she saw the grin on my face. "You think you're so funny, don't you?"

I chuckled. "Would you really refuse it if I bought you a sailboat?"

"I don't know." She sighed, smiling now. "Please don't ask me that. I don't even want to be tempted."

"I'll buy you a sailboat," I teased, bringing my bike even with hers, "as long as you promise to take me sailing with you. It's in my blood, after all." For a moment I imagined the two of us on a sailing adventure, cruising around the Caribbean. She wore a white string bikini, her hair in braids, and a relaxed smile on her face. We'd explore the various ports every day, then drink rum and make love under the stars every night. "I'll bet we'd have a great time," I murmured, caught up in my fantasy.

"Someday I'll buy myself a boat." She gave me a defiant look. "Just because I'm struggling now doesn't mean it's forever."

"I agree."

She glanced over at me. "You do?"

Over the years, I'd dealt with enough entrepreneurs and business owners to have an instinct about who was going to make it and who wasn't. Claire had the kind of drive I saw in people who succeeded. "I wouldn't say it if I didn't mean it."

"Thank you. I appreciate that."

"I think you're going to do well. Except I still don't like the name of your maid service."

She went quiet and seemed frustrated. "Do you really think it's that bad?"

People asked my opinion all the time, and I knew the best thing I could do was give it to her straight. "It's not strong enough, Claire. You need something with more punch. Something that's not ambiguous."

"But I had my car painted with that name, and I've bought all those T-shirts." Her voice rose. "And what about the website?"

"Write it off as a loss on your taxes. You can't stick with a lousy name just because you bought some T-shirts or painted your car. And you can always change your website."

"I suppose. This sucks," she grumbled.

"Better to figure it out now though."

"Why should I even listen to you?"

I shrugged. "You don't have to—except I know what I'm talking about."

We were riding through trees along the path, but I could see what looked like an opening up ahead.

She motioned with her chin toward it. "Do you see where that park begins up there?"

"Yeah, I see it. Why?" The trail curved around to the left, but I could just make out the park entrance.

She laughed. "Because I'll race you!"

My brows went up. I was going to tell her to forget it, that my bike was ten times faster than hers, but I didn't get the chance because she shot out in front of me.

I let out a shout of amusement. I should probably have ridden slowly, but I didn't. I was naturally competitive and suspected she wouldn't like it if I let her win anyway, so I sped up and passed her easily. I rode around the path. It veered to the left, and I figured I'd wait there for her at the park entrance and ask for a winner's kiss when she arrived.

But then something strange happened. Just as I rounded the corner, Claire came out of nowhere right at the entrance. I couldn't believe it.

"How the hell did you do that?" I asked, laughing as I slowed down and stopped beside her. I glanced around. "Did you find a wormhole?"

Claire was out of breath and laughing now too. "Sort of." She pointed to my right, and I saw a narrow opening that ran straight through the woods and let out here. "It's a secret path. It used to be dirt, but they paved it a while ago."

"Damn, I can't believe it. And here I was ready to ask for a winner's kiss." I let my eyes linger on hers. "I guess I can't do that now."

Her smile turned shy. She was still catching her breath, and I watched as she licked her bottom lip. "It turns out I'm the winner."

"I'd be happy to offer *you* one." I moved closer. She didn't back away, and I got as near to her as I could with the bikes between us. I gently tugged on one of her braids. "I like these."

"You do?" She was watching me with that same smile.

I nodded, my voice rough when I spoke. "Very much." And then I leaned down and lightly brushed my lips against hers. They were soft and minty. She responded right away, her mouth like velvet.

We kissed for a short while, until I felt myself getting aroused and drew back. I gazed down at her. She was pretty with her braids and cheeks flushed from bike riding. The classic girl next door. Something about her still reminded me of unicorns and rainbows, but I decided I liked it. "You're cute," I said.

"Thanks." That dimple appeared. "So are you."

"I'm glad you think so."

We continued to study each other. She licked her pink lips, and I was tempted to kiss her some more. I wanted to. Except I didn't want to deal with an erection while wearing bike shorts. I forced myself to look away and motioned toward the center of the park. There were people and food vendors, the aroma of fried onions drifting toward us.

"Do you want to stop and get something?"

She nodded. "That sounds good."

We headed over and claimed a bench, parking our bikes next to it. I asked her what she wanted and told her I was buying. "No refusals allowed."

She gave a dramatic fake sigh. "All right, fine. Get me a bottle of water."

I got in line while she stayed with the bikes.

I came back with not only water bottles but a couple of soft pretzels. "Here you go." I handed them over as I took a seat on the bench beside her. "Nourishment."

She took them, blinking prettily at me. "Thank you, my sugar daddy."

I chuckled. "I think you're a little mixed up about what a sugar daddy is."

We sat eating our pretzels and drinking water. It was a sunny weekend, so the park was filled with people out enjoying themselves. Some of them were picnicking in the grass while others played Frisbee. There were kids and dogs everywhere. I swear, it felt like I'd landed in Mayberry.

Claire was eyeing me. "I have a confession to make."

I squeezed mustard from a packet onto a corner of my pretzel and took a bite.

"I looked you up on the internet last night."

I nearly choked. "You did?"

"I hope you don't think I was spying. I was curious about you."

For a split second, I went into a panic. "What did you find?"

I tried to think of the worst it could be. Mostly women. I wasn't a dog, though some might disagree. I'd dated a lot in the past. The vapid women my sister was always complaining about. They usually didn't show up until at least page three or four on a search though. The first couple pages were typically stuff about NorthStone with various bios of me and some of the most successful investments we'd made.

She brushed some of the salt off her pretzel. "Leah was right about you and Gavin. It turns out you are a big deal."

"I suppose." I took another bite. I didn't like to think of myself that way. I'd seen how someone could get screwed up when they stroked their own ego, telling themselves they were better than everybody else. If you were lucky, it only turned you into an asshole. If you were unlucky, it turned you into something far worse. Unfortunately, my mom, Eliza, and I had to experience that shit firsthand.

"I guess I should listen to you about changing my business name. You probably do know what you're talking about," she muttered.

I grinned at her with affection. After everything she'd read, I liked that she still used the word "probably" about me. She was smart enough to want proof. "Let me ask you something. How big do you see your maid business growing?"

"I'm not sure. Why do you ask?"

"Because the name you chose is fine for something small. If that's what you want, then I wouldn't worry about it. Keep the name. But if you want to take it all the way, you need a different one."

She went quiet, her brows drawing together as she considered my words. I took a sip of water and continued to eat my pretzel.

She stared at me with determination. "I want to take it all the way."

I nodded, not surprised. Claire struck me as someone who was ambitious but only recently seemed to understand this about herself.

"Then do me a favor," I said. "You don't have to take my word for any of this, but make a list of your top ten competitors across the board. The most successful maid services, franchises—all of them. Then compare your name to theirs."

She nodded, swallowing a bite of food. "I could do that."

"That's information you should know anyway. Always know your competition." She didn't comment, but I could tell she was listening. I waited as she finished the last of her pretzel. "Do you want to head out again?"

"Okay." Claire put the cap back on her water bottle, nodding. "Maybe we can catch up with Gavin and Eliza."

"They're probably down by the harbor." I thought about my sister and Gavin, remembering the pest's squeals of laughter from earlier. "Can I ask you something?"

Her brow creased. "What is it?"

"I feel weird even bringing this up, but do you think there's something going on between my sister and Gavin?"

"Like something romantic?"

"Yeah."

She tilted her head. "I don't think so. To be honest, I don't know."

"You seem to have become friends with her. Has she mentioned anything?"

"Not at all."

I felt relieved, even though this was hardly definitive.

"Why do you ask? Is it bad if they get together?"

"Hell, yes, it's bad." I snorted. "He's my best friend. I don't want him dating my little sister."

"Don't you trust him?"

"Of course I trust him. But he's too old for her. There's an eleven-year age difference." I shook my head. "He's like a brother to me, and we know everything about each other."

She nodded. "I doubt Eliza sees him as a brother. I think they kind of flirt a little."

My relief evaporated. "They do, don't they?" I glanced around the park in frustration. "Dammit, I knew I wasn't imagining things."

"I don't know if it's an actual romance though."

"This is unacceptable." I frowned. Gavin definitely knew better. He knew I wouldn't want him going after Eliza. So what the hell was he thinking?

Claire was watching me. "Don't take this the wrong way, but you're kind of a control freak, aren't you?"

I didn't reply right away. It wasn't exactly the first time I'd heard that. "I just want the people I love to be happy and safe. Does that make me a control freak?"

"It does if you're trying to control them."

"You don't understand." I shook my head. "My mom and sister have been through enough. I want to protect them."

"From what?"

I let my gaze wander around the park again. Mayberry. Filled with perfect families, but not all families were perfect—especially not the one I grew up with. But I didn't want to get into all this right now.

"Nothing," I said. "Let's go ride some more."

Her gaze lingered on me, but thankfully she didn't push further.

We walked our bikes as we headed out of the park. Just before we reached the edge, there were some trash containers and a kiosk with information about the town. I threw my water bottle into a recycle bin across from a large poster announcing a town meeting.

"I think I'm going to that." Claire stopped in front of the poster. "Something needs to be done about all this. Did you know a bank in Hong Kong owns the land that's for sale here? Isn't that crazy?"

I didn't say anything. Obviously I knew who owned the land.

I studied the poster. It had a replica of the town on it with the areas for sale outlined in red. It showed what sort of development was being planned. I'd seen similar blueprints from the real estate group Gavin and I met with.

"How did that even happen?" Her hands flew up with exasperation. "How did a bank in China come to own half our town?"

"I'm sure they bought it from a domestic bank as part of a larger holding." In fact, that was exactly how the bank in Hong Kong had acquired a large chunk of the town.

"It doesn't seem right," she said. "Somebody way over in China deciding our fate. Hopefully we can stop them."

"I doubt it."

"There is a way." She told me how the town was planning to become a historic district. I listened, though I had to admit I was skeptical. "In fact, we're having a Pirate Days party at Sullivan House next month as a fundraiser," she continued. "The first in ages. You should come!" But then her expression changed. "I mean, if you're still here."

"Sure, I'd love to come."

She smiled. "You would?"

"Definitely." I smiled back, pleased to get an invitation. Hopefully it meant those walls she'd built were starting to come down.

"Shall we head out now?" she asked, putting her bike helmet back on.

"Sounds good."

I looked at the poster again, and just before I was ready to slip my helmet overhead, something caught my eye. At the bottom it listed all the companies that were bidding on the land. My gaze locked on one name.

Geldnor Investment Group.

"Are we riding down to the harbor now?" Claire asked.

My blood ran cold. I hadn't seen that name in a long time.

"Philip, are you all right?"

I was being sucked underwater, her voice coming at me from a great distance.

I should have known.

It was my father's company. And I shouldn't have been surprised to see they were bidding on the land here. They specialized in commercial real estate—one of the reasons I'd consistently steered NorthStone away from it.

"Philip?"

Finally, I dragged my eyes back to Claire.

"Is everything okay?" She glanced at the poster and then back to me with concern.

I put my helmet on, ignoring the poster. "Let's bike down to the harbor. I'll buy you another rum raisin ice cream cone." I tried to smile, though it felt false.

"Oh no, you don't. I'll buy *you* one."

I nodded, getting settled onto my bike. "Whatever you want."

She gave me a strange look. "Are you sure you're all right?"

"Yeah, I'm good. No problem at all."

NINETEEN

~ Philip ~

Claire and I headed back down the trail together, and while I tried to put that name out of my mind, to forget about it entirely, I couldn't. It was like a mosquito buzzing in my ear. Incessant.

After we found Eliza and Gavin down by the harbor, I pulled off on my own for a minute and texted Sam. I told him to dig up all the information he could about Geldnor Investment Group and send it to me ASAP.

All these years, I'd avoided having anything to do with my father. I never followed him in the press or the papers. Back when I was a teenager, I decided to find him, a part of me still not wanting to believe what he'd turned into. It was a mistake though, and one I'd never forgotten.

"Should we go out for dinner?" Gavin asked, glancing around the harbor as we all met up on our bikes. "I see a few restaurants."

"I don't think so." Eliza smoothed her forehead with the back of her hand. "I'm too sweaty in these bike clothes."

"Me too," Claire agreed. "I don't feel dressed up enough to eat out."

"How about we all head back to the house and barbecue," I offered. "There's a grill on the back deck we haven't used yet."

"Who's going to grill though?" my sister asked. "Mom's going out for dinner with Elliot tonight."

I opened my mouth in surprise. "She is?"

Claire smiled. "I'm so glad those two are seeing each other."

"Wait a minute," I said. "Who the hell is this Elliot guy? I don't want Mom going out with someone I've never met."

The pest shrugged. "I'm sure we'll meet him if she wants us to."

"That's unacceptable. I don't know anything about him. What if he's an asshole?" Claire's eyes were on me. In fact, everybody's eyes were on me until *I* felt like the asshole. "Am I the only one concerned that some strange guy is making a play for our mom?"

"Elliot's not some strange guy," Claire told me. "He's really nice. And it's obvious he and your mom are hitting it off."

"I think it's about time," Eliza said. "I'm so glad she's finally dating someone."

I gripped my bike's handlebars with displeasure and turned to Claire. "What does he do for a living?"

"He's a professor of archeology at the university. He travels all over the world searching for artifacts."

My sister seemed to think this was wonderful. "Wow, really? He sounds super interesting. I can't wait to meet him."

Claire nodded. "You'll like him. Elliot's fun to talk to. Plus he's sort of handsome and dashing. Some of the items he's found on archeological digs are worth a fortune, but he always gives them to a museum."

"Great," I muttered. "So our mother is dating Indiana Jones."

Everybody laughed, but I didn't see the humor.

"I suppose I could manage to barbecue," Eliza mused. "I've seen mom do it."

"I'll help," Claire offered. "I've only done it once, but it can't be that tough."

"What are you two talking about?" I said. "Barbecuing is men's work."

"Yeah," Gavin agreed. "Philip and I will handle the cooking."

The pest seemed amused. "You two? You must be joking."

"Don't you remember our beef jerky? Gavin and I know our way around a barbecue grill." Back in high school, one of our various entrepreneurial efforts was making beef jerky. Admittedly it didn't go over so well.

My sister looked appalled. "That gross stuff? It tasted like burnt shoe leather."

"It wasn't that bad," Gavin said.

"Yeah." I shrugged. "It was just a little chewy."

Claire watched us. "You guys made beef jerky?"

"A little chewy?" Eliza laughed. "Even Bailey wouldn't eat it. And he actually *did* eat people's shoes."

Unfortunately, that was true. Our dog, Bailey, wouldn't go near the beef jerky no matter how hard Gavin and I tried to convince him. In fact, nobody would go near it, human *or* animal.

We decided to bike back to the lot where our cars were parked and then hit the grocery store. Claire knew a shortcut through town, so the three of us followed her.

An hour later, we were on the back deck getting everything set up to grill. Gavin and I still insisted on manning the barbecue, but we made burgers since they were easy. Claire and my sister were in the kitchen making a salad and putting together some side dishes.

I told Gavin what I'd seen on that poster, how my father's company was bidding on the land here.

He took a sip from his beer. "I'm not surprised they want in on that deal. It's going to make everybody a lot of money."

"I can't believe they have that much cash."

He shrugged and flipped a couple of the burgers on the grill. "I don't know much about them. Maybe they're fairly liquid."

"Maybe." I was quiet, mulling things over.

He glanced at me. "Are you changing your mind about investing? Because the last I heard, Atlas was considering a partnership with a group in London."

"They are?" I turned to look out at the picturesque harbor.

"It's not official yet, but that's the unofficial word."

Once the food was ready, the four of us sat on the back deck, talking, drinking beer, and eating the burgers Gavin and I managed to only slightly burn. At least there were plenty of side dishes we'd picked up. After dinner, Eliza said she needed to run lines for her play, and Gavin offered to help. I tried not to get irritated as I watched the two of them disappear inside the house together.

At least it meant Claire and I were finally alone.

The sun was low in the sky, the colors straight out of Monet. I leaned back on a deck chair. "The sky here is fantastic."

"It is," she agreed. "Just wait until there's a storm. You can see the weather coming from miles away."

I turned to gaze at her. Under a golden sunset, she was prettier than ever, her cheeks flushed pink from the sun, those braids making me crazy. "What should we do now?"

I watched her glance at the darkening horizon. "I should probably get going."

"What?" That was not what I wanted to hear. "Stay a little longer."

She sighed. "I wish I could, but I still need to move all that stuff out of my living room. I was planning to do it today."

"Do it tomorrow. In fact, I'll help you."

"I couldn't ask that."

"Sure you can. I want to help."

Her walls were crumbling but not enough. I needed more time. "Stay," I said, then thought of something that might convince her.

"We never did watch another movie. In fact, there's a copy of *Pirates of the Caribbean* here."

"You've really never seen it?"

"I never have. I'm a... pirate virgin, if you will."

She laughed and then bit her lip. "Okay, maybe I could stay a little longer."

It was dusk when we went inside the house. I didn't see any sign of my sister or Gavin, but I figured they were downstairs. I grabbed a couple more beers for us while Claire went to the bathroom.

Soon we were settled on the couch together, snacking from a bowl of potato chips, as the movie played on the large flat-screen in front of us.

I tried to concentrate on the film. I honestly tried. And for about fifteen minutes, I managed it. But then my eyes began to go to Claire sitting next to me, my gaze discreetly roaming the length of her. She was barefoot with her feet up on an ottoman. That blue top dipped low enough to show a nice eyeful of cleavage, smooth and slightly sunburned. I wanted to lick every sun-kissed part of her—including the parts that had never seen the sun.

Images from the other night were coming back, turning me on even more.

"Are you taking notes?" she asked, glancing at me.

"Huh?" My gaze quickly moved to her face, and I hoped she hadn't noticed me staring at her breasts. "Taking notes on what?"

"There's some real pirate stuff in these movies."

"There is?"

She nodded. "You can learn what life was like for your infamous great-grandfather."

Claire turned back to the screen, and I took a draw from my beer, trying to put my sexual frustration aside and focus on the movie. I was sure Quicksilver—God rest his blackened soul—would understand if I was more interested in her than him.

Eventually, I leaned back and stretched my arm out, using a move I hadn't had to utilize since high school. It came down directly behind her, and my eyes kept going to her profile. I watched her smile at something on screen. My pulse kicked up. She was so damned cute. That dimple and those braids would be the death of me.

Somehow I'd become an awkward fool around this woman. It was crazy. I was turning into Doug.

I didn't get to mull over this strange notion, because Claire asked, "You're not watching the movie at all, are you?"

"I'm trying," I said. "But I'm too distracted."

"By what?"

"You."

She turned me. "How could I be a distraction? All I'm doing is sitting next to you."

"Believe me, that's enough."

Her eyes stayed on mine, and something in her gaze softened. Finally, I couldn't stand it anymore. I leaned in and kissed her, brushing my lips over hers.

Her body stilled, but then she shifted position, angling toward me. "Don't you want to watch the movie?"

"I do," I murmured. "But I can't resist you."

She seemed to consider this, and then she slid her arms around my neck, a teasing smile on her face. "I don't know if Quicksilver would approve of us ignoring your heritage."

I snorted. "Trust me, he'd approve." And then I bent down and kissed her again.

Right away she opened to me, and I couldn't stop the low rumble of pleasure in my throat. I wanted her. I wanted her so damn bad. My hands slid down her body, enjoying every sensual curve.

Thank God for bike shorts. Thank God for tight women's clothing too. And most of all, thank God for the way they looked in a pile on the floor when they hopefully came off.

We went at it for a while. Tongue kissing each other, teasing and rubbing our bodies together. Necking like a couple of teenagers in the back seat of a car. Normally the women I slept with were aggressive, and we got to the sex fast. I imagine it was what they thought I wanted, and usually it was, but this was different. I enjoyed taking my time with Claire. I wanted to savor her.

It wasn't long before I had her on her back on the couch, the movie long forgotten. Her soft body was luxurious beneath me. My hard-on felt heavy pressing against her. We were still fully clothed, but I wanted to explore every inch of her. In the back of my mind, I knew we couldn't stay out here in the living room like this. Gavin and Eliza could walk in on us any minute.

"Let's go upstairs to my room," I breathed. "We need more privacy."

"Your room?"

I chuckled. This whole thing really was starting to feel like high school. "I'd invite you to my house, but it's a plane ride away."

"You have a house?"

"Yeah, of course."

She smiled and stroked my hair. "I haven't really thought about where you live. Isn't that weird?"

I kissed her again, then nuzzled her neck. "You'll have to come visit. It overlooks Puget Sound." I knew Claire would enjoy that. "Plenty of sailboats for your viewing pleasure."

"Maybe." She smiled up at me. "It depends on my work though."

"Sure. We'll figure it out." I went back to her neck, then slid my mouth down to her cleavage, caressing her breast over the top she was wearing. "Come on, let's go upstairs."

"Oh, I almost forgot to tell you," she said, sitting up a little. "I found a lawyer."

"Great," I murmured, wanting to get her out of her clothes.

"He seems good, and his prices are reasonable. He thinks he can help me with the lawsuit."

"Lawsuit? You don't have to worry about that anymore." I slide my fingers over her top. The problem with all this tight fabric was I couldn't get my hands underneath it.

"Of course, I do."

"No, sweetheart, I fixed it." I kissed her throat again, inhaling the scent of sweat and arousal clinging to us both. If I'd been a little less turned on, a little less caught up in my own lust, I would have stopped talking, but I didn't. "I already took care of the whole thing."

Claire went still against me. "What do you mean, you took care of it?"

"Just what I said. You don't to have to worry about that lawsuit anymore. By next week it'll be dismissed."

She stared at me with confusion, her hands still on my shoulders. That was when it dawned on me that I might have made a mistake.

"What exactly are you talking about?"

"It's nothing," I tried to backpedal. "I just made a quick phone call to one of our lawyers."

"You did *what?*"

She pushed away from me and brought herself to a sitting position. My lust haze was clearing. "Look, it was no big deal. One phone call, that's all."

"You told them about my lawsuit, and they're going to make it go away?"

"Basically."

"But how would they even know the details?"

"I emailed them a copy of the letter."

Those gold flecks in her eyes caught fire, and I knew I was fucking this whole thing up.

"How?"

"You left it on the kitchen counter, and I took a picture with my phone." My gut could always tell when a deal was going south, and this one was going south faster than a sleigh ride to hell.

She gawked at me. "Are you crazy?"

"No, I'm not. I was helping you out."

"Helping me out? I didn't ask for your help."

I thought back to the way she'd been crying that morning, hugging me tight. Every instinct in my body told me I needed to fix it for her. "Look, I promised you I'd take care of it, and that's exactly what I did. You told me those women were bullying you."

She didn't seem to hear me though. "This is my business, and you had no right to interfere. I can't believe you'd do that!"

I rolled my eyes. "Stop being so stubborn. You think you're the only one who's ever needed help? You think most people got to where they are alone? Hell, you think no one ever helped *me*?"

"I don't care. I didn't ask for your help!"

"Maybe not, but you needed it." My voice grew quiet. "No offense, but you fucked up, Claire. Dropping your liability insurance was a rookie mistake. All I did was get you back on track."

Her mouth opened and then closed. "You're an asshole!" She pushed past me and scrambled up from the couch.

I got up too, stood there watching as she stomped around the room, grumbling about finding her socks and shoes.

"Come on, don't be angry."

She ignored me and sat down in one of the dining room chairs, pulling her socks on.

I went over to her. "Don't you think you're being a little unreasonable? All I did was make your lawsuit go away."

"You really are a control freak, you know that?"

"I wasn't trying to control you." I gripped my hair in frustration. "I was trying to help you. I didn't want to see your business fail."

She yanked on her shoes. Her innocent braids swung against her shoulders. Didn't she understand the world was big and ugly? That little mom-and-pop companies like hers were chewed up and spat out all the time? They were a dime a dozen and sank every day. One misstep. That was all it took.

She stood up and glared at me. "My business wasn't going to fail. I had it under control. And even if it did fail, then it's on *me*." She pointed at her chest.

The two of us stood there, eyes locked. I wanted to reach for her, to dial this whole conversation back. She was breathing hard, and even though she was furious, I still wanted her. I wanted her more than ever. I liked how she didn't back down from me, how she held her ground. I understood where she was coming from, but I wasn't going to apologize for something I didn't regret.

"You should be thanking me," I said. "I saved your ass, and you know it."

"It's too much, Philip, and you can't even see it." Her voice shook. "It was a mistake getting involved with someone like you. I don't know what I was thinking."

"What?" I blinked at her in shock. "Are you kidding?"

"No, I'm not kidding." She reached over to grab the small backpack she wore biking earlier and slipped it over her shoulder. "I'm going now. Please don't call me anymore."

"Claire, this is absurd."

But she walked past me, walked straight out of the room until I heard the front door slam.

It was like a blow to the chest. "Jesus...." I could barely believe it. *What the hell just happened?*

I WAS in a black mood the next day, blacker than my ancestor's infamous soul. I tried calling Claire and then texting her, but she ignored every message. I was tempted to drive over there and plead with her, but I still had a little pride left.

"What did you do to her?" the pest wanted to know. "Are you still being a dog? How could you chase her off like that? You're hopeless!"

"I didn't do anything to her," I said, irritated that I was being blamed. "All I did was help her with a problem."

The three of us—Eliza, my mom, and I—were all in the beach house's living room. I had my computer open in front of me, not that I could concentrate on work. I tried to explain what had happened, but neither of them seemed to hear me.

I told Gavin about it before he headed back to Seattle, but he only shook his head with disappointment. "Dude," he said, "she was great."

"Claire is not like all these other women you're used to dating," my sister ranted. "She's the real deal. You have to treat her differently!"

"I treated her just fine." Or at least I thought I had. Maybe I did come on too strong sometimes, but I wasn't used to holding back when I wanted something.

My mom studied me. "I'm sorry this happened, Philip. I really like Claire."

"Me too," I said.

"Maybe you could try calling her again?" she suggested. "Or send her an email explaining yourself?"

"Yeah," Eliza said. "Send her an email explaining what an idiot you are. And then you need to apologize."

I scowled. "I'm not apologizing. That's not going to happen."

"See? You're still acting like an idiot."

"Eliza," my mom reprimanded her. "That's enough. There's no reason to be insulting."

My sister huffed and then sat on the couch. She seemed to calm down a little before turning to me again. "Look, Claire's just not used to you yet. She doesn't understand your control-freak nature like we do. That it's endearing, and one of the things we *love* about you," she added quickly after my mom frowned at her.

I shook my head. "Why should I apologize for something I don't regret?"

"The problem is you never regret anything," the pest shot back.

"That's not true."

"Oh really? When's the last time you regretted something? Anything at all?"

I regretted this conversation, but I figured there was no point in mentioning that. "Who cares? I don't want to live a life regretting my decisions. The fact is my decisions are typically excellent."

My sister rolled her eyes. "See? It's like I said. Hopeless!"

Despite my protests, I did send an email to Claire. I didn't apologize, but I explained my actions—or my interference, as she saw it.

Not that I'd admit it to anyone, but I was hurt that she was angry at me. I figured she had trust issues from that bonehead ex-husband of hers, but I wasn't that kind of man, and I thought we'd spent enough time together that she could see that, could see I was only trying to protect her like I protected everyone I cared about.

She never responded.

And so my mood remained dark. I threw myself into work for the next few days—studying the marketing data on Drink Virtue and speaking with their CEO, going over the numbers on some start-ups an angel sent me, speaking with our investors. I flew up to Vancouver, BC, for the day to meet with that tech company that needed capital to move into the States.

On Wednesday afternoon, just as I was getting ready to fly back from Canada on a private charter, there was a call from Doug.

I stared at my phone for a few seconds and then declined it.

I'm making him plenty of money, I told myself as the plane took off, *so I have nothing to feel guilty about.*

That night I got an email from my assistant, Sam. I'd almost forgotten about my instructions to send me everything he could find on my father's company. But there it was—Geldnor Investment Group's entire portfolio, along with every scrap of data Sam could dig up.

I spent all night reading and crunching numbers, a change of pace from brooding about Claire. It was oddly fascinating to see what my father had been up to all these years, and I had to admit, he'd made a lot of money. Geldnor had some impressive holdings. The closer I looked though, I noticed strange irregularities—too many. Finally, I discovered what he'd managed to hide from his own investors.

He was in trouble.

Geldnor was leveraged to the max. They'd made a string of bad purchases over the last five years, bad real estate deals and some overseas junk bonds once worth millions that were now worth nothing.

He needed this current land deal. He'd have to sell and leverage every piece of property he could to come up with the cash, and even then I doubted it would be enough. If he lost, he'd be bankrupt.

I leaned back in my chair.

Sonofabitch.

After everything he put us through—my mom especially—I didn't want to say I was gleeful to discover he was on the verge of bankruptcy, but I didn't feel sorry for him. That bastard deserved to be miserable.

I decided to sit on this information. I could do nothing and let the dice fall, or I could bring the full weight of NorthStone back in and crush him.

There was no way he could outbid us.

Friday afternoon I drove through town in Doug's old pickup truck, hopeful and eagerly on the lookout for Claire's little turquoise car.

Pathetic, yes, but I missed her. I missed those rainbows and unicorns.

I kept noticing a bright yellow Ferrari driving around town. Apparently the head coach for the Seattle football team owned a vacation home here, so I figured it belonged to a player.

Imagine my surprise when I pulled up to the beach house and discovered that same yellow Ferrari sitting in our driveway. I got out and studied it. I liked the look of a nice car as much as anyone, but flashy automobiles had never impressed me. They were a lousy investment.

I didn't see him until I was nearly up to the front door. He was sitting on one of the porch chairs. It took me a moment to put it together who he was, which was strange as I'd just finished reading about him.

It had been well over a decade since I'd last seen my father. And as far as I was concerned, that wasn't long enough.

TWENTY

~ Claire ~

I spent the next couple days using the energy from my anger to help move all the boxes of cleaning supplies into my spare room. Philip kept trying to contact me, but I didn't want to talk to him.

It sucked, but this whole thing brought back too many bad memories.

When it came out that Ethan was cheating on me, it seemed like I was the last person to know. I felt deeply betrayed, but I also felt stupid. Completely blindsided. And I told myself I never wanted to feel that way again. I didn't want anyone going behind my back, making decisions about me or my business without my knowledge.

As Philip liked to say, it was unacceptable.

So I avoided his messages.

After I moved the boxes, I stood in my small living area with my arms stretched out. There was so much space now. Granted, my house was tiny by most people's standards, but it seemed huge to me.

Even my birds seemed pleased, twittering and flying from one perch to the next.

I needed a desk for my new office and a shelving system to organize all the cleaning supplies I'd bought wholesale and in bulk. I also had boxes of T-shirts that said Your House Sparkles on them. I hadn't taken Philip's advice to look up my competitors yet.

I was too angry at him to take his advice about anything.

The new lawyer I'd hired called on Tuesday and told me Mona withdrew her lawsuit. It was a relief, but it didn't change how I felt. Apparently Philip's lawyers countersued for defamation and made it clear to Mona that any claim on her part would involve a long and expensive legal battle.

The bully got bullied herself. Ironic.

At least it was over. Back to my regularly scheduled life that didn't include hot, meddling billionaires.

"But Philip made your problem go away," Theo said, putting down her glass of lemonade. "Why are you mad at him?"

We were at Leah's house, where she and I were coloring each other's hair. She painted bleach on mine while I put dark color over the silver streak she had in front. Theo's gorgeous red hair was natural, so she didn't need any color.

"It's the way he interfered," Leah told her matter-of-factly. Being a small business owner herself, she explained how Philip crossed the line. "Are you really going to stop seeing him though?" she asked, looking up at me. "I get why you're angry, but don't you think you're overreacting?"

I took my gloves off and checked the time for Leah's color. "He's too much for me. I'm not ready for a relationship anyway."

Theo reached over to pet one of Leah's many cats. "It's strange to admit this, but I liked him. Both of those guys were all right company for a couple of money-grubbing capitalists."

"Maybe you should at least talk to him some more," Leah said. "Philip seemed really into you."

A memory surfaced of the two of us dancing. The way he'd gazed at me that night. It made my stomach flutter just thinking about it.

Later, after Leah helped me wash the bleach out of my hair, I realized I'd never paid her back for the pizzas and beer. "Sorry, I forgot. How much do I owe you?"

"Nothing." She shrugged, handing me a towel. "Philip slipped me a hundred before I left."

"He did *what*?" My mouth gaped. "But I told you I wanted to pay!"

"I know, but I didn't think it was that big of a deal."

I was mad all over again. What was his problem? I knew I was overreacting, but did he have to interfere with everything?

Despite telling myself I was done with Philip, the next day I found myself driving by the beach house in stealth mode. I couldn't see any cars in the driveway, and I wondered if he'd finally gone home to Seattle. There was an ache at the thought of him leaving, that I might never see him again, but I forced myself to ignore it.

I'd been through much worse things than losing a fake boyfriend.

That night, as I sat outside in front of the carriage house with my Kit Kat bar, my gaze kept going to the patch of grass where Philip and I were on the blanket. I smiled, remembering the way he'd spoken in that silly pirate's voice. And then I remembered the way his body had felt against mine, the way he'd started a bonfire in me. Philip was the first guy I'd had an orgasm with since Ethan.

"So what?" I said, feeling surly as I broke my Kit Kat into four pieces, nibbling the chocolate around the first one. "I don't need a man for that."

THE NEXT EVENING, I was busy in my new office when Daphne called, sounding excited. "Guess what? Something wonderful happened last night!"

"It did?" I was reorganizing my cleaning supplies for the third time as I tried not to think about you-know-who.

"Doug and I went out for our nightly walk after dinner last night. Our walks are usually quiet, but this time one of the neighborhood dogs followed us."

I listened, still organizing. I really needed new shelves for this room.

"I told him how dogs make me nervous., " she went on. "So he took it back to the neighbor's yard, and you should have seen him, Claire. He was magnificent! The way he defended me. He told his neighbor in a stern voice how it wasn't right to let it wander around without a leash, that some people were frightened by dogs."

"What kind of dog was it?" I figured it was something large and vicious, because I'd never known Daphne to be afraid of dogs. "Was it a big dog?"

"No, I think it was a beagle."

"A beagle made you nervous?"

"Guess what happened after that?" I could hear her breathing rapidly. "Doug held my hand for the rest of the walk!"

My brows went up as my confusion cleared. "Wow, that's great." Apparently Daphne was craftier than I ever gave her credit for.

"He told me not to worry, that he'd make sure none of the neighborhood dogs ever bothered me again. Isn't that sweet? He's such an amazing guy." There was a note of triumph in her soft voice, but then she sighed. "Unfortunately, my mom is getting suspicious. She doesn't understand why it's taking so long and thinks I'm spending too much money here in the city."

"What are you going to do?"

"I told her I'd moved out of the hotel and was staying with a friend of yours."

I'd given up reorganizing and had gotten out the measuring tape, but I stopped as her words. "Wait, you told her a friend of *mine*?"

"I'm sorry, I hope that's okay. I didn't have any choice. My mom already knows all my friends in Seattle."

How was I getting pulled into this? I hoped Violet didn't start quizzing me about this supposed friend. "How much longer do you think you'll be there?"

"I'm not sure." She seemed to think it over. "Doug says he's nearly finished fixing up his mom's house, so not too much longer."

Sure enough, the next morning Violet texted me and asked me to join her for breakfast. And I was using the word "asked" loosely. She basically ordered me to breakfast. I considered ignoring her but knew she'd only hunt me down.

It was Friday, so I took a quick shower, then put on a turquoise Your House Sparkles T-shirt to remind her I had to work that day.

It'd rained the night before, and the ground was damp as I walked up to the main house, slipping in through the back door.

To my dismay, Violet wasn't alone at the dining room table. Ivy sat next to her, staring at her phone. There was a plate of uneaten fruit in front of her. I sighed to myself, wondering what this was all about.

Violet looked up at me over her glasses. "Good morning, Claire. I'm happy you could join us."

Ivy glanced at me but didn't say anything.

I considered turning around and walking right out of there, but to heck with that. I owned half this house, and I wasn't going to let Ivy chase me away.

I nodded at Violet. "Good morning." I went to the sideboard and got myself a plate of food and a cup of coffee, then sat down at the table across from Ivy.

Violet watched me as I added cream to my coffee, then doused my eggs with pepper. "How is Philip doing?" she asked. "I'm glad I could finally meet him last week."

A pang of longing stabbed at me. "He's fine." I figured I'd keep the fake boyfriend thing going as long as possible.

Ivy shifted in her chair. She was still studying her phone, and I couldn't stop myself from glaring at her. In a way, everything that happened with Philip was *her* fault. I was certain she was the one who'd convinced Mona to sue me in the first place.

Violet nodded. "I hope he'll be coming to Pirate Days in a few weeks. I'm looking forward to getting to know him better."

I couldn't stand it any longer. "How can you just sit there like that?" I sniped at Ivy. "Don't you have anything to say to me?"

Ivy glanced up from her phone with a haughty expression. "And what might that be?"

"An apology would be a good place to start."

Violet's gaze shifted between the two of us with concern. "What's going on here? Did something happen that I'm unaware of?"

"Ask your daughter." I motioned at Ivy. "She's been trying to put me out of business."

Ivy gave a forced laugh. "Delusional as always."

But Violet wasn't laughing. "What is Claire referring to?"

She shrugged. "How should I know?"

I studied Ivy as she pretended to have no idea what I was talking about. She wore a navy tank top with red straps from a pushup bra showing beneath it. Gold aviator sunglasses perched on top of her silky hair. I used to envy her easy sex appeal, the way she always drew attention wherever she went. Now I could barely stand the sight of her.

"I thought Ivy sent clients your way," Violet said to me. "That she was helpful to your maid business."

"Hardly." I explained how all those clients Ivy recommended had canceled, how Mona sued me for twenty grand.

To her credit, Violet looked visibly shaken. "Is this true?" she asked, turning to her daughter.

"I have no control over what Mona or any of my friends do." Ivy glanced up from her phone. She seemed bored with this conversation.

Violet slammed her newspaper down.

Ivy flinched in her chair.

"I've had just about enough of this!" Violet snapped. "We all know you've put poor Claire through enough misery, and I want this antagonism to end."

I wasn't crazy about Violet referring to me as "poor Claire," but I agreed with the rest of it.

"I mean it," Violet went on. "This mistreatment of Claire is going to stop. Do you hear me?"

"What have I ever done that would make you hate me so much?" I asked Ivy.

She glanced at her mother. "Nothing, of course. You're always the innocent one."

As far as I knew, I *was* innocent. "What are you talking about?"

Ivy grabbed her purse and pushed her chair out. "Never mind." She stood up. "I didn't come here to be lectured."

Violet's eyes were intense on her daughter. "I don't care whether you want to be lectured or not." Her expression eased a little. "This is no way to live. Can't you see that?"

There was uncertainty in Ivy's gaze, but then it hardened. "I'll stop when *she* acknowledges what she did."

"Me?" I was genuinely shocked. "What did I do?"

Ivy smiled without humor. "You may be fooling everybody else with your Little Miss Perfect act, but I'm not fooled."

I gaped at her, completely mystified. "What act?

But she only shook her head. "Let's just say I have a long memory." And with that, she left the room.

"Do you have any idea what she's referring to?" Violet asked me.

I shook my head. "None whatsoever."

Violet sighed and leaned back in her chair. "I should tell you she and Ethan are seeing a marriage counselor. I'm not trying to excuse my daughter's abhorrent behavior, but I do know she's under quite a bit of strain."

Obviously, I already knew about that. There was such great irony in Ethan and Ivy seeing a marriage counselor that I had to bite my lip to avoid smiling. Finally, I went back to eating my breakfast.

Violet seemed contemplative as she sipped her tea.

"I have to ask you something, Claire." She studied me. "Do you know what's going on with Daphne in Seattle?"

"Um... what do you mean?"

Her voice softened. "I think you know very well what I mean."

I didn't want to lie to Violet. She was obviously under strain herself. I knew she'd been working with the town council and some of the local businesses to try to get the downtown declared a historic district. And it couldn't be easy planning a Pirate Days party without my dad.

"Daphne's okay," I told her. "In fact, I think she'll be home soon."

Violet nodded. "In other words you do know, but you don't want to tell me." She glanced around the room. "I don't know where I've gone wrong with my children."

"You haven't gone wrong, at least not with Daphne." Ivy was another story, but I didn't blame Violet.

She studied me for a long moment, then reached out and put her hand over mine. "These last few years have been difficult for both of us."

My throat went tight. She was talking about my dad. "They have," I agreed.

"Your father would be proud of you. And I'm glad you've moved on from everything that happened with Ethan and my daughter."

I nodded.

"Philip seems like a fine young man."

"Sure." I swallowed. "He is."

"You're still young, Claire. Still so much ahead of you. Don't let anything stop you from enjoying your life."

I let Violet's words sink in. She was talking about Ivy and Ethan and what they'd done to me, but all I could think about was Philip. How that spark inside me was still there, how I didn't want to go back to the way I'd felt before I met him. Frozen inside.

When I left to go out front and get my mail, I was still thinking about him. To my surprise, Ivy was there in her red BMW with the driver window rolled down, smoking a cigarette.

I walked past her to get the mail and felt her eyes on me. She was talking to someone on the phone. Probably her daily chat with Satan.

"How did you manage it?" she asked when I walked by her again.

"Manage what?"

"Mona just told me she's been forced to withdraw her lawsuit." Ivy blew out a stream of smoke. "And who the hell is NorthStone Capital?"

"It's Philip's company." I couldn't keep the smug note out of my voice.

Her brows rose at this news.

I stepped toward her, gripping the mail in my hand. "Look, I'm tired of all this animosity. You need to stop trying to destroy my life."

She took a drag from her cigarette and studied me.

"You've got Ethan. What more do you want?"

"That's right," she said with satisfaction. "I've got Ethan."

"We've all moved on. Can't you just leave me alone?"

Her eyes narrowed. "Stop pretending you're the victim, like you didn't betray me first."

"How? What did I do to betray you?" Part of me wondered why I even bothered talking to her, but the other part wanted to know where all this hatred came from.

She blew out more smoke. "You're claiming you don't remember?"

"No, I don't. So why don't you enlighten me."

"You don't remember the summer before senior year?"

I thought back. The only thing memorable about that summer was I caught Ivy having sex in the carriage house with her boyfriend. "Are you talking about when I walked in on you in the carriage house?"

She nodded. "So you *do* remember."

"But I kept your secret. I never told anyone."

Her gaze hardened as she took another drag of her cigarette. "Well, wasn't that *nice* of you."

"I'm telling the truth."

"Sure you are."

"You don't believe me?"

Her eyes slitted like a serpent's. "Everybody always thinks I'm the bitch, but we both know you took full advantage of that situation." She flicked her cigarette on the ground. "I'm done here."

She drove off. I watched her red taillights glow at the end of the driveway before her car peeled left onto the main road.

Sighing to myself, I walked over to step on her cigarette butt, then picked it up and threw it in the trash.

Later as I worked, scrubbing and dusting for my clients, I tried to make sense of our conversation. *Am I missing something? She thinks I told someone about what I saw?*

"Whatever," I muttered. "Who cares?" Even if I'd done what Ivy accused me of, she was still crazy to be angry about it all these years later. What she did to me was a million times worse.

I had to admit I enjoyed the look on her face when I told her it was Philip's company that ended the lawsuit. It was satisfying to have someone on my side for a change. An outsider. Somebody who didn't think of me as "poor Claire."

That was when the yearning started again. I missed him. In only a short time, Philip had changed me, changed how I looked at things.

I tried to push down these feelings, but it wasn't easy.

When I drove home from my last job that afternoon, a smattering of dark clouds moved overhead. A strong breeze blew past, rustling leaves as I unloaded my groceries. I stopped and gazed up at the sky. Gray with patches of blue, but those patches would soon change.

I could always tell when there was a storm coming.

TWENTY-ONE

~ Philip ~

"Where the hell is everyone?"

After more than a decade, those were the first words my father said to me from his seat on the front porch.

He wore an arrogant expression and seemed put out that there was no one here to greet him, as if he'd expected a hero's welcome.

"What do you want?" I was relieved my mom and sister weren't home, and I could take care of this alone.

His dark eyes came to rest on me. "Philip? It's good to see you, son."

My jaw clenched at the word "son." I ignored the impulse to bodily remove him and kept my temper in check. "As I said, what do you want?"

"I wanted to see how my kids are doing. How's Eliza?"

I was surprised he remembered her name. He hadn't seen her in a very long time, and believe me, I intended to keep it that way.

"Nice place." He glanced around. "A bit small for my taste, but not bad."

I studied him. His skin was too tan, his hair too black, a man in his sixties trying to look younger than his age. My father was in a midlife crisis that never ended.

"You need to leave." I took a step closer. "Nobody wants you here."

He smiled, his teeth unnaturally white. "I've been following you over the years. NorthStone has done very well."

I remained silent.

"You should be proud of yourself. From what I understand, you've built up quite a company. Not bad."

He got up from the chair so I wasn't looking down on him anymore. We were the same height and stood eye to eye. All that alpha male bullshit, but this wasn't a game he could win. Not this time.

Because I knew why he was here now. The second he'd mentioned NorthStone, I knew.

He walked over to the porch rail and rested his arm on it, gazing up at the house. "I understand your sister has become an actress and even did a television commercial recently."

I waited him out. A strong breeze swept past us, blowing around the bushes near the front. Dark clouds churned above us.

"Does she ever mention me?" His gaze met mine. "She sounds like quite a young lady."

I could smell the alcohol on him. *So he needed a drink before he came to see me. Good.*

"I missed out on a lot with you two."

"You made a mistake coming here," I informed him. "NorthStone already pulled out."

"What's that?"

"You heard me."

He'd gone still, and I saw the information wash over him, saw the way he instantly knew what I was talking about. His expression turned shrewd. "That's not what I heard."

"Then you need better sources."

"I heard you were getting in over your head. I came here to try and talk some sense into you."

I almost smiled that he thought I'd be so easy to manipulate, that he still thought of me as some naive kid. "Is that right," I murmured. I'd done my homework, but he hadn't done his. I knew he was in trouble, and I knew the kind of man he was.

Apparently he knew nothing about me. It stung a little that he hadn't bothered to figure me out before showing up.

"This deal is going to blow up in your face," he went on. "I'm only here to warn you away."

"Warn me?" Now I wanted to laugh.

"Hell, yes." He kept talking, telling me how he regretted the things he'd done in the past, how he didn't always make the best choices, how he wanted to change all that, and so on.

I cut him off. "You can stop the bullshit. I've heard enough."

"What do you mean? I want to get to know—"

"Shut the hell up!" My temper flared. "I already know you're in trouble, all right? You're hanging on by your fingernails, and that's why you're here."

His eyes narrowed, and finally I saw the real man, the one who always put himself above everyone. His mouth closed, his jaw ticking.

"You're on the verge of bankruptcy, so stop fucking lying to me." I tried to rein in my anger, but it was like opening Pandora's box. Years of it simmered to the surface.

He moved closer, pointing at me. "Now you listen to me, Philip. I need this deal to happen, so you're going to step aside. Do you hear me?"

"Like I said, we've already pulled out."

He nodded. "Good. And you're going to keep it that way."

"Except you never should have come here." I glanced up at those storm clouds brewing and then met his eyes straight on. "Because now I'm rethinking our position."

He shook his head, smiling without humor. "Jesus, you've turned into a real bastard, haven't you?"

It didn't matter if I was lying. I doubted he'd be able to raise the amount of capital he needed. He stood close enough that I could smell him. Sweat and alcohol. The smell of desperation.

His smile disappeared. "Stay out of this deal. I'm warning you. Things will get ugly."

"There's nothing you can do to stop me. Things are already ugly."

"No they aren't." He studied me. "Maybe it's time I called my daughter to see if she'd like to have dinner with her old man. What do you think? We have a lot of catching up to do."

I blinked, immediately concerned about him contacting my sister. He didn't care about her and never would. Besides himself, money was the only thing he cared about.

He nodded. "Just as I thought. Looks like we finally *do* understand each other."

With that, he walked past me, his footsteps moving down the wooden stairs. I heard the Ferrari's engine roar to life.

I remained still until he drove off, my muscles tight with fury.

"Goddammit!" I slammed my fist into the porch rail. There was a loud crack, and pain shot through my hand as the wood broke away from its base

Ignoring it, I pushed my way into the house, seething.

I didn't do well with threats. Never had. That bastard should have taken the time to learn about me. If he thought threats would work, then he was dead wrong.

I yanked open the fridge, searching for a beer, but the only thing with alcohol were those dog-piss wine coolers. I grabbed one anyway and took it outside to sit on the back deck, trying to calm myself.

Vanity. Greed. Narcissism. There was a dark side to money. One I hated but saw too often in people. It had turned my father into something grotesque.

The wind was stronger and when I looked up at the sky there were black clouds moving in. Claire was right. You could see the storm coming from miles away. It looked like it was headed here fast.

At the thought of Claire, I leaned forward and closed my eyes. My chest ached. I missed her. I missed those rainbows and unicorns. That sweet voice. That tantalizing body. She was the exact opposite of all this darkness.

I set the bottle down. I didn't want to drink anything.

Instead I locked the house up and headed down to the beach. The wind was powerful out near the water, and I stood at the edge, letting it pound me.

Without thinking about it, I began to walk toward Sullivan House. In the back of my mind, I knew it was foolish to be out here like this, that only an idiot went out in this kind of weather, but I kept moving anyway. The wind grew stronger, clawing at me, but I'd decided I had to see Claire.

I didn't know what I would say to her. I didn't even know if she'd be there or if she'd speak to me. An instinct drove me, told me to keep going, and that was what I did.

The tide was high, and water crashed farther up the shoreline. Something bright flashed nearby. A loud snap followed by the smell of burning ozone. Startled, I realized it was lightning.

Thunder boomed overhead.

I clenched my jaw with determination, pushing forward even harder.

When I arrived at the back gate, I called her phone, but there was no answer. I texted and told her I was out here. *I need to see you.*

Because I wasn't turning back. Not a chance. Not now.

The gate was locked, so I did the only thing I could think of—I climbed it. I gave myself a running start and scaled the damn thing. The sky boomed overhead just as I landed on the other side.

Trespassing on private property. Quicksilver would be proud.

There were two paths. I took the one less used. The one I hoped would lead me to the carriage house.

It was only late afternoon but already dark as I made my way through the woods. I was nearly there when I saw a figure up ahead, coming toward me.

It was Claire, hugging herself against the wind.

"Are you crazy?" she yelled as soon as we were close enough. "What do you think you're doing out here?"

"I had to see you."

She was right in front of me, and it was all I could do not to reach out for her. She was so beautiful, so right in every way.

"Now?" She gestured at the wind pummeling us. "It couldn't wait?"

"No, it couldn't." I knew it was nuts coming here like this, but I didn't care. I needed to explain myself. "I was only trying to protect you when I got our lawyers involved. That's all. I swear I didn't mean anything else by it."

The wind whipped her hair around, but her eyes never left my face.

"I'm sorry," I said, speaking loudly over the storm. "Though I should tell you I don't regret it. In fact, I'd do it again the same way."

She seemed incredulous. "What kind of apology is *that*?"

"This isn't the end for us, Claire. It can't be." I reached down and grabbed her hands. "It's the beginning. Don't you see?"

She didn't reply, and I thought, *Shit, I'm fucking this whole thing up again.*

But then she smiled, and relief blew through me stronger than the wind.

In that moment, I knew I'd walk through any storm, slay any dragon, as long as it brought me to her door.

There was a loud boom above us, a cracking noise, and then it poured. Buckets of rain falling.

"Come on!" she yelled.

I still held her hand as we ran through the woods together. Her little house waited for us in the distance—a fairy-tale cottage, lit up and cozy.

Once inside, I pulled her into my arms. Stumbling over the threshold, I didn't care if we were soaking wet. I didn't care about the storm. All I knew was I needed to feel her against me.

Our mouths found each other, and I kissed her senseless. She tasted like heaven. Like a miracle.

"You're a lunatic," she told me, her lips moving against mine. "Completely crazy. I can't believe you."

"Don't talk, sweetheart."

She laughed, and I couldn't help laughing too, our faces close.

But then our laughter faded and our mouth came together, the kiss turning into something else. Something hungry. My tongue sought hers, and I held her while still ravaging her mouth, not holding back anything.

She whimpered, clinging to me, her arms tight around my neck. The scent of wet cotton surrounded us, more erotic than I could have imagined.

The sky thundered again as my hands roamed over her soaked clothing, then beneath them. I wanted to touch her everywhere, feel her against me.

"Let's get you out of these wet clothes," I said.

She nodded, helping me pull off everything until she was naked. Nothing but creamy white skin, every part of her plump and pretty, and damp from the rain.

I swallowed, trying to steady myself.

I slid my hands down over her shoulders to her breasts. She seemed to have grown shy before me, but I knew how to fix that. "You're beautiful, Claire," I said, my voice rough with honesty. "So beautiful."

Her eyes widened, and then she smiled as she pushed her hands beneath my shirt. "We need to take your wet clothes off too."

I reached behind my head and tugged my T-shirt off. Claire's hands went directly to my chest before moving lower to unfasten my belt. Her fingers slid over the front of my jeans, tracing the outline of my hard-on. A low groan escaped me.

She unfastened the top button, sliding the zipper down. I watched her face, my breath shaking, as she pushed her hands beneath the waistband of my boxers. Her cool fingers found me, stroking my length, and I groaned again.

"Sweetheart...," I murmured.

Claire continued to stroke me while I closed my eyes and gave in to the sensation.

Eventually she pushed my jeans and boxers down. Then I took over, kicking off everything else.

When we were both naked, my gaze went over to that brass bed of hers. It just sat there waiting for us. I couldn't help my grin when I saw it.

"What is it?" she asked.

I pulled her in to me. "I've had a lot of fantasies about the two of us in your bed."

Her brows went up. "You have?"

I slid a hand down over her ass and nodded.

"Like what?"

I licked my lips. "Are you sure you want to hear them? They'll make you blush."

I noticed her breath had picked up. She pressed her body closer. "Will they?"

"They will." I brought my mouth to hers, nipping at her lower lip.

"Go on, tell me."

With one hand on her ass, I moved the other between her thighs. "I've thought about tasting you a lot."

Her eyes grew heated.

"I want to lick you everywhere." I let my fingers slide through her folds, fondling her as her breath grew shaky. "I want to lick you until you're soaking wet, until you're screaming and coming all over my face. And then I want to do it again."

She moaned softly and yanked me in hard, crushing her mouth against mine.

Our tongues sparred with each other as my cock throbbed. I was glad she enjoyed my fantasy. I continued to play with her while her hips moved against me with need. She was responsive and slippery as hell, and it was making me crazy.

When our kiss broke apart, I brought my hand up to my mouth. Musky and sweet. The smell of her arousal sent a jolt of lust straight through me.

Despite what I'd just told her, her eyes widened as she watched me lick my fingers. "You're kind of dirty, aren't you?" she said, sounding breathless—and, if I wasn't mistaken, thrilled.

There was another loud boom of thunder. Rain pelted the windows and roof. Her birds squawked, and Claire turned toward the cage, which was covered with a white sheet.

"I should check on them."

I watched her walk. Those breasts and that ass bounced and jiggled, sending more jolts of lust through me. I grabbed my dick, trying to ease myself. I'd be happy to sit and watch her walk around this room all day.

She lifted the sheet on the cage, and I went over to stand behind her, my hands resting on her hips as I peered at the two birds over her shoulder. "How are they?"

"They get nervous during storms, but they seem okay."

Claire spoke softly to them, telling them everything was fine and the storm would be gone soon. I watched the parakeets flutter around.

"Kiss, kiss," squawked the green one—Calico Jack.

"Did you teach him that?"

She nodded. "I did. He's a fast learner."

"Does Quicksilver ever talk?"

"No." She turned and looked at me over her shoulder. "He's too busy being a delinquent."

As she gazed up at me, I was struck all over again by how pretty she was, how saucy and sweet. My chest ached with tenderness.

I was in the middle of a storm in a tiny house that looked like a lollipop with a woman who reminded me of rainbows. A month ago I never would have dreamed I'd be happy here, but I was. It was perfect. Better than perfect.

I lifted my hand to stroke her cheek, turning her toward me all the way. "Thank you for giving me another chance."

"It's okay." She took a deep breath. "I'll tell you a secret. I missed you."

"You did?" I searched her eyes. I wanted this to be true, wanted it more than anything.

She nodded. "A lot."

"Because I meant what I said. This is the beginning for us, Claire."

She slid her arms around my neck, pressing her soft body into mine. "I know. I'm glad you came back for me."

I let my breath out with relief. And then I kissed her again. I took my time exploring her mouth, savoring everything about her.

Thunder boomed. A gust of wind rattled the whole house, and then the lights flickered before going out completely.

"We've lost power," she whispered.

I glanced around the room. It was dim. Early evening, but there was still daylight. "You're right."

The birds began to squawk again. "I'm going to put the sheet back on," she said. "It usually calms them."

I nodded and watched as she turned back around to cover the cage. When she was finished, I stood behind her, whispering in her ear. "And now I have plans for you, my pirate princess."

"You do?"

"Aye, wicked plans."

She giggled. "Philip...."

I took her hand and pulled her over to the bed. I'd never been on it before and was pleased to discover the pillows and bedding were soft as we sank into them.

She was on her back and I lay over her, both of us kissing and caressing each other. Our hands slid everywhere, learning one another's body. A sexy torture.

I was aroused but trying to pace myself. When she slid her hand down to grasp my cock, I allowed it for a little while. Her fingers stroked me, exploring. It felt too good.

I moved her hand away and sat up partway, still wanting to savor this. Our first time. "Do something for me. I want you to grab the bed frame above your head."

"You do?"

I licked my lips, getting excited at the thought. "Yes."

She seemed concerned though. "Why? You're not going to tie me up, are you?"

"What?" I was taken aback. "No, I wasn't planning on it."

"Because I just... well, I want you to know I'm not into any of that weird stuff."

"Weird stuff?"

She nodded. "You know, that stuff billionaires do in movies."

I chuckled. I hadn't seen any of those movies, but I'd heard enough jokes about them. "Don't worry," I assured her. "A beautiful, sexy woman is all I need."

"Okay, good. I just wanted to be clear."

"So no whips or chains, huh?"

"Maybe in the future. After pigs grow wings and learn to fly."

I laughed some more and then gazed at her with affection. She was smiling too. That ache in my chest came back. I couldn't remember the last time I'd felt like this with anyone.

We both quieted, and I asked her again to grab the bed frame above her head again. "Do you trust me?"

She eyed me. "Apparently I do."

She reached overhead, and when she grabbed the brass frame, it was just like I'd imagined. Only better, because it was real. Beautiful and erotic. Her back arched, thrusting those perfect breasts up high. If I were an artist, this was what I'd paint. I'd create a dozen canvases with her just like this. A voyeuristic fantasy.

Her knees were bent, legs parted, and I moved between her thighs. My eyes roamed over the length of her, enjoying myself. Thank God it wasn't dark yet and I could see her clearly.

"This is all you wanted?" she asked softly.

I nodded. "To see you in this bed."

She watched me then as I leaned closer and slid my hand down from her shoulder, gliding over her breasts, then lower to her stomach. I stroked her everywhere, caressing and admiring her skin.

"You're lovely," I said, my voice rough to my own ears. "Truly lovely."

She squirmed beneath my attentions, getting aroused. I stroked her thighs but didn't touch between them yet.

"I think you're forgetting someplace," she breathed as I slid my hands up to her knees.

I grinned a little. "I'm saving the best for last."

When I bent down and took one of her nipples in my mouth, she sighed. It pebbled as I began to lick and suckle her, molding her breast with my hand.

I moved my mouth lower. My cock had gotten so hard it was painful. She wasn't shy anymore and seemed eager, but I took my time, stroking along her inner folds and then circling her clit before licking it. She was wet and musky on my tongue.

A breathy sound escaped her throat, something between a whimper and a moan that made my balls ache it was so sexy. I didn't want to come yet, but I didn't want to stop tasting her either.

Her hands came off the bed frame and grabbed my head, pulling my hair as she continued to moan and squirm against my mouth. I slid my tongue inside her, then replaced it with my fingers.

When I went back to licking her clit, she moaned louder. Her legs shook, and I kept at it until she cried out, bucking against me, doing just what I'd told her to earlier, coming and coming until my face was damp from her.

After she slowed down, I lifted up. I was panting, and all I could think about was fucking her. Making her mine. My heart hammered in my chest. I was trying to calm the hell down because I knew I didn't have any kind of protection.

"You don't have any condoms, do you?"

She nodded, still catching her breath. "There's some in the night-stand." She motioned to the side.

Relief flooded through me. I rummaged through her drawer and found a strip of them shoved in the back. I tore one off.

She stroked my thigh, watching as I rolled it on.

My excitement had turned into a kind of fever, heating my blood, driving me like the storm outside. When I was on top of her, I told myself to go slow, that she probably hadn't had sex in a while, but my body didn't want to listen. I managed a few short strokes, but then my control slipped and I took her in one hard thrust.

She gasped in my arms, grabbing my shoulders. I thrust again, sinking deep.

"Claire," I breathed, fighting for control. "God, I can't stop." She was hot and tight as a fist. A fierce instinct took hold of me, one I'd never experienced, and I wanted to possess her. I needed it.

Her nails scored my back as I began to move. "Yes," I groaned, my voice ragged. "Scratch me up, sweetheart."

Her legs wrapped around my thighs and then my waist as I thrust into her.

She went wild beneath me, moaning and crying out, "Yes," urging me on. When she bit into my shoulder, I lost it. My vision swam, my entire body consumed by the climax. Surreal in its intensity. Hot sparks burst in front of my eyes, blinding me completely as I emptied into her.

Afterward, I kissed her throat, inhaling her scent. "Claire," I whispered in her ear. "My sweet Claire." I smiled with satisfaction. Everything in my gut told me this was right.

Reaching down, I quickly took care of the condom. When I rolled back to her, I kissed her lips and then her cheek, stroking her hair. To my surprise, her face was damp.

I sat up on my forearm to look down at her. It had gotten dark, and I could just make out her features. "Are you okay?" I asked.

She sniffed, gazing up at me, and to my horror, I realized she was crying.

TWENTY-TWO

~ Claire ~

"Did I hurt you?" Philip's face hovered over me in alarm.

I rested my hand on his shoulder. "No, I'm fine." I smiled, even though I was crying.

"Sweetheart, what's wrong?" He stroked my hair and then my cheek. "Are you sure I didn't hurt you?"

"Not at all. That was wonderful." And it was. The hottest sex of my life. Which was mostly why I was crying.

He remained still, studying me in the dark. Then he sat up, glancing around the room. "Where's my phone? I want to see your face and make sure you're telling me the truth."

I laughed, though it sounded more like a croak. "What are you going to do? Shine your phone's flashlight in my face?"

His voice was tender. "Only if I have to."

I laughed some more and then sighed. He was something else.

But I could tell he was concerned, and I had to admit, it was probably freaky for him that I was crying.

"There are some flameless candles," I told him. "One on my nightstand and a few more on a shelf over there. You can light them with a switch at the bottom."

"Flameless?"

"I can't burn real candles around my birds."

"Ah, I see." He got up and padded across the room. Unfortunately, it was too dark to make out his naked body again, though I'd seen plenty earlier. And let me just say, while he looked spectacular in clothes, he looked even better without them.

Philip lit all the candles, saving the one on my nightstand for last. The storm continued outside, but the room now had a cozy glow.

The mattress dipped as he climbed into bed again. I tossed some extra pillows aside and pulled the covers up, and he slid under them next to me.

"Are you really okay?" he asked quietly, propping himself up on one elbow. His eyes roamed my face. "Tell me why you're crying."

"It's just...." I swallowed. How did I explain this? I took a shaky breath, trying to quell my emotions. "I just never thought I'd feel like this again."

"Like what?"

Tears stung my eyes. "Like this. Everything. Sexy and turned on. Wanting to be with you."

The play of shadows on his face made him look even more handsome.

Tears ran into my hair as I gazed at him. I was crying because I was glad, which seemed crazy.

"Am I the first man you've been with since your divorce?"

"No." And then I told him about my one-night stand and how awful it was. "I felt nothing when it happened. Nothing." I started to cry again. "It's like I was dead inside."

"Sweetheart," he murmured. He kissed my cheeks, my forehead, then stroked my hair. "What were you thinking? You should have waited for me."

I laughed though it sounded more like a sob. "I didn't know you were coming!"

"Damn." He shook his head. "I should have gotten here sooner." And I could tell he was serious, his voice thoughtful, like he blamed himself for being unable to fix the past.

"I didn't want Ethan to be the last guy I was with. I was trying to move on, you know?"

He nodded. "Yeah, I would have done the same thing."

"If only I'd had a crystal ball. I would have waited for you."

He stroked my hair, his eyes soft. "I'm here now. That's what matters."

I let out another shaky breath, nodding.

And then I rolled toward him, burying my face in his neck, inhaling his delicious scent while his hand stroked down my back. I let myself relax. The weather still raged outside, but I felt safe and warm. My birds had calmed down too.

We lay together, just listening to the storm, to the rain showering the roof and windows. Somewhere in there I dozed for a while.

When I woke up, we were in the same position. Philip's eyes were closed, and I studied him in the candlelight, his black hair and thick brows. Even asleep he had an air of command.

I kissed his jaw and then ran my tongue along the edge of his ear, nibbling the lobe. His breath hitched, and I knew he was awake.

He pulled back to look at me. "My pirate princess is feeling better?"

I nodded, winding my arms around his neck. "Much better."

"Good." He reached around to caress my ass.

I kissed him and then bit his lower lip, sucked his tongue until he grunted softly.

When I drew back, his gaze was on my face but then slid lower to my chest. One hand came up, caressing my right breast, lightly squeezing.

"They're perfect," he murmured, still looking down at them. "You have a perfect rack."

My brows went up. "Did you really just refer to my breasts as a *rack?*"

"A *perfect* rack." He grinned. "Don't forget the word 'perfect' was in there."

To be honest, my breasts were pretty nice. Definitely my favorite body part. There were plenty of other parts I could complain about—my height, for example—but I got lucky in the boob department.

"Are you going to hang your umbrella on them?" I questioned. "Or your coat and hat?"

"No." He chuckled, then gave me a wicked look. "But I can think of plenty of other things I'd like to do with them."

"You're being dirty again, aren't you?" Despite feeling mildly shocked earlier, the things he said and the way he'd licked his fingers after touching me were the hottest thing ever.

"That depends. Did you like it?"

"Of course not."

He snorted softly. "Liar."

I tried not to smile.

"Should I tell you what I'd like to do with these perfect breasts of yours?" His eyes were on mine. They looked dark in the candlelight, his pupils huge. "Because I have a few ideas."

"Like what?" Excitement sparked through me.

He licked his lips as he continued to caress me. "Well, I'd start slow... because I enjoy taking my time with you." His thumb circled my right areola. "I already know you like your nipples played with."

I gripped his shoulder.

"Don't you?"

"Yes."

He lightly pinched me between his thumb and forefinger, sending sparks through my center and down my spine.

"And I'll bet you liked it when I used my mouth on them too, licking these pretty pink buds." He leaned down to put his mouth on one of them again. His tongue swirled and then gently suckled.

My eyes fell shut as more sparks flew.

"Do you like that?" he asked softly.

I nodded, my stomach tight.

"Tell me."

"I like... it." His body felt sexy against mine. Solid and muscular. His cock, large and hard, pressed against my thigh.

"Good," he said huskily. "I like it too."

His gaze went down to my breasts again. He slid his fingers between them, back and forth.

My breath caught at what he was showing me.

"There's something else I'd like to do," he whispered, his eyes on mine, dark and absorbent. "But only if you'll let me."

I already knew I'd let him. I'd let him do anything he wanted, because I wanted it too. I wanted to do it all with Philip. Even the dirty things.

Especially the dirty things.

In that moment, something gave way, my passion overwhelming. After not feeling anything for years, it was like a dam had burst inside me. I couldn't stand it any longer, and I grabbed him, kissing him fiercely.

Philip groaned, his arms crushing me against him. Our mouths were a tangle of tongues and teeth, reckless and wanting more. I couldn't get close enough.

He broke the kiss and rolled onto his back, grabbing a condom from the nightstand. His hands shook as he yanked it from the wrapper and rolled it over himself.

"Climb onto me," he panted.

I straddled him eagerly, a thigh on each side while he grabbed my hips.

The storm raged outside, except now it raged inside too.

"Oh, God, *now*," I begged, and before I knew it, I was impaled. I gasped as my eyes fell shut. The pleasure was exquisite, flooding all through me. I savored it. Sweet as molasses. I could hear Philip breathing hard, feel him trembling, but he didn't move. He waited, letting me take the lead.

Finally, I began—slow at first, leaning over him to get the angle I needed. And then I let myself go. I took him in a completely selfish way, in a way I didn't think I ever had in my life.

His hands were on my ass, then my breasts, and then it was his mouth. Teasing and suckling me, urging me on. I saw stars when I came. Brilliant stars. Philip was nearly there with me, groaning with every stroke. So close. His cock swelled, and then I heard him growl as he grabbed my hips, thrusting deep.

"Goddamn, Claire," he breathed as we collapsed onto the bed with me still on top of him. I could feel his heart hammering in his chest. "Are you trying to kill me?"

"No." I laughed and lifted my head. "Why do you say that?"

He brushed the hair off my face. "That was the sexiest thing I've ever seen."

"It was?" I doubted it. I was sure he'd seen all kinds of sexy stuff. "I can't believe that's true."

"Trust me." He smiled. "That was hot."

"Really?" I was pleased, but I wasn't sure if he was just saying that.

"My sweet girl next door," he murmured, grinning at me. "Watching you get wild was erotic as hell."

My brows went up at his description. I'd never thought about it, but I guess I sort of was the girl-next-door type. "I guess when you put it that way...."

He chuckled and closed his eyes, still catching his breath. "Now you understand."

I laid my head back down on his chest and smiled. His fingers grazed lazily down my spine. I felt happier than I had in a long time, practically bursting with it, but there was this little bit of fear too. I was afraid to trust my happiness.

"I guess all of that was bottled up inside of me." My voice quivered. "Who knew?"

"Hey." Philip's fingers slowed their lazy pattern. "Are you all right?"

"I'm fine."

"Let me see your face."

I lifted my head to look at him.

His eyes searched mine, assessing. "Are you sure you're all right?"

I nodded, though my throat was tight. "I'm the happiest I've been in a long time."

"Are you going to cry?"

I nodded again and tried to smile as emotion welled up in me. "I think I am. I'm sorry."

"Don't be sorry." His voice was tender as he stroked my back. "You've been through a lot."

Tears ran down my face. I couldn't seem to stop them. It was like I was finding myself again after a long and terrible journey. I was so glad to be here with him in this moment. "I'm glad it's you," I whispered.

His gaze was full of understanding. "Me too."

And then I cried. Full-on tears. The storm inside me still raging, not finished yet. Philip held me the whole time, caressing me, telling me I was okay. I cried like I hadn't in years. I cried for everything. All the struggles I'd had, but mostly I cried because the past was behind me and the future ahead.

Eventually I calmed down and sat up next to him. I leaned over his chest to grab some tissue from the box on my nightstand and blew my nose. "You must think I'm a total basket case."

"Not at all."

"Really?" I croaked with laughter. "Do women usually cry after they have sex with you?"

His mouth twitched. "I can't say they ever do."

"Oh my God, I'm sorry to put you through this."

"Don't say that." His eyes met mine. "You're worth it, Claire."

"Thanks." I sniffed and smiled at him. I could tell he meant it. "You're so nice. That's not at all what I read about you online."

His brows furrowed. "What did you read online?"

I thought back to my Google session where I tried to learn more about Philip. "I read that you're a hardass. That most people are intimidated by you."

He shook his head and frowned. "That's because most people don't like to hear the truth."

"You tell them the truth?"

"I do." He sighed. "Though it's not always easy."

I thought about my own reaction to the advice he'd given me.

"Would you like anything?" I asked, gathering my used tissues to throw away. "I'm going to get a glass of water."

He sat up. "I can get it for you."

"I have to go to the bathroom anyway."

I got out of bed and, after using the bathroom, went into the kitchen to get us both some water from the fridge. It was still cold even though the power was out. When I came back into the main room, Philip's eyes were on me as I walked toward him.

"Thanks," he said, taking the glass from me.

I climbed in bed beside him. Amazingly, it was still raining outside. "It sounds like this storm is going all night." I glanced at my birds' cage. "At least the thunder stopped."

"I take it they're asleep now?"

I nodded. "Thank goodness."

He put his water glass on my nightstand and lay down in bed again, putting his arms out to me. "Come here, lie next to me."

I scooted down until we faced each other, both of us under the covers. His body was warm and solid against mine as I stroked his jaw.

We gazed at each other for a long while.

The candlelight cast a cozy glow while rain tapped steadily on the roof. It was like we were lost in our own world.

"What are you thinking about?" I asked, curious. He seemed deep in thought.

"You." His voice rumbled between us. "I was thinking how I'd like to take you away someplace warm and sunny."

"Steal me away like a pirate?"

"If I have to. Is there any place you'd like to go? The Caribbean maybe?"

I sighed with pleasure at the idea. "I've never been there."

"I'm sure there are lots of sailboats. We could rent one."

I closed my eyes and imagined it. The turquoise water. The endless blue skies. It would be wonderful.

"You could teach me how to sail," he coaxed. "And I'll teach you how to drink rum and curse like a sailor."

I laughed. "I think I could figure that out on my own."

"Hey, who's got the pirate blood, you or me?"

I smiled, then thought of something. "I can't leave my business." I knew it was crazy to turn down a trip to the Caribbean, and I could already hear Leah and Theo having a conniption. "I'm the only one running things, you know?"

"I know, but it wouldn't be for that long. Just a week or so."

"I thought you were this crazed workaholic, that your mom and sister had to kidnap you into taking a vacation."

He chuckled. "I am."

"So now you're trying to kidnap me into taking a vacation?"

"I guess I'll do anything to see you in a string bikini," he teased, sliding his hand along my hip. But then he looked at me with interest. "You don't happen to own one, do you?"

"A string bikini?" The only thing I had was a worn-out one-piece that didn't fit anymore. "No."

"That's okay, I'll buy you one."

"I can buy it myself."

He shook his head. "I know exactly the kind I want you to wear, so I'm buying it."

I watched him as he seemed to go over the whole thing in his mind. I played with a strand of his black hair, silky beneath my fingers. "You have a rich fantasy life, don't you?"

He wore a hint of a smile. "I do."

"I wouldn't have guessed that about you." Few people would guess it, I was sure. Despite his success, it occurred to me that Philip was a very private man.

He jokingly batted his lashes. "What can I say? I'm an enigma wrapped in a riddle tied in a bow."

I laughed at his expression. "I don't know if Quicksilver would approve."

"Then to hell with him." He shifted position a little, his arm still around me, but then he winced.

"Hey, are you in pain?"

"I'm fine." He shook his head. "I hurt my hand earlier, but it's nothing."

"How did you hurt your hand?"

"Something stupid. You don't want to know."

"What do you mean?"

He leaned in and kissed me. "Let's talk more about string bikinis and our trip to the Caribbean. I'm not done with that subject."

"Which hand did you hurt?"

He drew back and sighed. "My right one."

I looked over my shoulder. I was lying on his right arm with his hand on my pillow. I sat up a little. "Let me see it."

"It's fine," he said, though he gave it to me anyway.

I gently examined it, and even in the candlelight, I could tell it was more than he was letting on. "This doesn't look like nothing. You obviously injured yourself. It's swollen."

Philip took his hand from me and looked at it. He flexed it a little and winced again. "It wasn't bothering me much earlier, but it's starting to ache like a sonofabitch now."

"What did you do to it?"

He was quiet. "I punched the porch rail in front of the beach house."

"You did?" My eyes widened. "Why would you do that?"

"I had an unwelcome visitor today."

"Who?"

He shifted on the bed again and let his breath out. "My father."

I watched him. His jaw was tense, body rigid. His entire demeanor had changed. A few seconds ago, he was relaxed and playful, but now he was back in command mode.

"Do you want to talk about it?"

"No."

Philip seemed guarded. I knew what that was like, so I tried a different tactic. "You said this is the beginning for us, right?"

His eyes went to mine. "Yes."

"Isn't this the kind of thing you'd share with me, then?"

He remained silent. "It is. And I will tell you about him, but not tonight, okay?" He took my hand in the one he hadn't injured. "This is our first night together. I want it to be special."

I considered his earnest expression. I wanted it to be special too.

"He doesn't deserve our time, Claire. Not one minute of it."

I looked down at his swollen right hand. I couldn't imagine Philip so angry he'd punch a porch rail. "Let me at least get you some ice for your hand."

"I'm fine. Do you have any kind of food though? I'm starving."

"Mmm, I guess I'd better feed you." I leaned over to kiss him. "Because I'm definitely not done with you yet."

We both got up. There was a chill in the air, so I put on my white satin bathrobe. "I have another robe. Would you like to borrow it?"

He shrugged. "I doubt it would fit me."

"It might. It's bigger than this one." I went over to my closet and pulled out the robe Violet gave me for Christmas last year. It was a pink fleece, so I only wore it during the winter months.

Philip slipped it on. It was tight around his shoulders and stopped above the knee but otherwise fit okay. "How do I look?" he asked.

"Very pretty."

He ran his hand down the front of the robe, over the ruffled lapel. "It's soft." He grinned. "I'm feeling glamorous."

I laughed. Despite the girly bathrobe, he looked more masculine than ever, like it emphasized his maleness.

We went into the kitchen together. Despite what he'd said, I gave Philip an ice pack from the freezer and a couple of aspirin, which he accepted without complaint, so I figured he was in real pain.

"Would you like a sandwich?" I was glad I'd gone grocery shopping earlier. "Or there's hummus and pita bread."

"Let's have both." He stood next to me, leaning against the kitchen counter and holding the ice pack against his hand. His silver eyes found mine in the darkness, and there was a smile in them. "I've worked up quite an appetite."

"We should probably eat the ice cream for dessert too. I think it's melting."

We took all the food back over to the bed. As we ate, Philip checked his phone to make sure his mom and sister were okay.

I texted Violet, though Sullivan House had a generator, so I doubted the storm even made much of an impression on her.

"Anything from your mom and sister?" I asked, opening the bag of pita bread.

"They're fine." He was reading from the screen. "My sister's staying with a friend—one of the actresses from the play—and my mom is at the beach house." He put his phone down. "Elliot is there with her."

I leaned over to dip some pita bread into the hummus. "That's a good thing, right? She's not alone."

"I guess. I'm trying to be open-minded about this."

"Come on, be happy for her. I know you haven't met him yet, but you'll like him." I told Philip about some of my elderly clients, how their children were barely in the picture and seemed like jerks. "He's not like that. He's a good guy."

"All right, I believe you."

I grinned. "They're probably up to the same thing we are tonight."

"Shit." He smiled and tore off a chunk of pita bread, digging it into the hummus. "Probably, but I do *not* want to think about it. This is my mom we're talking about."

"Sylvia's also a grown woman who deserves love and happiness."

Philip paused and looked at me. "You're right, she does."

"Did you tell her you're over here with me?"

He nodded. "I let my mom and sister both know."

"What'd they say?"

"They're happy for me. They like you." He bit into the sandwich I'd made for him.

"I like them too." Sylvia and Eliza were great. I was glad they liked me. I suspected it would be difficult for Philip to be seriously involved with a woman they disliked.

His phone buzzed, and he picked it up again.

"What is it?"

"Dammit." He sighed and shook his head. "My mom wants to know why the porch rail is broken."

"You actually broke it?"

He nodded and texted something back to her. "Yeah. I'll have to make sure it gets fixed."

"I take it she doesn't know your dad was there today?"

"No." He glanced at me. "And I don't intend on telling her either."

I stayed quiet. I didn't understand the situation, so I figured the best thing was to keep my mouth shut.

We finished the rest of the food, and then I got the melting ice cream from the freezer. It was a single container of chocolate, and we sat next to each other in bed as I took turns feeding us.

"I have to confess something to you," he said, swallowing a bite. "You might not like it."

I paused with the spoon in midair to glance over at him. "What?"

"It's not a big thing, but since we're starting fresh, I want to be truthful."

"All right." I remained still, wondering what this could be.

"There was no meeting with a bike company on Saturday morning. I made the whole thing up." He smiled uncomfortably. "It's just that I was desperate to see you again."

"Oh, that. I already know about that." I dipped my spoon back into the ice cream.

His brows went up. "You do?"

"Eliza told me when we were riding together." I hadn't even been that surprised. The whole thing sounded odd from the start.

"You're not angry?"

"I was initially." I offered him a spoonful of ice cream, and he opened his mouth. "But then I thought about it and realized you did it because I gave you no choice." I was starting to understand Philip's nature, how single-minded he could be, how driven. "You don't let much stand in your way, do you?"

His eyes stayed on mine. "I don't. Especially when I want something."

"I expect nothing but the truth from now on though."

He nodded. "Of course."

"Good." I scraped the bottom of the container with my spoon. "Do you want the last bite?"

"Only if you don't."

I raised a brow. "Are you being truthful?"

He chuckled. "All right, I want it. But only because I need to keep my strength up." He leaned closer and slid his hand over my hip, lowering his voice. "The night's not even half over, and it turns out you're one hell of a handful, sweetheart."

"Here." I offered him the last spoonful with a smirk. "You're right. You *are* going to need your strength."

TWENTY-THREE

~ Claire ~

The next morning, I woke up to the sound of my phone buzzing.
Philip appeared asleep, but his hands were awake. They slid down my body as I reached over him to grab the phone from my nightstand.

"Who is it?" he asked, his voice husky. His eyes were half-lidded, watching me.

"Violet." I declined the call and put the phone on the bed beside me so I didn't have to reach over him again.

"You're not going to answer it?"

"No, I'll check my messages later." I snuggled down beside him, so warm and solid. I'd forgotten how wonderful it was to have a man in my bed. My hand drifted over his stomach, then lower to discover morning wood. "Mmm, what have we here?"

"A present for you."

"I like these kinds of presents."

He chuckled softly. "Don't I know it."

I smiled to myself. It had been quite a night. After years of feeling no passion at all, the floodgates had opened in a big way. It occurred to me that while I may have moved on from Ethan, I'd never moved on from the betrayal of a lover, from the way it froze me inside.

Happily, the thaw had arrived.

He shifted on the bed so we were face-to-face. "Be gentle with me, my pirate princess."

"Oh, I think you're up to it."

His eyes were on me with affection. "Look at you," he whispered. "Such a lusty wench."

"It's your fault."

"I'm glad," he murmured, rolling me onto my back, "because now I plan to take full advantage."

Later, after we'd had our fill of each other, I got up to remove the sheet from my birds' cage. They were both flittering around, chirping enthusiastically. "Do you mind if I let them out?"

"No, go ahead." Philip was sitting up in bed with a pillow tucked behind his back, studying his phone.

I opened the cage door and then climbed in beside him again. It felt luxurious to be lazing around like this. "I can't remember the last time I slept in late and hung out in bed."

"Same here." He pulled me in close so my head rested on his shoulder, then kissed my hair. "This is nice."

"How's your hand?"

"A little sore."

I noticed he was holding his phone with his left. "Can I see it?"

He moved his arm from around me and held his right hand out for both of us to study.

"It still looks bruised," I commented, "but I think it's less swollen than last night."

"I think you're right." He turned his hand this way and that, making a fist for a moment. "It was an idiotic thing to do."

"Should I get you more aspirin?"

He shook his head. "It's fine. I'll probably take some later."

I lay back down on his shoulder, and he went back to reading his phone. A thrill went through me as I studied his profile. My stomach tingled. I still couldn't believe he was here beside me, that last night happened at all.

Philip was reading something with his brows furrowed. I didn't even have to ask what he was doing. After being raised by a news junkie, I could tell he was getting his daily fix. I was tempted to pull my phone out too, but instead I continued to watch him. So handsome. I stroked his bristly jaw, reveling in the way I felt this morning. Happy and alive.

I thought about yesterday, that determined expression he wore as he'd trudged through the woods toward me with the wind howling. "That was very romantic what you did—coming to find me in the storm like that."

"Mmm," he rumbled, distracted.

"Romantic but stupid."

He glanced at me. "Excuse me?"

"Do you have any idea how dangerous it is to be out near the shore in a storm? What were you thinking?"

"As a matter of fact, I do know." He put his phone down. "I nearly had my ass fried into a piece of bacon."

"What do you mean?"

"I mean lightning struck close enough to me on the beach that I could smell it."

I blinked at him, sick at the thought of what could have happened. He wouldn't be the first person struck by lightning out there. "Please don't do that again, okay? Promise me."

His eyes lingered on mine. "I promise. It's just that I had to see you, and it couldn't wait."

"Next time drive."

He chuckled. "Let's hope there won't be a next time."

I imagined him braving the elements. Despite everything, I had to admit it was romantic. No one had ever done anything like that for me.

My birds were both out from the cage now, and I watched them fly to each of their favorite perches in the room, twittering happily. Quicksilver squawked a few times. They had pellets there for breakfast, but I figured I should get them some fruit too.

There was a buzzing noise from the phone tucked beneath my pillow, and I reached for it. It was a text from Violet. *Is your power still out? Come up to the house for a hot breakfast.*

I stared at her message and then glanced over at Philip, wondering if I should tell her he's here. She'd probably be scandalized. But then I thought of how she'd referred to me as "poor Claire" the other day and felt a wave of irritation.

I thumbed in my reply. *Philip stayed over last night. Is it all right if I invite him too?*

There was a long pause on Violet's end, and I waited to see what she would do. Eventually I could see she was typing something.

Certainly. Please extend the invitation to Philip.

Well, that was interesting. "Violet invited us up to the house for a hot breakfast. Would you like to go?"

"Sure." Then he turned to me. "How does she know I'm here?"

"I told her."

He put his phone down. "We can go up there if you want. I could definitely eat something."

I texted her back and said we'd be there in a little while. Philip and I got out of bed to take a shower together, though he started cracking jokes when he saw the size of my shower.

"This is pitiful." He held the glass door open, laughing at the tiny space. "I've seen phone booths bigger than this."

"Hey, no dissing my shower."

He grinned. "You'll have to come to Seattle and try mine. You'll love it. It has multiple sprayers and lots of space."

I rolled my eyes. I could only imagine. His shower was probably bigger than my whole bathroom.

He got in first and then pulled me in with him, our bodies

pressed tight as he stood behind me. "Maybe this isn't so bad after all," he murmured, closing the door. He slid soap over my breasts. "It has its perks."

Somehow we got each other clean without too much damage, though I nearly gave him a black eye with my elbow when he reached down for the shampoo.

"I'm sorry!"

"It's okay." He held the washcloth up to his face. "I still have one good eye left. Plus now I get to wear an eye patch."

Eventually we figured out a way to coordinate ourselves so there were no more injuries. I had to admit it was fun and sexy taking a shower together. I helped him wash his hair since his hand was still sore.

Afterward, I put on clean clothes and let my hair dry naturally so it was long and curly. Unfortunately, Philip had to wear the same jeans and T-shirt from yesterday, both horribly wrinkled from lying in a pile on the floor all night.

As we walked up to the main house, our feet crunching on the gravel, he reached for my hand. "Damn, you're cute." He pulled me in close to steal a kiss. "I'm in big trouble here. You know that, don't you?"

"Is that so?" I teased. My whole body felt warm and tingly, and I couldn't wipe the smile off my face for anything.

As usual, Violet was at the table in the dining room reading the paper. She did a double take when she saw the state of Philip's clothes.

"Good morning," he said to her. "Thank you for the breakfast invitation."

"Of course," she murmured, still agog at his severely wrinkled T-shirt and jeans. "Please... help yourself. There are eggs and bacon, or I could have my cook prepare an omelet if you'd like."

My brows went up with surprise. She'd never offered to have her cook prepare *me* an omelet.

"That won't be necessary. This is great."

We both went over to the sideboard and grabbed plates. When we were done getting food, we joined Violet at the table. She was still eyeing Philip when she asked if the power was still out down at the carriage house. He told her it was, and she explained how she'd been on the phone half the morning with the other town council members, coordinating cleanup efforts for the storm debris.

"At least it's Saturday," I said, swallowing a bite of toast. "Fewer people on the roads."

Violet nodded and then turned back to Philip. "Will you be joining us for our Pirate Days party?"

He glanced at me. "Yes, Claire invited me."

She picked up her teacup. "Did she also explain that it's a fundraiser for Truth Harbor?"

He nodded, picking up his glass of orange juice. "She did."

"We're trying to stop these horrible real estate developers from destroying our town. They seem to think *money* is the only thing in this world that matters." Her southern drawl was strong, and there was a hard edge to her voice that confused me.

"Is that right." He put his glass down.

"Yes, it *is*." Violet put her cup down as well.

The two of them seemed to be having a staring contest.

"Is something going on here?" I asked, my eyes flashing between them.

"Perhaps you should have Philip tell you."

"Tell me what?"

Violet sighed. "I'm sorry to have to inform you of this, Claire, but I've done some digging. It turns out Philip and his company are part of the real estate group that's planning to tear down our town."

My mouth fell open with astonishment. "What? That's not true!" I turned to Philip. "Is that true?"

He shook his head. "No, it isn't."

Violet snorted. "Please. I just read an article about it online. I was quite shocked." She leaned toward him, pointing. "You weren't being honest with me, young man, when I asked you about yourself the other night."

Philip's brows slammed together. "I was completely honest. I told you Gavin and I own a company called NorthStone Capital."

"Wait, are you part of the group that's planning to destroy our *town*?" My voice rose an octave. I could barely believe this. All my newfound happiness was going up in flames.

"We're not." He turned to me. "Gavin and I considered it for a short time. Word of our possible involvement leaked to the financial press, but we're not a part of that deal and never have been."

"Okay." My pulse rate began to go down. "So you're not buying that land?"

He shook his head. "No."

"That's not what I read online," Violet countered.

"What you read online was inaccurate. You're hearing it directly from *me* now."

She sniffed. "And how do you explain the way you acted the other night? You led me to believe you worked for Doug, that you were just starting out with your business."

"No he didn't," I said to Violet. "You assumed that was the case based solely on the way they were dressed, but he never said that."

She went silent.

To be honest, I was ready to get up and leave. I didn't enjoy coming here and having Philip accused of things he didn't do. Appearances were overly important to Violet, always had been. She was so rigid with all her rules and supposed standards that even my dad used to complain about it.

"My apologies," she said stiffly to Philip. "It appears I was mistaken, though you certainly could have corrected me instead of letting me make a fool out of myself."

"There's no apology necessary, and you weren't foolish. I understood you were only looking out for Claire."

Violet nodded in agreement and seemed somewhat placated. "I was, and I still am."

"Good. So am I."

The two of them continued to assess each other. Violet's eyes flickered over him, but I sensed she was backing down. Ethan had always been intimidated by Violet. During our marriage, he tried to avoid her, so it was ironic that he was now married to her daughter. Philip was clearly unfazed by her though.

"Oh, and there's a town meeting in ten days." She turned toward me. "You might like to come to that, as we'll be discussing the land purchase."

"I'll be there. I was already planning on it." Unlike my dad and Violet, I'd never been interested in town politics. Not to mention, the last time I went to a town meeting, people were still reeling from the scandal of Ethan dumping me for Ivy. There were a lot of sympathetic smiles, people clucking and whispering, "Poor Claire," under their breath. I knew they meant well, and most everyone made it clear they were on my side, but it still wasn't easy.

Violet seemed more relaxed now that she'd said everything she needed to. I could tell she'd finally decided what box Philip fit into, and since it was a successful, wealthy one, she was turning on the charm. She regaled us with the story of how she'd first met my father on a cruise ship, a story I'd heard many times but didn't mind hearing again.

We said our goodbyes after breakfast and were walking back down to the carriage house when I asked Philip about the real estate deal. "How come you never mentioned that before?"

He shrugged. "I didn't see any point in it."

"There's no chance you guys will still be part of that, right?"

"No."

"Because I don't think I could handle it if you were lured into making money off the destruction of my hometown."

"I don't want to see the destruction of your hometown." He stopped walking and faced me, pulling me in closer. "And the only thing I'm being lured in by is *you*."

TEN DAYS LATER, the town meeting ran late into the evening. There were so many people I hadn't seen in a while, so many of my dad's friends and associates. Happily, not a single person referred to me as "poor Claire." I figured it was because I was a bona fide business owner now, a real contributor to the local economy, but that turned out to be wrong. Word had gotten out that I finally had a boyfriend.

"It's a miracle!"

"We can't believe it!"

"Just when all hope was lost!"

"Don't let this one get away!"

"Ethan and Ivy are having marital problems!"

Of course, that last remark was made out of Violet's earshot.

By the time the evening wrapped up and I headed home, it was after nine. My heart skipped a beat when I saw a certain someone in front of my house. Someone with black hair and blue eyes. Someone who looked an awful lot like a pirate. A thrill went through me at the mere sight of him.

It was just before sunset, the sky golden and the air scented with the lush green of a summer evening.

I walked up to where he was sitting on one of my Adirondack chairs. Even sitting, Philip exuded a strong male energy. I shouldn't be surprised to see him here, since he'd been coming over every night for the past week and a half. I knew we were moving too fast, that we should put on the brakes, but I couldn't seem to resist him.

"How did it go?" Philip asked, his eyes roaming over me with interest.

I shrugged. "It was okay."

"I brought you something." He motioned down to the bag on the ground beside him. "I thought you might be hungry. It's Pad Thai from your favorite restaurant."

"You got me Pad Thai?" For someone with the reputation for being an intimidating hardass, he was astonishingly thoughtful.

"And for dessert...." He reached into the bag and pulled out a couple of Kit Kat bars. "Who's your sugar daddy?"

I squealed with delight. "You are!"

He grinned and picked up the bag. We went into the kitchen together to make up plates, though Philip mostly stood behind me and kissed my neck while I dished out the food.

"I missed you," he whispered in my ear, sliding his hands down to my hips. "I've been thinking about you all day. You're my new obsession."

I smiled. I'd been thinking about him all day too.

"After we eat, I'm going to take you to that naughty bed of yours and make you scream my name."

I chuckled. For some reason, he was really into my bed.

"Laugh all you want, my pirate princess, but soon you'll be overcome with passion."

I put the peanut sauce down and turned around to face him, still smiling. "What am I going to do with you?"

He wore a playful expression. "You're going to fuck me senseless."

"Is that right?" I asked softly. Then I stepped closer to him and slid my arms around his neck. Resting my head against his shoulder, I sighed.

"Hey, what is it sweetheart?" he murmured, stroking my back. "Is something wrong?"

I didn't reply right away, taking a moment to gather my thoughts. "I'm just worried we're moving too fast. That maybe we should slow down. We've been together every night."

He went still against me. "Do you want me to leave?"

"Of course not." I glanced up at him. "Don't be ridiculous."

"I can go. Maybe you want a night to yourself."

"No. Don't go." I hugged him tighter. I didn't want him to leave. That was the last thing I wanted.

"I don't think we're moving too fast," he said, stroking me again. "I think you're amazing, and I want to spend all my time with you. That's why I can't stay away."

That was the other surprising thing about Philip. He didn't seem to hold anything back. It was unnerving. The other night, when we were in bed together, he'd told me about his past and how he used to date a lot, how he's been called a dog. "Are you always like this with women, then?" I asked.

He went quiet and reached for my hand. "I've never been like this with anyone, Claire. Ever."

"You haven't?"

"No." He seemed thoughtful, studying me. "This is a first."

As I stood in the kitchen hugging Philip, I wished I could be as fearless as he was. He seemed to embrace our relationship with genuine gusto. "Have you ever had your heart broken?"

He shook his head. "Not like you. But I watched my mom go through it, so I have some idea of how bad it can be."

"It's the betrayal. It makes it hard to trust someone again."

He nodded. "I know, but I'm not Ethan. I'd never betray you like that."

I wanted to believe him.

"Come on," he said. "Let's eat dinner, and then I'll replace every bad memory you have with a happy one."

I smiled and leaned against him again, closing my eyes. He really was something. Of all the fake boyfriends I might have conjured up, it turned out Philip was better than any I could have imagined.

We pulled apart, and I finished putting together plates for us. After giving my birds some fruit, we took our meal outside.

We sat out front, and I told him about the town meeting, describing some of the people and how the plans were moving forward to have the downtown area officially made into a historic district.

Philip mostly listened while he ate noodles with chopsticks.

"Oh, and there was this older guy there," I said. "Apparently he's one of the real estate investors. He spoke to everyone about what his plans were if they won the bid."

"An older guy?" He took another bite of food.

"Yeah, he came and spoke to a few of us after the meeting. I told him I owned a maid service, and he said he was a big supporter of small businesses like mine."

"What did he look like?"

"Black hair with brown eyes. Very tan. He was probably in his mid sixties."

Philip's face changed upon hearing this. "About my height?"

"I think so."

"Son of a bitch." He put his chopsticks down. "I don't believe this."

"What is it?" I stopped eating too.

"You said he spoke to you?"

I nodded. "He spoke to a few of us afterward. He seemed nice enough. What's wrong?"

Philip's jaw clenched. He shook his head.

"Do you know him?" I asked. "Who is he?"

He went silent. "My father."

"Really?" My eyes widened with surprise. "What a strange coincidence he was there."

"What else did he say? Tell me exactly."

"He said he was partnering with another real estate group. He was trying to convince people they didn't need to worry about turning the downtown into a historic district, that he and his investors weren't planning to make any changes downtown."

He snorted. "I'll just bet he was."

I studied Philip as I tried to reconcile him with the man I'd met earlier. Oddly, now that I thought about it, there was a vague resemblance between them.

He remained quiet and appeared to be going over something in his mind.

"So your dad's a commercial real estate developer?" I asked.

He nodded. "Listen to me, Claire. If you see him again, don't speak to him. He's not a good man."

"Really? He didn't seem that bad."

"Trust me, everything he says is a lie. He can be charming, but none of it's real."

"So the things he told everyone about leaving the downtown area alone weren't true?"

"They weren't. He's only telling people what they want to hear. If he gets a hold of that land, he'll tear down everything and build whatever he deems most profitable."

"So he's just like every other developer."

Philip nodded. "Only worse because you'll never see him coming."

We finished eating and brought everything inside. The conversation between us had grown stilted, as Philip now seemed unhappy and distracted. After putting the plates in the sink, I told him I was going to take a shower. He nodded. He had his phone out, texting someone. Usually he joined me in the shower, but finding out his father was at that meeting had obviously upset him.

When I emerged twenty minutes later, he was sitting on my bed against the pillows, still fully dressed and on his phone.

"Are you going to put that away?" I asked, climbing in beside him wearing my satin robe.

He glanced at me. "I'm almost done."

I watched his tense profile as he continued texting. He had the air about him of a general marshaling his troops. "Is everything okay?" Hearing about his dad had changed the whole tenor of our evening.

He didn't reply. I doubted he even heard me.

I was tempted to go over work stuff, but instead I got up to visit my birds. Quicksilver was chewing on the new wooden perch I'd put in a few days ago. "Caught you," I said to him as he continued to chew. "That's the third perch I've bought you, young man."

"Kiss, kiss," squawked Calico Jack. "Kiss, kiss."

"Talk some sense into your friend here, will you?" I told Calico.

Behind me, I heard movement. When I turned around, Philip had finally put his phone down and was lying on the bed with his eyes closed.

I went over to him. "Are you all right? Tell me what's going on."

He opened his eyes and smiled when he saw me. "Come here." He put his arm out, and I climbed in beside him. "Mmm, you smell nice," he murmured. "I can't believe I missed my nightly eye gouging in the shower."

I couldn't help my laughter. I kept elbowing him in the face every time. It was terrible.

He shifted position and rolled toward me, sliding his hands down my body over the outside of my robe, then beneath it to caress my bare bottom. "You feel good," he said, moving closer, his lips pressed to my ear. "You always feel so good."

I wanted to talk though. I tried to ask about his father, but he must have sensed my intentions, because he immediately kissed me, moving from my mouth to my neck, sending hot shimmers through me. It was always like this. I grew aroused so quickly. *Making up for lost time,* I told myself, though I suspected it was Philip himself I found so arousing.

"Take your robe off. Let me see you," he said softly.

I sat up partway and did as he asked, loosening the tie and then letting it slip down over my shoulders.

Philip's eyes were on my face but then dropped lower, watching as the robe slid all the way off. He wore the same mesmerized expression every time he saw me. Every single time. I didn't even know couples were like this together. I'd always thought Ethan and I had a good marriage, but he never looked at me like Philip did.

Like I was a gift.

"Beautiful," he said, reaching for me and pulling me closer. "So beautiful. I want you all the time." He was still dressed, and it felt erotic and naughty being the only one naked.

I put my hand over his erection, measuring the column beneath his jeans. When I unzipped his pants, he didn't stop me, and when I pushed his jeans lower and took him out, he didn't stop me either.

"Is this for me?" I asked, stroking his hard length, smooth and thick in my hand.

He nodded, his eyes half-lidded. "Only you."

I smiled and then bent down and took him in my mouth. I heard his intake of breath as I gave him a blow job. He was always going down on me, but I hadn't returned the favor nearly as often.

"Sweetheart," he murmured. His hand came up to stroke my neck as I continued my administrations. I felt his eyes on me, and when I glanced up, his mouth was open, his jaw flushed with arousal.

After a short while, I stopped and moved over him, straddling his hips as I pushed his shirt up so I could see his chest. We were still using condoms, and he immediately reached over to the nightstand and grabbed one out of the drawer.

"Hurry," I said, desire rushing through me.

He chuckled at my impatience, but when he finished and I sank down onto him, his whole face changed. His body tightened, and when his eyes flashed to mine, they were glazed with pleasure. "God-damn," he breathed. "I love it when you do that."

"Grab my hips," I told him, a catch in my voice.

I was never like this with Ethan, never this pushy or insistent. With him, I was giving all the time, and in the end, what did it get me? But Philip seemed to enjoy it when I took what I wanted from him, seemed to encourage it even. It was like he understood something about me I was only now starting to see myself. That I needed this.

He grasped my hips, urging me on.

Then I leaned over him and did exactly what he'd said I should do earlier—I fucked him senseless.

TWENTY-FOUR

~ Philip ~

I listened as Claire fell asleep beside me. Her ass was tucked into my stomach, my arm lying across her hip.

There was a full moon outside, so the room wasn't as dark as usual. The sheet draped over her birdcage had become a canvas for trees to cast long shadows upon.

I shut my eyes and tried to sleep, except I couldn't stop thinking. It looked like my father was going to win that land bid. It turned out he was trying to join with Atlas—the same commercial developers we'd been planning to partner with. The group of investors in London had dropped out, and somehow my father had stepped in.

I should have predicted he'd figure out a way. He always did. Until now, I'd had every intention of staying out of this whole thing. Except everything changed when Claire told me he was at that meeting. It enraged me to think of him charming her, charming everyone and landing on his feet once again.

Before I knew it, I was texting Gavin and the CEO of Atlas on a fact-finding mission. I discovered things weren't settled. Contracts hadn't been signed yet, and my father was overconfident.

Claire made a huffing noise in her sleep. It reminded me of how she sometimes snorted when she laughed. It was cute, though she didn't think it was cute when I'd teased her about it the other day.

"Instead of pirate princess, I think I'll call you piggy princess."

Her expression had turned indignant. "Excuse me, but I do *not* sound like a piggy."

She was so fun to tease. I loved her snorting laughter, how she could be sweet one minute and sexy the next. The way she never played head games or pouted. If she disagreed about something, she stood her ground. It was relaxing to discover I could be myself around her. And then there was the way she'd sometimes smile at me with a sideways glance, or I'd watch her walking toward me and it took my breath away.

Somehow in a short time, Claire had become very important to me. She was quality. The kind of woman you kept. I understood completely why Doug had fallen for her, why he'd been so desperate to win her heart. He obviously saw the same things in her as I did.

Damn. I blew my breath out roughly.

I felt sick thinking about my cousin. What the hell was I going to say to him? I glanced down at Claire as she slept, her soft body tucked into mine, and guilt burned through me. At the same time, I was grateful. Grateful for my good fortune, because I was happier than I've ever been.

I had no idea how to tell him about Claire and me. Doug had called twice this past week, and I let both calls go to voice mail.

At least I'm still making him money. I was still running his business, and things were so busy I'd had to hire two more contractors.

Claire shifted in front of me. "Are you awake?" she asked softly.

"Yeah, I can't sleep. Did I wake you?"

"No, I don't think so." My arm was still around her, and she slid her fingers down to entwine with mine. "Is your hand still bothering you?"

"A little, but it's mostly healed." I leaned closer to stick my nose in her hair. She smelled like shampoo mixed with her own clean scent.

"Are you thinking about your father?"

I stiffened.

"Don't shut me out like this, Philip."

It wasn't about shutting her out. I just didn't want the stain of him anywhere near her.

I took my hand back and brushed her hair aside, kissing the nape of her neck, knowing full well it turned her on. I heard her intake of breath, and my cock stirred.

I ran my fingers down her back, enjoying the feel of her smooth skin. I wanted her again. I wasn't surprised anymore by the strength of my desire, that it never waned. By now I would have lost interest with the women I'd dated in the past. It was strange to even think of them. They all seemed interchangeable.

I slid my hand around to caress her breast, but she wasn't having any of it this time. Instead she rolled over and faced me.

"You're changing the subject," she said flatly.

"I know."

"Please talk to me. What caused this rift? Why did you punch that porch rail?"

I licked my lips but didn't say anything.

"Is it because he cheated on your mom?"

I could just make out the curve of her cheek, her eyes on me, and even in the dark room, I saw the compassion there. I looked away from her, over to the shadows falling across her birdcage.

We were both quiet as she waited for me. I knew this was one of those moments in a relationship where you either moved forward or you didn't.

I took a deep breath. "Yes, he cheated on her, but it went way beyond that. He left her, but he left all of us." My jaw tightened. "*Abandoned* would be a better word."

"How old were you?"

"Thirteen. I was thirteen, and Eliza was two."

She reached out to stroke my hair. It felt strange to talk about it, and I realized it was because I hadn't for a long time. It was private and not something I shared.

"Do you know why he did it?" she asked softly.

I thought back to when I was a kid and how, as my father's business grew, he acted different toward us, like we weren't good enough. "Sometimes money changes people. The more successful he became, the more he treated us like useless baggage. He was especially cruel to my mom."

She quieted. "Was he abusive?"

"Not physically but verbally. He decided he was in the top percent of earners, so he should have a woman who was in the top percent for looks."

I heard her soft intake of breath. "That's terrible. Your mom is so nice."

"We came home from a school field trip one day and discovered he'd moved everything out of our house. The only thing left were the beds. What's even worse is he took all the money—every single cent."

"What do you mean?"

"I mean he cleaned out all the bank accounts. He left my mother penniless."

She sounded outraged. "But how? He can't just do that!"

"He did." I still felt the weight of those memories like a shackle. A stone around my neck I dragged everywhere. The anger and shame. "We stayed in our house as long as we could, but he stopped paying the mortgage and the utilities." I turned to Claire. "Do you see now why he's poison? What kind of man takes everything and abandons his wife and baby?"

"And you too," she added softly. "He also abandoned you."

"My sister was only two." My throat went tight, remembering

what Eliza had been like back then. A toddler just learning about the world. So trusting. I closed my eyes.

Claire's warm hand stroked my face, and I reached up to slip my fingers through hers, held them to me.

"I wanted to protect them," I told her, my voice rough, "but I didn't know how."

"You were just a kid yourself."

"I know, but it's not how I felt. Eventually we were evicted from our house." I forced myself to continue, pushing forward to tell her the rest of it. "The utilities were shut off. My mom had been looking for a job, but it was difficult with a toddler to take care of, and I was in school all day, so I couldn't help." I licked my lips. "We wound up in a homeless shelter."

Claire's eyes were on me, and I saw them widen in the dark.

"Seven days. The worst week of my life." I'd never forget that first night, the helplessness I felt. I blamed myself for letting it happen, for not knowing what to do or how to prevent it.

And then there was the rage toward my father. Even now it was like pouring gasoline on fire. "I found out later he'd been on a ski vacation that same week."

"You're kidding," she breathed. "That's horrible."

"It *was* horrible," I acknowledged. "The only way I could get through it was to use my anger, to tell myself I'd get even someday."

She went quiet. I tried to imagine what she was thinking, trying to process the selfish monster I was related to. "What happened after seven days?"

"My aunt Linda—Doug's mom—took us in. She's my dad's sister. She agreed to watch Eliza during the day. Long enough that my mom could find work and eventually get her teaching certificate."

Claire nodded. "Doug's mom sounds like a kind woman."

I snorted softly. The dragon lady was a piece of work, but I'd never forget what she did for us. *And of course, she's never let us forget it either.* "She has her moments," I admitted in a dry voice. "Not all of them good."

I thought of how she told me I was selfish on the phone not long ago. A selfish boy who had turned into a selfish man. But then I thought of Doug, of how I'd agreed to help him win Claire's heart, yet here I was lying in bed with her.

Aunt Linda was right. I was selfish.

For a split second, I even considered giving Claire up, somehow turning things back around in my cousin's favor.

I won't do it.

A powerful stubbornness took hold of me. Selfish or not, I didn't care. I wanted her. Consequences be damned.

"What is it?" she asked, obviously sensing my churning emotions.

"Nothing."

"I'm so sorry for what the three of you went through."

In the night's quiet, surrounded by angry memories and guilt, our conversation brought out fears I seldom examined in the light of day. Vulnerabilities I didn't like to think about, how the rug could be yanked out from under me at any time.

I pulled her in tight. "Stay with me," I whispered fiercely. "Stay with me always."

My gut told me this was right. She was right. It sucked that it had to come at a cost to Doug, but what was I supposed to do? Give her up?

I pulled back to look at Claire, our faces close in the dark.

"I'm here," she said softly, stroking my jaw. "I'm not going anywhere."

I nodded with relief and then kissed her. Tenderly at first, her lips petal soft.

She let me explore her mouth and then her body, so warm and willing. Every night I wanted her, but tonight was different. Tonight I needed her, and she gave herself to me with sweet abandon.

I'd been with so many women, but none of them had ever been like this. None of them had ever felt so right.

I WAS on the edge of sleep, lying on my back with my eyes closed. Blood pumped through my veins thick and slow. I felt peaceful. Satisfied. Claire was beside me, and all that anger and guilt seemed miles away.

"Did you wear a condom?"

My eyes jerked open. Any sense of peace evaporated. "I forgot." I sat up, a wave of panic gripping me. "Goddamn, I completely forgot."

Her head was turned, and she appeared to be thinking things over. "It's probably okay," she said finally. "My period is due any day now."

"It is?"

She nodded.

I relaxed a little. "All right."

We both lay back down with Claire's head on my shoulder. I tried to relax again but found myself staring up at the ceiling. I couldn't believe I'd forgotten protection. I never forgot. Someone in my position was vulnerable to all kinds of craziness.

I began to imagine what would happen if Claire got pregnant. Obviously I'd handle every expense. That wouldn't even be an issue. No child of mine would ever have to worry about money or wind up in a homeless shelter.

But then a peculiar thing happened. I began to imagine an actual child. A little girl. What would she look like? Would her hair be dark like mine? Or maybe blonde curls like Claire? With the two of us as her parents, she'd be a pistol, that was for sure. I imagined light blue eyes smiling up at me. Hopefully she'd get Claire's pretty voice and maybe my head for numbers. I pictured the three of us out on the beach together. Laughter and little yellow rain boots splashing along the water's edge.

"Have you ever wanted kids?" Claire asked, startling me out of my fantasy.

The little girl faded, and I was reluctant to let her go. In the past when people had asked me that question, I'd always given a careless affirmative, but now I gave it real thought.

"Yes, when the time is right," I said, realizing it was true. I wanted them. "How about you?"

"I've always wanted them. Ethan and I were trying for a baby when he cheated on me."

I shook my head. Jesus, could that ex of hers be any more of a loser?

Both of us were silent, and I sensed awkwardness, especially in light of my forgetting the rubber. "Listen, if something happened, I'd take care of everything. You know that right?"

"Take care of everything?"

"If you were to get pregnant accidentally. You wouldn't have to worry."

She was quiet, and I found myself imagining it again, how much it would change my life. With amazement, I realized my earlier sense of panic had been replaced with a kind of yearning.

Claire still hadn't spoken. "Are you okay?" I asked.

"I'm *not*, actually." There was a strange note in her voice.

I changed position and faced her. "What is it, sweetheart? Are you worried?"

"No, it's not that."

"Because everything will be all right. I promise."

She moved away from me and sat up. "I have to tell you something, and you aren't going to like it."

"What?"

"If I get pregnant accidentally, I'm keeping the baby. You should know that."

My brows went up.

"Because I've wanted kids my whole life, and not having them has been my biggest regret. So if you want to get careless with condoms, you better prepare for the results." She gave me a weighted look. "And it won't be something you can just 'take care of' because the timing isn't right."

I sat up too. "That's not what I meant when I said I'd take care of everything. I meant I'd take care of you and the child."

"You did?" Her eyes widened, and I could see I'd knocked the wind out of her argument. "Oh." She went quiet.

"I don't run away from my obligations."

She nodded. "I just didn't want any misunderstandings."

I smiled. "Damn, listen to you. You're like a mama bear without her cub."

"I guess I am. I can't help it." She threw her hands up. "Am I totally freaking you out?"

"No. I like that you speak your mind."

She turned to me. "You do? Even now?"

"Absolutely." I thought of all the women I'd dated over the years who played head games or told me what they thought I wanted to hear. Until this moment, I'd never realized just how much I hated it. I leaned forward and kissed her shoulder. "I don't even mind your occasional temper. In fact, I like that too."

"My temper? I don't have a temper!"

I gave her a look, and she laughed.

"Okay," she conceded, "maybe I do have a temper. It's weird because I was such a doormat during my marriage."

"You were?" I had to admit I was surprised. "I find that hard to believe."

"I was always trying to keep the peace. I gave in to Ethan with practically everything."

"Then it sounds like you've changed."

That gave her pause. "You're right, I have changed. I don't put up with anyone's crap anymore." She pointed at my chest. "Even yours. I don't care how intimidating people say you are—you don't bother me a bit."

I chuckled. "I've noticed."

We were both smiling, but then she sighed. "I should get an IUD or go on the pill again to be on the safe side."

"Probably," I acknowledged.

Our eyes were still on each other when my stomach took a dip. My chest went tight, and I couldn't look away. Everything about her moved me. She was so pretty and tough sitting here in the middle of her fairy-tale house. I already knew I was losing my head.

"Is that really your biggest regret?" I asked, genuinely curious. "Not having kids?"

Claire nodded and then glanced toward the window. "It is. I know how crazy that sounds, since my divorce was so ugly, but I've always wanted them." She turned back to me and appeared to be considering something. "What's your biggest regret?"

"I don't have regrets," I said immediately.

"Really? Eliza once told me that. So there's nothing?"

I shrugged. "I don't think so."

"You're lucky."

"I suppose I am." I was silent then, thinking it over. But then my breath halted as a terrible truth struck me. A boom of thunder.

I *did* have a regret.

But only one.

I regretted not making my father pay for what he did to us. All those years he spent living like a king, he never suffered any consequences for his actions. In my eyes, he'd committed a crime against us and got away with it.

I thought about my texts with the CEO of Atlas earlier. Just gathering information—or at least that was what I told myself. But now I understood what I'd been dancing around all night.

A situation this perfect wasn't going to come along again.

To be honest, I relished the poetic justice of NorthStone—the company I'd helped build from nothing—being the one to crush him, to leave him bankrupt and penniless just like he'd left my mom, Eliza, and me.

"What are you thinking about?" Claire asked. "You're scowling."

My eyes flashed to hers, and I realized I couldn't tell her any of this. Not yet. I'd have to figure out a way later though if I went ahead with this land deal. "Just the past."

"I know I kind of forced it out of you. I hope you're not angry."

"No, I'm glad I told you." And I *was* glad. She needed to know, to understand where I was coming from. I reached for her hand. "I want us to be close."

"Me too." She smiled and then yawned. "Do you want to try and get some more sleep?"

"Sure."

I spooned her from behind again, and it wasn't long before I heard her soft, even breathing, but I didn't sleep. Instead, I spent the rest of the night going over what I knew had to be done.

TWENTY-FIVE

~ Claire ~

T he next morning when I woke up, Philip was already awake and dressed. We usually lingered in bed until my alarm went off, but this morning he was sitting at my kitchen table texting someone.

"You're up early." I touched his shoulder on the way to the bathroom.

"I had a few things to take care of." The phone rang in his hand—that western tune. "It's Gavin." He stood up. "I'm going to take this outside."

He kissed my forehead before heading out the front door. I went into the bathroom and wet my hair a little, trying to comb down the wild mess it had become. Afterward, I went to the kitchen and started fresh coffee. There was an empty bowl with bits of cereal in the sink.

From the front window, I could see Philip on his phone, pacing the front yard like a caged tiger. He wore dark slacks and a gray button-down shirt.

A twinge of worry needled its way into me. Ethan used to take phone calls in private too, and stupid me, I'd always believed him when he'd told me they were clients. Later I figured out he was talking to Ivy.

I shook my head and turned back to the coffee maker. I needed to stop thinking like this. Philip wasn't cheating on me. That was absurd.

I could hear my birds getting restless beneath the sheet and went over to remove it for them.

"Kiss, kiss," squawked Calico Jack.

"Good morning to you too," I said. I didn't let them out, just stood and cooed to them for a little while.

By the time Philip came back inside, I was dressed and sitting on my bed going over my schedule for the day, coffee and a bowl of fruit nearby. I'd cut up a portion for my birds and was eating the rest myself.

"Is everything okay?" I asked when he came over to sit on the edge of the bed next to me.

"It's fine. I have to go to Seattle."

I put my fork down. "Today?"

He nodded. "Something's come up. I'm flying there this morning."

"Nothing bad, I hope."

"No." He let his breath out. "Just something that needs my immediate attention."

Logically, I knew he and Gavin were running this successful venture capital firm, that their main offices were in Seattle, and that he had to go there sometimes. I mean, he couldn't just spend every night here with me.

His phone rang again, and he stood up to pull it from his front pocket. I watched him answer and start talking to someone named Bob about a house remodel. They went over a schedule for the next week.

"Who's Bob?" I asked after he hung up.

"He's the head contractor I hired to oversee all the jobs for Doug's business. It's gotten too time-consuming for me."

"There's that much new work?" Philip had told me how Doug's business was languishing before he stepped in.

He nodded. "Yes, quite a bit."

"That's amazing."

Philip seemed almost embarrassed. He glanced down at his phone again before slipping it into his front pocket. "It's no big deal. It's just what I do."

"But how did you do it?"

He sat down on the bed again and shrugged. "It's like being a mechanic."

"A mechanic?"

"The way I see it, every business is like a machine, and sometimes certain parts aren't working properly. I figure out which parts are broken and then fix them."

"You make it sound so easy, though I'm guessing it's not."

He moved closer. "Listen, I've been thinking about something. It's Friday. Why don't you fly out and join me tonight? We can stay at my place for a change."

My eyes widened. "Your place?"

"You haven't been there yet."

I thought about it, and my interest was piqued. "It would be nice to see where you live."

"The house is all right. It's been a good investment." He grinned. "However, it does have a spectacular shower."

That was when I noticed his hair was damp and he smelled like green apple shampoo. "Did you already take a shower?"

He nodded. "I missed you in there, but I didn't want to wake you. You were sleeping so hard."

I thought back to last night, to the way we'd been up talking. "Is everything really okay?"

His brows came together with concern. "Why would you think otherwise?"

"I don't know. It was kind of intense last night." All those things I'd said about wanting kids had probably freaked him out. Most guys would be running for the hills after having a discussion like that.

"If you haven't noticed, I like intense. It was good we talked. I want us to know everything about each other."

"Are you sure I didn't scare you away?"

He gave me a considering look. "Do you honestly think I scare that easily?"

"No." I suspected when Philip dug in his heels, he'd be very difficult to scare.

He took the bowl of fruit away, moved my planner aside, and then leaned in and kissed me.

"You taste like cereal," I whispered.

"And you taste like a sexy woman." He slid his hand beneath my shirt and kissed me some more. "I wish I could spend all day here with you."

I wound my arms around his neck, a delicious heat moving through my limbs. "How soon do you have to leave?"

"Too soon, unfortunately." He sighed, but then his expression grew serious. "Listen, I seldom share the things I told you last night."

"I know." I played with the curling ends of his dark hair.

"This is new for me... the way I am with you."

I didn't say anything. Instead, I ran my hand along his jaw. He'd shaved this morning, and his skin was smooth for a change.

"It's obvious I'm crazy about you."

I nodded. "I'm glad."

"You're glad?"

"Yes." I knew I should say more but didn't.

Philip's eyes stayed on mine, and his mouth kicked up at the corner.

"What is it?"

He shook his head. "You *do* realize I'm the woman in this relationship."

"Really? I don't know about that." Leaning forward, I ran my hand over his thigh, then cupped his genitals. I lowered my voice. "You don't feel like a woman to me."

He licked his lips. "Keep your hand there. Let's make sure."

My eyes widened "Oh my gosh. What's happening?" His cock grew hard beneath my palm. "These womanly bits of yours are starting to concern me."

"You may need to examine them more closely."

I slid my fingers over the erection now tenting his slacks. "I think I better," I said, reaching for his belt buckle. "For science."

I unfastened his pants and pushed them down while he watched me with half-lidded eyes. My desire for him was this persistent ache that never went away. I didn't know what had gotten into me. "I feel like a sex maniac around you."

He grinned. "Thank God."

He was trying to tug my jeans and panties off, and I helped kick them aside. I reached over and plucked a condom from the nightstand. After rolling it onto him, I straddled his hips, but Philip had other ideas. Before I knew it, he'd flipped me onto my back, his chest over me, his hand gripping the brass headboard for traction.

I gasped as the full length of him thrust into me. Pleasure flooded every nerve ending, and all my senses lit up. I had to catch my breath. He stifled a groan when I grabbed at the muscles in his back, digging my fingernails into the shirt fabric.

Philip wasn't rough, but he took me hard, both of us losing our minds. Our moans and panting noises filled the room, along with the persistent rattle of the bed hitting the wall. When I came, it was with violent intensity. I might have even screamed.

He collapsed onto me with a loud groan. "Jesus... fuck."

From a distance, I realized my birds were part of the cacophony. I tried to move to check on them, but I was too exhausted. "My birds... I hope they're okay."

Philip's low chuckle vibrated against my chest. "Sweetheart, those birds know exactly what we're up to."

I sighed. He was probably right. They didn't sound distressed, more like they were cheering us on. My eyes fell shut. "They *are* both males."

"It might be time for a female parakeet."

"I can't. They'll start laying eggs and having babies."

He turned his head to the side so our faces were close. "Is that right?"

"It is." He was still lying on top of me, but I didn't mind his weight. It felt good.

His lips parted as he fought to catch his breath. His mouth looked so sexy, I leaned in and kissed him. "I was noisy. Maybe that's what got them going. I think I might have screamed."

"You definitely screamed."

My eyes widened. "I did?"

He nodded. "Trust me, that scream is going into my memory bank for future use."

I pushed against his shoulder and laughed.

"You think I'm joking, but I'm not." He was grinning at me.

"All right, fine. I might have some future-use memories of you too," I admitted.

His brows went up, and his grin grew wider. "This is news. Tell me, what are they?"

I shook my head and looked away, though I couldn't stop smiling.

"Come on," he coaxed. "I need to know."

I turned so our faces were close again. "This," I whispered. "Right now."

His eyes stayed on mine.

We fell quiet. This was incredible between us, and we both knew it. The stuff artists and poets had been inspired by for centuries.

Philip's gaze grew intense. "I love you, Claire."

"You do?"

He nodded, his voice rough. "I do."

I didn't reply. My heart was pounding. I wasn't quite sure what to say.

"You've captured me."

I stroked his face. "You've captured me too."

───────

I'D NEVER BEEN on a privately chartered plane before, and it wasn't what I expected.

For starters, both pilots came out and shook my hand, introducing themselves. One was named Benjamin, though everyone called him Ben. The other was Jason. They each wore a white shirt with a dark tie and pilot insignia on their shoulders.

The flight attendant's name was Marnie, and she asked if I'd like anything to drink before takeoff. "There's wine, or we have chilled champagne, if you prefer."

"A glass of white wine, please," I said.

I glanced around the inside of the plane. I'd only ever flown commercial, and this was a very different experience. I was sitting in a big leather chair with a table in front of me. There were five more leather chairs, two of them across from the couch.

Yes, the couch.

Marnie brought me my wine with a smile. She was very pretty. "It's only a short flight to Seattle. Not enough time for a meal, but would you like some chocolate truffles?"

"Okay."

I was trying to act cool, like this was all normal for me. She brought me the truffles, and I offered her one, but she declined. Then I felt stupid because I realized I probably wasn't supposed to offer her one.

The flight was a little bumpier than I was used to, but luckily it was short. In thirty minutes we were preparing to land.

I looked out the window. It was early evening, and the buildings were lit up. We landed smoothly, and once we were on the ground, it was obvious we were in a part of the airport surrounded by other private jets.

Ben, Jason, and Marnie all lined up by the door and wished me a great weekend.

"Do you know where I'm supposed to meet Philip?" I asked them.

Marnie smiled. "Mr. North left instructions that he'd meet you on the tarmac."

I nodded. "Okay, thank you."

I walked down the metal stairs into the warm summer evening like an astronaut descending onto the moon.

I mean, Mr. North?

I looked around the tarmac but didn't see Philip. All I saw were more planes. Between the noise and the smell of jet fuel, it was disorienting. My head swam. I nearly got my phone out, but finally I saw him a short distance away in front of a dark SUV, waving me over.

He wore the same clothes as earlier and looked just like his normal self, like the guy who'd told me in bed this morning that he loved me. Not this Mr. North person.

I walked toward him, and he watched me with a grin.

"Hey, sweetheart," he said, pulling me in for a hug. He smelled like home, like the apple shampoo from my tiny shower, and it helped. I felt better. He drew back and gazed down at me. "I missed you, my pirate princess."

"It's only been a few hours," I said with a smile.

"I don't care." He stroked my hair. "Did you miss me?"

"Yes."

"How much?"

"A lot." In truth, I've been obsessing about him all day. I couldn't stop reliving that "I love you." Even on the plane ride here, I was going over it again in my mind.

"Good." Then he kissed me, his lips warm and sensual.

I responded to him like I always did, like a flame ignited.

"So how was the flight?" he asked, reaching down to take the overnight bag from my hand.

"It was nice. They served me wine and chocolate truffles." My gaze went to his car, a dark green Range Rover. He opened the rear and put my bag inside. It looked like his was in there too.

"Is that your bag?"

He nodded. "I just came from work and haven't been home yet."

We climbed into the car, and I checked out the interior while Philip drove us out of the airport. There was an opened bottle of water in the seat between us and what looked like a granola bar wrapper stuffed next to it.

I told him how I'd let Violet know I was coming here and that Leah agreed to check on my birds. "Do you think you'll be in Seattle all week?" I asked. "Because the Pirate Days party is next weekend."

"I know." He glanced at me. "I'll be there."

We talked some more. I told him I'd invited his mom and Elliot to the party and that Eliza was bringing a fellow actor from the theater as her date—which I figured would make him happy, since he was so weird about the idea that she and Gavin might be interested in each other.

As we headed into Seattle, he asked me about my day. I described it, and as usual, he listened with real interest. That was something I'd learned about Philip, and I'd bet it was a big part of his success.

While most people only half listened, waiting for their turn to talk, Philip actually listened. He had an incredible memory for details too. He probably knew as much about my clients as I did. It was amazing.

"How was your day?" I asked. "Why did you have to come to Seattle?"

He shrugged. "It was fine. Meetings mostly." He glanced at me. "Are you hungry? Because I'm starved. I haven't had dinner yet."

He seemed evasive, but I told myself to calm down. Between all my trust issues from Ethan and the general newness of being on Philip's turf, it had me on edge. "I'm kind of hungry. I haven't had dinner yet either."

After some discussion, we went to an Italian restaurant near his house. "It's a small mom-and-pop place," he told me. "The food is excellent."

I knew he lived on the water in Magnolia, and I had to admit I was curious to see his house. By the time we drove to the restaurant, parked, and were seated at a booth by the window, I was feeling better. Less on edge.

"Do you eat here a lot?" I asked, glancing around the restaurant. It was Friday night, and the place was busy.

"No. I mean, I do, but it's always takeout. I've never eaten inside like this."

I nodded and turned back to him.

He leaned forward with his arms on the table, and I was struck all over again by how sexy he was. Every little movement. His shirt sleeves were rolled up, and even the dark hair on his forearms was turning me on.

"Is everything okay?" he asked. "You seem a little weird since I picked you up."

"I'm fine." I wasn't sure how to explain my astronaut feeling without it sounding bad.

He reached for my hand with concern. "It's not because of what I said this morning, is it?"

"No, that's not it."

He nodded, his eyes still on mine.

"I'm glad you said what you did. I've been thinking about it all day."

"And what have you been thinking?"

I licked my lips. "I want to be more like you."

"What do you mean?"

"Less afraid. You never worry that we're moving too fast, or worry about holding anything back."

"You're right. If I want something, I go for it."

I took a deep breath and let it out. "I want to go for it too."

He grinned. "Now you're speaking my language." His gaze dropped to my mouth. "I have an idea. Let's get takeout instead."

My breath caught at his expression. The promise of intimacy and pleasure.

We told the waitress when she came back and then waited for our food up front by the cash register, standing close together while he held my hand.

Once we were back in his car again, Philip leaned over the seat, reaching for me and kissing me hungrily. "What have you done to me? I can't get enough of you." He shook his head and seemed to force himself to turn away. "Let's go before I completely lose my wits and take you right here in this car."

He started the engine, and we headed out. I tried to look around the neighborhood, to absorb my surroundings and calm myself, because I'd already lost my wits. Was I really going to go for it? Risk another broken heart? Or even worse, a betrayal? Did I even have it in me to approach this relationship with the same gusto as he did?

Philip kept looking over at me as he drove, our eyes catching. Each time, a spark of excitement flew through me.

Eventually we turned onto a small road dotted with nice homes on one side, all of them along the water. He took a left into a narrow driveway that led down a short hill and through a keypad-locked gate. It leveled off in front of a house that was not what I expected.

"This is it," he said.

My mouth fell open with astonishment. "Wait, this is your house?" It was a giant glass and cement palace.

He turned the engine off. "Come here." He tried to reach for me again, but I was too busy gawking.

It was way bigger than Sullivan House. It was enormous. "And you live here *alone?*" I was expecting his house to be impressive, but nothing like this. "Are you planning to start your own religious cult? Is that it?"

He chuckled. "No."

"Because I think you could."

He rolled his eyes. "Very funny."

We got out of the car, and I held the takeout food while he grabbed our bags from the back. I felt disoriented again like I had at the airport. All this show of wealth didn't seem like Philip. It was too much. Where was the guy with the beat-up sneakers? The one who laid down the floor in my spare room?

At the entrance, he stood and gazed up into what looked like a small camera.

"What is that?"

There was a click and the front door opened.

"Iris scan," he explained. "I have it set up for keyless entry."

"Like a retina scan?"

He shook his head. "That's an older technology. This is better and more secure. It's one of our investments."

Inside the house smelled like lemons, and right away I wondered what type of cleaning products were used to leave that scent. It was nice. Fresh and clean.

"Do you have a maid service?"

He carried our bags along with what looked like an extra computer case. "Of course."

"Do they leave you a list of products they use?" I glanced around the entryway. The floors were marble tile that I knew from experience dulled easily, but they were nice and shiny. "Could I see the invoices they've given you?"

Philip went still, and I glanced over at him. I realized it was probably weird that I was asking about his maid service. I mean, here he was living like a king in this palace while I lived like a peasant in a tiny carriage house.

But he was nodding at me with approval. "Sure, I'll have a few of them forwarded to you."

He led me through the main living room, which was like a hotel lobby except it was completely empty.

"Why don't you have any furniture?" I asked. There were large windows everywhere looking out onto the water. The view was magnificent.

To my surprise, instead of going into the kitchen to drop off the food, he led me up a staircase. "Where are we going?"

"I mainly hang out upstairs."

"You do?"

At the top of the stairs, he took a turn and led me down a long empty hallway. It let out into another living area like the one below us but smaller. As we walked through, I could hear him giving voice commands about the lights and temperature. Various lamps flicked on.

I glanced around the room. A couple of nice leather sofas were in the center with a group of flat-paneled televisions mounted on the wall across from them. Shelves were filled with books and other items. Some photos and prints hung on the walls, and Persian rugs lay over shiny hardwood floors. The overall aesthetic was pleasing.

I followed him to a kitchen area. It was state-of-the-art and certainly bigger than mine but not overly grand. More like a fancy mini kitchen.

"Why do you have six televisions?" I asked, glancing back to the living room.

He took the food from me and put it on the counter. "You'll see." He motioned with his head. "Come on, I haven't shown you my bedroom yet."

We walked past the kitchen and through some double doors, and there it was—the master bedroom. Large windows dominated the space along with a king-sized bed. The room colors were shades of blue and green with a lot of dark wood.

He brought the bags over to a small sitting area. I started to walk around the room, but he pulled me in close and tried to kiss me again.

"So you have this giant house, but you only live in a small part of it?" I asked, avoiding his kiss.

"I bought the house purely as an investment." He brushed my hair aside and kissed my neck.

My eyes fell shut against my will. His lips felt so nice. "Has it been a good investment?"

"I paid cash when the market was depressed, and the value has more than tripled." He pulled back and seemed to consider his own words. His brows furrowed. "It may be time to sell soon," he murmured.

Watching his face, I recognized that expression. He wore it a lot when he was talking about his various business interests. I realized it was true what he'd told me that night on the blanket in my front yard —making money was like a hobby for him.

I felt myself relax. This was the guy I knew and cared about. Obviously this crazy house was just part of his hobby.

I stroked Philip's hair with affection. "You're an unusual man, you know that?"

That seemed to pull him out of his thoughts, and his mouth kicked up at the corner. "You're only now figuring that out?"

"I guess I am."

His gaze softened. "Am I unusual enough for you to fall in love with?"

"We'll see." I smiled. "Maybe."

"Maybe?" He studied me with a devilish grin. "It's clear you're going to need more convincing."

"And how are you planning to do that?"

"You'll see." He leaned down and kissed me.

I wrapped my arms around his neck and didn't want to talk anymore. Instead I let him convince me as much as he liked.

A LITTLE WHILE LATER, I discovered why Philip had six televisions. We were sitting on the couch, both of us wearing sweatpants and eating our Italian takeout.

"*Screens on*," he said in a commanding tone, and all six televisions flickered to life.

"Does everything in your house run on voice commands?"

He shrugged. "Some things are automated, like the windows. Most everything else uses voice, or there are tablets for more options."

I glanced around and saw what he meant, noting a tablet on the coffee table and one on each end table.

"*Standard channels*," he said to the system, and the screens appeared to be automatically changing stations. He turned to me. "Each screen is programmed to connect to a different news network."

"But how can you watch all six at the same time? Isn't it too noisy?" I took a bite from the plate of eggplant parmesan on my lap.

"I keep them muted with the captions running, and if something interests me, then I unmute it."

He showed me using both voice commands and a remote controller. He unmuted various news stations—one of them C-SPAN, of course.

I studied the screens in front of me. The channels were varied and included both international and domestic news stations. "My dad would have loved this," I said. They reminded me so much of him, that a wave of sadness washed over me. I looked at Philip. "I wish you could have met my dad."

"Me too." He reached over and took my hand, squeezing it. "I think I would have liked him."

I nodded, my throat going tight. "You guys would have gotten along great."

"Are you okay, sweetheart?"

"I'm fine." I looked at the screens again. "I have these moments, but then they pass, you know?"

"Is there anything I can do?"

I shook my head and took a deep breath. "I'm okay."

He turned back to the televisions now on mute once more. With a command, he told them to shut down, and they all flickered off.

"Hey, I have an idea." He turned back to me with interest. "What do you say we watch *The Godfather*?"

I laughed.

"Is that funny?"

I shook my head. "Just look at us. We're sitting here wearing sweats, eating takeout, and watching television. Is this the glamorous life or what?"

Philip stroked his chin and appeared to be thinking it over. "I could spill some food on myself. Burp and fart a little. Would that be glamorous enough for you?"

I sighed. "Would you do that for me?"

"Anything for you, my pirate princess." He gave me a quick kiss before picking up his plate of food again.

"That's so sweet."

"And besides"—he leaned back on the couch, resting his bare feet on the large stone coffee table—"not only will you not let me buy you anything, but you refuse to let me take you anywhere—not even the Caribbean."

I didn't bother to respond since it was a discussion we'd had a few times. He wanted to spend money on me, but I wouldn't let him.

Instead, my eyes roamed the length of him. He wore gray sweats and a black T-shirt that had a circuit board with the logo of some company on it. Despite what I'd just said, he looked incredibly hot. "Seriously though, aren't you supposed to be out at a charity event somewhere cutting ribbons and donating giant checks?"

Philip raised an eyebrow at me as he took a large bite from his plate of spaghetti.

"Fighting crime every night while your butler irons your clothes and polishes your weapons."

He nearly choked with laughter. I watched him reach for his glass of water and take a drink. "You seem to have me confused with Batman."

"Do I?" I tilted my head.

In the end, I agreed to watch *The Godfather* in his movie theater.

Yes, his movie theater.

It was in another part of the house. Small and cozy, decorated with side columns like a Greek theater. The ceiling had twinkling lights that looked like stars. The chairs were attached to each other, but if you lifted the drink holders, they converted into couches. We curled up on one together, munching on a bowl of grapes. I grabbed a couple of Kit Kat bars too. I'd discovered his kitchen was full of food, and he admitted he'd had his assistant, Sam, fill it with groceries before I arrived today.

"I told him all about your Kit Kat bar habit," Philip said with a grin.

To my surprise, the film wasn't boring like I remembered. It was engrossing.

"I don't understand why the Mafia would consider it business and not personal," I said, breaking off half of my chocolate bar for him. "Even when they lose the people they love."

"Because it's the life they chose."

Afterward, when the credits were rolling, he studied me. "So tell me I was right. Is that a great movie or what?"

"You were right. I loved it."

He nodded. "The second film is just as good. We'll have to watch that too."

We were lying on the couch. It was late, and I was tired but still felt this excited energy like I always did around Philip.

"I still have one thing left to show you," he murmured, lightly trailing his fingers down my arm.

"You do?"

He nodded. "My special room."

"Special room?"

"You're going to enjoy it, trust me."

A sense of unease shot through me. "This special room's not red, is it?"

"Red?" His brows came together.

"Because I'm not interested in any kind of special room that's red."

He gave me a strange look. "No, it isn't red."

I sighed with relief. "Okay, good. Just checking."

"It's mostly light tile. The sauna is wood, obviously, but the shower is going to blow your mind."

"So this special room is your bathroom?"

He nodded. "What else would it be?"

TWENTY-SIX

~ Claire ~

Philip's special room was green and white tile. The toilet flushed silently, and the towel warmers turned on automatically with the shower. There was also a sauna and a sunken tub that overlooked the water. It was great, except for the ridiculous size.

"Are you planning to play hockey in here with your religious cult?" I asked.

"As a matter of fact, I am. As soon as the new uniforms arrive."

The shower was huge too, though I didn't mind that. It even had a place to sit down, which I loved for shaving my legs. Shaving in my tiny shower at home involved gymnastic-style contortions.

And then there were the shower sprayers, not just on top but down the sides of the wall. If you turned them all on, it sprayed you from every angle.

"This is like heaven," I said standing with all that warm water jetting on me.

Philip came up behind me. "See, I knew you'd love it."

I turned to face him. "You realize my whole bathroom would fit in this shower."

"It would," he agreed.

I pulled away from him to pick out some shampoo from a rack on the side that contained all sort of bottles. I chose one to put in the shower holder near us. When I came back, he reached for me, but I pulled away again.

"Hey, where are you going?"

"I forgot the conditioner." I stood for a moment, looking through my options. Almost all of them were salon brands and high-end. "Do you really use all these?"

"No. I had Sam take care of it before you arrived."

"Sam sounds like a great assistant. Most men don't know a thing about hair products."

"He's excellent, though I'm sure it was his assistant, Lorna, who picked those out."

"Wait, your assistant has an assistant?"

"Of course." Philip pulled me into his arms again. "I'm a demanding tyrant who needs a dozen minions scurrying around me. Haven't you noticed?"

I didn't reply. The truth was just the opposite. Most men in his position probably did a have a dozen minions, but it was clear Philip enjoyed his privacy.

"Oh, wait, I need one more thing," I said, slipping out of his arms.

"What now?"

"Well, there's some very nice soap, and I forgot to grab a bar."

When I finally came back to him, he wrapped his arms around me and sighed. "I can't believe I'm saying this, but I think I miss your tiny shower."

PHILIP'S BEDROOM windows were so huge it gave the illusion of being outside on the water at night.

"Why are there no curtains?" I asked. We were lying in bed together, though he was texting with someone on his phone. "Don't you feel weird walking around naked? What if somebody flies a drone out there to spy on you?"

"Then the antiaircraft gun on the roof will shoot it down."

I rolled back to look at him. "Tell me you're joking."

"I'm joking."

I stared at him.

He snorted. "What do you think I am, *a superhero?*"

I laughed but then quieted as I glanced at the windows again. "You probably are a superhero," I muttered.

He smirked but couldn't be deterred from his phone. I was beginning to understand why his mom and sister had buried it on the beach. I was tempted to do the same thing.

"Who could you be texting with at this hour? It's the middle of the night."

"Work."

"What are you working on?"

He stopped what he was doing. There was a strange expression on his face. It almost looked like guilt, but that couldn't be right.

"What is it?" I asked.

He shook his head. "Nothing."

Like before, I had the sense he was being evasive. "Is there something you're not telling me?"

"There is something."

"What?"

He put his phone down, and his expression grew serious. "I *am* Batman."

I groaned and rolled my eyes. Reaching around, I grabbed my pillow and smacked him with it. "You asshat."

He laughed, putting his arm up to defend himself. I hit him again.

I tried to hit him a third time, but he was faster and grabbed the pillow from me, tossing it aside. He pushed me down on the bed and lay over me. "Did you really just call me an asshat?"

"Yes, I did." My voice turned sassy. "What are you going to do about it?"

He held my hands up so I couldn't get away. Laughing, I squirmed, trying to release my wrists, but his grip was too tight.

"I wouldn't mind wearing your ass as a hat," he murmured, his face close to mine. "In fact, I've worn it a number of times already."

"You have," I admitted.

"So technically *you're* the asshat."

I giggled, still squirming.

"In fact, I love wearing your ass so much I'm going to put it on tonight."

"You are?"

He grinned. "Definitely."

———

LATER, after he got creative with the hat wearing, we both fell asleep. Except I woke up. The room was dark and unfamiliar. I glanced over at Philip. He was sleeping soundly on his side, facing me.

Quietly, I slipped my sweatpants and tank top back on. I left the bedroom, figuring I'd get a drink of water.

He'd given me a tour of the house earlier and showed me his exercise room and his office. There were some guest bedrooms on the other side next to the movie theater. Apparently Eliza stayed over with friends occasionally. Mostly it was empty though.

I poured myself a cold glass from the fridge and decided to wander through his living room. The lights were off, but he'd taught me how to turn them on using voice commands, so I put them at a low setting.

I scanned his books—mostly nonfiction titles about business and economic theory. Apparently Philip wasn't big on reading fiction, though I did see a couple tech thrillers.

I looked at the photos next. There were a few of him when he was younger. I picked up one for a closer inspection.

It was a frame with a set of three pictures. The first one showed Philip as a little kid, smiling at a birthday party. In the second one, he was older with a little girl, obviously Eliza, in the woods near a lake, the two of them laughing. The last photo was of him as a teenager. He was standing with his mom and sister in someone's backyard. Everyone was smiling at the camera except Philip, who wore an intense expression.

"Claire?"

I turned my head.

"What are you doing out here, sweetheart?"

He walked toward me, and I couldn't help but admire the view. He hadn't bothered with a shirt, and his sweatpants rode low on his hips. His body was solid and muscular. His chest had a smattering of dark hair, and there was a happy trail that ran down from his belly button.

"I couldn't sleep."

I placed the photos back on the bookshelf as he came up and stood behind me, slipping his arms around my shoulders. He yawned. "I figured I wore you out."

"It's just being in a new place. Where were these photos taken?" I asked, pointing at the ones I'd put back.

He rested his cheek against my hair. "Let's see... the first one is my sixth birthday. The second one was camping in eastern Washington, and that last one was in our backyard right before my high school graduation."

I studied the photos some more. "The three of you have always been close, huh?"

He nodded. "We have."

"You're lucky to have them."

"I know."

I leaned back against him and closed my eyes. "I hate that I've become an orphan." I hated that I sounded so pitiful too. "I'm sorry, I shouldn't have said that. I'm just having a weird moment."

"That's not weird." He turned me around and held me close. "Do you want to come to bed and try to sleep again?" he asked softly.

"Okay."

I brought my glass of water with me and put it on the nightstand. We climbed back into the center of his huge bed, where I lay facing the windows while Philip spooned me.

Instead of sleeping, I looked out at the night sky, though I noticed a change. "Are the windows darker than they were before?"

"They are. It's electrochromic glass."

"What's that?"

"Smart glass. I have them set on a timer, so they get darker close to sunrise. It's a company we've invested in. They're still working out the kinks, but they're going to be very profitable once they do."

We both went quiet after that.

I closed my eyes and tried to sleep, but I was still too restless. "I'm sorry if I'm keeping you awake."

"That's all right," he murmured. "Would you like me to stroke your back?"

I looked over my shoulder at him. "Aren't you tired?"

"I don't mind. I like doing it."

"Okay, that would be nice."

It was something I'd recently discovered relaxed me—or more accurately, Philip discovered it.

He sat up partway, propped up on one elbow, while I pulled my tank top off. I lay on my stomach, facing him.

My eyes fell shut as soon as his hand slid down my back. It felt so good. He stroked my shoulders and then slowly down my spine. It wasn't a back rub, just a soft caress, and I loved it.

I sighed with pleasure, purring like a cat. Philip was so tactile and sensual. It was a new experience being with someone like him.

"Sweetheart, can I ask you something?"

"Yes," I murmured.

"What happened to your mom?"

My eyes drifted opened. "She left when I was a baby."

"Do you know why?"

"Apparently she couldn't handle being a wife and mother."

His hand still caressed me. "I'm sorry to hear that."

"It's okay." I took a deep breath. "I had my dad, and he was wonderful. I know it sounds hard to believe, but he made up for her not being around."

"I'm glad. Do you ever hear from her at all?"

"No, though I used to get occasional birthday cards. And then when I was ten, I visited her."

"What was that like?"

"Not great." I closed my eyes and told him the story of how I went and saw her in Oregon, where she lived in a hippie commune. "The whole thing was weird. I only had one day with her, and even then she didn't want to be around me. I spent the entire time playing with some kid named Mica." I remembered something and laughed. "It was the first time I ever smoked pot."

"You smoked pot when you were ten?"

"He offered it to me. I didn't know what it was, but I figured it must be okay with her."

"Jesus."

"Later I realized she probably didn't know anything about it."

"Did you hear from her after that?"

"Not really. A couple birthday cards. She never invited me again —not that I would have gone." I was quiet, thinking it over. "Some people just aren't meant to be parents."

"True."

"When I was younger, I used to feel sorry for myself that I missed out on having a mom, but now I feel sorry for her."

We both fell silent.

"I wonder if it has anything to do with your strong desire for kids," he murmured.

"What do you mean?"

"You were so close with your dad, but you missed out on what it's like to have a mother. Maybe you want to satisfy that desire by being one."

"I don't know. A lot of people want kids."

"It might not be the whole reason." He brushed my hair aside, his warm fingers caressing my neck.

I considered his words. It was true that I was intense about my yearning for children. "Maybe you're right. I've never thought of it like that. A part of me doesn't want to miss out a second time, you know?"

"That's understandable."

My eyes fell shut again while his hand stroked my body. Finally I began to fall asleep, and while I might have only dreamed it, just before drifting off, I could have sworn I heard him whisper, "Someday, Claire, if you let me, I'm going to give you everything you've ever wanted."

THE NEXT MORNING, as we waited in line at a coffee shop near his house, Philip informed me that we had theater tickets that night and then dinner reservations at one of Seattle's finest restaurants.

"We're not hanging out in our sweats again?" I teased.

"Sweetheart, I'd be happy to hang out in our sweats anytime." He leaned forward and whispered in my ear, "Though I prefer to hang out with you when you're wearing nothing at all."

I smiled up at him. Our eyes stayed on each other, and I knew we were both thinking of all the time we'd already spent wearing nothing at all.

After leaving with our drinks, we strolled down the sidewalk. I asked Philip if I could see his office downtown.

"You want to go to my office?" He took a drink from his bottle of orange juice and seemed surprised. "Now?"

"Is that weird? I just want to see where you work."

"I don't think I've ever dated a woman who wanted to see where I work."

"Really?"

"No." He was staring straight ahead and seemed deep in thought. Then he turned to me. "I'd love to show you our offices."

It turned out they were only a fifteen-minute drive from his house. For some reason, I'd expected them to be in a high-rise downtown, but he pulled up to a three-story building near Lake Union. It was modern and kind of funky, with glass and decorative metal beams across the front of the windows that ran from floor to ceiling. There were trees planted around the outside along with other foliage.

"This is it?"

He nodded. "It's new. We just moved here a year ago."

Looking around, I had to admit I liked it. "This is cool."

"Thanks. We wanted someplace more relaxed. We're not your typical venture firm, and it was time our offices reflected that."

After parking in the underground garage, he took me around the building. Although it was Saturday, there were still people around. He said hello to the ones we ran across, and no one seemed surprised to see him. I suspected he worked a lot on Saturdays.

His office was big but not crazy big. A large window faced toward Lake Union. There was a wall of flat-screens on one side, and I could tell it was the same setup he had at home. His desk had two other large screen monitors on them. The room's feel was modern. A rug with a multicolored geometric design dominated the space. There was a seating area to one side with a colorful glass sculpture that looked like a Chihuly in the corner.

Then it dawned on me. It *was* a Chihuly.

I stood gazing out the window. "So this is where you conquer the world?"

"It is."

I glanced over at him. He was sitting on the edge of his desk watching me. "What?"

"I like seeing you here."

"You do?"

He nodded, then held his hand out to me. "Come closer."

"Uh-oh. I know that look." I glanced at the door. It was closed, but there was an artsy glass wall next to it, and I wasn't sure how well people could see in if they walked past.

He chuckled. "I just want to kiss you, that's all."

I took his hand, and he pulled me against him. "Are you sure that's all?" I slipped my arms around his neck. He smelled like the fancy soap from his shower.

"Maybe grope you a little too." He slid his hands down over my bottom and squeezed.

"Hmm... kissing and groping. You're asking an awful lot."

"Am I?"

We smiled at each other. Except I noticed the smile didn't quite reach his eyes.

"Is everything okay?"

He shook his head. "Everything's fine."

He pulled me closer and hugged me tight. I wasn't sure what was going on, but I hugged him back. It reminded me of that night when he'd told me about his father.

"We don't have to go out later," I said. "If you want to hang out in our sweatpants again and watch movies, it's fine by me."

"No, I want to." He drew back. "I want to take you out for a nice evening. You deserve it."

I stroked his neck. "I always have a nice time with you no matter what we do."

"I know, but I don't get to spoil you enough," he whispered. "Let me spoil you for a change."

It had never occurred to me that my resistance to Philip buying me things might be a real problem. "Is that what's bothering you? That I don't let you spoil me?"

He gazed over my shoulder toward the window, his eyes

reflecting the sky. Finally, he shrugged. "Even though I understand it, I guess it does bother me."

I took in his handsome features, thought about how kind he always was to me. I made an instant decision. "Okay, I'll let you spoil me as much as you want for the rest of the day." That got his attention. "Except we can't leave the country, and you can't buy me a sailboat."

He nodded. "I can work with that."

"And no crazy-expensive jewelry or houses or cars. Or anything that costs more than—"

He kissed me, cutting me off, which was just as well because I'd probably have whittled it down to a bag of peanuts.

"Did you bring anything dressy to wear?" he asked, his face still close to mine.

That gave me pause. I'd packed a sundress, but it wasn't exactly dressy. "Not really."

He grinned. "Then let me dress you for tonight."

"Dress me?"

"Yes." He was already reaching for his phone. "Would that be acceptable?"

I didn't have time to think it over, because he was already speaking to Sam about taking me shopping.

"Tell him thank you for getting all that food at the house too," I said, interrupting. "And for the Kit Kat bars and the great shampoo."

I watched as Philip relayed my message to Sam. His eyes flashed to mine. "He says you're welcome."

I nodded and listened as they finished their conversation.

"Does Sam ever get a day off?" I asked after he hung up.

"Sure. He takes Saturday and Sunday off."

"But today's Saturday."

"Well"—he shrugged—"unless I need something."

I rolled my eyes. "What did you say about being a demanding tyrant?"

He smirked. "Trust me, I'm a generous boss. Sam is very well-compensated."

After we left his office, the afternoon became like something out of a movie. He took me to a ritzy clothing store downtown, where we apparently had an appointment. To be honest, walking in the shop, I was concerned. The clothes on the racks looked expensive and weird. I wasn't exactly into high fashion.

After being led into a private dressing room, we were offered coffee or champagne.

Apparently rich people drink a lot of champagne.

Luckily, Sasha, the saleswoman who helped me, knew what she was doing. After an hour of trying on clothes and shoes, we found a half dozen dresses that made my short, curvy body look more stunning than I ever thought possible. I picked out the dress I liked best, but to my surprise, Philip told her we'd take them all.

"But I only need one for tonight," I said.

"What about next time?" he countered.

He began asking Sasha about lingerie, telling her we needed bras and panties to go with everything. She nodded, taking notes on an iPad.

I put my hand on his arm to stop him. "Listen, I just want the one dress. That's it."

He turned to stare at me. I could feel Sasha staring too. For some reason, she seemed more interested in me than before.

Philip nodded and changed his instructions, telling her we'd just take the one dress and the shoes.

"Hmm, this one's different," I heard her murmur to herself as she changed the information on her iPad.

That comment didn't sit well. I wondered how many other women he'd brought to this store.

I began to get that strange feeling again. Disoriented, like I didn't belong here. Like I was only a tourist.

It didn't help that when we'd arrived, I saw a player from Seattle's football team, and then when leaving the shop, there was a famous rapper and his entourage headed back toward one of the dressing rooms.

"Have you shopped there before?" I asked once we were in Philip's car with the boxes in back.

He glanced at me. "Yes."

I nodded and took a deep breath, trying to push down any feelings of jealousy or insecurity.

He reached over for my hand. "Thank you for letting me do that. It was a pleasure to spoil you a little."

"The dress is gorgeous. I'm the one who should thank you."

He shook his head. "That's not necessary."

"I guess you really are my sugar daddy now." I meant it to come out light and teasing, but it came out with an edge.

Philip heard it too. "It makes me happy to buy you nice things." He lowered his voice. "Let me have this, Claire."

I studied him and realized it really did make him happy, that I was being peevish. "I'm sorry." I squeezed his hand. "You may continue with this day of spoiling me."

That night when we went out to the theater, I was glad for the new dress, the new shoes, and the sparkly new earrings I let him buy me at another shop. The dress was pink and black lace, tight in the waist with a low neckline. I felt glamorous beside him in his light gray suit. He wore a white shirt below it with an open collar and was deliciously handsome.

"Wow, you're like a total fox."

He laughed, then put his mouth to my ear and whispered, "More like a wolf to you, little girl."

Everything was going great, and we were having a fantastic time —until we got to the restaurant.

As we walked through the door, some other couple was already there, waiting for the maître d' to seat them. All night long, people had been coming up to Philip, so I thought nothing of it at first when this pair seemed to know him. The guy was older, probably in his fifties, though the woman was around my age. Both of them were dressed for a night out like we were.

Introductions were made, and it soon became obvious this woman, Madison, seemed to think she had some kind of claim on Philip.

"I heard you were dragged off to some god-awful town in the middle of nowhere," she said to him with a laugh. She was medium height with long blonde hair, a pretty face, and big boobs. Basically everything I already knew he liked.

I tried to hear what his response was, but her date, a guy named Edward, started talking to me about the show we'd just seen. All I knew was my alarm bells were going off. She was standing too close to Philip, touching his arm, and when we left to be seated, I watched the way her eyes stayed on him in a predatory way.

"Where do you know her from?" I asked after we sat down, trying to sound casual.

He shrugged. "Just around."

"Around where?"

He was looking at his menu. "She's just someone I know. I met her at a dinner party a few months ago."

We ordered our meal, and I excused myself to go to the restroom —which was super fancy. There was a crystal chandelier and bottles of expensive perfume on a shelf for the patrons. Except the whole room was done in red, which didn't help my discomfort. I told myself to calm down. And then I had a stern talk with myself about jealousy and all my worries about being cheated on again. Philip had never given me any reason to distrust him. He didn't deserve to be punished for what Ethan had done.

When I went back to our table, Philip was looking at his phone. He put it down when he saw me. "There you are. I was ready to send out a search party. Is everything all right?"

"Of course." I took my seat again and reached for one of the breadsticks, trying to appear nonchalant.

The waiter came over and filled my wineglass. I picked it up and drank, except I took too large a gulp. To my embarrassment, wine spilled out the sides of my mouth and onto my chin. It even dribbled down the front of my chest and into my cleavage. "Dang it!" I quickly grabbed the cloth napkin from my lap and dabbed myself, trying to mop up the wine now pooled between my breasts. For some reason, I still held the bread-stick in my other hand and accidentally smacked myself in the face.

Philip was silent watching this spectacle.

Eventually, I put the napkin down and let out a sigh of relief. I took a bite of the breadstick and chewed, venturing a glance at him.

He grinned. "Damn, you're cute."

"Really?" I swallowed. "Because I think I just put on a skit for you."

He laughed and leaned forward. "I love everything about you, Claire."

I gazed at him. His eyes were like a calm sea. Whatever his outer trappings were, the inner Philip, the one I'd gotten to know, was the absolute best.

"Are you really okay?" he asked.

I took a deep breath and decided to tell him the truth. "To be honest, I've been feeling a little out of my depth since I arrived yesterday."

His brows came together. "What do you mean? Talk to me."

And so I did. I told him how I'd been disoriented since I stepped off the plane, that I wasn't used to his lifestyle.

"Sweetheart, why didn't you say something sooner?"

"I figured I'd get over it. I mean, I will. It's just a passing thing."

"You never have to hold back from me. Don't you know that?"

The rest of our dinner was good. We talked quietly, and Philip kept insisting I tell him the next time I felt the least bit uncomfortable.

Before dessert, he got up and left to use the restroom. I sat alone, sipping my wine and feeling a whole lot better. I should have told him about my discomfort sooner. It was silly to hide it. After all, I'd said I wanted to go for it, right?

There was buzzing on the table, and I noticed Philip had left his phone behind. It buzzed again, and I reached over to pick it up, glancing at the screen. Someone had texted him. I didn't mean to, but I couldn't stop my eyes from scanning the words. It was from Madison.

Ditch your date and meet me at the bar. I have a sexy surprise for you.

TWENTY-SEVEN

~ Claire ~

My stomach lurched as I stared at the message with disbelief. This couldn't be happening.

A wave of nausea came over me so strong, I thought I might throw up.

The phone buzzed in my hand again, and another text from Madison appeared.

Where are you, baby? My surprise is I'm not wearing any panties.

My hand shook, and I dropped the phone like it was radioactive. It hit the table with a loud thud.

It all came flooding back to me. The emails I'd seen on Ethan's computer—the sexy ones from Ivy. I went to her apartment that day to confront her, because like a fool, I still thought Ethan was innocent. I thought he was innocent until the moment I discovered him fucking her. That was how dumb I was.

My skin broke out in a cold sweat. I knew this couldn't be true.

Philip would never do this to me, not after knowing what I'd been through. He wasn't that kind of man.

Except that was the same thing I'd told myself about Ethan.

My eyes searched the restaurant for an exit. I had to get out of here.

Fumbling around for my purse, I was ready to leave when Philip appeared and sat down.

He took one look at me, and his brows slammed together. "What's wrong?"

I shook my head, trying to catch my breath. My heart was beating so hard it felt like it was trying to jump out of my chest. "Your phone," I managed to say.

Philip grabbed his phone from the table in front of me. His face hardened when he read the messages. "Claire, this is not what you think. You know that."

I held my hand over my chest, still trying to catch my breath. "I have to leave. I need air."

"I had nothing to do with these messages."

"Please, get me... out of here," I said, my voice strangled.

He jumped up quickly and came to my side. I let him rest his hand on my back and guide me toward the entrance. The small rational part of me knew he was telling the truth, but the rest of me was freaking out.

A group of people was entering as we tried to leave, and naturally, one of them knew Philip. The guy started talking to him as we moved past. "I've heard rumblings on the street. The word is North-Stone is going to make a killing!"

Philip's expression remained stern. "Excuse us" was all he said as he pushed through the crowd. His hand was still on my back, but as soon as we were outside, I broke away.

The cool air felt good against my face. I went to the side of the building and leaned against the wall, still trying to catch my breath. I was scared. Everything around me was a blur, and I couldn't focus.

"Sweetheart, listen to me. I think you're having a panic attack."

"I am?" My voice shook.

"I want you take a deep breath and hold it for five seconds, then let it out slowly."

I tried to follow his instructions. At first I struggled, but by the sixth time, I was managing it. Somehow I was getting my breath under control. I kept at it, focusing on the ground at my feet.

"What's four times eight plus three?" he asked.

"Are you crazy? I don't know!"

"Just breathe and then multiply and add the numbers. It'll help," he said. "Trust me."

I closed my eyes and did the math. "Thirty-five."

"Good." He gave me another simple math problem, and I did that one too. We did a few more, and I was starting to feel better.

Finally, I was able to focus on Philip and could see the way he was watching me with concern. "I need to get the car from the valet and take care of the check. Are you going to be okay here for a minute?"

"I think so."

He left me with another math problem. It was longer, and I slowly worked it out in my head.

When the car arrived, he asked if I wanted to go to the ER, but I said no, that I just wanted to go back to the house.

"How did you know how to do that?" I asked once we were driving.

"My mom started having panic attacks when my dad left. Sometimes we'd wind up in the ER, but other times I could talk her down." He glanced at me. "Have you ever had one before?"

I nodded. "Once, after my dad died. I didn't know what it was. Violet gave me something, and it helped me relax."

Soon we went through the gate and were pulling up in front of his house. At least I was feeling better. Drained and tired, but not overly anxious anymore. Once upstairs, I went straight to the bedroom to change from my dress into something more comfortable—a tank top and pajama bottoms.

I sat on the end of the bed, watching Philip as he stripped out of his suit and thinking about those texts. They had Madison's name on them, so she was obviously in his phone contacts. "How well do you know her? Why do you think she sent you sexy messages like that?"

He shook his head. "Let's not talk about this anymore. I don't want it to upset you again."

"No, answer me."

He pulled on a pair of clean athletic pants and a white T-shirt, then came over and sat next to me on the end of the bed. He didn't look happy. "I dated her for a short while."

"What?" I blinked in surprise. "Are you serious? Why didn't you tell me when I asked you about her?"

"Because we only went out a few times. It wasn't worth mentioning."

"Did you sleep with her?"

He glanced toward the windows. "Once."

The room went silent. I put my hand to my stomach, which had tightened into a knot. "You should have told me who she was. I don't understand why you didn't."

"I was trying to protect you."

"From what? Former girlfriends?"

He nodded. "You're not going to want to hear details about every woman I've been with in the same way I don't want to hear about every guy you've been with."

"Except you've already heard about all the guys I've been with. There are only three, and you're one of them!"

He sighed. "Well, it's been more than three for me. I've told you about my reputation as a dog."

I considered his words. Did I really want to know his number? "How many are we talking about?"

He didn't reply.

"Less than a thousand?"

That made him chuckle. "Yes, definitely less than a thousand."

"Less than a hundred?"

He nodded.

"Less than fifty?"

He looked at me.

"More than fifty and less than a hundred?"

He nodded again. "Let's settle somewhere in that range."

"That's a lot of women."

He remained silent, but then he turned to me. His voice was rough when he spoke. "None of them were *you* though."

A warmth spread through me at his words, starting in my chest and moving out to my fingertips and toes.

I focused on the cool hardwood beneath my feet and tried not to let emotion overwhelm me. "So how long ago did you date Madison?"

"We were dating when I met you."

My brows shot up. "Well, no wonder. She probably thinks she still has a chance with you."

"She doesn't. I have zero interest in her."

I didn't say anything, still stewing over this new information. I thought about my reaction to those texts. Not only was Philip handsome, but he was rich and successful. Women probably came on to him all the time.

"Look at me, Claire."

I took a deep breath and turned to him.

"I've fallen in love with you."

"I know," I whispered.

"I don't want anyone else." His eyes stayed on mine. "Only you, sweetheart."

I nodded. "It just reminded me of everything that happened with my marriage. Next time just tell me if we come across someone you've dated, okay? I don't need protecting."

"I will." He sighed deeply, then gazed toward the windows again. He was silent for a long moment before asking, "I screwed up earlier taking you to that dress shop too, didn't I?"

I studied his handsome profile and told him the truth. "It was weird finding out you'd brought other women there."

"I'm sorry, Claire." He leaned forward and scrubbed his hands over his face. "*Fuck.* This is all so new for me." He looked over, his eyes worried. "I might make some mistakes."

Philip was always confident, so it was strange to see him vulnerable like this. I scooted closer on the bed. "This is new for me too." I slipped an arm through his and leaned my head against his shoulder. "We'll figure it out together."

We were both quiet. I put my hand in his, and he threaded our fingers together.

"How are you feeling now?" he asked. "Still anxious?"

"Mostly tired."

"That's understandable. Do you want to lie down? I can get you something."

"Like what?"

"A glass of wine or maybe a whiskey. It might help you relax."

"That's okay." I lifted my head. "All I want is you."

He smiled gently. "You have me."

WE WENT TO BED. I wasn't in the mood for anything intimate, so Philip stroked my back for a while. Instead of getting sleepy, I rolled over to face him. The room was dark, but with the starry sky outside, we could still see each other. He didn't say anything when I moved closer, when I slipped my arms around his neck, his body warm and solid. We were both naked since we usually slept in the nude.

He grunted softly when I kissed him, our tongues slowly exploring each other's mouths. I drew back to caress his jaw, then his cheek and forehead.

His eyes fell shut.

"I really like you," I whispered.

"I like you too."

"You're different from anyone I've ever known."

His eyes slid open. "I hope that's all right."

"It is."

I took my time when I kissed him again. His mouth was silky, and he tasted so good. Like the lover I didn't know I'd been waiting for, like the future I'd only dreamed of in my quietest moments. We took it slow, neither of us in a hurry. And the whole time, there was this current flowing through me, flowing through us both. Even the room seemed alive with it.

"I love you, Claire," he whispered. "That's never going to change."

I hugged him close. He felt so right.

Later, as I was drifting off to sleep, I thought about falling in love with Philip, how easy that would be. Easier than anything. He was wonderful. I still wasn't ready, but with time... maybe I would be.

UNFORTUNATELY, Philip wasn't able to fly home with me Sunday afternoon. I was disappointed, but he promised he'd be back in time for the Pirate Days party the next weekend.

We spent all morning in bed together and then had a long parting kiss at the airport.

"I'm going to miss you, sweetheart," he said, still holding me close. "Text me as soon as you land."

"I will."

"And then when you get home too."

I smiled. "Maybe I'll send you a photo or two when I get home."

He drew back from me with a wicked grin. "I'd like that." His eyes dropped to my mouth, and soon we were caught up in another searing kiss.

I pulled back, breathless. "I should go before the plane leaves without me."

He seemed to find this amusing. "Don't worry, that plane's not going anywhere."

Eventually we parted. I climbed the stairs, then waved goodbye to him still down on the tarmac. He waved back.

Once on board, it turned out it was the same crew as before—Ben, Jason, and Marnie. I was delighted.

"Hi, guys," I said with a grin.

They greeted me with enthusiasm, and we exchanged pleasantries about our weekends.

Marnie didn't offer me chocolate truffles this time but had a selection of pastries available. I chose a delicious apple tart.

By the time we landed back home, I felt like a seasoned vet with all this flying by private charter stuff. In truth, it was pretty nice. No long lines at the airport, no worries about lost luggage. I just got on a plane and went.

I'd left my Kia parked at the small airport in Truth Harbor, and it was still there waiting for me. I was only gone two days, but somehow it felt longer.

I texted Philip from my car, then again when I got home. That time I included a selfie of myself with some cleavage showing. He responded right away.

You're killing me, sweetheart. I miss you so much already.

I smiled to myself, my grin a mile wide. *I miss you too.*

When I went to work the next day, that smile was still inside me. I carried it within me like a lit candle. People commented on it everywhere I went.

"You look so pretty. Have you done something different with your hair?" a couple of my clients asked.

"Are you on a new diet?" Luanne, the checker at the grocery store, wanted to know, even though she'd just put six Kit Kat bars in my grocery bag.

Violet was studying me with a shrewd expression when I dropped off paper plates and cups that evening at Sullivan House. She'd had me pick up extras for the party on Saturday. "I gather your weekend with Philip went well?"

"Yes, it did," I said, my outer smile matching my inner one.

She reached over and put her hand on my arm. "I'm so pleased for you, Claire. Truly."

Later, Leah and Theo came over for dinner. The three of us sat outside eating Chinese takeout.

"So how was your weekend with Philip?" Leah asked.

I told them both about the high-tech stuff at Philip's house and about the show we went to in Seattle. I mentioned the clothing boutique with the famous Seattle rapper I saw.

"Wow," Theo said, digging into her rice with chopsticks. "I'd probably be impressed if I knew who that was."

"I'm sure you've heard his songs on the radio," Leah said. She sang one of his tunes.

Theo shook her head. "Nope, still no clue."

"I saw one of the Seattle football players there too," I said. "I think it was the running back."

"Really?" Leah nodded with approval. "Some of those guys are so hot."

Theo rolled her eyes. "Please. There's nothing hot about millionaire jocks running around tackling each other. Football is barbaric and idiotic."

"No, it's not," Leah said. "They're incredible athletes."

Theo gave her a look. "Who cares? I doubt they even have two brain cells to rub together.

"You guys always argue about the same things," I said, shaking my head. I heard music for a moment and gazed toward the main house. "I think the DJ is here setting up the sound system for the party."

Leah looked at me with sympathy. She'd been to Pirate Days parties in the past and knew how hard this was for me. "Are you okay?"

I nodded. "It's just weird having this party without my dad."

"I know." She reached over and touched my arm.

Theo was eyeing me with sympathy too. "I wish I was going to be here. I can't believe the timing for everything." It turned out she'd accepted a guest lecturer spot at a university in Montana before she knew about the party.

"Me too," I said. "We'll have to share a bottle of rum when you get back and then have our own bonfire on the beach."

She nodded. "That sounds fun. Should I invite Clement? He'll be back from Guatemala by then."

I cringed a little. Clement was Theo's boyfriend. I didn't know him that well since he was gone a lot—usually to Central America. Last time I saw him, he talked to me for two hours straight about the acoustic signals of the horned passalus beetle. "Let's just make it a girls' night. What do you think, Leah?"

She shrugged. "Sounds good. I don't have a boyfriend anymore anyway."

My mouth fell open. "What about Neil?"

"I broke up with him."

"You did? You never said a word. When did this happen?"

"About a week ago. It just wasn't working out anymore." She picked up her water bottle. "To be honest, I think I was only dragging the relationship out because he was giving me such a great deal on my vet bills."

I couldn't help smiling, since it was the exact thought I'd had myself. "Are you okay, then?"

"Sure. I'm fine. It's not like it was true love or anything."

BY THE TIME Friday rolled around, Philip still hadn't flown back. I'd invited Gavin too, but he'd never returned my text.

I called Philip, worried. "Are you still coming to the party?" I asked.

"Of course." There was a pause on his end of the phone, and I heard someone else talking. "It's been crazy here. I'll be there, I promise."

"It's tomorrow night."

"I know."

I realized he was busy, but I thought he understood how Pirate Days was an important part of my past, how it would be difficult enough not having my father there. "This is a big deal to me."

"I know it is, sweetheart. Trust me, I wouldn't miss it for anything."

"Plus the ticket sales are paying for the cost of turning our downtown into a historical district."

He didn't say anything to that.

"Have you spoken to Gavin by chance? I texted and invited him, but he never answered me."

"Gavin's been in Hong Kong all week."

"Hong Kong?"

"He gets back later tonight though. I'll let him know."

I nodded, not sure what else to say. I wondered why Gavin needed to fly to Hong Kong, though I knew some of the tech companies they invested in were overseas.

Philip and I only sent a handful of texts all week, and we'd barely spoken on the phone. I was trying not to read anything into it or let my fears run amok since I knew he could be obsessive when it came to work.

"You'll be pleased to know I have my pirate costume all ready to go for tomorrow," he said. "I think you'll approve."

"You do?" I smiled with relief. "What does it look like?"

"It's black with sapphire blue accents, cuffed sleeves, and a long jacket. It's definitely something a pirate would wear." He chuckled. "Or a rock star."

"That sounds great. Where did you find it? Or let me guess, Sam found it for you?"

"That's correct."

I smiled. "I want to meet Sam sometime."

"He wants to meet you too."

"He does?"

"Yes, he thinks you sound delightful."

"Well," I said teasingly, "I *am* delightful."

"Mmm, that you are." I could picture Philip's grin on the other end of the phone. "I miss you so much, sweetheart. I know I've been consumed with work this week."

"What is that you guys are working on?"

He hesitated. "I'll explain it to you later. Tell me about your week instead. Anything new to report with your clients?"

"Not really." I thought over my week and then perked up as I remembered something interesting that happened. "I think I might have found a new employee."

"Is that so? I didn't know you were looking to hire someone new."

"Not right away, but soon. I met her when she was a nanny for Mona. I gave her my card that first night we met, and she called me a few days ago."

"Why did you do that?"

"Because I could tell she was responsible. She had a good vibe about her." I told him how I'd read online that successful business owners were always on the lookout for good people, always thinking two steps ahead. "Is that true?"

"Absolutely."

"It is?"

"Let me tell you a secret. When I invest in any venture, it's with the person as much as the idea. Sometimes even more so."

"Really?"

"If I meet someone and their business doesn't impress me but they do, I always get their contact information and keep in touch." I could hear him shifting the phone around to get more comfortable. "Just because their first idea isn't a winner doesn't mean their second or third idea won't be. That's paid off more than a few times."

I thought about how, when I'd spoken to Taylor recently, she'd told me she was glad to get my message, that she was thinking about quitting her nanny job. "I'm going to meet her for coffee next week. I figure I'll put her on the schedule with a client or two and see how it goes."

"That's great thinking, Claire."

I could feel his approval emanating through the phone, and I had to admit I liked it. Philip's approval was addictive. "Thanks for being so supportive of my tiny business. I know it's nothing compared to what you do."

"If it's important to you, then it's important to me. You know that."

"I know," I murmured.

"I always enjoy hearing about your maid business. In some ways you remind me of myself in the early days before NorthStone."

"Really?" I felt both surprised and complimented. "Even when I don't take your advice? You realize I still haven't changed the name."

"And we all have to learn from our mistakes, don't we?"

I laughed. "Probably."

He sighed. "God, I love hearing your voice. I can't wait to see you tomorrow. This week has been taking its toll on me more than I thought it would."

"What do you mean?"

"Nothing." He went quiet. "I miss having you beside me all night."

"Me too."

"You and that naughty bed of yours," he purred. "I've been thinking about all the things I want to do to you when I get you in it again."

"You're bad." Though I couldn't stop the tingle of anticipation.

"I've never felt like this about anyone. You've done a real number on me."

"I can't wait to see you tomorrow. We haven't been on the phone much this week."

"It's my fault. But I'm going to make it up to you, my pirate princess. You'll see."

I smiled again. "You better."

TWENTY-EIGHT

~ Claire ~

"Where's your new boyfriend?" Delores, the unofficial town gossip, was studying me. "He's still coming, isn't he?"

"He'll be here," I said.

"Everything's okay, I hope." She leaned closer, lowering her voice. "You two haven't broken up, have you?"

"Of course not." I tried to sound light and airy, but she was the sixth person at the party to ask me about Philip. Apparently everybody was excited to meet him.

"Good, I'm glad. You deserve some happiness. Have you heard Ethan and Ivy are having problems?"

I murmured something noncommittal, then took a sip of rum punch.

"I always thought you were too good for Ethan anyway," she said, holding up her own punch. There was red lipstick smeared on the front of her small white teeth. It matched the red in the pirate scarf tied at her waist. "He never should have left you for her. What a mistake that was."

I motioned to the front of her mouth. "You have some lipstick on your teeth."

"I do?" Her hand shot up, and she scrubbed her front teeth with her finger. "Is it gone?"

"I think it's still there. You might want to check in the bathroom mirror."

"I think I will. Thank you."

She hurried off, and I was relieved to end the conversation.

Ironically, in that moment I saw Ivy across the room. The she-devil herself. She wore a tight red leather corset over a short black skirt. Pirate-style boots encased her long legs. As always, she looked perfect. Her hair fell down her back and shoulders like pale silk.

She must have sensed my gaze, because she turned in my direction. We stared at each other.

But then she smirked and turned away.

If it had been up to me, I'd never have invited her or Ethan to this party.

He was there too, standing beside her as they talked to some people I didn't know. He wasn't dressed up at all and wore a T-shirt and cargo shorts.

My stomach tightened. Resentment burned through me at their presence. How could I ever forget what they did to me when I had to see them all the time? It was like I would never get rid of this burden. Their betrayal was going to plague me the rest of my life.

On a happy note, the party was a smashing success. The place was packed with people. The great room had all the furniture pushed aside, and a DJ spun a mixture of dance music along with the occasional sea shanty. The food and alcohol were flowing. People were dancing. Apparently they'd sold every single ticket and had gotten a number of donations.

Everybody was having a good time, and I knew many of the faces. Most of them, like Delores, I'd known since childhood. A lot of my father's friends and clients. He was popular even before he became mayor. Seeing and talking to everyone again made me miss my dad.

After a couple hours, I went upstairs to my old bedroom and closed the door. I needed a break. It smelled faintly of the floral perfume I wore in high school. I mostly used the room as extra storage space since the carriage house was so small.

I sat on the bed and checked my phone again. Philip had texted me that afternoon saying he'd be here by six, but it was nearly seven. *Where is he?*

It was starting to feel like I did have a fake boyfriend.

I knew he wouldn't stand me up though. Philip wasn't made that way. If he was late, it had to be for a good reason. Something serious must have delayed him, and I hoped he was okay.

There was a knock on the door, and I glanced up.

Leah's head peeked inside. "I thought I might find you here."

"I just needed a break."

She closed the door and came over to me. "How are you?"

"I'm fine." I scooted over to make room for her on the bed.

"Wow, I haven't been up here in ages." Her eyes scanned my former bedroom. "It takes me back to the good old days when our biggest worry was whether the guy we had a crush on noticed if we were alive or not."

"I mostly remember that Danish exchange student you had a thing for. What was his name again?"

She grinned. "Tobias."

"He was cute. Didn't you kiss him once?"

"Yes, at a party. Ivy's friend Amber wound up dating him though."

I snorted. "Don't feel bad. Amber put out. That's the only reason he liked her."

Leah leaned back against the headboard and sighed. "Sometimes I wish I'd put out more."

"What?" I gave her a look. "That's silly."

"Think about it. Girls like that have all the fun."

"No they don't. Everybody looks down on them."

"Oh really? Whatever happened to Amber?"

I thought about it. "I think she married Derek." Ivy's old boyfriend, the captain of the football team. "He owns an appliance store now."

"See? She's happily married with kids. None of it hurt her at all."

I thought about those days, and something occurred to me. "I wonder why Ivy didn't marry Derek. She dated him through most of high school. It must have been weird for her when he and Amber got married."

Leah shrugged. "Maybe she didn't want to. Or maybe Violet didn't approve of Derek as marriage material."

"Maybe." Violet had particularly high standards for her daughters. She even had them travel back to the south with her for a debutante ball.

Leah was watching me. "There were a couple guys you liked in high school. It wasn't just Ethan."

"None of them liked me back though." I thought about my various crushes. Ironically, Ethan hadn't been one of them. I'd barely even noticed him until senior year, when he started showing an interest in me.

There was a loud boom outside.

"What's that?" Leah looked toward the bedroom window.

We both got up and looked out to the beach behind the house. It was still early evening, and I could see all the stacks of firewood along the water, ready to be lit into bonfires later. "I think someone blew off a firework early," I said. "There's going to be a show later tonight."

People were walking around the backyard and then meandering down to the water. I caught a glimpse of Violet giving orders to one of the caterers. It was amusing to see her in a pirate's costume. She wore it with surprising panache. My dad used to tease her and say it brought out her true nature.

It occurred to me that I wasn't the only one missing him tonight.

Violet would be missing him too. And then I felt bad for hiding up here.

"I need to get down there again," I told Leah. "I should be helping."

I MADE my way down the stairs alone, Leah having stayed behind to use the bathroom. It was a wide staircase with a rich green carpet and a decorative wooden rail befitting a home as grand as Sullivan House. As a little girl, I used to pretend I was a princess gliding down these stairs, and a handsome prince would be waiting for me at the bottom.

Just a foolish daydream.

I slid my hand along the rail, my eyes scanning the crowd, and that's when I saw Philip by the front door.

A thrill ran through me.

He'd obviously just arrived. It had only been a week since we'd seen each other, but I missed him. I missed him a lot.

He stopped past the threshold, his eyes searching the room.

I knew he was looking for me, and that made my breath catch with excitement. He wore a black coat with wide lapels and large buttons down the front, the cuffed sleeves adorned with blue accents. His description was exactly right. The coat hugged his broad shoulders, then tapered down at the waist.

Instead of rushing down the stairs to meet him, I stayed where I was.

He took in his surroundings with the same keen interest he did everything in life. It occurred to me that Philip had never seen this part of Sullivan House. We'd gone in through the backdoor for breakfast that morning with Violet, which was the only time he'd been inside.

I remained still, waiting for him to find me, my heart pounding.

Other people had begun to notice him, some of them whispering to each other.

Finally, his gaze went to the top of the stairs, and I could tell the exact moment he saw me.

His face changed to the expression he wore so often when we were together. The one where he looked at me like I was a gift.

And that was when the truth struck me.

I've fallen in love with Philip.

I clutched the bannister in shock.

How could this have happened?

Of course, I knew exactly how. He was devious. A thief since the day I met him. He'd snuck past all my defenses.

Now that he'd seen me, he made his way through the crowd with determination.

I headed down the stairs at a quick pace. As I approached the bottom, he was already there waiting for me. The prince I'd dreamed of so long ago.

He grinned as he took in my clothes. "You really are my pirate princess."

I was wearing a black dress with a corseted top. It was flattering, even if it did display a little more cleavage than I was used to. I wore gold hoop earrings, a linked gold chain around my waist, and bandanas tied at my hip.

His eyes stayed on mine. "I've been going crazy all week without you."

I nodded, still coming to terms with my realization that I'd fallen in love.

His brows came together, misinterpreting my silence. "I'm sorry I'm late. I hope you're not upset."

I shook my head and flung myself into his arms.

"Sweetheart," he murmured, stroking my back. "Are you okay?"

"I'm glad you're here," I whispered.

"Did you get my texts?"

I pulled back a little. "Texts? No."

"The plane I chartered was grounded with mechanical problems, and for some reason, they couldn't get me another flight. It was ridiculous." His expression turned stern. "As you can imagine, I raised hell."

I could imagine.

"Eventually it got resolved, and I texted you from the air. I tried calling, but the line kept getting dropped." He shook his head with frustration.

I nodded and put my hand to his cheek. "It's okay." He'd let his beard grow out a little, and it was scratchy beneath my fingers.

Philip's eyes roamed my face. "What is it? Something's changed."

"I'll tell you later." I could feel people watching us. "We seem to be the center of attention."

"Are we?" He raised a brow. "Well, then let's give them a show."

His grip tightened, and then he kissed me. A real one too, long and lush. I didn't even care that the whole room was watching. Let them watch. At least no one would be calling me "poor Claire" anymore.

After the kiss, we held hands, and I figured I'd give him a proper tour of Sullivan House. I didn't get very far though, because we were surrounded.

"You must be Philip!"

"It's nice to meet you!"

"We're so happy Claire's found someone!"

"My goodness, don't you make a dashing pirate!"

That much was true. Philip looked hot. All that indomitable energy poured into pirate garb was definitely working for him.

He shook a lot of hands and responded to everyone's comments politely, then firmly when they tried to get too nosy. Most people meant well though. Living in a small town wasn't always easy, but I knew they wanted to see me happy.

"You look sexy," I told him when we had a moment to ourselves again.

He chuckled. "I had a feeling you'd like it. Oh, that reminds me." He reached into his coat pocket and pulled out a couple of items, handing them to me. "Sam told me you'd know what to do with these."

I examined them both. One was a bandana that matched his coat, and the other was a black kohl eye pencil. "Are you willing to wear eyeliner?"

He shrugged. "Sure, why not."

I thought about where to put this on and realized I couldn't take him to my bedroom, since everybody would notice. I wasn't willing to be that scandalous.

"Come on." I grabbed his hand and led him toward the small bathroom near the kitchen. It was the only place I could think of with a mirror, and I doubted anybody would be using it.

As soon as we were alone inside the small space, Philip pulled me against him. "Finally," he murmured. "I have you to myself."

We kissed like we were on fire, both of us grabbing each other with a crazed passion, until he had me pushed against the bathroom door. "We can't do this right now," I said in a fluster. "It has to wait until later."

"Just let me have you once," he growled. "I want you so much."

Desire tumbled through me like a kaleidoscope. My body was saying yes, but my brain was saying no. "I have to get back out there. People will notice if I'm gone too long."

He pulled my skirt up with impatience. "Trust me, this isn't going to take long."

I laughed. "You really know how to woo a girl, don't you?"

There was a flash of white when he grinned. "I'm just telling you the truth."

"Well, that's not going to convince me."

"You need more convincing, do you?" He stroked my bare bottom. "Shall I sweeten the deal? Add an extra addendum?"

I didn't reply because his fingers had slid lower and were stroking me right where it mattered. My breath caught.

Philip was watching me.

Then he looked down, and I knew what he was going to do.

"We shouldn't," I said, though it sounded weak even to my own ears.

He sank to his knees on the floor in front of me, pushed my skirt up, tugged my panties aside, and put his mouth right on my clit.

My eyes fell shut. I tried not to moan as he gently tongued me, but a whimper escaped anyway.

"This isn't fair," I said, though it was the last thing I said, because when I opened my eyes, I remembered there was a mirror next to me. For the first time in my life, I watched myself being serviced by a pirate.

Let's be honest, it wasn't exactly an unfamiliar fantasy. I may have had it a time or two.

The more excited I got, the more excited Philip seemed to get. He gripped my ass with one hand, grunting when I grabbed his hair. When he slipped his fingers inside me, I began to come, moaning and pushing my hips out. He was groaning against me just as noisy as I was, probably even more so. The whole thing was dirty as hell.

In the next moment, he was on his feet. I was loose limbed, barely recovered, but he was all business. He retrieved a condom from his wallet though his hands were shaking.

"Bend over the sink," he told me.

I did as he asked, watching him in the mirror behind me—his jaw flushed beneath that stubble, his dark head bent in concentration. A hand grabbed my hip, and when he thrust into me, it was over the top. Erotic pleasure spiraled through me, lighting me up.

But then his movements slowed, stopping altogether. His gaze found mine in the mirror's reflection. I could hear party sounds in the distance. People laughing. But here we were alone together.

His eyes softened, his voice rough when he spoke. "*God*, Claire."

I nodded, because I knew what he meant. This was so intimate. So intense. So good.

He slowly began to move again at a measured pace, trying to make it last. He was doing it for me.

"Don't," I said, urging him on. "Take me hard."

His face changed at that. His mouth closed, stifling a groan, and then he began to pound into me. He shook his head as the climax approached, trying to deny it, but his body wouldn't let him.

Afterward, he spun me around, pulled me in close, and kissed me deeply.

He held my head as we gazed at each other.

"You're the one," he whispered. "The only one."

"I love you, Philip."

His breath went still. I saw my words working their way through him until he nodded with understanding. "That's what's changed."

"Yes." My voice shook. "You and your sneaky ways."

A grin pulled at the corner of his mouth. "It's about time."

I rolled my eyes, though they were brimming with tears. "It's crazy. I haven't even known you very long."

"That doesn't matter." His voice was quiet, his gaze steady and true. "We're meant for each other."

WE SPENT the next hour of the party holding hands, sneaking kisses, and acting like the kind of lovesick couple that was annoying to be around.

I introduced him to more people, friends and acquaintances. We hung out with Leah for a while before she went over to talk to the owner of the local yarn shop. Eliza found us and introduced us to her date, a skinny young actor named Will who spouted Shakespeare in a pompous voice, calling her his Juliet. After Will recited his fifth sonnet, Philip scowled at him. Unfortunately, with the black eyeliner, it made him more intimidating than usual. Will ran off to get something to eat and never came back.

Philip noticed himself in a mirror. "Maybe I should wear eyeliner more often," he said to me after Eliza left to go search for her date. "I'm enjoying the effects."

"You scared that poor guy half to death."

He chuckled.

"That's not funny." Though my reprimand would have carried more weight if I hadn't been laughing too. "You should feel ashamed of yourself for chasing him away like that."

"Believe me, I'm doing him a favor. If he scares that easily, my sister will walk all over him." He popped the last bit of food from the paper plate into his mouth. "Besides, that guy was annoying as hell."

I had to admit he was.

"Would you like more punch?" Philip asked, noticing my cup was empty.

"That depends. Are you planning to get me drunk and take advantage of me later?"

"Of course."

"Then okay." I handed him my cup, and he left to get more. My eyes followed his broad shoulders as he disappeared into the crowd. I had to admit I was having a great time. It was like the universe was finally smiling on me.

"Claire!"

I turned at the sound of my name. To my delight, it was Daphne. We hugged each other, and her lemony perfume surrounded me. "I'm glad you're back from Seattle. It's about time."

She smiled her shy smile and looked as pretty as always. Her strawberry blonde hair was curled and flowing around her shoulders. She wore a long peasant dress with multicolored beads around her neck. "It's good to be back."

Behind her stood Doug, dressed in a billowing white pirate's shirt and black pants, his hair slicked back in a style I'd never seen before.

I said hello to him, but he only nodded.

My eyes flickered between the two of them, pleased to see them together. It was obvious they were a couple.

"So have you talked to your mom?" I asked. "I'm sure she'll be thrilled to know you're home."

Daphne told me she'd spoken to her briefly, then gushed about all the decorations for the party and how she wished she'd been here to help. She told me how Doug's mom had changed her mind about moving out of her house, and that was why they were able to come back.

The whole time we talked, Doug kept fidgeting beside her, watching me, though when our eyes met, he looked away.

Daphne asked me how business was going. "My mom said you lost clients because of Ivy."

I shook my head. "I can't say I miss them. They were—"

"I can't stand it anymore!" Doug burst into the conversation. "I've just got to say it, Claire." He took a deep breath. "I'm *real* sorry for everything."

My brows went up with surprise. He looked miserable, though to be honest, that was how he always looked. "Sorry for what?"

"I didn't mean for it to happen. Honest, I didn't." He swallowed. "It's just that Daphne and I hit it off with each other. I hope there's no hard feelings."

"Um... that's okay." I was confused, then decided he must have been talking about how he had to leave town, how Philip had to finish my room. "I totally understand."

"You do? I'm glad to hear that." He nodded his head bobbing. "You're not upset?"

"No."

"Because I still think you're a sweet girl, and I wouldn't want you to think I led you on."

It dawned on me then that he was talking about our canceled movie date. I'd completely forgotten about it. "Don't worry. I'm happy for you and Daphne."

Just then I glanced behind him and saw Philip coming toward us with my rum punch.

He didn't seem to notice Doug as he bent down to kiss me. "Here you go, sweetheart," he said, handing me the cup. "And you'll be pleased to know I coaxed Will out from where he was hiding in the bushes. I think he's less afraid of me now."

"Look who's here," I said to him. "It's your cousin."

"My what?" He turned to Doug, who was standing there with a strange expression on his face. Philip went silent. When he spoke, his voice sounded forced. "Hey, Doug. How's it going?"

Doug didn't reply. His eyes had grown as big as saucers, and he was staring at us with his mouth hanging open.

"It's been a while." Philip smiled, but seemed uncomfortable. He cleared his throat, then glanced at me.

Meanwhile, Doug's face turned bright red as he continued to gawk at us.

"So, uh, is everything settled with your mom?" Philip asked. "We should get together soon and go over the changes I've made to your business."

"You... you," Doug stammered, pointing at Philip. He was breathing so hard he seemed on the verge of hyperventilation. "You... *betrayer!*"

A few people turned in our direction as his voice carried. I was confused. Doug was obviously upset, but it made no sense. From everything I'd seen, he should have been grateful. His construction business was running like a well-oiled machine.

"*Traitor,*" Doug spat again. "I trusted you!"

Philip put his hand up. "Look, it's not what you think, okay? Calm down."

"Not what I think? It's exactly what I think!" He grew even more agitated, his hands clenched at his side. "You've been *lying* to me this whole time."

"Let's talk about it rationally."

"I'm not talking to *you!* You're a damn liar. A backstabber. I'll never trust you again!"

"There's more to the—"

Doug punched Philip in the face. A loud smack with a crunch as his fist hit skin and bone.

I gasped, and I wasn't the only one. The blow knocked Philip to the side. He didn't go to his knees, but stumbled backward.

The whole room seemed to go silent. Even the DJ's music

stopped, though I think it already had. I'd never seen anyone punched in my life.

I rushed over to where Philip stood rubbing his jaw. I wondered what I should do. Was he all right? But he barely even noticed me. Instead, his eyes narrowed in on Doug. Their pale blue had turned to icy glaciers.

Despite Philip being the one who had gotten punched, I was more worried for Doug. I glanced over at him. He looked worried too. In fact, he looked terrified, bouncing up and down on the balls of his feet like a jangly marionette.

"You... you... deserved it," Doug gulped. "You know you did!"

Philip was still rubbing his jaw in deadly silence.

I was ready to tell Doug to go run and hide in the bushes, that maybe I could try to talk Philip down. I couldn't understand why he'd punched him in the first place. Had he lost his mind?

But then something surprising happened, something I could barely believe.

Philip smiled.

TWENTY-NINE

~ Philip ~

"That was a helluva punch," I said, rubbing the part of my jaw where Doug's fist had just landed. Pain radiated up the side of my face and into my mouth.

He nodded with obvious uncertainty. "I... I... guess it was."

"A few inches higher and you would have broken my nose."

"You think so?"

"I do."

Doug looked scared, and he had good reason to be. Two seconds ago, I was ready to knock his head off.

"Are you going to *kill* me?" he squeaked.

"No." I smiled again, though it hurt. "I'm not going to kill you."

"Okay... thank you. I'm real glad."

"The fact is you're right." I studied him. "I deserved that punch."

He didn't reply, probably too much in shock over what he'd done.

Hell, even I was in shock. I could sense people watching us. Claire was at my side, but this was between my cousin and me.

"I'm impressed," I told him. "I didn't know you had it in you."

He stood up straighter. "Well, I guess I do." His chest puffed out. "It... had to be done."

Claire's sister Daphne was there. I noticed the way she moved to Doug's side. The way she slipped her arm through his. They were obviously together.

Good. I was glad for him. "Are we straight with each other now?"

He seemed to ruminate on the idea, glancing at Daphne. "Okay." He nodded. "We're straight."

The crowd, sensing the drama was over, seemed to lose interest. Claire was speaking to a few people, telling them everything was fine. I nodded and tried to smile reassuringly despite the pain. Somebody mentioned getting the police, but I shut that down quickly.

Daphne led Doug off somewhere, her gaze admiring. I noticed how he seemed to walk taller beside her. He looked happy, the happiest I'd ever seen him.

Meanwhile, Claire was studying me with concern. "Should I take you to the hospital?"

I moved my jaw around a little. My molars felt strange, and I checked to see if they were loose, but they weren't. "No, I don't think it's necessary. I could use an ice pack though."

I followed her into the kitchen, ignoring the stares from people. I could tell Claire had questions too, but to her credit, she remained silent, intent on getting me what I needed first. Afterward we headed down to the beach. She led me to a secluded spot near a fire pit that hadn't been lit yet, and we both sat on some blankets.

"Are you in a lot of pain?" she asked, twisting the cap off a bottle of water before handing it to me.

"Let's just say getting punched in the face hurts like hell."

"Is there anything else I can get you?"

"I'm okay." I put the bottle down and held the ice pack up to my jaw, reliving the whole thing with amazement. "I can't believe Doug had the balls to punch me."

"You almost sound like you're proud of him."

"I guess I am." I thought back to when his fist came in my direction. The surprise of it. I'd moved my head but not fast enough. At least he got me in the jaw instead of the nose.

"I can't believe you'd feel that way. Especially after everything you've done for him."

"Trust me, I had it coming." As odd as it sounded, I was glad Doug stood up for himself, glad he had the backbone for once, even if it meant I had to take a punch.

"But why? What was he so mad about?"

I turned and studied her, so pretty out here under the summer sky. "You, sweetheart."

"Me?" Her golden brown eyes widened, clearly trying to make sense of it all.

I nodded. And then I told her the whole story, or most of it. I took a few shortcuts because my jaw ached when I talked.

Claire seemed dumbfounded. "You were helping Doug win me over? But I was never romantically interested in Doug to begin with."

"I know, but he thought he was in love with you and enlisted my aid."

"That's crazy. He barely even knows me." She gazed out at the water. "I only agreed to go to the movies with him because he begged me, and I felt sorry for him."

I shrugged. "It doesn't matter. What matters is I told him I'd help him win your heart. Instead, I decided I wanted you for myself."

"Doug and I would never have been romantically compatible. This whole plan you guys cooked up was doomed from the start."

An amused snort escaped me. "Isn't that the truth. Turns out you're way too much woman for Doug." I shifted the ice pack. "Too much for most men, actually."

She raised a brow. "Is that so?"

"You're lucky I came along. At least I don't back down from a challenge."

Claire moved closer so she was directly in front of me. My eyes flashed lower, admiring her cleavage, but then they moved up to her face. She wore a teasing smile. "So I'm not too much for *you* to handle?"

Her hair fell in waves around her shoulders. The gold flecks in her eyes sparked. Everything about her moved me. Turned me on. Mesmerized me.

"No, sweetheart," I said softly. "You're just right."

She reached out and stroked the side of my face that didn't ache. "So you got punched in the face for me?"

"Basically."

Her eyes searched mine. She appeared to be contemplating something. "Men are such odd creatures."

I chuckled. "Don't make me laugh. Seriously. It's too painful."

She moved back and sat with her legs folded. "Well, they *do* say love hurts. I can't decide if I'm complimented or angry after hearing all this."

I moved the ice pack from my face and reached for her hand. "Be complimented. I know I'm glad things turned out the way they did. Aren't you?"

WE WERE STILL HOLDING hands when I decided it was time to explain what I'd been working on the last week and a half. Negotiating the largest commercial real estate venture NorthStone had ever been involved in. Our investors were thrilled. Gavin had been right all along. It would make everybody a ton of money.

But this deal was going to do a hell of a lot more than that. It would finally settle the score with my father.

"Listen, Claire, I need to talk to you about something. I know you've been wondering—"

"Look." She pointed toward the house. "Isn't that your mom and Elliot over there?"

"Huh? Where?" I still hadn't met Elliot yet. To be honest, I'd had him discreetly checked out a week ago. Thankfully, nothing bad turned up.

"By the edge of the fence."

Finally I saw them, or I thought I did. "Is that my mom?"

Claire stood up and waved them over. I stood too as they headed toward us.

Glancing at Claire, I realized I would have to wait until later to tell her about the deal with Atlas. I hadn't wanted to discuss it with her until it was a sure thing, and I knew she'd be upset, at least at first, so I didn't want to tell her over the phone.

"Mom?" I said when the two of them got closer. "Is that really you?" She was dressed like a real old-fashioned pirate wench with a white blouse that came off the shoulders and a long blue skirt. I'd never seen her in anything like it. Her hair was pulled up with curls falling down around her face. She looked pretty and younger somehow.

"Philip, I just heard what happened with Doug," she said, coming closer with a worried expression. "Are you okay?"

"I'm fine. It was nothing."

"Did he really punch you?" She examined my face. "I couldn't believe it when I heard. Do you need to see a doctor?"

"I'm okay," I assured her. "Just guy stuff. That's all."

My mom nodded, but I knew there would be more questions later.

"You must be Philip." Elliot stepped forward and put his hand out. "It's great to meet you finally."

His grip was firm. I took his measure, still not quite sure what to make of him. He wore the most realistic pirate costume I'd ever seen. From what I could tell, Claire had described him fairly accurately. He was in his late fifties and ruggedly handsome.

"That's quite a costume," I said to him. "Probably the best one I've seen tonight."

"You guys both look amazing," Claire enthused. "Like real pirates."

Elliot chuckled. "I have some friends who make historically accurate clothing. They're both professors, and it's become something of a side business for them."

We talked a little more. I asked questions about his work with the university, and he told me about some of the places he'd traveled to. He was articulate and entertaining. I imagined his classes were popular.

Most importantly, my gut told me he was all right. I didn't sense anything that worried me.

The sun was starting to set, and I was ready to suggest we go back inside and get more food when a bell clanged. It sounded like it was coming from the house.

"What's that?" I asked Claire.

She didn't answer right away, a wistful expression on her face. "It's the town crier bell. My dad used to ring it in the past." She sighed. "Violet must be doing it now. Afterward they'll light all the bonfires."

"What's it for?" my mom wanted to know.

"Mostly announcements about various things in the community. Come on." She took my hand and motioned at the others. "We should head up to the house."

The three of us followed her, and everyone gathered in the main room. Violet, who was dressed like a male pirate, including a sword at her side, was standing partway up the staircase. She held out a sheet of paper.

"Ahoy there, mateys." She spoke in a loud voice tinged with a southern drawl. "I have news for all good and upstanding citizens, and even for those citizens who *aren't* so good and upstanding." She stopped and gave a sly wink as people clapped and whistled. "Let me begin with the retirement of our current mayor." She went on to talk about how the mayor and his wife planned to travel the country in their new motorhome as people clapped and hooted.

I stood next to Claire, holding her hand and listening as Violet continued with the announcements. There were engagements, weddings, anniversaries, and babies being christened.

It was an interesting experience for me, as I'd never been part of a small community like this. The closest thing I've experienced were some of our company parties at NorthStone. I had to admit, it wasn't bad. Nice, even.

People continued to clap, cheer, and make jokes at the various announcements. About fifteen minutes into the whole thing, some guy walked up to Violet with another piece of paper. I watched as she read it. And then I watched as she looked down into the crowd, searching. Her eyes didn't stop until they found mine.

We studied each other from across the room. Judging by her expression, I knew what was on that paper.

I glanced down at Claire. We were still holding hands.

Violet spoke again. "I've been given some information from our lawyers."

As I listened, I thought about how I'd spent my whole adult life taking calculated risks. It had gotten me to where I was now. It had made NorthStone a success.

"They say they've been informed by the bank that a deal's been made. The land in our historic district is being sold to two companies. Atlas Investments and... NorthStone Capital."

Silence engulfed the room. There were a few mutterings. Mostly, I sensed confusion. My mom and Elliot were looking at me.

"That's not true," Claire spoke up. "Do we have to go through this again? Philip's already explained to you he has no part in any of it."

"I'm sorry, but I have it right here in black and white," Violet said. "Let's ask him whether it's true." She turned to me. "What do you have to say, Philip?"

I felt the whole room full of people turning in my direction. As ridiculous as it sounded, it only now occurred to me that I'd made a colossal error in judgment. I should have told Claire about all this sooner. Much sooner. I should have prepared her. What the hell was I thinking? I'd gotten so caught up in my own priorities, I'd lost sight of the obvious.

"Come on," Claire insisted. We were still holding hands, and she tugged on mine. "Tell them you have no part in any of it."

I studied her. This woman who'd captured my heart, who'd brought so much joy and light into my life that the days before I met her seemed murky and dark.

"I can't." I knew it was another calculated risk, that Claire might not stand by my decision. But I also knew she'd understand why I had to do it.

"Why not?"

"Because it's true, sweetheart."

She blinked at me in bewilderment. "What are you talking about?"

"NorthStone is partnering with Atlas. We're buying that land together."

"That can't be right." But then her eyes lit up. "Did you do it for me? If NorthStone's involved, you can stop them from tearing everything down, right?"

I shook my head. "That's not how it works. It isn't structured that way. We offered it to our investors as a package."

She yanked her hand from mine.

"I should have told you sooner," I admitted, "but I didn't want to tell you over the phone."

"That's all you have to say for yourself?" Her voice rose an octave. "This is what you've been working on so obsessively?"

I sensed everyone around us watching and listening to our conversation with keen interest. "Let's discuss this in private."

Claire glanced around too. Violet was still on the staircase, ready to spring into action. I heard someone in the crowd mutter, "Asshole," and knew it was directed at me. I ignored it. I hadn't gotten to where I was in life without pissing people off.

"Fine," she said, her face stony. "Let's go."

Conversation around us picked up as we left out the back door. I was glad to be leaving, though I was concerned about Claire.

We walked down the dirt and gravel road toward the carriage house in silence. It was a nice night, and I figured we'd sit outside, but she walked over to the driver side of her little turquoise car.

"Are we going someplace?"

"Yes, we are," she snapped. "Get in."

I opened the car door. Once inside, I glanced around with interest. I'd never been inside her car before. It smelled like stale coffee and cleaning supplies. There was a pirate charm hanging from her rearview mirror.

"Do you always keep your keys in here?" I asked as she started the engine and backed us out of the driveway.

"What's it to you?"

"It's not safe. You should bring them inside."

She rolled her eyes after pulling onto the main road. "Who's going to steal a turquoise car with the name Your House Sparkles on it? It's a little conspicuous, don't you think?"

"Screw the car. It's *you* I'm worried about."

Her head spun toward me. "Oh, no you don't. You don't get to act like you care about me, like you're concerned for my welfare. Not after what just happened."

"Don't be like that. Of course I care about you. I'm in love with you."

She shook her head, staring at the road. "You have a funny way of showing it."

"Claire, you know why I had to do this. You know *exactly* why. I couldn't let my father land on his feet again."

She went silent after that. I didn't say anything more either.

Eventually she parked near the ice cream parlor where we went on our first date. We both got out of the car.

I glanced around in confusion. It was a quiet summer night. The scent of saltwater drifted in on a breeze. We appeared to have the streets to ourselves. "You brought me here to get ice cream?"

"Everything is closed tonight for the party."

I stood next to the car and crossed my arms. "Then what are we doing here?"

"We're here because I want you to take a good look at everything you'll be destroying."

"I've already been down here. I don't need to see it again."

"Tonight you get to see it through *my* eyes."

I took a breath and held my hand up. "Look, Claire, I know you're upset, but this is pointless."

She ignored me and strutted off, leaving me no choice but to follow.

We passed a number of shops, and she told me the history behind each one. "See this shoe store? I bought my first pair of high heels there when I was fourteen. And that flower shop across the street? Three generations have owned it. They do all the weddings in our town."

I remained silent as I listened, letting her lead me wherever she wanted to, telling me about each place and its significance. The cafe where she'd been meeting friends all her life, the movie theater where she had her first kiss with some guy named Caleb.

I wasn't a monster. I didn't enjoy hearing all these stories. I didn't enjoy knowing I was part of destroying all these places. I knew most people living here were against the land development.

I didn't like being the bad guy, but I didn't get rich being the good guy.

Eventually we stopped in front of a classic old brick building with tall, narrow windows, and white trim around the edges. There was an ornate white paneled front door. A For Rent sign was taped to one of the windows.

Anger had been fueling her as she led me around, but I sensed it sputtering out.

"What is this place?"

She pointed at the gold lettering above the door where it said Sullivan & Tunney Attorneys at Law. "My dad's old law office."

I moved closer and tried to wrap my arms around her. "I'm sorry, sweetheart."

She shrugged me off. "No you're not. This is one of the buildings you'll be destroying." She turned to face me. "How could you not tell me you were doing this? You honestly thought I'd be okay with it?"

I rubbed my jaw, which ached and felt swollen. "I knew you'd be upset, but I also knew you'd understand where I was coming from."

"Why would I understand?"

"Because you've been betrayed too. You know the wound it leaves behind."

Her breath trembled. "But you're betraying *me*."

"No." I shook my head. "I'm not. I'd *never* do that. This has nothing to do with you."

"Of course, it does. How can you say that?"

"Because this is how the world works, Claire." I laid my hand on the brick wall beside me. "You can't stop change. These old buildings aren't going to last forever."

"You don't know that," she said stubbornly. "What if they declare this whole area a historic district?"

"It won't make any difference. Our lawyers have already looked into it." I gestured around. "Many of these buildings aren't old enough, and even the old ones have been significantly altered. The fact is, if it's not NorthStone tearing them down, it'll be my father's company doing it."

She licked her lips. "Then let it be his."

I gave her a long look. "You can't possibly mean that."

"I don't want it to be *you*."

"This deal is going to be extremely profitable. I can't turn my back on that. I don't want to."

Her eyes blazed. "So that's all you care about? No wonder green is your favorite color. It's the color of *money*."

I ignored the dig. "There's too much at stake here. I'm flying to Seattle tomorrow to sign contracts."

"You haven't signed anything yet?"

"Not until Monday."

She moved closer, her face stamped with hope. "So there's still time for me to change your mind?"

I looked away from that hope, staring out at the street, surrounded by this town's infamous past—its history both good and bad. Oddly, I'd soon be a part of that history.

"Please, Philip," she whispered. "Don't do it. If you love me, don't do it."

"Stop." I took a deep breath, feeling like shit. "You can't ask this of me."

"It's a mistake on so many levels. One you'll regret. You think it'll fix the past, but it won't."

"Are you kidding? The only thing I regret is that I didn't find a way sooner. I can't let him win." My voice hardened. "Not *this* time."

She studied me and then took my hand. I slipped my fingers through hers. We gazed at each other. I hated the unhappy expression on her face. I hated that I was the one putting it there.

"You've already won. Can't you see that?" Her voice carried into the night. "You have your mom and sister while he has no one. Your father lost everything a long time ago."

"It's not enough, Claire. I wish it were, but it's not."

"Listen to yourself. When is it ever enough? How much money will it take for you to feel safe? To be happy?"

I didn't reply.

"The wolves aren't howling at your door anymore. It's nothing but revenge."

"No." I pulled my hand from hers. "That's where you're wrong. This isn't revenge. It's *justice*."

"You're better than this. I know you are."

I walked a few paces from her and gazed at the gold lettering above that solid and respectable doorway. Claire's father was a good man. I could tell without ever having met him. I could tell from the way she spoke of him, from the kind of person he raised in her.

"I left something out of the story I told you that night." I turned to her again. "After my mom, Eliza, and I were forced out of our home, and after we moved in with my aunt, I went to see my father. He'd moved into a high-rise downtown. I snuck past the building's security and made my way up to the top floor, to the penthouse. Do you know what I found?"

She shook her head.

"He was having a party. Just him and a bunch of women—hookers, I imagine. One of them let me in." I closed my eyes. Nausea cut through me at the memory of it. The stink of booze and perfume in that apartment. "He was in bed with two of them. I should have left right then, but I didn't. I told him what had happened to us. I asked him—" I swallowed, shame burning through me, "I asked him for money."

Claire's eyes were on me, but I couldn't look at her.

"My father got out of bed and wrapped a towel around himself. He grabbed his wallet from the dresser. Then he handed me a single twenty-dollar bill and said, 'That should be enough for a taxi home.'"

I finally met her eyes. "I took the twenty dollars, because we needed it, and rode the bus home."

"Philip—" Claire tried to reach out for me, but I wouldn't let her touch me.

"I have to do this. I *have* to."

"You're not that thirteen-year-old boy anymore."

"You asked me if it will ever be enough?" I shook my head. "No, it never will be. Those wolves are always at my door."

"But they aren't real." There was compassion in her gaze. "You think you have to take care of everybody. It's just like that Monopoly game. You want to control everything. You think it's all up to you, but it's not."

"Of course it is."

"Take a look around. Your mom and Eliza are fine. Both of them are living happy lives."

I didn't respond. She couldn't possibly understand the fear I've had to live with. Those wolves were plenty real. I was glad for her though. I would never want her to have those kinds of worries.

"And now you're going to destroy everything," she went on heatedly. "Not only this town but you and me. Just to get back at a man who isn't even worth it!"

"It *has* to be done."

"No, it doesn't. You can still drop this whole thing." She threw her hands up. "How can we be together otherwise?"

"Don't ask this of me, Claire. Anything but *this*!" I slapped the brick wall beside me. "What has this town ever done for you? Is it so much that you're willing to sacrifice your own happiness?"

She went still. Right away I realized my mistake. I'd questioned her loyalty to her home.

"Sweetheart," I pleaded. "Choose *me*." But I knew it was too late. I knew the same way I always knew when a deal was dead in the water. It was finished. Over.

"That's the problem," she said, her gaze level on mine. "I shouldn't have to choose at all."

THIRTY

~ Claire ~

The next morning was bright and sunny, though it shouldn't have been. The birds were chirping in the woods, and Quicksilver and Calico Jack were singing right along with them.

I'd been awake all night, lying in bed going over everything.

In one day I'd gone from the dizzying heights of happiness to the depths of despair.

Philip would be back in Seattle by now, back to that big empty house of his. He'd only have his religious cult to keep him company. I smiled a little, remembering our joke.

My phone buzzed, and I reached for it, hoping it was him telling me he'd changed his mind yet knowing it wasn't. It was Violet. She wanted to see if I was okay and invited me up to the house for breakfast. There were other messages too. Four from Leah, a few more from Eliza and Sylvia.

I rolled onto my side, staring at the empty half of my bed.

How could I be with a man who planned to destroy my home-town? I loved him, but I couldn't accept that.

My heart ached at the expression on his face last night. That wounded thirteen-year-old boy was still there, plain as day.

I decided to get up and join Violet. There was no point in lying here feeling sorry for myself. I'd felt sorry for myself a lot after Ethan left, and I didn't want to fall into that black hole again. She probably needed help getting the house back in order anyway.

After feeding my birds, I threw on jean shorts and a white T-shirt, slipped on a pair of flip-flops, and headed up to the main house.

I could tell it was going to be a hot day. Bees buzzed near the flowerpots, and the air felt thick as honey. There was a hint of wood smoke from the bonfires last night. Normally I loved mornings like this.

I entered through the back door, glancing around the great room. It looked like they'd already cleaned up, though there were still some decorations to take down, a few clothing items left behind to return, and furniture that needed to be moved back into place.

When I heard voices, I followed the sound into the dining room, figuring it was Violet and Daphne. Instead there was a table full of people.

To my dismay, two of them were Ethan and Ivy. I stopped in the doorway, instantly realizing my mistake. I'd forgotten it was Sunday. Their day to have breakfast here.

"Come on in, Claire." Violet motioned me over. "Join us."

I was tempted to grab a cup of coffee and go. I didn't want to deal with those two. But then I thought, *No, this is my house as well.*

"There's plenty of food on the sideboard," Violet said as I walked over to get a plate. "I can have Esmé make more eggs if those aren't enough."

"This is fine," I murmured. I felt everyone's eyes on me.

Violet began to discuss some people she'd spoken to at the party last night, and I sensed awkwardness in the room. It was like no one knew what to say now that I was here.

I brought my plate and mug over to the only empty chair at the table. To my surprise, it was right next to Doug. I hadn't even noticed him.

Unfortunately, Ethan was on the other side, and he jumped up and pulled the chair out for me. "Let me help," he said eagerly, trying to take my mug, but I moved it out of his reach.

"It's fine, I've got it." I took a seat, ignoring him.

"Would you like cream?" he asked, bringing it over. I didn't look at Ivy, but I could sense her disapproval.

"Thanks." I poured cream into my coffee and then turned to Doug. "It's nice to see you this morning."

He smiled nervously. "How are you, Claire? I hope... you're okay."

"I'm fine," I said, peppering my eggs.

Violet was talking about the places our mayor was traveling to in retirement, but it seemed like she was filling the air with words.

Daphne was sitting beside Doug, watching me with compassion. "Are you really okay, Claire?"

I chewed my food. Of course I wasn't really okay, but how was I supposed to answer that? "Well." I shrugged. "You know how it goes."

She nodded.

"How is... Philip?" Doug asked. "I mean... after I punched him last night. I hope I didn't hurt him too much. Was he in pain?"

Ivy snorted. "Who cares if he was in pain? That asshole deserved a lot worse than a punch in the face."

I glanced over at her, ready to get into it, but then realized the strange position I was in. I couldn't defend Philip's actions. I was breaking up with him because of them.

She smirked at me. "You sure know how to pick 'em, don't you?"

"Let's not start this," Violet said to her daughter. "We need to give Claire whatever space she requires. This can't be easy for her."

"Philip is not a bad person," Doug spoke up. "He's helped me a lot. In fact, he helps people all the time."

Ivy rolled her eyes while she absentmindedly shredded a napkin. The plate of food in front of her was barely eaten. My guess was she needed a cigarette. "Yes, Mr. Moneybags sounds like a real prince. We should ask him if he'd like to run for town mayor."

"I'll remind you, Philip is still Doug's cousin," Violet said in a stern voice. "And it's rude to besmirch a member of his family."

I had to admit, it surprised me that Violet was so solicitous toward Doug. She must have really mellowed out. That he was here at the table next to Daphne said it all. There was no way she would have approved of him as a suitor in the past.

"Whatever," Ivy muttered. "I'm not going to pretend to like the guy."

"Have you and Philip broken up, then?" Ethan asked, leaning toward me.

I swallowed a bite of food. "We have."

"I'm really sorry to hear that. Is there anything I could do to help?"

"Help?" I picked up my mug of coffee and glanced at him. "Like how?"

"I'm not sure. I could mow your lawn or something."

My brows went up. "You want to mow my lawn?" I sensed Ivy's eyes on both of us, her body tensing as she watched this conversation.

"Sure. You might not be feeling up to it."

"No, that's okay." I put my mug down. The last thing I wanted was Ethan going into his good-guy routine and hanging around the carriage house.

"I might be able to help in other ways too."

Ivy snapped, "Are you *fucking* kidding me with this?"

Ethan and I looked at her. The whole table did. Violet put her hand up in warning. "Ivy, this isn't the time or place, and I don't appreciate that sort of language."

She threw down the napkin she'd been shredding, turning on Ethan. "You want to mow her lawn? Wax her car? Maybe you guys should have a sleepover and braid each other's hair."

He opened his mouth. "It's not like that. I just want to help."

"And I don't *want* his help," I added.

"Oh, please." Ivy glared at me. "You'd love any excuse to be around him. Once a betrayer, always a betrayer."

"You would know, wouldn't you?"

She scoffed. "Like you didn't start this whole thing. There's no need to keep pretending you're innocent."

I rolled my eyes. "You're crazy. Are you still going on about me catching you with Derek in the carriage house? Nobody cares about that anymore."

"Derek?" Ivy laughed. "I wasn't with Derek, and you know it!"

I blinked at her. "What do you mean? Who were you with?"

She glanced at Ethan, and I went still. Cold awareness flooded through me. The truth sank in with a shock. It made sense now. I didn't know why it had never occurred to me before. After all these years, so many puzzle pieces fell into place.

I looked at Ethan. "My God, it was *you* that summer, wasn't it?"

He licked his lips and seemed nervous. "I thought you knew. Or I did at first anyway."

"Why would you think that?"

"Because you ratted us out to my mom," Ivy interjected. "Even after I begged you not to. But you wanted him for yourself, didn't you? It wasn't enough you had *everything* else. A wonderful father who loved you. This amazing house. But you wanted Ethan too. You knew my mom would tell him to stay away from me, and that's exactly what happened."

Her outburst flabbergasted me. I never knew Ivy felt that way. I glanced at Violet, who appeared deep in thought. "I never said anything to your mom. I didn't even know that was Ethan with you in the carriage house."

"Stop lying!"

"I'm not."

"Oh really? Then who told my mom about us?"

"I did," Daphne's soft voice said.

Ivy startled and turned to her sister. "What?"

"I'm the one who told Mom about you and Ethan that summer."

The room went so quiet, I could hear the lawn sprinklers out back. My mind was still processing that Ethan and Ivy had a relationship all those years ago before we did. Not to mention this jealousy toward me. If only I'd known.

"Why?" Ivy asked her. "Why would you do such a thing? How could you?"

Daphne glanced at Violet. "Because it wasn't right what you two were doing. None of it."

Ivy leaned back in her chair. "This is unbelievable. My own sister."

Violet nodded. "Daphne came to me and told me what was going on, but don't blame her. I did what any mother with a sixteen-year-old daughter would have done."

"And you." Ivy turned to Ethan. "You never told Claire about *us?* In all that time you were together?"

Ethan shifted uncomfortably in his chair. "Well, I figured she knew. After a while, it became obvious she didn't know, but how could I tell her then?"

"So you kept the lie going." Ivy seemed to get more upset. "You didn't want her to know. She really meant that much to you?"

"We were married. I didn't want to hurt her."

"And now *we're* married, but you don't seem to mind hurting *me.*" Ivy shoved herself up from the table, bumping it and rattling the dishes. "I've had enough. If you still want Claire so much, then go back to her. I don't care anymore."

I opened my mouth in protest. I didn't want him. She couldn't unload him on me.

Ivy tried to leave, but Ethan's hand flew out and grabbed her wrist.

"Let go!"

"No." Ethan's face was intense. "I'm not letting go. Not now, not ever. That summer meant just as much to me as it did to you."

She stood there, and I watched as her gaze settled on him.

"I'm not losing you again," he told her. "If I have to fight for you, then I will."

He held her wrist, and in that moment, something passed between them. Something intimate that I recognized. Ivy's eyes softened, and I had a revelation.

They loved each other.

As strange as it sounded, I'd never quite gotten that before. I guess I didn't want to think about it. Or I wanted to pretend it was lust or some kind of affection, not real love. And my heart grieved because the thing I recognized between them was what Philip and I had. It was the way *we* looked at each other.

Ivy's gaze hardened. "And what about Claire? Do you still love her too?"

Ethan shook his head. "No, I don't. Not like this." He glanced at me. "Sorry, Claire."

Ivy pulled her wrist away. "Then why did you go to her house? Why all this attention on her?"

"Because I feel guilty. I never wanted to hurt her. Claire and I were once close."

That didn't seem to placate Ivy. Just the opposite. Her scowl deepened.

"Listen to me." Ethan lowered his voice. "You've always been the one I wanted. But you have to stop pushing me away, stop this pointless jealousy, because you're *ruining* everything."

Ivy blinked at him.

"I fell in love with you that summer," he said, his voice heated, "and that's never changed."

I couldn't explain it, but as I watched the two of them, I had a moment of clarity. I decided to forgive them both. Forgive them for everything. I thought I'd moved on, and I had, but a part of me was still angry. As long as I carried that anger, the wound from their betrayal would never heal.

I took a deep breath, and it was like a great burden had been lifted from me. Let them be happy. Their paths and mine had diverged. Our lives were separate.

Ethan and Ivy.

Ivy Spivy.

Okay, I'm allowed a little pleasure at that name.

MY WAY of handling the breakup with Philip was to keep busy nonstop. Scrubbing and cleaning with a fervor, it was like I'd gone back in time, trying to find my Zen place again, creating order in the universe where there was none.

I met with Taylor too and gave her a couple of shifts. I was right about her. She was energetic and responsible. Both of the clients I spoke with afterward said they really liked her. I could tell she was going to be an asset to my business. It turned out she was older than I'd thought too. She looked like a teenager but was nearly my age.

Thankfully, nobody in town called me "Poor Claire." Instead they were helpful and kind. Isabel came by and brought me some of her family's famous strawberry shortcake. Even Delores, the town gossip, brought me a casserole and didn't pump me for too much information.

Philip became public enemy number one. Especially after contracts were signed and somebody sent around the video link from YouTube, a short clip taken from some financial news network. I watched it, though I shouldn't have. To my surprise, Philip and Gavin were both wearing suits. What happened to the outlaws? Philip looked pale, and his expression remained stony even when Gavin was speaking to him about something.

I decided the best thing I could do was move forward, so that was what I did. I went to the movies with Doug and Daphne one night. And then I met Leah and Theo for dinner a couple nights later. I told them I didn't want a pity party.

"But pity parties have ice cream," Theo pointed out.

"And alcohol," Leah complained. "You can't deny us the right to throw you a pity party after a breakup this momentous."

I sighed. "Fine."

We had the party at Leah's house, since my place was too small, and Theo's boyfriend, Clement, was back from Guatemala. I didn't want to risk another two-hour dissertation on the horned passalus beetle. There was ice cream, fancy drinks, and a stack of chick flicks we binged on until everyone fell asleep.

The next day, despite being tired, I finally finished organizing my spare room. And then I put the rest of my focus on coming up with a new name for my business.

Yes, I was taking Philip's advice.

I got out some paper and wrote down different names and then looked them up online. I tried drawing some of my ideas with a logo, but I wasn't much of an artist. A couple hours into it, I heard a car coming down the driveway.

I wasn't expecting anyone.

I got up and peeked out the window, and when I saw Sylvia's silver SUV, my heart stopped. I could barely breathe. *Is it Philip? What's he doing here?* I went into a blind panic. I hadn't showered since yesterday. Sticky with sweat and no makeup, I ran around the room, fanning myself with my hands. Quickly I pulled my hair out of its bun and flipped my head upside down, trying to fluff it out.

Turned out it was only Eliza.

She took in my flustered appearance. "Is everything okay?"

"Oh, fine." I tried to catch my breath. "I was just... exercising."

She nodded and came inside.

"Would you like anything?" I asked, moving into my kitchen. "Lemonade or water? I might have some soda left."

"Lemonade sounds good. I can't believe you're exercising in this hot weather."

"Oh." I shrugged. "I just felt like it."

We both went into the main room, where I put our glasses on the table next to my bed while she talked to my birds, both of them chirping and fluttering around.

"Would you like to hold one of them?" I asked.

She turned to me with excitement. Her topknot wasn't as high today, bouncing instead of wobbling. "Do you think they'd mind?"

"There's one way to find out." I came over and opened the cage door, letting Calico Jack step up onto my finger. "He's a little friendlier than your great-grandfather's namesake."

"Kiss, kiss," he squawked when I passed him over to her.

She giggled. "His claws are scratchy. And he's so light."

I nodded. "They weigh practically nothing."

I left for a second to close all the curtains and cover the mirror, making sure things were safe before my birds flew around.

Meanwhile Eliza was gently petting Calico. "He's really soft," she whispered.

By now Quicksilver was sticking his head out of the cage, looking for trouble as usual. To my amazement, he flew out, then came back and landed on my shoulder.

"That's sweet," she said. "Does he always do that?"

"He never has." I petted and cooed to him, pleased that he was warming up.

After a few minutes, I set both birds up on the rope I had strung over the room, and Eliza and I took a seat on the bed. I gathered up all the papers spread everywhere, the ones filled with business name ideas and drawings.

She seemed interested. "What is all that?"

I told her how I was trying to find a different name for my maid service. Something stronger. "It was your brother's idea," I admitted. "He never liked Your House Sparkles."

"It sounds like it could be a good tagline though." Then she rolled her eyes and laughed. "Wow, listen to me. I've spent too much time around him and Gavin. Do you mind if I look at what you have?"

"Sure." I handed the stack of papers to her.

As she read through them, it was on the tip of my tongue to ask how Philip was doing. I knew I shouldn't though. I was supposed to be moving on. To be honest, I was worried for him after seeing how he looked on that YouTube clip.

"What about this one?" she asked, pointing to one of my top picks. "I like that."

"I like it too, but I don't know what kind of logo I could make."

Eliza studied the paper. "Would you mind if I played around with it for a few days?"

"Sure, but do you know how to draw?"

She nodded. "I was an art major for two semesters."

As she went back to looking through my notes, I couldn't stand it any longer.

"How is Philip doing? I mean, I'm just wondering."

She turned to me, her eyes filled with concern. "That's the reason I came here tonight." She put the papers down. "He's not good, Claire."

"What do you mean?"

"He's in terrible shape. He doesn't want to talk to anybody. And when we do talk to him, he's always in a bad mood. Even Gavin's been walking on eggshells around him."

If I were a different kind of person, I would have been glad to hear that, but I wasn't. It made me feel worse.

"He's holed up in that big empty house," she continued. "My mom and I don't know what to do. We tried going over there, but he won't talk to us. He just sits there all day watching those stupid news channels."

"I'm sorry to hear that."

"Gavin told me he hasn't been to work in two weeks."

"Really? That doesn't sound like Philip."

"No, it doesn't." Eliza's pale eyes, so much like her brother's, fixated on me. "We know he got involved in that big land deal to get back at our father, but it was a mistake. My mom and I told him so." She glanced over at my birds, who were sitting at the highest spot on the wall, their favorite perch. "Everybody here in town is still nice to us. Nobody blames us for what he's doing."

I nodded, glad to hear that.

"I wonder if you could try talking to him." She bit her lip. "Maybe it would help."

"What would I say?"

"I don't know. I mean, I know you guys have broken up, but I've never seen him like this."

"It's probably not a good idea," I said, being honest. "I think dragging this out will only make things harder for both of us."

ABOUT A WEEK LATER, when I drove down the driveway toward my house after work, there was a car sitting there I didn't recognize. A black Acura. A middle-aged man sat in the driver seat.

I pulled up alongside it and paused. *This is weird. Who is he? What am I supposed to do?*

I didn't have long to think about it, because he got out of his car and walked over to my side. He wore dark slacks and a beige button-down shirt.

I cracked my window a couple inches. "Can I help you?"

The man smiled. He was handsome in an older guy kind of way. Balding, and when he ran his hand over the top of his head, I saw he wore a wedding band. "Sorry, I hope I didn't alarm you. I'm Sam."

I blinked at him. "Who?"

"Mr. North's—er, Philip's personal assistant." As he spoke, I realized he had an Australian accent.

Sam! My eyes widened. I couldn't believe it. "Yes, I know who you are."

"I've brought a few of your things. Clothing and a couple of other items. Philip asked me to see they were returned to you."

I rolled my window back up and got out of the car.

"It's nice to meet you finally," I said, holding my hand out. He was on the short side, only a few inches taller than me.

"You too." He grinned as we shook hands.

"Philip never told me you were from Australia."

"Didn't he?"

I shook my head.

"Let me get those items for you," he said.

I followed him over to the rear of his car, where he opened the trunk. Inside was a brand-new Coach bag. He handed it to me.

"What's this? This isn't mine."

"It is now." He smiled and seemed a little embarrassed. "I needed to put them in something. My assistant, Lorna, suggested it."

Thank you, Lorna. Curiously, I looked inside the purse. There was a peach T-shirt, a hairbrush, and the cord to my cell phone, which I'd already replaced.

"You didn't have to come all the way out here for this," I said, mystified. "You could have mailed it."

He closed the trunk and turned to me. "I certainly could have done that, but I wanted to meet you in person."

"Okay." I nodded slowly. "Why?"

"I had a theory about you, and now that I've met you, it's been confirmed."

My brows came together. "What theory is that?"

"You're completely different from any woman Philip's ever been with."

"I'm different?"

"I'll say. Very different."

I took that in, thinking back to Madison. I was certainly different than her.

"I've worked with Philip for years now, and it's almost like he's been waiting for something, for *someone*. And it's obvious that someone is you, Claire."

I was taken aback. Was this really the place of a personal

assistant? My guess was Philip would fire him on the spot if he knew he was here saying these things.

"I see you're surprised by my candor." He grinned. "Sticking my nose in where it doesn't belong, eh? What has Philip told you about me?"

"To be honest, all he's told me is that you're an excellent assistant."

Sam nodded and tipped his head forward. "And now you get to see *why* I'm an excellent assistant." His brown eyes met mine. "In action."

I smiled. I couldn't help it. He was more charming than I'd expected.

"He needs you, Claire." His expression turned serious. "This mess with his father is only going to get worse. He's made a mistake, and now he's drowning in it. Stuck in the past and can't move forward."

I took a deep breath. This sounded like the same thing Eliza told me.

"You need to go to him," he said.

"I can't do that. Not after what he's done. This is my home, and he's destroying it."

"I understand. But you should reach out to him anyway."

"You're kind of pushy, aren't you?"

He grinned. "I've always liked the word 'persistent.'"

AFTER HE LEFT, I slipped into my normal evening routine, fed my birds, made my dinner. It turned out Eliza had come up with some amazing artwork ideas for my new business name, and I was thrilled as I studied the pages.

Eventually I'd have to go to bed though, and that was the hardest part of my day.

The part I dreaded.

That was when I missed Philip the most. I missed lying together and talking. I missed our occasional wrestling matches, and, of course, I missed being intimate. Finding that part of myself again with him was something I'd be forever grateful for.

Some nights I cried, but others I lay awake as memories swam to the surface. I kept thinking about that crazy day when he came to me in the storm. His expression when he found me. No one had ever wanted me that much. It wasn't the kind of thing you forgot.

I remembered other times too. Sitting outside together late at night enjoying the woods. And then there was the time we got into a debate over the most satisfying way to eat a Kit Kat bar. Philip insisted on biting the whole thing, whereas I preferred breaking it into pieces and nibbling the edges.

"It takes forever to eat it that way," he'd pointed out.

"I know. I like savoring it."

He'd leaned in, nibbling my neck. It tickled, and I couldn't stop laughing. "The only thing I'm interested in savoring is *you*."

Even if we couldn't be together, I hated the idea of him miserable and lashing out at everyone. I thought about how I'd moved past my anger toward Ethan and Ivy. I wished Philip could do the same.

Impulsively, I grabbed my phone off the bedside table. It was the middle of the night, but I opened a text message to him.

I stopped for a second.

And then I typed five words.

I stared at it for a long time before I finally touched Send.

I hope he reads it, and I hope he does exactly what it says.

THIRTY-ONE

~ Philip ~

"I have *employees*?" Doug's voice warbled over the phone. "Since when do I have employees?"

"Since I hired them." I reached for the remote control to turn down the volume on screen three. It was a financial news update but appeared to be a repeat of the same one I'd seen a half hour ago on screen two.

"How... how many do I have?" He sounded scared to find out.

"Five."

"I have *five* employees?" He gulped.

"That's correct. Are we done now?" Glancing over, I could tell C-SPAN had started live coverage of a congressional hearing. I wanted to get back to my screens, but Doug wouldn't stop talking.

"What is this Bradley Renovations name I keep seeing on every-thing?" he asked. "I've never heard of that."

"That's your new business name."

"My *what?*"

"I had to rename it." I got up and went into the kitchen since I couldn't concentrate on the news anyway. I opened the fridge. There wasn't much food. Some Italian takeout, but when I looked inside the box, it had hair growing on it.

"But my business name is Bradley Wood & Paint."

"Not anymore."

"That's not... I don't... how...?" he sputtered.

I sniffed at the Italian food. It smelled okay. Maybe I could scrape off the bad parts. But then I remembered my food poisoning in Mexico City and decided not to chance it.

"You've gone too far, Philip. This is *too* far." I pictured him pacing around his living room with his usual unhappy expression. "I can't believe you would do that!"

"Look, I had to. The old name was fine, but it wasn't working anymore." I opened the garbage can and dumped the leftovers inside. "Things change."

"And who asked you to make these changes? I sure didn't."

"You left me in charge of a business that was barely solvent. I turned it into a highly profitable enterprise."

"So? So what? Nobody asked you to do that!"

I rolled my eyes. So now Doug was angry at me? After that punch in the jaw, I thought we were straight, but I should have known better. Nothing with Doug was ever straight.

"I'm just a simple guy," he ranted. "I don't know anything about running a business this size. Do I have to give stock options? I don't even know what that is!"

"Calm down. Jesus, you're acting like I put you on the *Forbes* list." I opened the cabinet to see if there was a can of chili or soup I could warm up, then wished I hadn't when my eyes landed on a stack of Kit Kat bars.

I went still. I hadn't realized those were there. My chest tightened, and the back of my throat closed up. I blinked a few times, then forced myself to take a deep breath.

Doug was still carrying on about stock options, corporate taxes, and 401(k) plans.

I closed the cabinet door. "Look, you can do whatever you want with your business. Sell the damn thing for all I care."

"Sell it?" That seemed to give him pause. "I could sell it?"

"It wouldn't surprise me if Bob wanted to buy it."

"Who's Bob?"

"Your general manager."

"Oh."

We both went quiet. I kept thinking about those chocolate bars and Claire. Always Claire. I didn't want to think about her, but she found ways of sneaking in.

Watching the news seemed to be the only thing that kept her at bay.

Because it'd been hard without her. The days had been terrible. The nights were even worse. Somehow my life had gone to shit.

It didn't help that everyone was angry at me. My mom and sister —even Gavin was acting strange. When Mom and Eliza came to stay, they both voiced their disapproval over what I'd done. They wanted to talk about my "feelings," but that was the last thing I wanted. Finally, they went back to Truth Harbor.

"Could... could you ask Bob if he'd like to buy it?" Doug ventured. "I think I might like to sell."

"No," I said irritably. "Ask him yourself."

There was a doorbell in the background on his phone. "I have to get that. Daphne and I are going to the movies with... um... with no one. We're going with no one!"

I remained silent, though I could feel my heart pounding.

"It's just the two of us tonight," Doug carried on. "That's right, Daphne and me all alone at the movies."

I still didn't say anything.

"Fine! I admit it. We're going with Claire. Daphne thinks she could use a night out."

I licked my lips and lowered my voice. "Is she there?" I imagined

Doug handing the phone to her. I imagined hearing her pretty voice again. A terrible yearning took hold of me. My grip tightened. I shouldn't be allowing this. An addict hoping for one last fix.

"No, we're picking her up at the carriage house."

Disappointment echoed through me. But then I realized what he'd just said. "Why does Daphne think Claire needs a night out? Is she okay?"

"Oh, sure. She's okay. It's just that she's working all the time. Daphne said she even hired a new person."

That's my pirate princess. Using her energies to build something. Meanwhile, I was watching television day and night. I couldn't muster the energy for anything. Not even work.

"I have to go," he said. "Would you... um... ask Bob if he'd like to buy me out? I'd really appreciate it."

I nearly said no again but then stopped myself. It wouldn't kill me to help. "All right, fine, I'll talk to him."

———

THE NEWS WASN'T the only thing I watched. I also watched my father. I tracked his financial health closely. Not long after we signed that partnership with Atlas, rumors swirled that his company was in trouble.

I was glad to hear that, but it wasn't enough.

A few days later, the people I had monitoring him told me the banks had begun seizing his assets. Not only his business assets but his personal ones too. He'd been living in a house of cards, and it had come crashing down.

I was glad, but, of course, it wasn't enough.

When my people got back to me a week later and told me he'd declared both business and personal bankruptcy, I was glad again.

But it still wasn't enough.

I didn't understand.

Why wasn't it enough?

I SOON HAD MY ANSWER.

It was a hot summer night. I had the air conditioner blasting and didn't notice how warm it was outside until I answered the door for the pizza delivery guy.

"Wow, this is some place," he said, his eyes bugging out of his head. He was dark-haired, portly, and covered in zits. "A real palace."

I didn't reply as I signed the credit card receipt.

"Where's your furniture though?" He craned his neck around me, trying to see inside. "That's weird. Why don't you have any furniture?"

"None of your fucking business is why." I slammed the door shut.

I ate the first slice of pizza in silence, chewing slowly since my jaw still bothered me. Popping open a can of soda, I took a swig. Sam made sure groceries were delivered once a week, though I mostly ordered out. It occurred to me that the only people I saw anymore were delivery people.

Gavin came by the other day, but his visit was short.

"What the hell is going on with you?" he'd wanted to know. "When is this self-imposed exile going to end?"

"When I'm good and ready. Anything else?"

He sighed. "C'mon, Philip. We're all worried about you."

"Don't be."

He studied me. "Is there any way you and Claire could patch things up?"

I turned my head. "I don't want to talk about it."

"Then what do you want to talk about?"

"Nothing."

Gavin sighed and ran a hand down his face. He leaned forward. "This isn't healthy. Eliza tells me all you're doing is watching the news day and night. You should at least come into the office."

I rubbed my jaw, which ached like a sonofabitch. I knew I should have it X-rayed, but I didn't want the hassle. "My father declared bankruptcy recently."

Gavin's brows went up. "Really?" He leaned back. "Well, you should be pleased. That must be very satisfying."

I nodded. But it wasn't satisfying. Not at all.

"Come into the office Monday. Drink Virtue is presenting their new flavor fixes to a group of our investors. We could use your input."

"Fine, I'll be there."

"Really? Great. I'll send you the details."

I'd agreed to look them over, but it was mostly so Gavin would leave. I already knew I wasn't going anywhere Monday.

I picked up another slice of pizza, which had cooled considerably. *Maybe I should turn down the air. It feels like winter in here.* Instead I leaned back on the couch with a blanket and watched an analysis on the Fed and current interest rates.

Somewhere in there I must have dozed off. When I woke up, there was drool on my chin, and I heard the sound of someone calling from the main gate.

I sat up, disoriented. *That's strange.* I wiped the spit off my face and checked the time. It was the middle of the night. I grabbed my iPad to see who was at the gate.

"Let me in, Philip."

I stared at him on screen. The black hair and overly tanned skin.

"What do you want?" I asked.

"Just let me in." He smiled, his teeth a garish white. He looked like the headliner for a Las Vegas act. "I'd like to talk to you."

I hesitated. Did I really want to deal with this? But then I buzzed him in, realizing a part of me had been waiting for him all along.

As soon as he entered the doorway, I could tell he'd been drinking. The stench of booze and cologne clung to him like acid rain. He whistled with approval as he took in the house. "Nice place. Bigger than I expected. I like it."

It figured that he'd approve of this ridiculous house.

His brows rose when he followed me upstairs and realized none of it was furnished, that I only lived in a small part. "You're kind of eccentric, aren't you? I'm not surprised. You get it from your mother. She's always had a weird bohemian streak."

I had a flash of memory from when I was a kid. Anything out of my father's wheelhouse was referred to as "bohemian."

He followed me into the living room, and I wished I'd picked up. I'd had a maid service, but I'd canceled it, and the place was a mess. I didn't want him knowing I was in such bad shape.

He glanced around and didn't seem to notice the mess. He walked over to one of the French doors and opened them to look outside. "It's dark out, but I can tell the view isn't half bad either."

"Why are you here? Are you planning to buy the house?" I smirked at my joke. There was no way he could afford this house. Not anymore.

He turned back to me. "Do you have anything to drink? How about you pour me a glass of whatever you've got."

I considered him, deciding I could be generous now that I was the one holding all the cards. I went to the kitchen and poured a couple fingers of single malt Scotch into a glass. Then I thought, *What the hell*, and poured myself the same. After handing him his drink, I took a seat on the couch.

He continued to wander around the room, examining various objects. "I've been thinking things over. Do you know what my biggest mistake was?" he asked, glancing over at me.

I took a sip of Scotch, smooth as silk with a hint of wood smoke, and waited.

He picked up one of the framed photos from the shelf. The one Claire had asked about with my mom, Eliza, and me from years ago. I expected him to tell me his biggest mistake was dumping his family. I hoped that was why he came here, to throw himself at my mercy, to ask me to bail him out.

I'd enjoy that.

It might even be enough.

"My biggest mistake was underestimating you." He put the photo frame down and walked toward me, took a seat in the nearest chair. "I should have figured you out before I came to see you that day."

I studied him. The room lights were set for evening, but it was enough to see how his eyes were bloodshot, how the lines on his face ran deep.

"I still thought of you as a boy," he continued. "I hadn't realized you'd turned into a man, and a formidable one at that."

I didn't say anything.

"I'm impressed. And I don't impress easily."

I took another swallow of Scotch, irritated. Praise was the last thing I wanted from him. When was he going to ask for money?

"I shouldn't have threatened you that day," he said. "I realize that now. I've never responded well to threats either."

I tapped my glass with impatience.

He leaned forward, still holding his drink. "Let me ask you something. Do you have many regrets in life?"

I already knew why he was asking. He was playing on my sympathies, but it wouldn't work. My voice hardened. "No, I don't have *any.*"

He nodded. "I figured as much. You're just like me. Regrets are for the weak-minded."

I didn't want to hear this bullshit. "Did you come here for my help? Is that it? Because I know you've been forced into bankruptcy."

"No, I came here to congratulate you."

Unease settled in the pit of my stomach. "What do you mean?"

"Just what I said." He leaned back in his chair. "You're right, the banks have seized all my assets. There's even a padlock on the front door of my house."

"So why are you congratulating me?"

"Because you did a hell of a job taking me down, Philip. I know you hate me, and I don't blame you. But I'm still proud of you." He smiled. "You did exactly what I would have done."

My breath slowed. The room seemed to have grown smaller.

"And now here we are, father and son. A couple of high rollers who don't take shit from anybody." He held his glass up to me in a toast. "Congratulations. It turns out you're a true North."

He finished his drink, then stood up. "You might like to know that I'm leaving the country tomorrow. The vultures have moved in, and they're welcome to the carcass." He smirked. "Besides, there are some offshore accounts of mine they *won't* be able to get their filthy hands on."

He walked out of the room, and a moment later, I heard the front door open and close shut.

After he left, I didn't move at all as the large house closed in around me. Every room and window. Every door. All of it as suffocating as that first night my mom, Eliza, and I spent in a homeless shelter. I sat on the couch, trying to control myself, to breathe.

Then I stood up. An explosion of sound shattered the silence when I hurled my glass at the wall of televisions. Shards rained down as one of the screens splintered.

I stalked into the kitchen, grabbing more glasses and smashing those too. Next it was the mugs and every single plate I owned. Serving dishes I'd never seen before, bowls I'd never used. The noise was loud, an unnerving racket.

When I finished with the kitchen, I destroyed every item I could find, grunting and growling like an animal, until eventually the floor was littered with broken glass, splintered wood, plastic—all the remnants of my fury.

I collapsed into a heap, dripping sweat despite the frigid air conditioning. I thought of all I'd given up. The mistakes I'd made. The people I'd hurt.

All my talk of justice had amounted to nothing.

There would never be any justice.

My throat went tight. When I squeezed my eyes shut, the world was black. My future sprawled before me in darkness. How could I live with myself? How? Was I really so much like him?

I thought of Claire. That was the worst pain of all. The beautiful life we would have shared. Laughter and those little yellow rain boots splashing along the water. I already knew I'd never love like that again.

A buzz came from my pocket. Somehow my phone had escaped destruction. I pulled it out, stunned to discover a text from Claire. I was even more stunned when I saw what she'd written.

Forgive him. Then forgive yourself.

I blinked at it, staring in disbelief.

I put my head down and did something I hadn't done in a long time.

I cried.

I cried for that helpless thirteen-year-old kid I used to be, and then I cried for all the things that might have been.

OVER THE NEXT FEW DAYS, the fog lifted. I took Claire's advice and began to feel like myself again, except different. Somehow better. Changed. I'd been carrying that stone around my neck so long, I'd forgotten what it was like to live without it. To be free.

I knew I had a large problem to solve. Luckily, I was good at solving large problems. And for once, I wanted to be the good guy, the one who rode in on the white horse, the one who thought past improving his bottom line.

Because no matter what he'd said, I wasn't like him. I wasn't my father, and I never would be.

I told Gavin about it when I went back into work on Monday, right after I went to the Drink Virtue presentation. Happily, their fixes were brilliant. They needed a new production facility, and tooling costs had to be nailed down, but we were moving forward. They decided to put out both a regular and nonalcoholic version of their health drinks. The plan was to get them in every grocery store on the West Coast and expand from there.

We were sitting in Gavin's office when I told him what my plans were.

His brows shot up. "That's going to cost you. Are you sure about this?"

I nodded. "I've already spoken with the head of legal to figure out the best way to approach it."

"The investors will make you pay more than it's worth."

I rubbed my jaw, which still ached. I'd finally had Sam set up a doctor's appointment for me this afternoon to have it checked out. "I know."

He studied me and then grinned. "I never thought I'd see the day. You of all people, purposefully losing money."

I shrugged. At some point I'd tell him what happened with my father, but not now.

"Listen." I leaned forward. "I also know the perfect place for Drink Virtue's new production facility." I told him about the closed bottling factory on the outskirts of Truth Harbor.

"Damn, that does sound perfect." He tilted his head. "I wonder what Claire will say when she hears about all this."

"I think she'll be relieved, but that's not why I'm doing it."

"It's not?"

"Well, not the whole reason." In truth, I *was* doing it partly for Claire, because I loved her and didn't want to be the destroyer of her hometown.

"Then why are you?"

"I'm doing it because it's the right thing."

THIRTY-TWO

~ Claire ~

Everybody was going crazy with the news. The whole town had come alive with it.

"Have you heard?"

"You must be so proud of him, Claire!"

"What a generous man!"

The land that had been for sale in Truth Harbor was now being given to us all. The town would be its new owner.

On top of that, a beverage company had begun moving into the old soda bottling factory, and they were planning to hire hundreds of people.

This was all because of Philip.

He'd gone from public enemy number one to the town hero.

I didn't know what to make of it. From everything I'd heard, he was losing money, and that didn't sound like Philip.

"I think donating that property is a magnificent gesture," Violet said. "Our lawyers are setting up a permanent legal entity to manage it."

"Great," I murmured. I was glad, but also unsure. Was there some angle here I couldn't see?

"I have something to talk to you about." Violet pushed her empty plate out of the way. "Two things really. It's the reason I asked you here to breakfast this morning."

"Oh?" My stomach tightened. Usually when Violet had something to tell me, it wasn't good.

Her eyes met mine. "The first one is Ivy's pregnant. She and Ethan found out a few days ago."

She quieted, waiting for my reaction.

Was that it? I hoped her second thing was as easy as that one, because it was nothing. "Congratulations," I said and meant it. "You get to be a grandmother."

I could tell by her expression that she was pleased. She considered me for a moment. "I was concerned you might not take the news well, but I see I had nothing to worry about."

"You're right, I'm fine with it." And I truly was okay. Ethan and Ivy could have ten kids for all I cared.

"Good. I'm glad to hear that."

I picked up my glass.

"My second item to discuss with you is the house."

"What about it?" I took a sip from my orange juice.

"I've decided to sell."

The juice turned bitter in my mouth. I wanted to spit it out but swallowed instead. "Why?" I asked, though I already knew why.

"It's too much for me. Daphne's taken an apartment in town, and I can't see any reason for me to live here all alone anymore."

"But I'm here."

She smiled gently. "Yes, you're in the carriage house. But I don't need this much space." Leaning back, she sighed. "It's just me, ghosting around these big rooms every night. There are so many memories here, most of them good ones, but still."

I knew she was talking about my father, and I could see how staying here might make it hard for her to move on.

I took a deep breath. "When are you planning to put it on the market?" There was no point in discussing whether I should keep the house and buy her out, since we both knew I couldn't afford it.

"Soon. I've already spoken to Daphne about listing it. I wanted to tell you before that happens."

"Where are you planning to live after it sells?"

"Probably a condo by the water. Something smaller and closer to town." She turned to me. "After the sale, you'll have enough to buy something. Or you could rent for a while."

I nodded and smiled for her sake. I felt ill though. I didn't want strangers living in my home. And I couldn't even imagine myself happy anywhere else.

DAPHNE LISTED the house right away. She asked me if I'd like to start looking at places, said she could help, but I declined her offer.

They might have to drag me kicking and screaming out of my little fairy-tale cottage.

I spent Saturday morning doing yard work. The carriage house probably wouldn't be mine much longer, but I was going to enjoy it up to the last minute.

I mowed the small lawn and weeded around the flower beds. A client had given me some pansies, and I was planting them when I heard a car turn down my driveway. Glancing over, I saw it was Sylvia's SUV. For a second I went into a panic, then realized it was just Eliza again. We'd talked on the phone earlier, and she said she might drop by with some more sketches for my new logo.

I went back to planting flowers and wondered if she'd spoken to Philip. Everybody kept asking me about him. They all seemed to think we were back together.

The car door closed, and I was on my hands and knees trying to get the last pansy in the ground when I heard a familiar voice behind me.

"Hello, my pirate princess."

I sucked in my breath and went still before whipping my head around. "Philip?"

He grinned. "How are you, Claire?"

My mouth hung open. Then I realized how I must look—kneeling on the ground with my ass sticking up. Embarrassed, I sat back, trying to appear dignified. It wasn't easy. I was covered in dirt, sweaty with no makeup, my hair pulled back into a messy bun. Of all the times I'd imagined seeing him again, none of those fantasies looked like this.

He moved closer, and excitement drummed through me. He had on dark jeans and a short-sleeved T-shirt. I had a memory of the way his body felt pressed against mine. Big and solid.

"It's good to see you. I've missed you, sweetheart."

I was ready to tell him I missed him too, but then I remembered how I hadn't heard from him. "Don't 'sweetheart' me." I stood up and brushed the dirt off myself. "Where the heck have you been? Everybody keeps asking me about you, and I have no idea what to tell them."

He seemed puzzled. "People have been asking about me?"

"The whole town is ready to throw you a ticker tape parade for what you've done."

His confusion cleared, and he seemed embarrassed. "It wasn't much."

"I disagree. It's wonderful."

He only shrugged.

"Thank you. It means a lot to everybody. I heard you lost money though. Is that true?"

He moved closer until he was standing right in front of me. "I didn't come here to talk about money. That's the last thing I want to talk about."

"Then why did you come here?"

"I think you know."

Our eyes stayed on each other. His matched the color of the sky above us, rimmed with those sooty lashes.

"Have you missed me at all?" he asked, his voice low. "Tell me you've missed me."

"I might have missed you a little," I conceded.

"Is that so?"

"Maybe."

He smiled at me. "Look at you. So pretty as always." He reached out, and I thought he was going to stroke my cheek, but instead he pulled a weed from my hair.

I laughed lightly, trying not to be embarrassed. "I'm sure I look a fright."

"You're beautiful. I've been dreaming about your face."

"You have?"

He nodded. "Every night. It's all I can think about." His gaze dropped lower, a rascally smile on his lips. "And maybe a few other parts of you too."

I rolled my eyes, but I couldn't stop the feeling of warmth gliding through me. "I see some things never change."

"Not when it comes to the way I feel about you." He grinned, but then the levity vanished and his expression grew serious. "I'm so sorry, Claire. For all of it. You were right about everything you said to me that night. I'm done with those wolves at my door. I've chased them off for good."

I didn't know what had happened or what brought him to this state, but it must have been cataclysmic, because I could see he meant it. "I'm glad to hear that."

He reached for my hand, and I let him take it. "Tell me it isn't too late for us, sweetheart. That we can still make this work."

If I were a different kind of woman, maybe I would have made him beg for it, get on his knees, apologize more, but I didn't play games like that. I didn't want to waste any more time. We'd wasted enough.

I smiled and squeezed his hand. "It's not too late."

NATURALLY, we wound up in bed. Me with weeds in my hair and dirt on my skin. Philip said he didn't care, that he liked the weeds and the dirt.

Early afternoon sunlight filtered through the windows, illuminating my little fairy-tale cottage like a box of jewels.

His eyes were on me the whole time, and I could see them changing colors. Light blue to a deep violet. Magic.

It wasn't long before his clothes were on the floor, his scent all over me. Clean and familiar. His strong body moved over mine, and I pulled him in close, gasping when we came together. We moaned at the intensity, at the rightness of each other.

Later, when we were lying in bed, he trailed his fingertips down my arm. "Do you think you can ever love me again?" he asked quietly.

The room was warm and still. Even my birds were subdued. I was lying next to Philip, tucked into his side, watching dust motes float on a ray of sunlight.

"I know a lot's happened," he went on. "I understand if you need time."

I lifted my head so I could see him clearly. "I don't need time." I reached out to touch his face. "I never stopped loving you."

Our eyes met, and there was relief in his. "Then I'm grateful. Because you're it for me, Claire. I'll never love anyone else like this."

I moved up to kiss him. He opened his mouth to me, and we explored each other. As it grew deeper, he winced.

"Are you okay?" I moved back.

"It's my jaw. It's still sore from getting punched."

"Really? That was a while ago."

"Yeah, it was." He rolled his eyes. "It turns out Doug has a wicked right hook. Who knew?"

"Have you seen a doctor?" I asked with concern.

Philip nodded. "Apparently the bone is bruised and takes time to heal. It's a lot better than it was, at least."

"Does that mean we shouldn't kiss anymore?"

He shifted position and ran his hand down to my ass. "Just the opposite. In fact, we need to be kissing as much as possible."

"Oh really? Is this what your doctor said?"

"Not exactly. It's my own kind of therapy." He lowered his voice. "In fact, my therapy involves things so dirty they'll make you blush."

I laughed. I couldn't help it. "And that's supposed to help heal your jaw?"

"Trust me, I'll feel a lot better."

I shook my head as he grinned. So handsome. In that moment, I realized how much I'd missed him and how hard it'd been without him. As much as I'd tried to fill my days, it was never enough.

It must have shown on my face. "What is it, sweetheart? My jaw really is okay, honest."

I shook my head. "It's not that. I just thought this was over between us, you know? I tried to move on, but I couldn't."

That quieted him. "It's been terrible for me too. More than you can imagine." Our eyes stayed on each other. He stroked my hip. "Come lie down on me again."

I did as he asked, laying my body over his. Despite our difference in height, we'd always fit together so well. I could hear his heart beating, steady and true, as he caressed my back. I thought about the last few weeks apart and then remembered something. "Did you ever get the text message I sent you?"

His hand stopped on my lower back.

I lifted my head to look at him and was surprised by the raw emotion on his face. "What is it?"

He licked his lips. "I got it."

"Was that a weird thing for me to send?"

"No, but I'm curious. Why did you send it?"

I sat up a little more. "Something important happened to me

while we were apart." I rested my hand on his chest and told him about the revelation I'd had regarding Ethan and Ivy.

His fingertips traced my skin again as he listened. "I didn't realize you were still holding so much anger toward them."

"I was, but I've forgiven them, and it's helped me so much. I thought maybe it would help you if you could forgive your father." I put my hand over his heart. "And I knew you'd start blaming yourself."

"That message...." His voice shook, and he stopped talking.

"Are you all right?"

He nodded and took a deep breath. "That message was amazing. You saved my life that night."

"I did?"

"I was in a dark place. It was a miracle." He smiled softly. "You were my miracle."

I stroked his hair. "What happened?"

"My father came to see me. I thought he was there for money." He told me the rest of the story, how his dad was there to congratulate him, how he said they were alike.

"I don't think that's true."

He took another breath. "For one horrible hour, I believed him."

"So where is he now?"

"Who knows? South America probably. With all my talk of justice, I should have known he'd have funds hidden in offshore accounts. I was too caught up in the destruction I could do."

"I'm glad he's out of your life."

"So am I."

"How do you feel about him now that it's over?"

Philip didn't reply right away and appeared to be thinking about it. "I realize he's a damaged person. I decided to forgive him because in some ways, he's his own worst enemy." He turned to me. "But to be honest, I'll never forgive him for what he put my mom through. I can't. I'm not made that way. The irony is I think she's forgiven him. I think she did it years ago."

WE TOOK A SHOWER TOGETHER, and it was just like old times. I even elbowed him in the face accidentally.

"I'm so sorry!" I was horrified. "Did I hurt you?"

He held the washcloth up to his eye. "Are you kidding? It wouldn't be a real shower if you didn't give me at least one black eye."

"Are you really okay? I feel terrible."

He pulled me in close, our slick bodies pressed against each other. "Don't worry, I'm fine." And then he kissed me, our mouths slippery and wet. "I missed showering in a phone booth with you."

"Me too." I played with the hair at the nape of his neck. "And I promise I'll be more careful where my elbows land."

We kissed some more. His erection poked my stomach, so I stroked it for a while. His eyes were half-lidded with pleasure as he soaped my breasts. But the shower was too small to have sex. Instead, we went out to the bed, both of us steamy and damp, mingling with the hot summer air.

"I love this bed," he said afterward, sighing with contentment. "It's perfect. Let's never leave it again."

I laughed. "You and my bed should run away together."

He glanced at me. "Where did you find this brass bed anyway? It looks like something from an old-fashioned bordello."

"It was in the attic at Sullivan House. I guess it belonged to a former owner. Violet was going to toss it because it was old and discolored, but I polished it and brought it back to life."

"What about all the pillows and everything?"

I smiled with embarrassment. "It's my fantasy idea of the bed on a pirate's ship. That's why I set it up this way."

"Well, I highly approve. And I've got pirate blood, so my approval is what matters."

I laughed. "Do you really like it that much?"

"I do. It's naughty as hell." He gave me a wicked look. "I want to ravage you every time I see you in it. But then I always want to ravage you."

"I wonder which owner of Sullivan House had this bed," I mused. "I should try to figure it out."

Philip seemed distracted by something. "What time is it?" He sat up. "I need to check my phone."

I watched him walk across the room naked, enjoying the sight. Those powerful shoulders and back tapering down to that perfect butt. "Is it something for work?"

"Sort of. I have a few things in the air right now." He found the phone in his jeans pocket and stood there checking his messages and then texting.

I sprawled across the sheets and put my arms out. "Come back to bed," I complained. "That's enough work." But that reminded me of something. "Do you mind if I get your opinion on an idea?"

"Sure, what is it?" He came back over beside me.

I sat up, and then, just because I could, I kissed him. His hair was still wet, and he smelled like himself mixed with the apple shampoo from my shower. One whiff and my heart swelled with happiness.

"I love you," I whispered.

His eyes were steady on mine. "I love you too."

We gazed at each other, the summer light reflecting around us.

"I'm sorry for everything," he said. "I wish I'd listened to you from the start."

I nodded. In truth, as hard as it was, I believed Philip had to go through what he did to bring him to the place he was now.

He ran a hand down my leg. "So what's this thing you want my opinion on?"

"Oh, I took your advice." I reached over for the folder on my bedside table. "I've decided to change the name of my maid service."

"Interesting."

I handed him the folder. "I came up with some name ideas. Your sister was here, and we both liked one in particular. She came up with a logo and marketing idea for it, and I think I'm going to use it."

"What's the new name?" he asked, opening the folder.

I took a deep breath, excited but nervous that he might shoot it down.

He glanced at me.

"Maids of Truth." I pointed at the artwork. "Eliza had this whole superhero idea. Like a maid superhero. It works for the town, but also if I want to expand."

Philip was quiet, studying the pages. "My sister drew these?"

"She's a very good artist."

Finally, he nodded. "I like it."

"You do?"

"It's excellent. The name and the concept go well together. It's both eye-catching and fun."

I was excited. "So, you really like it? You aren't just saying that?"

He gave me a look. "Have you ever known me not to be brutally honest with my opinions?"

I laughed. "No."

I was still bouncing on the bed in excitement when my phone buzzed. I reached over and grabbed it from my bedside table.

There was a text from Violet. *Could you come up to the house? There's something I need your assistance with. It's urgent.*

"That's weird. I just heard from Violet."

He was watching me. "What did she say?"

"That she needs me right away, and it's urgent."

He nodded. "I'll come with you."

We both got off the bed. I walked over to my dresser and pulled out a clean T-shirt and shorts while Philip slipped his clothes back on.

After getting dressed, we headed up to the main house.

"I wonder what it could be," I said, walking up the graveled driveway. It was late afternoon but still hot outside. The air smelled good, sweet and summery and full of promise.

Or maybe I was just happy.

Philip took my hand as we walked up, and we kept glancing at each other, smiling. It was like those few weeks apart were only a bad dream.

When I tried to open the French doors in back, I discovered they were locked.

"Let's go around to the front," he said.

We walked around the side, and just as we headed down the path toward the front of the house, Philip let go of my hand.

I turned to him, but to my astonishment, he swooped in and plucked me right off the ground.

"Aaah! What are you doing?"

He grinned. "You'll see."

I wrapped my arms around his neck as he carried me to the front door.

"I'm perfectly capable of walking myself, you know."

"Yes, but I want to carry you over the threshold."

I stared at him mystified. "Why?"

He didn't reply. I liked being carried by him. It reminded me of the day we first met. "Are you going to steal my phone again?"

He laughed heartily. "Not this time."

When we reached the front door to Sullivan House, it must have already been unlatched, because he pushed it open with his foot.

After walking inside, he gently put me down. I was a little flustered. We were in the great room, but I didn't see any sign of Violet.

Philip was eyeing me with barely contained excitement. "Violet's not here. It's just the two of us."

"What do you mean?" I looked around the room. "Is something going on?"

"Yes, there is." He led me over to a table that had a vase of wild-flowers on it. Right next to it were some documents with a pen. And next to that was a small gift box with a red ribbon.

I looked at it questioningly.

"This is for you." He handed me the box.

My adrenaline skyrocketed. Was he proposing? But the box

looked too big for a ring. I opened it, and inside I found a key. "What is this?"

"It's your new key. Sullivan House is now completely yours, Claire."

My head jerked up. "What are you talking about?"

"I bought out Violet's half, and I'm gifting it to you. She's already deeded the house in your name. Just sign the papers and it's yours."

"Seriously?" My eyes widened. "How did you manage all this?"

He rubbed his jaw. "I have to admit, I had a little help from Sam. He's the one who told me Violet had put the house on the market."

"Sam?" I thought of that day he came to see me.

He nodded. "So I contacted her, and she agreed to let me buy her out."

"Philip, it's incredibly thoughtful, and I appreciate it." I put the key back inside the box and closed it. "But you know I can't accept a gift like this. I'm sorry, but it's too much."

"I thought you might say that." He took a deep breath. "How about accepting it as a wedding present?"

My heart stopped. "A wedding present?"

He took my hand. "I want to marry you, Claire. Tell me you'll be my wife." His eyes met mine, and he seemed nervous. "Please say you'll marry me, sweetheart."

I was stunned into silence. I never thought I'd get married again. Especially not to someone this wonderful. "Yes, I will," I said, finally finding my voice. I couldn't contain my smile. "I'll marry you."

He pulled me in close, and we hugged each other tight. "I don't know how I ever lived without you," he said. "But I never want to again."

"But, Philip, are you sure you want to do this?" I asked when we pulled apart.

He gave me an incredulous look. "I've never been more sure of anything in my life."

"You'll have to move to Truth Harbor. I don't want to live in the city."

He chuckled. "Maybe you haven't noticed, but I'm crazy in love with you. I'll live anywhere you want. Hell, we can even live in that tiny fairy-tale cottage of yours."

I could see he meant it.

"I might hold you to that," I teased.

"I don't care. I want to be with you, my pirate princess. Always."

EPILOGUE

~ Philip ~

Seven Months Later

"I t feels like I've learned a new language," I said, gazing out at the turquoise waters of the Caribbean. "If you'd asked me a week ago, I never could have told you what aft was, or bowlines, or halyards, or how to hoist a mainsail."

Claire smiled. "You're picking it up fast. I guess that pirate blood of yours is good for more than just drinking rum."

It was true. I felt remarkably at ease on the water. Not quite like Claire, who had grown up sailing, but surprisingly comfortable. Now that I'd experienced it, I planned to make it a permanent part of my life.

The sun was getting low in the sky as we tied our rented sailboat to a mooring ball off the coast of St. John's for the night. We'd picked up supplies in town yesterday and were eating dinner on the boat tonight. Tomorrow we were planning to sail over to the British Virgin Islands.

It'd been an incredible honeymoon. Every day an adventure. Some days we sailed, while others were spent swimming and snorkeling in these crystal blue waters, or exploring the various towns and beaches.

Before flying here, I married Claire at a small chapel in Truth Harbor with only close family and friends around us. Afterward, we had a large reception at Sullivan House and invited everyone. It was a lively party, with Doug and Daphne announcing their own engagement. They'd asked us in advance if it was all right. I was glad my cousin found the love of his life in the same way I found mine.

Because that was what Claire was. The love of my life.

I watched her check the lines once more while I stood behind the helm. It usually took us a few tries to get moored, but tonight we got it on the first go-round.

"That was easy," she said, coming over to me. "I think we're finally getting it down. I hope the ones in the BVI are the same."

I nodded, unable to take my eyes off her. She wore her hair in braids to please me and looked so damn pretty. She had on a crocheted white string bikini top and shorts. I'd bought her half a dozen string bikinis before we left for our honeymoon. I couldn't help myself. Her skin was tan despite all the sunblock we lathered on every day, and her cheeks and the bridge of her nose were pink and peeling.

"What is it?" she asked, tilting her head.

"I'm just admiring my beautiful wife." My eyes roamed the length of her with pleasure.

She smiled, showing off that dimple. "You're not so bad yourself."

I reached out to draw her close. "It's like heaven here with you. I've never been this happy."

"Me either." She slipped her arms around my waist and sighed. "This has to be the best honeymoon of all time."

I stroked her back and thought about everything that brought us here. Sure, there were some bumps in the road, but we made it.

A lot had happened since the day I asked her to marry me.

For starters, Violet had become Truth Harbor's new mayor. A position which suited her in every way. After running a political campaign with all the vigor and discipline of a field marshal, she was elected last month. Claire said her dad would have been pleased to see it.

Doug and Daphne, besides getting engaged, had also gone into business together. After Doug sold Bradley Renovations to Bob, he and Daphne used the money to open a small health food store with a bakery attached. Doug now sold his kick-starter muffins to the world. And it turned out Daphne makes a delicious jam to complete those muffins. Their store was downtown in one of the old buildings that would have been destroyed. And even though Doug still worried a lot, I'd noticed these days he did it with a smile on his face.

Even better, my aunt Linda, the dragon lady, sold her house in Seattle and was moving to Truth Harbor. God help us. Apparently she adored Daphne though and was excited for grandchildren.

My mom finished the first book in her cozy mystery series and published it herself. So far it was doing well, and she was hard at work on the second one. A local bookstore hosted a signing. I was proud and happy for her. She and Elliot were still seeing each other and recently came back from a trip to Ireland. The more I'd gotten to know him, the more I approved. I suspected there might be marriage plans in their future.

My sister's play was so successful she stayed in town to be part of the next production. After creating the terrific logo for Maids of Truth, the pest was also considering a career in graphic art. She still hadn't gone back to college. It wasn't easy, but my lovely new bride convinced me to keep my opinions about that to myself.

Ethan, the bonehead, and his wife, Ivy, recently became the

parents of identical red-haired twin girls. Claire told me she was happy for them, so I was too.

I hadn't heard a word from my father, not that I wanted to. The people I had tracking him told me he was in Costa Rica, but that was months ago, and I'd long since stopped keeping tabs on him.

As for me, I sold my house in Seattle. The market timing was perfect, and to be honest, I made a killing. I'd already moved all my stuff into Sullivan House and planned to commute to Seattle and work from home.

Claire's maid business was continuing to grow. She'd added two more employees and was thinking ahead. She'd told me recently that if things continued on as they had been, she might open a second location. Taylor, who I'd met a few times now, was managing things for her while we were on our honeymoon.

And let's not forget our feathered friends, Calico Jack and Quicksilver. After some initial adjustments, both birds settled in happily at the larger house. I'd tried to convince my wife to get them a couple of lady birds, but so far, no dice. *Sorry, guys.*

Claire and I still slept in the carriage house sometimes. Eventually she planned to make it her office, but for now I liked to think of it as our den of iniquity.

Speaking of iniquity....

Dinner on the boat was fresh fish and vegetables we cooked on the small galley stove. We ate our meal under an orange and gold sunset, surrounded by other sailboats bobbing in the distance.

"That was the best meal ever," I said, patting my stomach with satisfaction.

She laughed. "You say that every time."

"That's because it's true." I reached over for her empty plate. "Would you like some rum?" I asked, getting up.

"Okay." She smiled and stretched her arms out before lying back on the pillows and blankets we'd set out.

I took our plates below, then came back with glasses and the bottle of rum we'd picked up on St. Thomas.

"There are so many stars out here at night," she said, gazing upward. "It's amazing, isn't it? More than back home even."

I poured a splash in each glass and handed one to her, then settled myself beside her to stargaze.

We'd done this almost every night. The two of us out here drinking a little rum and enjoying the cool breeze as we talked and made plans for the future. Later we'd make love, either up here or in the cabin below.

"I've been thinking lately." I set my glass down and turned toward her.

"Oh? And what have you been thinking about?" She put her drink down and snuggled next to me.

"Everything. Even though we just got married, I don't want to wait or put it off."

"Put what off?"

"All the things we want. You know how I am—I like to go for it."

She looked up at me, her eyes large and dark. I watched as comprehension sank in. The longing on her face. Then I thought about those little yellow rain boots splashing on the water's edge, and there was longing on mine too.

I held her close, enjoying the scent of coconut shampoo mixed with the sweetness of the woman I loved.

"Are you saying what I think you are?" she murmured, gazing up at me.

"Yes, I am." I put my lips to her ear and whispered, "Let's make a baby tonight, sweetheart."

The End

TRUTH ABOUT CATS & SPINSTERS

Read the next book! Leah & Josh's story TRUTH ABOUT CATS & SPINSTERS.

When rock star Joshua Trevant shows up at Leah's door to escape the paparazzi nightmare at his house... little does he know she caused it.

NOTE FROM ANDREA

Thank you for reading Philip and Claire's story! I hope you enjoyed it. I loved writing about those two.

The next book in the series is Leah's, and the third book will be Theo's. (And, yes, Gavin and Eliza will have a book too!)

If you enjoyed Philip and Claire's story, I hope you'll be kind enough to leave a review or rating on Amazon and/or Goodreads. I appreciate it.

If you have any thoughts or comments you'd like to share, feel free to email me at authorsimonne@gmail.com.

With so many books choices out there, thank you for choosing mine.

xo,

Andrea

SWEET LIFE IN SEATTLE SERIES

ANDREA SIMONNE

I hope you'll check out the first book from my series Sweet Life in Seattle, YEAR OF LIVING BLONDE.

Find out what happens when Natalie's husband leaves her for a much older woman...

Order YEAR OF LIVING BLONDE today!

STANDALONE

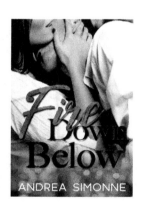

Read my steamy standalone FIRE DOWN BELOW!

Still single and just turned thirty-five, Kate suddenly finds herself engaged to one man, while obsessing over another...

ALSO BY ANDREA SIMONNE

Sweet Life in Seattle series

Year of Living Blonde

Return of the Jerk

Some Like It Hotter

Object of My Addiction

Too Much Like Love

About Love series

Truth About Men & Dogs

Truth About Cats & Spinsters

Truth About Nerds & Bees

Other

Fire Down Below

ABOUT THE AUTHOR

Andrea Simonne grew up as an army brat and discovered she had a talent for creating personas at each new school. The most memorable was a surfer chick named "Ace" who never touched a surfboard in her life, but had an impressive collection of puka shell necklaces. Andrea still enjoys creating personas though now they occupy her books. She's an Amazon best seller in romantic comedy and contemporary romance, and author of the series Sweet Life in Seattle and About Love. She currently makes her home in the Pacific Northwest with her husband and two sons.

She loves hearing from her readers! You can find her on the web at www.andreasimonne.com.

Email: authorsimonne@gmail.com.

Printed in Great Britain
by Amazon

41040428R00253